# UNEXPECTED ANSWERS

## Dee Rivers

All Rights Reserved.

No reproduction, copy or transmission of the publication may be may be made without written permission. No paragraph or section of this publication may be reproduced copied or transmitted save with the written permission or in accordance with the provisions of the Copyright Act 1956 (as amended).
Copyright 2017 Dee M Rivers
The right of Dee M Rivers to be identified as the author of this work has been asserted in accordance with the Copyright Designs and Patents Act 1988.

Revised Edition

ISBN -13: 9781983346262

# DEDICATION

TO MY PARENTS
WILLIAM AND MARY HARD

## ACKNOWLEDGEMENTS

My loving thanks to Sue, Matthew, Bill and Marty for their unstinting loyalty, support, encouragement and love.
Credit and love to my sister Ronnie who has championed me through thick and thin all my life.
Special thanks to Teresa, Jim, Bill and Grit for all the stories they shared, without which this story could never have been written.
Love and thanks to Beryl who has wholeheartedly welcomed her 'new' sisters into her world.
Lastly, thanks to ancestry.com who provided our miracle.

# REVIEWS

'I'm impressed with the book 'unexpected answers' by Dee Rivers. I have not finished the book yet but am enjoying every page so far. I think we all love a family saga. A bit of mystery is an enticement as well !!' *Margaret Clare UK*

'Thoroughly enjoyable read, lovely character development, and intriguing tale. Can't recommend highly enough.' *Ann Smith UK*

'Wonderful book, a real page turner to find out what happened in this amazing story. So well written for a first book. Highly recommended.' *Jean Phillips UK*

'I am hoping that we will see more Dee Rivers' novels. Unexpected Answers is a page turner, the writing flows and from the start one is in the story - made all the more interesting by the fact that this is based on a true story. I certainly recommend it.' *Nikki Clark France*

'Very intriguing story, keeps you on the edge of your seat. A real page turner.' *S Choi UK*

'Very good read, especially since I knew some of the people in the book. Enjoyed the story.' *V M Pearce USA*

'Very-well written and an amazing story. I was intrigued after the first sentence. It really makes you think of what people go through for so many different reasons. Thank you Dee (& Ronnie) for sharing your story -- I truly loved it.' *S Perrin USA*

'A Fascinating story from start to finish. I actually knew Bill and Mary, late in their lives in Ohio, but I would have enjoyed the book even if I didn't.' *Adrienne Nagy USA*

'I thoroughly enjoyed reading the book. I could not put it down. Understand Dee Rivers is writing another book.' *Andrea D USA*

'Difficult to put down! This book was a real rollercoaster of emotions and I love books that portray the complexities of individuals not simply as 'good' or 'bad' people. Dee has enabled the reader to empathise with all the individuals in Unexpected Answers and I found that I experienced so many different feelings as I was reading it, from hope, to anguish and to a sense of contentedness as well. I would definitely recommend this book, especially to those with an interest in genealogy.' *Amy C. UK*

# WHO'S WHO IN UNEXPECTED ANSWERS

**DAVIES FAMILY**
Will & Annie Bedelia Davies
Daughter Midge (Annie Mary Eugene)
Daughter Ronnie (Veronica died aged 7)
Daughter Grit (Gertrude)
Son Frank
Son James
Son William
Daughter Teresa Mary Veronica

**RIVERS FAMILY**
Halford & Ruby Rivers
Son Derek (stillborn)
Daughter Beryl Helen
Son Raymond

**HARD FAMILY**
Bill & Mary Hard
Daughter Ronnie (Veronica Mary)
Son John (William John Raymond died aged 21)
Daughter Doreen Mary Eugene (Dee Rivers author)

## PROLOGUE

6$^{th}$ March 1999 at 8.09am. 'You've got post'....
*Oh boy, this is great. Mom's line is busy, so I just keep redialling, but I know you are related to us. My Mom is Teresa, youngest in that family and I have seen a picture of Midge. Mom has so wanted to know what happened to her. Mom's maiden name was Teresa Mary Veronica Davies. Just got back from a visit to England the other day – only third since 1946. You have many cousins, in USA and others in NZ, France, South Africa etc.
Still trying to get through to Mom…
Denise.*
The sisters read and re-read the email.

6$^{th}$ March 1999 at 9.31am. 'You've got post'....
*Veronica, I just got through to Mom and she is VERY excited, not having heard anything in about 65 years. She will be writing you, and we are all excited to make contact and help fill in missing bits…The excitement in my Mom's voice was indescribable.*

6th March 1999 at 10.51am. 'You've got post'....
*Dear Niece Veronica,*
*You have no idea how thrilled I am to find you and to learn news of my older sister, 'Midge' after 65 years! My daughter, Denise forwarded your email and also phoned me with your news. I sat down and cried with joy.*
*I was only 10 years old when your mother left home and none of the family ever heard from her or anything about her until now. It's so wonderful to learn that I have two nieces, her daughters. You undoubtedly were named for another of our sisters who was named Veronica but died as a young child. This was why Mother named the house that Dad had built "Veronica". Just over a week ago I was in that very house and visited with John Stanley and his wife. They mentioned that someone named Veronica had been there from the USA and enquiring about the place and Blue House Farm not long ago. Was that you? Would you be willing to give me your phone number? We have so much to talk about. I find it hard to believe that I will finally, after all these years, be able to learn what had happened to my sister. So many questions come to mind.*
*Welcome to the family. It's a big one! Aunt Teresa*

**PART ONE**

**THE MEETING**

## CHAPTER ONE

## 1919...

'A mother should not have to bury their child,' Annie declared fiercely on that awful day. A vice-like grip encircled her chest, squeezing her breath away. Her whole body ached. Every movement was a struggle. She pressed her handkerchief to her mouth with a clenched fist, in an effort to halt the urge to scream. Will nodded his head in sad agreement, not trusting himself to speak. His role was to support his wife and family in their grief. His own mourning would be done in private.

Will Davies and his wife, Annie Bedelia walked through the wet grass side by side, away from the grave where a few minutes ago, they had thrown their symbolic handfuls of earth onto the small coffin of Veronica their second child. The boughs of the trees that lined the path drooped under the weight of the rain-soaked leaves. A chilling breeze scattered teardrops of water onto the heads and shoulders of the passing mourners.

Hearing her mother's words was a scary moment for Midge. Up until the death of her younger sister, Midge had led a carefree life, playing energetic games with Veronica and their other sister, Gertrude. There had been no dark shadows lurking and the sun always seemed to shine. Now, she cast her eyes around the shifting shapes of her extended family, saw the pain etched on their grey faces. Their black coats and hats fluttering in the wind appeared to her, like black birds, a dark and sombre presence. To her young mind, the graveyard was a desolate place. There was no pretty church, just a field with a low hedge surrounding it and a few trees. Her heart was pierced and as she followed her parents along the puddled path, she gripped Gertrude's hand a little tighter in protection. She sensed that her memories began that day there at the graveside of her sister.

With the funeral over, back home in Frinton after the mourners had quietly dispersed, having partaken of the customary drinks and snacks, even the normally boisterous youngsters were morose. The darkened rooms, with curtains drawn in reverence to the dead child, added weight to the already heavy atmosphere. Cousins, having attempted to play games, had gone away with heads bowed, awestruck by the solemnity of the occasion.

Will slipped into the parlour and slumped heavily in the worn leather armchair, resting his head on the antimacassar. Earlier, before leaving the house for the funeral, he had lit a fire in the grate in an effort to welcome any mourners who might want to sit, but now, just a few embers remained. The room was kept for special occasions and visitors like the Catholic priest. Today it seemed a gloomy, dim place, filled with cumbersome furniture.

He was about to close his eyes when a beam of light, stealing its way through a crack in the heavy velvet curtains formed a glow over a photograph on the polished oak sideboard. Wearily he stood and stretched out his hand to pick it up. There in the photograph was Veronica, rather Ronnie as he liked to call her, his little blonde angel. Her eyes twinkled at him and a gentle smile played on her lips. She stood with Midge and Gertrude, her two sisters and baby Frank propped up on a large chair between them. Will thought it must have been taken when Frank was about five months old.

Annie had been determined to secure a memento of their children's lives, and he remembered how he'd relented and taken them along to the studio. The three girls looked so pretty. Each of his daughters had a large ribbon tied in a bow on top of their heads. Their mother had knitted navy blue jumpers for them with a pretty collar and three-quarter sleeves.

*Yes,* he thought, *Annie always makes sure the children are turned out well.*

Despite his sadness, Will found himself smiling as he recalled how they'd struggled to keep Frank sitting upright, the girls giggling while Frank became more and more fretful. With a deep sigh, he sat once more, holding the picture carefully. As he studied the image, his chin dropped down into his chest and a sob, caught in his throat, escaped with a groan.

Outside the parlour door, Midge sat silently on the bottom step of the stairs. She drew her knees up to her chin, wrapped her arms tightly round her legs and gently rocked to and fro. She was frightened to learn that her strong, tall Papa could cry and in her young innocent mind she resolved never to cause him pain.

Her little sister's precious life had been snatched away by Scarlet Fever, a severe infection of the throat that had claimed the lives of several children in the area.

'Veronica is singing and dancing with the angels now,' the priest had announced in his sermon.

If there was anything to be pleased about on this tortuous day, Midge's mother was thankful that the mass had been said by Father Dempsey. He was a family friend and very aware of the depth of feeling that ran through them. He was there as their little girl took her last breath. He stayed with the couple when they tried to explain to their other children about the devastating event that had just taken place. And, he was there to help Midge through her pain on hearing the news that her sister of seven years was gone forever. At nine years of age, Midge was the eldest of Will and Annie's five children.

With Veronica now gone, Gertrude (nicknamed Grit) came next, followed by the two brothers, Frank now three years old and one-year old James. When Grit and the boys wanted to know where their sister was, Midge repeated the words of Father Dempsey, not only because she wanted to make her young siblings feel better but because she accepted it as truth.

'Veronica's singing and dancing with the angels in heaven now,' she would say. They in turn believed her implicitly, such was the bold impression Veronica had made in her short life.

Unlike her dark-haired siblings, Veronica with her blonde curls had looked like an angel even as she played with them. So, for the youngsters, the sadness of her absence was appeased by the image of her playing with the angels in heaven. However, in Midge the experience created a fierce protectiveness over her siblings, which gave her mother some comfort.

***

Annie was pregnant with her sixth child. Being a deeply religious woman, she prayed regularly, pleading with God to preserve the rest of her family in good health, especially the unborn baby that was now stirring in her womb.

Although her feelings had been raging in anger at the untimely death of her child, she wasn't angry with God. She couldn't be sure to whom or what she was directing her anger, but nevertheless, there were nights when she lay awake clamping her mouth shut, trying to subdue screams that threatened to burst her lungs. Strangely and in a contradictory way, she found that she had acquired a new fervour in her devotion rather than a weakening of her faith in God.

Sadly, Will did not share her commitment. His bereavement caused him anger and doubt in a God who could snatch away such a tender life. Veronica's death had left him with a deep uncertainty of his ability to be the protector and provider for his family. His disillusionment, set against his wife's piety was kindling to the flicker of despondency that was creeping its way insidiously between them.

Midge would watch them covertly, worry etched in her young mind. But time marched on and as the weeks moved into months following Veronica's death the family inched its way towards some sort of normality. With four lively children to care for, Annie had little time to brood on her missing child and her pregnancy was reaching full term.

Will immersed himself in the farm he'd inherited from his father. There was plenty of work to be done with the dairy herd and his milk round. He had no truck with sentimentality. Life went on.

Annie delivered another boy in 1920. They named this one, her sixth child, William after his Papa and grandfather. Midge helped her Mama as best she could and often took her younger siblings off on adventures to keep them occupied.

'Who wants to come with me to the park?' she called one day.
They raced to her side shouting and waving their arms.
'Yes, yes, let's go on an adventure.'
'Can we go Mama? We'll be good,' five-year-old Frank pleaded.

'Why, of course you can go. Midge and Grit will pack some drinks for you all. Take some apples too. You can make a picnic.'

She was baking cakes, and normally would be inundated with offers of 'help', but today she was grateful for Midge's suggestion to take them away, out from under her feet.

After packing the supplies for the picnic, the two girls took hold of the boys' hands and set off for the Frinton esplanade. Along the way, they played follow my leader, hopping over pot holes, dancing round trees, tapping on the railings along the gardens in front of the big houses. The sky was blue with cotton wool clouds, though the air was crisp on this May morning.

People passing by smiled at the happy-go-lucky little group. The children always said "Hello" very politely. When they reached the esplanade, Grit found the perfect spot to set down their picnic basket with its red gingham cover. They cart-wheeled and chased each other along the wide expanse of grass that reached to the edge of the cliff, all the while chattering and laughing.

Suddenly James began shouting exuberantly, 'I can fly. Look at me, I can fly. I'm a bird.'

James had undone the buttons on his navy-blue coat and with his arms outstretched and coat tails flapping, he was running like the wind towards the cliff edge.

'No, James, come back…James,' yelled Midge as loud as she could as she ran after him. 'Stop, you'll fall.'

As the tiny frame of her young brother disappeared from view, Midge raced to catch up. She knew there was a steep incline. Gasping for breath, she reached the place where he had gone over. Down the stony slope she clambered, sliding through prickly bushes. Her bare skin scraped across the rough ground. At last she reached him.

James was wailing loudly. His trousers were torn and his coat was covered in dirt and leaves. Blood from his scratched face and hands was staining his shirt. Gathering him up in her arms, Midge struggled along the beach until she found a safe route up to the top.

Grit, who had been anxiously waiting, grabbed hold of Frank's hand and the picnic things. They had to run to keep up with the older girl as she made her way back to their home with James held in her arms.

By the time they reached the house, Midge's arms and legs were trembling with the strain. Grit shoved open the door and the four children fell in, totally exhausted. Their Mama rushed out of the kitchen when she heard the commotion. Her hand flew to her mouth as she saw the blood on the child's face and clothes.

'Midge, what's happened to him?'

Sobbing with relief at reaching home and the pain in her arms and stomach, Midge tried to explain what James had done.

Grit took over. 'He said he could fly like a bird and ran over the cliff edge, the stupid boy.' She scowled at her brother in disgust.

'Let's get him into the kitchen and look at the damage,' said Mama taking the sobbing child from Midge's aching arms. 'Midge, go and get washed and change out of those clothes,' noticing her stained dress.

Midge was relieved to be free of the responsibility. James was three years old and always getting into some form of scrape or other. One of his sisters was usually saving him from disaster.

Sitting him on the edge of the kitchen table, Annie inspected him. This time he had bitten through his tongue and was covered in scratches and bruises.

'Oh, we'll soon get you cleaned up and good as new,' she said tenderly.

There wasn't much to do about his tongue though, and once he had stopped crying and the bleeding staunched, he began to boast of his adventure.

'It hasn't stopped you talking, has it?' teased Grit.

\*\*\*

Annie was pregnant again. Midge now thirteen continued to show her protectiveness over Grit and her three brothers. As her Mama's pregnancy progressed, they became more like sisters than mother and daughter. Will was away at the farm more than Annie wished for, but that was their livelihood so she wouldn't make trouble for him.

They had married in 1909 when she was twenty-four years of age and Will was twenty-nine. Midge arrived nine months later and now at thirty-eight, here she was expecting her seventh.

*This time is the last,* she vowed to herself.

One day in the heat of the summer, she was feeling especially weary.

'Midge, darling, would you be an angel and keep the little ones quiet for an hour or so while I go and put my feet up?' she asked.

Midge's eyes lit up with her mother's request. She was always willing to help with her younger siblings.

'Yes, Mama, they can draw some pictures for you. Shall I play the piano to soothe you to sleep?' she suggested, tenderly touching Annie's arm.

'That would be wonderful, my darling. You're such a good girl. What would I do without you? Thank you.'

Midge found the paper and crayons that were kept in a cupboard and sat the children down around the table. When they were settled she took her sheet music from inside the piano stool and began to play a gentle waltz. The household was lulled into blissful peace with four heads bent in concentration over their creations. A delicate scent drifted through the open kitchen door from the pink roses that grew round the frame. The garden seemed to sleep in lazy splendour as the music flowed.

Grit and Midge were having piano lessons at school, though Grit was not keen on practising and frequently had her knuckles rapped for mistakes. Her enthusiasm was waning, but Midge woke early every morning so that she could shut herself away with the piano for an hour before school.

After a while, she joined the others, inspecting their efforts fondly.

'Grit, what would you like to be when you grow up?'

'I want to be a nurse and make people feel better,' she replied. 'What about you, will you be a nurse, Midge?'

'Yes, that's what I'd like to be or maybe look after children.' Her easy answer was innocent of any doubts about her future. 'Not like you horrible imps though,' she teased as she tickled her brothers. As they squirmed and giggled, she narrowed her eyes and snarled.

'Or maybe I'll be a…' she paused for effect - 'Maybe I'll be a witch.'

This had them running around the room in hysterics.

'Shh, shh,' she said, while trying to smother her grin. 'We're supposed to be quiet. Mama's resting.'

'Can we have an adventure, Midge?' pleaded young William. He was learning about his sister's talent for making even the most mundane event exciting.

'Maybe we can when Mama wakes up. Tomorrow we might be going to Blue House Farm to help Papa.'

Just then the door opened and Annie entered the room with a smile on her face. The rest had refreshed her and the children echoed her smile with their cheerfulness. Her eyes roamed over the cosy scene and she felt a glow of pride at how her eldest daughter was proving to be such a blessing to her.

'Are we going to Blue House Farm tomorrow?' asked Frank excitedly.

'Papa has lots of things to sort out so he could do with some help, so yes, we'll go along and see what we can do. Grandma is feeling lonely without Grandpa so you little ones can keep her company. She'd like that.'

'Yippee,' shouted the boys, leaping round the kitchen.

Midge grabbed hold of James's arm. 'Whoa there, calm down or we won't be able to go anywhere.'

Their mother smiled gratefully. Now heavily pregnant again, it was difficult to cope with the liveliness of her boys.

\*\*\*

Will had worked alongside his father on Blue House Farm since it was purchased by his parents in 1918 after renting the property and land for several years but nine months ago, Bill Davies senior had died, leaving his son with sole responsibility for the running of the farm and milk round.

The children enjoyed visiting the farm. It was so different from the seaside, set in the middle of the countryside as it was, though only about three miles away from their home. The farmhouse was just off the main street of the village, surrounded by fields where the dairy herd grazed the soft lush grass. They delighted in seeing the animals and playing with the kittens that always seemed to be around, but the biggest bonus was the ride on the bus.

As promised, the next day they all piled on to the rickety old vehicle, clambering to fill up the back seat. Mama climbed the steps first to buy the tickets, followed by young William, James, Frank and Grit, eagerly tripping over each other's heels in a bid to get the best seat. Finally, in came Midge who patiently made her way to join the others.

There was always a certain amount of pushing, shoving and arguing until they were each settled and today was no different. The younger Davies children grabbed their favourite spot - kneeling on the back seat, watching the fields and houses racing by. They shrieked whenever the bus turned a corner but the loud noises didn't seem to bother the other passengers, some of whom even joined in the fun.

\*\*\*

On December 22$^{nd}$ 1923, Teresa Veronica Mary was born. Not a convenient date for a new baby to join a family already bursting at the seams, but Annie's mother came along to help out.

Annie confided to her mother. 'We could do with some extra space with this growing family. Although, this is definitely the last,' she added with a weak laugh.

'Will is thinking of building us a house on the farmland.'

Her mother nodded wisely.

'It'll be so much better than him having to drive over from Frinton every day.'

Annie silently hoped having him at home more would improve their relationship that had been rather strained of late, not to mention a welcome easing of her burden coping with such a large brood. Without Midge's help, she knew life would be almost unbearable.

## CHAPTER TWO

**1921...**
1st October 1921 was a grand occasion on the calendars of two families in Thorpe le Soken, a small village in rural Essex: the wedding of William Halford Rivers to Ruby Deal in St. Michaels' Church.

The guests were enamoured with the handsome couple. The blushing bride was a dainty twenty-eight-year-old, wearing a lace ankle-length dress, pulled in to accentuate her tiny waist. Her long blonde hair was caught up with a floral head-dress that supported a shoulder length veil. The spray she carried was created using white Lily's grown in her parent's garden.

The groom, a head taller than his bride, held himself proudly erect, his dark shining hair contrasting with Ruby's fair complexion as they posed for photographs in the October sunshine outside the old stone church.

As the happy couple walked with their guests to the Bell Inn for the reception, their friends and neighbours came out to toss pink petals of roses over their heads. The hotel was a stones-throw from the church, as was Oakley House that Halford was to move into with Ruby. The house had been Ruby's home for all of her life, so it had been agreed that she would continue living there and caring for her invalid mother with Halford. It was a solid, square building with a heavy front door between two windows. Two more windows stared out from the upper floor. Iron railings separated the compact front garden from the road to Frinton. Halford couldn't wait to start work on the large rear garden, where he had dreamed of all sorts of possibilities for his design flair to be worked out.

Mrs Deal, bed-ridden since suffering a stroke, was pleased with Ruby's choice of husband.

'I'm not losing a daughter, I'm gaining a son,' she would repeat proudly to anyone who cared to listen. She had been a widow for some years and found it soothing to think of a man about the house again.

Late that evening after the ceremony and celebrations were over, Halford took Ruby by the hand and led her to their room. Ruby squealed with delight when Halford swept her off her feet to carry her over the threshold. As he set her down, she was overcome by shyness. She lowered her eyes as her fingers twined together. Halford slowly unpinned her wedding veil and then removed the combs that gripped her hair. The gossamer veil fell to the floor and Ruby's hair tumbled down to her waist, covering her shoulders. Halford ran his fingers through the waves, feeling the silky sensuousness on his skin.

'You're the most wonderful girl in the world, darling,' he whispered cupping her face in his hands.

Ruby looked deep into his eyes and as Halford slowly moved his mouth to hers, she lost herself in his love. On her wedding night, she entered the room a virgin bride. Next morning, she came from it, a woman.

\*\*\*

Two weeks later, Halford dashed into Oakley house.

'Ruby, where are you? Come here quick. Get your coat on, I've got a surprise for you.'

She left her mother's room and found Halford greatly excited. She giggled to see the state of him.

'What's going on? What are you up to?'

'Wait and see,' he answered mysteriously, 'now put your coat on. Have you got your gloves? Yes? Very well, let's go.'

Suddenly, he put his arms round her.

'Wait...'

'Halford, what is going on?' she asked, beginning to get impatient.

'Shut your eyes.'

'What?'

'Just shut your eyes.'

Ruby obediently shut her eyes and with his hands on her shoulders, Halford carefully guided her outside.

'You can open them now.'

There before her was a gleaming motor car. It was a black two-seater Riley 11/40, open to all weathers. He'd bought a motor bike soon after he and Ruby had met, chosen especially because of the side car that was attached. They had spent many an enjoyable day riding out to the coast, with Ruby tucked safely inside, but this car was his dream.

His young wife almost lost her balance as he pulled her round to the passenger side of this beast and flung open the door for her with a gentlemanly flourish. He helped her into the seat, shut the door and swung himself to the front of the car. Ruby peered over the wind shield with fascination as Halford turned a handle with great effort.

'Shan't be long. I have to crank the engine to start her up,' he shouted after a couple of turns.

She had no idea what he was talking about but watched in awe as Halford's whole body was shunted up and down. In the brief glimpses she caught of his face, she could see he was becoming very red. She in turn was becoming rather agitated. A sudden banging and clanging startled her as the whole car began to rattle and shake.

'Oh, oh...' she screeched in panic.

'Hold on, Ruby,' shouted Halford breathlessly, laughing at her shocked expression. He leapt into the driver's seat next to her.

'Hold on tight,' came the instruction.

Ruby held on as she watched her husband struggling with a large handle, until with a shudder, the vehicle lurched forward. They were both thrown every which way as it chugged on at what she decided was an alarming rate. The houses and hedges were streaking by and a man on a bicycle was almost knocked into the ditch. She clamped her hat onto her head with one hand whilst the other grasped the top of the wind screen. The noise was deafening, but when she dared take her eyes off the road and turned towards Halford, she was amazed to see his face aglow with elation. With the wind blowing and the roar of the motor it was impossible to speak, so when Halford grinned and winked at her, she smiled back and relaxed a little.

There were very few cars travelling through their village and Ruby had certainly never had a ride in one. Once she had recovered from the initial shock, she thoroughly enjoyed the jaunt and couldn't wait to recount her amazing escapade to her mother on their return. As Halford pulled up in front of Oakley House he squeezed a rubber ball that was near the front windscreen. The tooting horn made Ruby laugh with delight.

Halford helped her down from the car and she rushed in to the house, up the stairs to her mother's room.

'Mother, Oh, wait 'til I tell you what an extraordinary experience I've had,' she declared breathlessly.

Mrs Deal nodded and smiled, making encouraging noises.

'I'm so pleased you're happy, dear. Halford is such a splendid chap. So generous and thoughtful,' she said when her daughter had finally run out of steam.

As if to prove her right, just at that moment Halford came in with a tray of tea and cream cakes. Mrs Deal glanced knowingly at Ruby.

'There, what did I tell you?' she said with a smirk.

'What did you tell Ruby, Mother?' Halford asked in a puzzled voice, looking from one to the other. He put the tray down on the table beside the invalid's bed. Ruby moved to pour the tea from the pot into her mother's china cup. The two women grinned cheekily.

'She's telling me what a wonderful man you are.'

'Ooh, don't let him know that, dear. He'll start getting too big for his boots,' Mrs Deal retorted with a wink. Despite being old and frail, she couldn't resist teasing her son-in-law. As she lifted the cup to her mouth, she shook her head, chuckling quietly to herself.

\*\*\*

Halford and Ruby enjoyed many outings and as the weather improved, they became more adventurous, happily tackling longer distances. By early spring of 1922, his good friend Jack Austin had also acquired an automobile.

One beautiful sunny morning, they set off in tandem on a journey to Brighton where they could stay overnight in Halford's fathers house. The following day they ventured up onto the South Downs for a picnic. Sitting on their picnic blanket amongst the wild flowers of the rolling hills of the chalk downland, Ruby and Gloria showed the children how to make daisy chains while Halford and Jack chatted and smoked amiably together.

'We've got to move with the times, Halford. I've been thinking of setting up a battery re-charging service in the village. It seems to me that now we're in the '20's, the wireless set is becoming rather popular and people are going to need the batteries. Instead of having to travel into Colchester, what would be better than having somewhere right on the doorstep?'

The friends gazed thoughtfully towards the sea. Halford inhaled on his cigarette.

'You might have something there, old thing.'

Jack paused before developing his idea further, tentatively weighing up his friend's reaction.

'What do you think about coming in with me?'

'It does sound like a very bright idea, but I'm not sure what role I would have or if it would support two families. I think we would have to have another string to our bow to make it a success. Let me sleep on it and see if we can come up with something that would work alongside it.'

A few days later, back home in Thorpe le Soken, Jack and his wife Gloria had accepted an invitation to dinner from Ruby and Halford. The four friends gathered around the polished oak dining table, chatting over local gossip and the state of the world. They were relaxed, sated by Ruby's scrumptious meal, enjoying each other's company.

'I've been giving a lot of thought to your idea, Jack,' Halford began as he took a cigarette from its packet and offered one to his friend. 'With our engineering background, there are two other possible services we could consider offering.'

Then after drawing deeply on his cigarette, with his eyes almost closed, he continued, 'Time-pieces need repairing, don't they? And what about bicycles?'

Up to this point, Jack had let Halford talk.

'So, does this mean you want to join me Halford?' he asked.

Halford flicked the tip of his cigarette into the ashtray that Ruby had placed between the two men.

'It certainly looks like it, old chap.'

'That's marvellous,' chuckled Jack. 'I agree with you about the clocks and bicycles,' he conceded. 'We'll need somewhere to work from, and I've been making some enquiries in the village. I believe old Roland Archer wants to rent out his buildings opposite the church for a nominal charge.'

'Mm. Sounds interesting… While we're talking of money, it would be an appropriate moment to say that I have some available cash for tools etc. We'd have to fit out the workroom and also do some advertising.'

'That's absolutely true. I have some capital that could go into the kitty,'

The two women had disappeared earlier into the kitchen to wash the dishes and now returned with a pot of tea, happy to see their men looking pleased with themselves.

'Are we in business then?' asked Gloria pleasantly.

Jack and Halford grinned at each other, stood up and shook hands heartily.

Gloria laughed loudly. 'I'd say the answer is "yes", wouldn't you, Ruby?'

For the next hour, ideas and opinions, designs and dreams flew across the table until the smoke hung hazily over their heads and the ladies both stifled their yawns.

Jack stretched his lean body. 'We'd best be getting home, Gloria love.'

After agreeing to meet again next week, the two couples said, 'good night.'

In the kitchen Ruby washed the teacups.

'If this doesn't work out, I'd really like to move back up north again, back to Lancashire, or even abroad to Canada. I've heard it's a beautiful country,' Halford said.

He had been born in Lancashire and spent many happy hours playing in the sand dunes, racing up and down the promenade on his bicycle. He'd joined the Royal Army Medical Corps, lying about his age. Had even been in France during the war. But then had followed his parents to Thorpe le Soken.

Ruby continued her task with her back towards Halford. This wasn't the first time he'd spoken of moving away and as always, she felt a tremor of fear gnawing inside her as she knew she could never leave her home in this village or her poor mother. Not wanting to spoil the mood she remained silent. She suddenly jumped when Halford came up behind her and putting his arms around her waist, pulled her close, kissing her neck.

Now in the third year of their marriage, she was aware that this dream of Halford's was the only subject that challenged her loyalty towards her husband. She would never consider defying him as it wasn't in her nature. In every other aspect she followed her wedding vows to love, honour and obey, but she wasn't sure of her reaction should he wish to bring his dream of moving away to fruition. She hoped and prayed she would never be put into a situation that would force her to choose.

Next day was Saturday. It was customary for Nell, Ruby's step-sister to spend the day with them. She arrived a little earlier than usual and found Halford and Ruby in the garden. Ruby was seated on a small stool directly in front of Halford who was perched precariously on the edge of a deck chair.

As usual, they were impeccably dressed. Ruby in a pretty pale lemon floral dress and Halford was suited with collar and tie. Nell was not surprised to spot the highly polished shoes on their feet. What was unfamiliar to her was a sight that stopped her in mid-stride. Ruby's eyes were shut, her hair unpinned and flowing almost to the ground. Halford was brushing it with loving strokes and as Nell watched this intimate scene, he began to braid her long locks. He was so lost in thought that he failed to notice Nell as she took the opportunity to speedily prepare her camera.

Being an avid photographer, this was one shot too good to miss. As Nell peered into her camera, Ruby opened her eyes and spotted her step-sister. Halford continued with the braiding, so deep in thought that he didn't raise his head until Nell spoke.

'Perfect!'

Halford immediately looked up in surprise.

'Good morning, Nell! You're up and about early, aren't you?'

Nell bent down to kiss Ruby lightly on the cheek and slapped Halford on the back.

'Just keen to get on with the day, you know. Much to do in too little time,' she replied briskly, replacing her camera back in its bag.

'How's mother today, Ruby?' she asked.

'Oh, not so good. She couldn't eat any breakfast. She couldn't even manage a cup of tea and you know how she loves her tea,' answered Ruby with a worried frown.

'Right oh. While you finish off here, I'll go and put the kettle on. See if I can cheer the old girl up,' said Nell, sounding more hopeful than she felt.

About half an hour later, Nell, leaning her heavy frame against the door, called out from the kitchen.

'Tea's up. Let's take it into Mother's room. She's been trying to say something and I can't make out what it is.'

Ruby sat on her mother's bed with Halford and Nell opting for chairs that had been placed especially for visitors since Mrs Deal had become bed-ridden. Ruby watched her mother's face. Asked if she wanted a drink, the old lady turned away and weakly lifted her hand from where it lay on the bed cover. Ruby took hold of it tenderly, stroking the thin papery skin. A fragile sound came from her mother's throat, forcing Ruby to lean in closely.

Nell and Halford glanced at each other.

'What is it, Mother? What do you want to say, dear?'

Mrs Deal spoke with tremendous effort. 'Mr Wrigley. Go and see Mr Wrigley.'

'Of course, Mother.' Ruby recognised the name of their family solicitor.

Her mother's breathing grew shallower. Ruby, Nell and Halford watched in silence. The sound of the clock ticking on the wall seemed to reverberate in their heads and a wren sang its morning song regardless of the emotions running riot within the room. They leaned forward as one, as the dying woman's eyes flickered open and searched the room.

'Nell, Halford are you there? Look after her, won't you?'

Before they had time to reply, she closed her eyes and with a peaceful sigh, she was gone. They sat in the stillness for several minutes while the clock continued to tick and the wren continued to sing his melody to the world. Ruby continued to stroke her mother's hand.

It was a few days later, that Ruby visited Mr Wrigley, the family solicitor and discovered that her mother had included a clause in her will. It stated that the house should stay in Ruby's name until such time as she, Ruby Rivers died. Learning this fact, Ruby had no idea how felicitous her mother's action would be in the future.

## CHAPTER THREE

**1925...**

'Oh, Mama, look at this,' Midge called breathlessly, picking an envelope off the floor that had at that moment fallen through the letter-box.

'It's a letter for me,' she exclaimed in a tremulous voice.

It was such an unusual event for one of the children to receive a letter that the whole family gathered round to see what it was all about. The little crowd followed her into the kitchen where Midge stopped to examine the white envelope, turning it over carefully. Her name and address were typewritten, giving no clue of the sender's identity.

Grit was the first to explode.

'Well open it then, you silly goose.'

'Grit!' admonished Mama.

Midge slid her finger carefully under the flap and biting her bottom lip she unsealed it and peeped inside. She could see a card with its scalloped edge bordered in gold. Time stood still as everyone held their breath in anticipation. The magic was harshly broken by a loud sniff coming from James.

'Where's your handkerchief, James,' exclaimed Annie as they all breathed out at once.

Pinching the card delicately between her fingers, Midge pulled it out of the envelope. She held it up in front of her face and began to read aloud the words printed in ornate script to the giggles of her younger siblings.

23

'It says....' More giggles were met with a glaring glance from Midge and Annie.

'It says...' she announced grandly –
>**"An Invitation to Miss Annie Mary Eugene Davies…"**

'Who's Annie Mary you Davies?' interrupted young William.

Everyone turned to look at him in surprise. Grit found her voice first.

'It's Midge of course, silly. And it's not you, it's Eugene.'

'But Midge is Midge, how can she be Annie as well?' he asked with a puzzled frown. 'I thought you were Annie, Mama'

'Of course, I suppose you are too young to know that when Midge was born she was a very big baby so we called her the opposite of big which is midget,' Annie explained.

'So, we call her Midge,' put in Grit.

They all laughed at young William's befuddled expression.

Finally, Midge's usual tireless patience gave out.

'Do you want to hear what the invitation says, or don't you?'

'Yes,' they chorused.

Midge gave an important sounding cough and continued:
>**"On the occasion of the sixteenth birthday of our son,**
>**Mr Charles Horace Winterton."**

'Oh, listen to this, Mama. It's at THE GRAND HOTEL.' This she pronounced slowly in a loud voice for extra effect.
>**"Frinton on Sea,"**

Her voice grew louder and more excitable as the words revealed the true nature of the invitation.

>**"A fancy-dress ball on June 23$^{rd}$ 1925**
>**at 7.30 pm until Midnight."**

'Midge's got a boyfriend, Midge's got a boyfriend,' Frank and James whooped with glee.

Young William and Teresa joined in the fun until Annie's head was whirring.

'Now children. Stop teasing your sister and calm down,' she said firmly.

Gratefully, Midge dropped onto the nearest chair and read the whole invitation again. Her elation suddenly changed to dismay, and she threw her hands to her face.

'What am I going to wear, Mama?' she wailed.

Annie leaned over Midge's back with her hands resting on her daughter's shoulders.

'Look, it's not for a few week's yet. We'll put our thinking caps on. We're sure to think of something and you'll look wonderful.'

Five-year-old William wanted to be helpful. 'You can borrow my school cap if you like,' he said thoughtfully,

'Mama doesn't mean a real cap, William,' Midge said, directing a frantic eye towards him. 'She just means we'll all have to think hard, but thank you anyway,' she added, ruffling his hair kindly.

Midge glanced round the room at her family.

'Has anyone got any ideas?'

Over the next few days, the fancy dress ball was the hub of conversation. Ideas for what Midge could wear were getting increasingly bizarre. The boys opted for a cowboy, a train driver or even a priest. This last was Frank's idea.

'You could borrow Cousin Hugh's cassock.'

'Oh, thank you so much,' replied Midge sarcastically.

Teresa was still too young to understand and so Midge was relying on Grit and Mama to have some inspiration. Up to date, Midge had rejected a fairy, Little Bo Peep, a nun and a ballerina, none of which appealed.

It was the sister's habit to sit on their big double bed to chat and gossip in their room while they ragged each other's hair. This was a cunning system to add bouncing curls. Midge would take a tress of Grit's hair and wrap it round her finger. Next, she would thread a strip of rag that had been cut from an old sheet, between her finger and the hair and tie it tight. Grit would repeat the process for Midge until their heads were covered in rags. Next morning the rags were removed, the hair was brushed and hey presto, the girls had a head full of curls.

'Do you like Charles very much?' Grit asked.

'He's all right I suppose,' Midge answered as she plumped up her pillow with her fists. Once they had dived into bed, Midge considered her feelings for Charles.

'I can't imagine why he's asked me to go. All the girls follow him around with droopy eyes. It makes me sick. Urgh,' she shuddered.

'What's he like?' asked Grit in her usual outspoken manner.

'You must surely know him. He's in Mr Vine's class. He's tall with dark hair. His father always drops him off at school in that big Jaguar car.'

'Oh yes,' laughed Grit knowingly, 'now I remember. Oh my! Who's a lucky girl then? Why, if you marry him you'll be rich. Rich Mrs Winterton.' She rolled round the bed, gripping her knees, convulsing with laughter.

Midge threw her pillow at her sister and said good-naturedly,

'He's invited me to the Ball not to get married, you twerp.'

While Grit struggled to contain her mirth, Midge sat thoughtfully.

'He's probably invited lots of other girls as well, so they can all follow him round with their giggles and goo-goo eyes and flirty moves. Well, I for one will not be joining them,' she added in a resigned voice.

Grit giggled as Midge fluttered her eyelids and pursed her lips in an impression of them.

'Anyway, how can I even think of going when I've got nothing to wear?' the older girl concluded before throwing herself back on her pillows and pulling the cover up under her chin.

The eldest Davies' daughter was not one to join with gossip of girlfriends. She preferred sportier past-times such as sailing, swimming, horse riding and tennis. Even working with her father on the farm was better than the boring chitter-chatter of the girls at school. But she had to admit that she did like Charles.

'Wouldn't it be marvellous if he has picked me over all those others? Don't you dare tell Mama or anyone else that I said that will you?' she gasped.

Grit sat up in bed, licked her finger and made the sign of a cross over her heart.

'Cross my heart and hope to die. I promise.'

Suddenly Midge wailed again. 'Oh, but what am I going to go as? We have to think of something. It has to be something glamorous.'

'Yes,' concluded Grit, warming to her sister's enthusiasm.

'Something that will knock the socks off those other girls.'

The two girls loved to share their secrets. At this point in their young carefree lives neither girl foresaw a time when one would betray the other and that an opportunity to forgive or be forgiven would never occur. Innocent of all thoughts of betrayal, they were as thick as thieves, as their father was often heard to say.

Annie loved her garden and next morning after seeing five of her six children off to school, she wandered outside, holding Teresa in her arms while admiring the flowers that were sprouting in the spring sunshine. She was mulling over the question of Midge's fancy dress costume. She strolled along the cinder path through the plants and came to a decision. Whatever Midge wore, it would have to be feminine. At times, she was exasperated with her eldest daughter's lack of interest in her appearance. She was more interested in mucking out the cowsheds than wearing pretty dresses, but Annie realised there was beauty hidden behind the façade of her couldn't-care-less attitude. At fourteen, Midge was now taller than her mother and though big-boned like all the Davies family, she was graced with glossy black hair and gentle brown eyes.

Annie's attention was drawn towards an early tortoiseshell butterfly basking in a sheltered corner of sunlight on a bush of lavender. The flowers were just beginning to open and as she stretched out her hand to pick a stalk of buds, she had a flash of inspiration.

'A lavender girl,' she said out loud to Teresa. 'That's it. I'll make her a beautiful gown in a delicate shade of lavender taffeta and she can carry a basket of lavender flowers.'

Rushing indoors, she put Teresa in her high chair where the baby caught on to Mama's excitement and began clapping her hands. Annie found her box of dress-making patterns and was soon fingering through the pile of packets.

'I'm sure I have one in here somewhere. Come on, where are you?'

She continued her search for another few minutes.

'Ah, here it is. That's the one I was looking for. Just the job.' Teresa chuckled and clapped again.

***

As Midge came out of the school main door that afternoon, she became aware of another body in close proximity to her own. On one side was her friend Maria with her arm linked through Midge's, so turning to see who was closing in on her other side, she was surprised and rather pleased to find Charles matching her pace.

'Oh hello,' she said pleasantly.

'Hello Midge. How are you?'

He had a strong deep tone to his voice and Midge made a mental note of the polite way in which he addressed her.

'Very well, thank you,' she replied equally politely, despite feeling Maria's hand squeezing her arm encouragingly.

'Oh, thank you for the invitation, Charles,' suddenly remembering why he was probably talking to her. *'That's all he wants.'*

He stopped walking and looked earnestly down at her face.

'I'd really like you to come,' he murmured, as if reading her thoughts.

As she gazed up into his eyes, she noticed how brown they were.

*So brown. So beautiful. So...*

'Midge,' hissed Maria shaking her arm.

'Er, right. Yes. Righto,' she stuttered and was relieved that the appearance of Grit at that moment was enough to hide her embarrassment.

'Bye then, Midge,' smiled Charles as he waved and walked off in the opposite direction.

Midge didn't dare look back and remonstrated when Maria and Grit sneaked a glance.

'Ooh,' Grit teased.

'He likes you…. a lot,' offered Maria knowingly, being a self-confessed expert on matters of love and ways of the world. Midge didn't see how that was possible because they were the same age but Maria had a favourite saying.

'Trust me. I know what I'm talking about.'

Midge didn't trust her in the subject of her personal love life but such as it was, she deeply wanted to believe that Maria was right this time. They continued on their way until Maria turned off at her house with a grin and a wave and the two sisters made their way to the boy's school to pick up their brothers.

As they charged noisily through the door of their home and into the kitchen they found their mother sitting at the table, grinning like a Cheshire cat that had been given all the cream. Teresa sat on her knee, banging her hands on the table while Annie jiggled her up and down. On the table, right in the centre was a packet. The boys crowded round and Midge stretched across their heads and picked the package up. The drawing on the cover of the packet showed a slim young woman wearing a long dress with a full skirt pinched in at the waist topped by a tight bodice with an off-the-shoulder neck-line. Midge was so busy looking at the picture that she hadn't noticed the sprigs of flowers that Annie had laid beneath the packet. Frank spotted them and picked them up.

'What are these, Mama?'

'Ah, now who knows what these flowers are?'

The sprigs were passed round.

'Smell them,' she urged.

The three boys made disgusted noises but Grit and Midge held the flowers to their noses and inhaled gently. They looked at each other.

'Lavender,' they shouted in unison.

'But I don't understand Mama,' cried Midge. 'What does it all mean?'

'It means, child, that you can go to the ball as a lavender girl,' said Annie.

Seeing their puzzled expressions, she laughed and explained.

'Years ago, girls would gather baskets full of lavender and walk round the streets selling it in bunches or cloth bags with the dried flower heads inside. We've made lavender bags, haven't we? Well in those days people used it far more. There were so many horrid smells that they would hold the lavender bag under their nose or hang them inside their cupboards to make their clothes smell nice. We don't need to hold them under our noses now but we still like to keep them in our wardrobes and drawers. So,' she continued, 'I'm going to make Midge a dress like that one in the picture out of lavender taffeta.'

Midge threw her arms round her Mama.

'You're the best Mama in the whole world. Thank you.'

***

Midge could hardly contain her excitement when she woke on the morning of the Fancy Dress Ball. Grit was almost as excited. They had both stayed awake for hours the night before and eventually exhausted themselves into a deep sleep. Annie had worked wonders on the dress and the two sisters went outside early to pick the fresh lavender stalks. The flowers were at their peak as they laid them in an open basket, finishing it off with a large floppy lavender ribbon tied in a bow.

As they were finishing it, there was a shout from the front hall.

'Yoo-hoo, anybody home?'

It was Aunty Kitty bustling through to the living room where they were all gathered.

'Now then, how's my little lavender girl?' she said, reaching out for Midge.

She smothered her niece in her ample bosom with a hug and a wet kiss, and then reached out to the others in turn. Annie and Aunty Kitty were sisters. She and Gabriel Bartrum had four sons, Hugh, Norbert, Maurice and Michael. With all these boys, Kitty always made a big fuss of their three nieces. The occasion of the Fancy Dress Ball was causing a stir throughout the whole family.

'I wouldn't miss this day for the world,' Kitty declared as she sat herself down in a comfortable armchair. Folding her arms across her chest, bosom resting on them, she almost appeared to hug herself as she contemplated Midge's grand entrance in the hotel. Annie and Kitty had been ensconced in the living room almost every day for the last two weeks cutting, pinning and stitching, occasionally calling Midge to stand on a chair for a fitting.

Now that the day had actually arrived, they were jittery with nerves.

'Anybody would think you and Mama were going to the Ball,' Midge joked. 'You're making me nervous. I'll go and get some tea brewed, Mama. I think we're going to need it.'

Later that morning Annie and Kitty's sister-in-law, Babs arrived with her sons. Midge offered to take the younger children out of the way with Grit, but the three women wouldn't hear of it.

'No, no,' Aunty Babs insisted. 'I've brought Boy and Eric to entertain them. You need to preserve your strength, lovie. We can't have you disappearing and getting into mischief or having to rescue someone today of all days. Please just sit down and relax. Have another cup of tea.'

After dinner, Midge made a face at Grit in a plea to be rescued from all the fuss and when the women fell into memories of their teenage years, the two girls crept out of the room.

Shutting the door of her bedroom Midge let out a big sigh.

'Oh, what a fuss. I wish they'd stop talking about it.'

Five minutes later, the door opened and Eric and Boy came bounding in, wanting to know what Charles was like.

'Will he make a suitable husband?' said Boy in perfect mimicry of his Uncle Bill.

They were laughing when Aunty Babs called out from the bottom of the stairs.

'Will you boys come down and take Frank and James and young William out to the park to play. We need to have a male-free house for a while. Hair-dressing and all that, you understand.'

They didn't, but decided they'd heard enough of dresses, boyfriends and girl talk for one day.

'Coming Mother,' they yelled as they clattered down the stairs.

***

Midge sat in the kitchen having endured hours with rags in her hair, then a further hour having it brushed and tweaked and tied up with a lavender bow. When she saw the result in the mirror that Grit held, she turned to Annie with a red face.

'Mama, do I have to wear this bow in my hair. It looks so…' She struggled for the right word, waving her hands in the air, '…babyish.'

Out came the bow and a new hair style was devised until all were satisfied. Next came the dress. Midge thought it looked exactly like the drawing on the pattern cover. The colour was exactly the right shade of lavender to match the sprigs in her basket. Mama had even bought her a strapless brassiere, because of the off-the-shoulder design. The bodice was slightly gathered, which contrasted with the tight waistline, giving her an enviable hour-glass figure. Annie had added a layer of fine lace to the yards of taffeta drawn into the waistband that made up the skirt.

'I'll have to keep visiting the ladies' room to hitch it up!' Midge said to Grit in a jittery voice as she wriggled into the dress.

Grit thought that was hilarious and they chuckled nervously.

'Babs, did you bring your bag of tricks?' asked Annie.

'Oh yes, of course. Come along, Midge. Let's put the finishing touches on.'

Without a moment's hesitation, Babs produced her make-up bag and after rummaging round for several seconds brought out a powder compact, lipstick, a pot of rouge and mascara. When Midge saw it all, she first looked at the items lined up on the table and then turned to her mother.

'Surely, you're not going to put all that on my face, are you?' she cried timidly.

Annie and Kitty laughed with a knowing look.

'Look at me, Midge,' ordered Babs.

In fifteen minutes, Midge had been transformed.

'Oh, Annie, will you just look at her,' sighed Kitty as the women stepped back to review their handiwork.

Just at that moment Midge's father walked in. All eyes turned towards him. They waited for his reaction. Annie silently shot up a hasty prayer asking for him to be pleased.

'Who is this beautiful young lady?' he beamed. 'Can it be my little girl?'

Aunty Babs countered, laughing raucously, 'Not so little now, eh Will?'

***

Will's chest swelled with pride as he pulled up in front of the impressive steps that led up to entrance of The Grand Hotel. It was an old mansion house that had been converted into a prestigious hotel many years earlier. Virginia creeper covered the face of the building and lights glowed in all the downstairs windows, revealing a hive of activity within.

'I'll be waiting for you at midnight. Mind your manners now,' he reminded his eldest daughter as she made her way into the foyer.

With a quick embarrassed wave, she disappeared amidst the throng of excited teenagers. Midge scanned the faces that surrounded her, searching for her friends. Maria spotted her first and shouted out across the bobbing heads. Battling their way towards each other they hugged and then leaned back to admire their outfits. Afterwards, they stood side by side praising or criticizing others, depending how well they liked the object of interest.

Suddenly Maria began jumping up and down, waving her hand high. In no time at all, the two friends were joined by several giggling girls and made their way into the ballroom. The orchestra was playing a lively quickstep as the girls tottered round the edge of the dance floor on unaccustomed high heels. Gradually, the young ladies dispersed as they were selected to dance.

Midge's heart leapt as Charles bowed before her and took her hand. He swept the long purple and gold cloak around his body as he did so. The golden threads woven through the cloth glittered as he moved. He was an Arabian knight, complete with a jewel encrusted black turban and carrying a sword in its sheath.

As he stood to his full height and looked at her, Midge saw the admiration in his eyes and blushed, thankful for the dimmed lights. As they twirled round the dance floor, she couldn't help a trace of smugness playing on her lips, when she spotted the jealous eyes of some of the other girls.

During a lady's 'excuse me' waltz, Midge struggled to maintain her dignity as girl after girl, tapped him on the shoulder in order to dance with him. As soon as the dance ended, Midge, who had been watching him out of the corner of her eye, suddenly found him towering over her once again.

'Thank goodness that's over with. I can't stand all those giggling girls,' he said with a shudder.

Laughing, Midge accepted his hand as they stepped onto the dance floor again. The Charleston proved to be a bit tricky to dance in her long dress. That was followed by the Black Bottom which was positively dangerous, but laughing and panting at their antics, they finally left the floor to revive themselves with cold drinks. It was necessary for Charles to lean low and close to Midge so that they could hear each other speak over the sounds of the orchestra. Before she knew what was happening, he had put his arm round her shoulders and pulled her even closer, planting his lips firmly on hers. Feeling flustered, she breathed deeply as he released her and gazed into her eyes.

*Mm,'* she thought, *'that was nice.*

It was nice, but not as wonderful as she had heard some of the girls telling each other about their experiences with boys. Not exactly earth shattering. Just nice.

*But still, things may get better,* she thought as she returned his smile.

The evening flew by. It seemed only a few minutes had passed before Midge was hobbling as delicately as she could, down the hotel steps towards her father's car at midnight. The evening had flashed by in a flurry of quicksteps, waltzes, foxtrots and those crazy dances. She and Charles had won the spot waltz. She had whispered a prayer of thanks for her school dancing lessons at the moment when they received their prize and Charles had kissed her in front of everyone. And when everyone had sung 'Happy Birthday' to him, he'd looked straight at her.

As she sat in her father's car on the way home, she shivered at the memory of the whole experience. She was so happy she thought she would burst, she could never be this happy again.

## CHAPTER FOUR

**1926...**
'We're going to call the house, "Veronica". What do you think of that?' Will asked his family as they gathered together for the first time in the living room of their new house.

Midge's eyes immediately filled with tears and she struggled to keep the lump out of her throat. Annie grasped her hand, understanding her daughter's emotion at the memory of their darling angel. The other children were racing round the house. They had watched in awe as it grew from a few marks on the land to the first layers of bricks, and then seen as it developed into a building with rooms and a staircase and finally the roof went on.

'That's a wonderful name, Papa. She'll be with us for ever and ever,' Midge ventured when she felt she had control of her voice.

The house had been two years in the building and Will and Annie were very pleased and proud of it. It was a square house with four bay windows at the front and a door with a porch. A narrow, smaller window peeped out above the porch. A slate roof topped it off with a chimney at each end. There was plenty of land surrounding the house in which Will planned to plant an orchard of apple trees. Midge and Grit would share one bedroom, the three boys in another, with Will and Annie sharing a third room with baby Teresa. That left one small room spare.

'When can Teresa come and sleep in our room, Mama?' Grit asked one morning as they cleared the breakfast things away. Will and Annie had been discussing this question, knowing that Teresa couldn't sleep in their bedroom forever. Annie now called Midge to her side next to Grit and put her arms round them.

'It's funny you say that, Grit, because Papa and I were talking about this very thing only the other day. Midge, we thought you might like to have a room to yourself now you're a teenager and Teresa can sleep with Grit.'

Midge pursed her lips and frowned thoughtfully, unsure of the idea. She'd shared a room with Grit for so long it would take some getting used to.

'Teresa's three years old. She's getting too big to share our room and you and Grit will still have lots of time to be together.' Annie assured her gently, seeing her hesitation.

'What do you think about it, Grit?' she asked, turning to the younger girl.

Grit was mulling it over. Silently she thought she would quite like to have her little sister to care for. She had been the younger one for so long, it would be fun to be a big sister for a change.

'You're nearly grown up now, Midge. I could still come in before we go to sleep and talk for a while, so I don't mind. Honestly,' Grit explained. She looked closely into her sister's eyes, searching for any sign of hurt feelings.

Suddenly, Midge reached her conclusion.

'Yes. I will then. Yes,' she shouted enthusiastically. 'Can we go and sort the rooms out now, Mama?'

'Yes, of course you can,' laughed Annie, pleased to see their plan work out well.

The two girls raced off up the stairs and began moving furniture and cupboards. It kept them busy for several hours until they charged back down the stairs announcing that all was ready. Little Teresa was swept up between them with shrieks of laughter and carried to her new bedroom. They fussed over her until Annie was forced to remonstrate with them.

'For goodness sake, girls you're smothering her. You must take it in turns to hold her. Poor child has three mothers.'

Frank, James and young William decided to join them. Amid much jostling and joking they all piled in. Teresa was very proud to think she was such a big girl to be able to sleep in a proper bed with her sister.

Grit helped to move Midge's things into the smallest bedroom in the house. There was just enough space for a narrow single bed, with a small wardrobe and a chair. Papa had built some shelves in a cupboard over the stairs that she immediately filled with her books. A long narrow window let in the morning sunshine and she couldn't have been happier with it.

The next day was a Saturday and after she had done her jobs for her Mama, Midge sat on the bed with her arms locked round her knees. Her eyes wandered around the room and she decided she liked the pale blue--e walls. It reminded her of the blue sky she could see from her window. Midge realised that if she sat in bed she could see the sky. Her attention drifted to the window again. She spotted a robin singing heartily on the branch of a tree very close to her window. She loved to watch the birds and butterflies and this was the ideal spot. As she gazed out she could see the branches of the trees swaying and dancing. It made her want to dance and sing. Sitting there alone, she treasured her thoughts of Charles. This was her very own world, one that she came to value more than she could have perceived in earlier days

It had been almost a year since her romance with Charles had begun at his birthday ball, when Midge had dressed as a lavender girl. She had to pinch herself occasionally to remind herself it was real. They enjoyed each other's company, horse-riding along the sands or across the countryside, at other times sailing out on the open sea. Daydreaming about that first time together suddenly gave her the idea for the new colour of her room. Although she had thought she was happy with the sky-blue, now she had a change of heart.

'Mama,' she yelled at the top of her voice. 'Mama, I know what colour I want my bedroom walls to be.'

She had finished her sentence even before she had found her mother.

'Midge. Stop shouting like a fish-wife! It's not lady-like,' Annie reprimanded. 'Now calm down and tell me quietly what it is you are trying to say?'

Midge took a deep breath to calm herself. 'Lilac. I'd like to have my bedroom in the colour lilac, please Mama.'

'We probably should have done the decorating before you moved all the furniture in there. Well it's too late now, we'll just have to do it as best we can,' replied Annie patiently.

***

Time passed quickly by for the Davies family in "Veronica". Midge left school and spent most of her time working with her father on the farm as well as running her own greengrocery round.

She had learnt to drive and could be seen trundling around the neighbourhood selling her fruit and vegetables. The younger children felt very privileged when she picked them up from school in her van. It was like one of their big sister's adventures. Her boyfriend, Charles was often to be found playing cricket or kicking a football with Midges young brothers. He was liked by her family which was an important fact for Midge.

With her seventeenth birthday approaching, she was excited to apply for enrolment at the Royal School of Nursing in London. A few weeks later a letter arrived for her, announcing an appointment for her to attend a medical examination. Travelling alone for the first time on the train to London, she felt the butterflies in her stomach but kept an outward appearance of quiet maturity. She watched the world pass by, occasionally having to peer through the smoke from the train engine for a glimpse of the landscape. But soon the green fields gave way to grim tall buildings, their dark, forbidding walls stretching high beside the railway lines. Then the whistle screamed, awakening a man sleeping soundly on the seat opposite to Midge. She hid a smile with her hand as he struggled to wipe a dribble of saliva that had run from his mouth. He coughed, embarrassed by his lack of control. Midge kept her eyes on the scene outside so as not to make him feel uncomfortable. As the train screeched to a halt, leaving her co-passengers to gather their belongings, she jumped down onto the platform and made her way out of the station and on to the next stage of her journey.

The hospital receptionist had given her directions and she soon found herself sitting on a hard, wooden, straight-backed chair in the austere waiting room. There was a smell of disinfectant that was making her feel slightly nauseous. After a short wait a telephone on the receptionist's desk rang giving Midge a fright.
'You can go in now,' the receptionist instructed as she led Midge through a dark green door. She found herself in a small room furnished with a table and chair on which sat a rather stern looking woman. There was a paper file on the table that the woman consulted as Midge walked in.
'Miss Davies?' Midge nodded with a quiet 'yes'.
'Stand over there by the wall,' the woman called as she stretched out a long arm with a pointed finger. 'I need to test your eye-sight first'.
Midge then spotted the chart on the opposite side of the room. Not moving from her chair, the woman instructed Midge to begin at the top and work down until she could not read any more Midge
breathed a sigh of relief that she had managed to read all the way down to the tiny print.
Next came a hearing test. This time the woman rose from her chair after first writing something down in the file. She came to stand behind Midge who felt slightly threatened by this woman's severe countenance.
'I shall now make some small noises. As soon as you hear something, I want you to raise your hand. Do you understand?'
Midge nodded her head. Her mouth was too dry to say anything now for she knew she was slightly deaf. Would this effect the result? Midge was able to raise her hand for the first few sounds then stood waiting for further noises. After a few moments, the woman walked quickly back to her seat at the table. She began writing again.
'Now I must listen to your chest. Please remove your blouse and come over here to me.'
Midge did as she was told and stood patiently while the cold stethoscope was pressed to her chest and back. The woman sat again and began writing in the file. Midge waited for her next instruction. Abruptly, the woman looked up, her eagle eyes searching Midge's eyes.
'What are you waiting for?' she tutted. 'Get yourself dressed and then go and wait outside until I call for you with your results.'

Midge did as she was told and made her way quietly to the door. Closing it as carefully as she could, she glanced at the receptionist who continued with her work without looking up.

*No encouragement from her*, thought Midge.

As she sat down, she suddenly felt weary and a little dejected. She was certain she had failed the medical examination.

It was a sad girl who retraced her steps on the return journey that she had begun so full of hope. She had failed the medical test due to slight deafness and a weak chest. Disappointed, she returned home to the farm but determined not to give up hope of working with children. In the meantime, she would continue to help her mother where she could with her younger siblings, and her father at the farm.

## CHAPTER FIVE

## 1930...

After four years living in the house called "Veronica", Annie had despaired of rekindling any intimacy in her marriage to Will. As the seasons advanced he became more distant than ever and she plunged further into church life, travelling on the bus to spend time with people who were responsive to her efforts. Nothing she did would please him anymore and he seemed to find the children to be a nuisance, except for Midge.

Sometimes Midge would take the boys with her to help on the farm, but their father was easily annoyed and impatient with them so they went there less and less. Annie's determination to continue in a loveless marriage was weakening rapidly, along with her resolve to obey the laws of a Catholic union.

The last straw came when she heard rumours of Will being involved with another woman and in 1930 she made the momentous decision to leave him.

It was a painful day for all the family when they packed their belongings and moved eight miles away to Walton on the Naze. Annie had found a house quite close to her brother and sister and their families who unselfishly offered welcome support. She would be able to take in lodgers, providing her with an income.

Midge helped her mother set the business up using her knowledge of book-keeping that she had learnt after her nursing career failed to get off the ground. It was useful in helping her father and now invaluable to her mother, but she was restless, still feeling the urge to work with children.

Grit had left home. She and Midge had always agreed that they would both like to be nurses but it was Grit alone who had achieved her ambition. She was now enrolled in the very nursing college where Midge had previously been denied access.

One day, Midge was sitting down to breakfast with her mother after the lodgers had left for work and Teresa and the boys were in school.

'Mama, my friend was telling me about a family who are looking for an au pair to care for their two little boys. You know how I've always loved looking after children. I think I'd like to apply for the job,' she said gently.

Annie laughed at her daughter's hesitancy.

'Well, you've had enough practice with all your brothers and sisters, haven't you? I think you'd make a wonderful au pair. Do I know the family?'

'Their name is Mr and Mrs Swain. They're American.'

'Oh, my goodness,' chuckled Annie. 'They must be the family that have recently moved here. I heard they were asking about a church and I was going to pay them a call. Shall we go together and introduce ourselves?'

The Swain family took to Midge instantly and she to them. Their two young sons, Hugo and Junior fell in love with her at first sight.

When Midge saw Hugo, she wanted to sweep him up into her arms. Mrs Swain immediately detected the emotion in Midge's eyes.

'Hugo was a premature baby which has made him frail and vulnerable to any illness. He's a little undersized for his age but he makes up for that with his intelligence,' she explained rather proudly. She paused to gaze lovingly on her little boy. 'I can see he's already concluded that he approves of you!'

Midge understood now the reason for his alabaster skin. His large, vivid blue eyes seemed to encompass his whole face and stared straight into hers as he stretched out his tiny hand to grasp hers in a formal handshake. He shared the red hair of his brother but there the similarity ended for though eighteen months younger, Junior was as solid as Hugo was slight and at least six inches taller. Junior stepped forward after Hugo, also offering a formal handshake.

'Your boys are such polite young gentlemen, such wonderful manners,' Annie said, as she watched this amazing spectacle. She turned with raised eyebrows towards Midge, thinking of her own boisterous family.

'How many children do you have, Mrs Davies?'

Annie smiled. 'Oh, I've had three girls, three boys and Teresa.' They discovered mutual interests as Annie shared her knowledge of the area and her church over several cups of tea.

'What work are you doing at the moment, Midge?' Mr Swain asked.

'I'm helping my father on the farm and doing his accounts. I also help Mama with her book-keeping, but what I really want to do is work with children.'

By this time, she had already made friends with the children and suddenly Mr Swain rose from his chair.

'Would you excuse us for a moment?'

The couple disappeared into another room while Midge and Annie chatted to Hugo and Junior, Annie covertly inspecting the room.

On their return Mr Swain said, 'We can see how the boys have already taken to Midge, Mrs Davies, and we think she would be an invaluable asset to our family.'

Turning to Midge, he continued, 'We'd like you to come and look after Hugo and Junior, starting as soon as possible, Midge. What do you say to next Monday?'

Midge felt a little overwhelmed, but receiving a gentle, encouraging nod from her mother, she grinned with relief.

'Yes please. I'd like that very much.'

Mr Swain excused himself and disappeared.

'Come along, honey. You can have a look at your room. Our other au pair was a gem but she decided she wanted to move into the medical profession caring for terminally ill children. She'd been with us since Hugo was born,' said Mrs Swain as she moved towards the door.

'Oh,' replied Midge rather despondently, feeling inadequate.

'Now don't worry about a thing, Midge. We're not expecting you to replicate her, just be yourself. Look at those two little guys. They know you're going to be just fine.'

Each child had scuttled nearer to grab hold of one of Midge's hands and was gazing up at her adoringly.

As they made their way home, Midge linked arms with her mother.

'Did you see the room they had for me, Mama? I didn't realise they'd want me to live there. Those boys are so lovely. I just wanted to cuddle them all the time,' she said dreamily.

Annie wanted to join her daughter's enthusiasm but it suddenly hit her that her little girl was a young woman and setting out on her own adventures in life. She found the thought a mite scary but didn't want Midge to notice her emotions. These were a mother's natural instincts, so she patted Midge's hand and agreed.

'They seem to be a lovely caring family. You're going to have a marvellous time.' She paused and took a deep breath. 'I'm going to miss you though. Terribly.'

'I won't be far away and I'll get time off so I can come home. And I'm sure to see you every Sunday at church.'

Annie was somewhat comforted by that thought.

*I shouldn't be so unprepared for Midge leaving home,* she scolded herself.

When Midge was set to go nursing, Annie had accepted the inevitable. But now, with Grit having moved to London a few months earlier to start her nursing training and this new position for Midge, it all seemed so final. Since leaving her husband, even though Annie firmly believed it to be the right course to take, she still felt vulnerable and at times even a little scared.

Later that day, Annie confided her thoughts to her own mother. 'I'm so thankful that the family Midge is going to live with is Catholic. I feel happier knowing that we'll see her every Sunday.'

Unwittingly, her mother cast a cloud over Annie's head once again. 'Of course, you never know if they might want to move away. I heard they'd moved quite a lot already.'

Annie took another sip of tea, staring blankly at the currant cake on her plate, having suddenly lost her appetite. For a minute or so, she sat silently while her mother pottered around her small kitchen.

'Have you finished with that tea, Annie? Oh, and look at that, you've not touched your currant bun.'

Annie was jolted out of her reverie. 'Yes, I've finished. I'm not very hungry, thank you Mother. I must get home quickly,' she said, realising she didn't want to waste a minute of these last few days with her beloved Midge. She knew Teresa would miss her big sister too. With Grit now living away from home, her eldest and youngest daughters were enjoying each other's company despite the thirteen years that separated them.

\*\*\*

Several months later, Midge was sitting in the garden on one of her days off. Times of being with her boyfriend Charles had long gone. It was simply a teenage fling. Now as she sat in contemplation, with the sun's rays filtering through the blossom of the overhanging branches of an apple tree, she watched the patterns of shadows as they danced across the flowers in her mother's herbaceous border. Her mind was on the news that Mrs Swain had given her that morning and was waiting to tell Annie. As her mother came down the steps to join her, Midge looked up and smiled warmly. Annie bent down to kiss her daughter's cheek in a tender welcome.

'Hello, darling. It's good to see you.'

'Hello Mama.'

After talking about the weather and the garden flowers, Annie glanced thoughtfully at her daughter.

'Midge, what's the matter? You seem a bit distant. Have you got something on your mind?'

Midge always shared things easily with her mother, but she knew this latest news would be hard for Annie. Slowly, she took a breath and revealed what was on her mind.

'The Swains are going on a trip round Europe for three months and they want me to go with them to help with the children.'

Midge stopped as she heard her mother's sharp intake of breath.

'Three months?... Oh, but it's a wonderful opportunity for you, Midge,' she said as she gathered herself together. 'We'll miss you of course. When are they planning to start the holiday?'

'We leave to spend a few days in London on the 5<sup>th</sup> June.'

'Oh, my goodness, so soon,' said Annie, all of a flutter. A sudden change of heart caused her to declare, 'How marvellous for you Midge.'

She stood, pulling Midge to her feet. 'We must go and tell Aunty Kitty and Aunty Babs. Come on, let's go.'

Later, as they prepared the evening meal together, Midge felt concern for her youngest sister.

'Let me tell Teresa, Mama,' she paused, and with a sigh, added, 'I wish I could take her with me.'

'You'll have to tell Papa as well, Midge.'

'Mm, that's true, though I suppose he won't miss me so much now that I'm not helping him on the farm.'

'Yes. He seems to be managing well with the young lads from the village helping him, doesn't he?'

The day of Midge's departure drew nearer and when she was allowed a weekend at home to be with her family she was glad to spend some time with Teresa and their mother as well as visiting her father. Midge found it difficult to come to terms with her parent's separated lives. But all her attempts at changing her mother's mind had met with a determination she had not witnessed before and her father refused even to discuss it. Midge was a happy young woman and wanted those she loved to be the same. The situation with her parents gave her a degree of uncertainty about her own life, though she had to concede that her mother was successfully striving to be independent.

When Midge told her father of her impending travels, his reply came rather grumpily. 'Ah well, I suppose I might have expected you'd leave sooner or later, though I don't know who's going to do my book-keeping now.'

As he turned back to the cow he was milking, Midge looked down at her feet, not knowing what to say. She listened to the gentle sound of the milk squirting into the pale for a few moments.

'Mm, I'm sorry about that, Papa, but I'm only going for three months, not for ever. You'll surely find someone else to take care of it for a while, won't you?'

Her father simply carried on milking without turning back to face her, effectively ending their conversation.

'Bye then, Papa,' she whispered, sighing tremulously.

When he made no reply, she spun on her heel and walked away. Grabbing her bicycle that was leaning on the cow shed wall she rode off as quickly as she could. She didn't see the expression on his face as he shifted his position in order to have one last glimpse of his daughter as she disappeared out of sight. He remained with his head leaning on the cow's warm flank for several seconds, staring in the direction she had taken, lost in thought, until suddenly shaking himself to return to his task.

***

'Mama, there's a post card from Midge.'

Teresa raced to the front door as she heard the letterbox rattle, clattering down the stairs and along the hall, yelling at the top of her voice.

Annie came into the hall, drying her hands on a towel, peering eagerly over Teresa's shoulder.

'What does she say, dear?'

Teresa read aloud:

*Dear Mama and all,*
*Been to London Zoo and cathedrals in Canterbury, York & Durham and castles in Chester and York. Marvellous hotels. Boys well behaved. Arrived in Bergen, Norway yesterday. Love Midge.*

Annie gasped in amazement.

'My goodness, they've done so much already and only just left the country. Let's see, when did she write this? Mm, 16$^{th}$ June. Oh, I expect she's started travelling through Europe now.'

Teresa was bubbling with excitement and studying the post card.

'Look, Mama, it's a picture of a place called Trafalgar Square in London. Do you think her hotel was there?'

'It could have been, I suppose.'

Ten days later as Teresa arrived home from school, she hung her satchel on the hall-stand and heard her mother calling.

'I'm in the sitting room, darling. There's something here you'd like to see.'

She skipped through the doorway and sat next to Annie on the sofa as her mother waved several sheets of notepaper in front of her. Her mouth opened wide and she let out a shriek of delight.

'A letter from Midge. Hooray!'

Annie had read the letter several times since it had been pushed through the letter box that morning, giving her time to savour her daughter's news. It was such a relief to know that Midge was relaxed and enjoying herself. Teresa began the letter:

*28/6/31*

*Dear Mama and all,*

*We've been to some beautiful villages since arriving in Norway. In one called Ulvik we watched a Norwegian wedding and, in the evening, I danced with a young German called Frederik. (Very handsome!!!) We have spent a lot of time travelling by car, yet Hugo and Junior have been so good. The scenery is breath-taking. We had extra excitement two days ago when we travelled by steamer to Leon. It's pouring with rain today and Junior has a cold. We hope it doesn't affect Hugo. I am packing (again) as tomorrow we have a long drive up to over 6000ft to Grocli. We're not expecting to get there until about 9 o'clock in the evening. Will probably fall into bed. I hope the boys settle down quickly.*

*Hope all at home are well. Mama, please give my love to Teresa, Frank, James and young William.*

*I've written to Grit and Papa.*

*I miss you. Love always, Midge.*

*PS We'll be staying at the Grand Hotel, Stockholm from 8$^{th}$ to 11$^{th}$ July if you want to write to me there.*

'Isn't Midge the luckiest person in the world, Mama?' asked Teresa in awe.

'She certainly is. She's having the experience of a lifetime.'

'Yes, but she is working,' reminded Teresa in a serious voice.

'I agree, but Hugo and Junior sound like little angels. I can't imagine even attempting to travel round like that with you rascals,' she laughed as she heard her three sons bounding into the house, back from school.

'Come and read the letter from your sister, boys,' she cried, trying to make herself heard above the racket.

They all missed their big sister. She had always been there for them, full of fun and laughter. Of course, since working for the Swain family, her time at home had been limited, but she continued to make each of her siblings feel special. They loved her and were eager to hear her news.

'Midge's twenty-first birthday is coming up soon. Shall we send her a birthday card through the post?' suggested Frank after reading her letter through. 'Look, she says she'll be at the Grand Hotel in Stockholm.'

'What a wonderful idea, Frank,' sighed Annie, kissing him briskly on the cheek. 'We'll all go to the shop tomorrow and choose a card for her. If we send it straight away, it should reach the hotel in time.'

The next day Annie took her four children to choose a card. After they had all signed it, the envelope was carefully sealed and addressed. With great ceremony they sent it on its way.

'D'you think she'll do something extra special to celebrate as it's her 21$^{st}$, Mama?' asked Teresa with concern.

'I don't know, Teresa. I hope she will, but with all that travelling, maybe there won't be an opportunity.'

The family waited with baited breath for the next instalment from Europe. They hoped against hope that their card would reach the hotel in time for Midge to receive it. They also prayed that Midge would be able to enjoy this major milestone in her life.

At last, eight days after Midge's birthday, Annie bent down to retrieve an envelope, addressed in Midge's familiar handwriting.

*13$^{th}$ & 14$^{th}$ July 1931*
*Dear All,*
*Thank you, thank you, thank you! Your delightful birthday card was waiting for me when we arrived at the Grand Hotel in Stockholm (and VERY grand it was too!). Thank God for the Royal Mail. On THE DAY, I took the children to the park in the morning, but in the afternoon, I went shopping alone. I treated myself to a beautiful dress. Mama, you'll love it. (You know I'm not one for wearing dresses, but I couldn't resist this one.) It's dark blue with small white spots, long sleeves, a gorgeous floating skirt and in a jersey material. Mr and Mrs Swain gave me a string of pearls which was*

*very generous of them. Today (14<sup>th</sup>), I'm brought back down to earth again, doing the ironing!*
*The weather has improved and after driving away from Grocli, where there was snow, we've been able to swim in the sea and the boys have played in the sand and had great fun building sand castles. We found a lovely park where I could take them every day. Wonderful – we were there for three whole days! I even took them to the museum that they enjoyed. Oh, I must tell you. I've had my hair waved. I look a real bobby dazzler! On the same day we visited some Viking ships in Oslo. Very impressive. Frank would have loved them. Tomorrow we leave for Dresden in Germany. We're staying there for five days. Hoorah! The next place we will stop for five days will be Lucerne in Switzerland. At the Grand Hotel again, (we've stayed at several).*
*I've written a few letters – Grit, Papa, etc. etc.*
*Give my love to all, from Midge.*

Annie placed the letter on the table in front of her, smoothing out the paper with the flat of her hand.

'Phew, it makes me breathless just listening to all that moving around,' said Kitty.

They sat on the opposite sides of the table, each cradling a cup of tea.

'Yes, me too,' conceded Annie. 'But what an opportunity, Kitty. There was nothing like that in our day, was there?'

'No, we were lucky if we had a trip to Southend.'

The two women laughed at their childhood memories.

'Well, I'm sure Midge appreciates the experience,' finished Annie as she stood up and collected the cups.

They moved into the scullery where Kitty helped Annie to sort out the laundry.

'The children will be excited to have another letter.'

'Yes, they will. It's the last day of school, so it'll be something nice to start the holidays off,' answered Annie as she folded the last of the towels in a neat stack.

\*\*\*

The children threw themselves into the halcyon, school-free days with wild abandon. There was always something to keep them occupied, whether it was helping Annie with the housework and garden or travelling on the bus to Blue House Farm to help their father with the cows or milk round or playing cricket and tennis, sailing and swimming in the sea. Having them around was a blessed distraction for their mother. There wasn't time to dwell on the absence of Midge and Grit.

'Is there a letter from Midge today, Mama?' Teresa asked as she came into the kitchen with tousled hair and sleepy eyes. She stretched and yawned before sitting herself down at the kitchen table. As she stifled another yawn, Annie turned from her task to view her youngest daughter.

'Teresa Davies, get your elbows off the table. What a blessing it's the holidays, you'd never get to school looking like that,' she declared with a frown. 'And that's the third time this week you've asked that question. You'll just have to be patient. She is supposed to be working remember.'

Annie didn't care to admit that she too was getting impatient for another bulletin. Stirring herself back to the state of her daughter, sitting in front of her looking like a scarecrow, she snapped rather more angrily than she intended.

'Teresa, go and get washed and dressed, and get those brothers of yours moving too.'

Muttering to herself, she returned to the breakfasts she was preparing for her lodgers, mentally ticking off a list of jobs she would get the children to do.

It was later, while Frank was sweeping the front steps and path that she heard a raucous shout.

'Mama, the postman's brought a post card from Midge.'

Everyone rushed to the front door, calling to each other on the way. This time, the family was a little disappointed.

'She doesn't say very much,' said a deflated Frank who had taken the card from the postman.

*Weather very hot. Driven from Dresden to Prague, then Vienna, Salzburg & Innsbruck. Now in Lucerne, Switzerland. Had to call doctor in for Junior. Mass in Lucerne cathedral. Love Midge.*

'That's all it says.'

Turning the card over, he looked at the picture of a large church in Vienna, before handing it over to his mother. Dejectedly, they returned to their jobs while Annie read the card again. She placed it on the mantelshelf alongside the first card they'd received, then folding her arms across her chest she stood quietly staring at the pictures. Minutes later, Teresa found her mother there. Even at eight years of age, Teresa was sensitive enough to note Annie's mood. Stepping forward, she hugged her mother. Annie raised her arms and put them round Teresa. They stood together, gently swaying.

'I wonder what's wrong with Junior. All that travelling round can't be good for those children. Midge must be tired too. We must pray for Midge and the family,' Annie whispered.

It was with surprise and some trepidation that Annie found an envelope on the doormat after only two days had passed since receiving the postcard.

The letter read:

*9/8/31*

*Dear Mama,*
*Thank goodness Junior recovered enough for us to leave Lucerne. We stopped off in Interlaker for three nights, but then Hugo started to feel ill. We made it to our next stop, Oberhofen, but had to rush him to hospital. He's had appendicitis, and looks terrible, poor mite. On top of that, it's been raining practically non-stop, though I did manage to take Junior to the beach yesterday for a short time. He was a bit lost without his brother. Tomorrow I am going to see Hugo in hospital. The doctors have told Mrs Swain that they will be taking his tubes out tomorrow but will probably have to stay in hospital for another four or five days. We all hope and pray he will recover his strength quickly.*
*We'll be spending about a week in Paris from 23$^{rd}$ August so I'll write again from there. I am looking forward to Paris, especially staying longer than one night. We'll have time to enjoy the place.*
*All my love, from Midge.*

Once again, Annie placed the letter with the others and the post cards on the mantelpiece, before going happily about her work but after shooting a quick prayer skywards for little Hugo. She made a promise to herself to sit down in the afternoon while the children were with their father and write to Midge in Paris. True to her word, later that day, she picked up her pen and paper.

*15th August 1931*
*Dear Midge,*
*How I envy you visiting Paris. I've heard such wonderful stories about the place, the Eiffel Tower and the River Seine with all the artists. We're all looking forward to hearing about it.*
*We hope and pray that by the time you get this letter, Hugo is fully recovered and playing with his brother again. That must have been a very worrying time for all of you.*
*Darling, we are missing you very much, even the boys sometimes seem to look a bit lost! I am keeping them busy with jobs around the house and garden. Sometimes they go to the farm to help Papa. He remains the same. Write soon then. I can't wait to have you back again.*
*All my love, Mama.*

They had to wait another ten days before Midge's final letter arrived. Annie read it with great relief to find that Hugo had indeed recovered. Their prayers had been answered.

*25/8/31*
*Dear Mama and all,*
*It's my day off today so I can catch up on my letter writing. Thank you so much, Mama for your letter. It is so good to know you have been praying for us and yes, Hugo is back to normal. Poor Mrs Swain was beside herself with worry, but it is all over now.*
*You are right about Paris. It is a wonderful place. Tomorrow we are going to the Louvre which I am excited about and there is a park nearby that I know Junior and Hugo would love to spend quite a bit of time there. On Wednesday, we are going to drive four hours to Rouen then four hours back. I hope it will be worth it!*

*After that there will only be a few days left before we set sail from Dunkirk to Tilbury docks and home. 90 days holiday ended! It feels like I've been gone for a lifetime.*
*Can't wait to see everyone again.*
*Love from Midge.*

*** 

Nothing was going to calm Annie's family this morning. Today, Midge would be coming home for a whole week and they were impatient.

'Now, children, your sister is going to be very tired after all that travelling, so don't you go pestering her for adventures and games as soon as she walks through the door.'

She spoke with such a stern voice that they knew they had better do as she said. Annie knew she would have to wait until much later in the day when the children had tired themselves out before she would get Midge to herself.

Once breakfast was over and the lodgers had disappeared for their day's activities, she busied herself preparing Midge's favourite meal of roast beef and Yorkshire pudding. Being a Tuesday, this would be a treat for the whole family as roasts were normally reserved for Sunday lunch. The children invited their father to the meal, but they came home disappointed with the news that he had told them he would be too busy, it being a weekday, and he had a farm to run, and milk to deliver, and if she wanted to see him she'd have to come to him.

Annie breathed a sigh of relief when she heard this diatribe as she guessed he would be unwilling to give Midge a warm welcome. His attitude infuriated her as she thought for the umpteenth time of all the hard work their eldest daughter had done for him, without begrudging him one moment. Well, she didn't want anything to spoil Midge's homecoming and soon the delicious smell of roast beef was wafting through the house. Frank peeled the potatoes, James peeled the carrots, young William popped the fresh peas out of their pods and had eaten several when James slapped his hand.

'Stop eating them. We want some too, you know.'

Teresa decided to pick some flowers to put in a vase for the table and then changed her mind and took them up to the bedroom she shared with Midge when her sister was at home. She put the vase on the dressing table and then flung open the window to let in the summer sunshine. Poking her nose down into the petals of the roses, she inhaled deeply, closing her eyes to get the full effect of the aroma. Giving them a final shuffle, she turned to inspect the room. It was a comfortable place. The two single beds were covered with prettily flowered eiderdowns with curtains to match at the window. There were books on a shelf that Midge had put up, with more on top of a tallboy chest of drawers. Both girls liked to read and now that Midge was living mostly away from home, Teresa was discovering all the stories that her older sister had collected. At last, feeling satisfied with the result of her efforts, she left the room and found her mother laying the table in the dining room.

'Shall I do that, Mama?'

Annie handed her the cutlery and after giving some instructions, made a hasty retreat to the kitchen.

Just at that moment, the front door opened and in walked Midge bringing the sunshine with her. Her four younger siblings almost knocked her over in their enthusiasm to be the first to greet her, while Annie stood back and drank in the scene. The sun formed a halo around her brood.

*This is what family is all about.*

As Midge embraced her siblings, a dark shadow flitted across the open doorway, causing a shiver to course down her back. She was at once aware of a sense of foreboding deep within her and glancing up she saw her mother folding her arms protectively around herself as if she had felt it too.

'Midge,' called her mother, breaking the spell. With tears spilling down their faces, they kissed and hugged, relieved and grateful for the warmth of each other's touch. Annie released herself and took Midge's face in her hands.

'Let me look at you.'

Suddenly Teresa grabbed her arm, and there was pandemonium.

'Mama, the water's boiling over!'

'Oh, good heavens. Quick! Let me get in there,' gasped Annie, rushing to the stove.

With everyone laughing and shouting at once, she rescued the dinner and before long, after a quick Grace was said, they were setting about demolishing the delicious food. As soon as the meal was over, Annie rested her elbows on the table and put her hands under her chin. She was ready to make an announcement. Her family turned to look at her.

'Now that we're here together, I'd like to get a photograph of us. We could sit on the back porch in a family group. Aunty Kitty and Uncle Gabriel are coming over to see you later, Midge, so I'll get him to take it. It'll be our memento of Midge coming home.'

Everyone spoke at once, but the general consensus of opinion was one of agreement.

Kitty and Gabriel wanted to know all about Midge's tour of Europe, but before her family disappeared to their own activities, Annie called them out onto the porch. Frank placed a basket-weave chair for her to sit at the centre. She wore a pale pink, long sleeved dress, with a necklace of pearls. James and Frank, standing tall positioned themselves behind her. They were dressed ready for their game of cricket later, in pullovers that Annie had knitted for them. Grit was between her brothers with a pretty white and navy cross-over dress. Teresa, wearing a blue sleeveless dress and young William, casual in his open-necked shirt and shorts kneeled on either side of their mother. Midge sat on the step below Teresa. She had succumbed to her mother's wish for her to wear a dress. Annie and her three daughters shared the same fashionable hairstyle. A short bob, cut just below the ear and parted on the right-hand side. The boys were joking and larking around, causing everyone to laugh. All except Teresa who was a little overcome with the sense of occasion.

***

Midge continued to enjoy her employment with the Swain family and was rewarded handsomely for her dedication to the children. Her pleasure was from seeing Hugo's health improve and by the time the new year of 1932 arrived he had almost caught up with his brother in size.

Just as Midge began to think her life was nicely settled she came downstairs one afternoon after settling Junior and Hugo in their beds for a nap, to find Mrs Swain pouring cups of tea in the kitchen.

'Come and sit down for a moment, Midge, honey.'

She slid a cup and saucer across the table towards Midge with a carefully manicured hand.

'Midge, Mr Swains' employers want him back in the States. Now, we are so pleased with the way you have cared for Hugo and Junior that we want to ask you to come with us.'

Midge almost choked on her tea. 'When are you going?' she asked nervously.

'In one month's time. But please, you don't have to give me your decision now. Just take your time and think about it.'

She stood up and came around the table to put her hand on Midge's shoulder.

'Take your time, honey. Let us know after you've been home at the weekend. Talk to your family about it and see what they advise.'

The week seemed to pass so slowly, that Midge changed her mind countless times. Yes, she should go. No, she couldn't possibly go. The arguments went back and forth in her head making her dizzy.

*'Mama will know what to do,'* she told herself desperately, trying to put the decision to rest.

When Midge returned home, she told Annie about the Swain's going back to America and their request for her to go with them.

'What do you want to do, Midge?' Her mother's calm expression belied the churning in her stomach.

Midge's face crumpled in agony.

'I don't know what I want to do. I've been going over and over it all week and I can't seem to come to any decision. Mrs Swain will want to know when I go back on Monday. Oh Mama, what am I to do?'

Annie went through all the objections to going away and then pointed out all the advantages that Midge would find living in another country, including the fact that the Swain boys loved her as she loved them. She reminded her that she had become as one of the family.

'The decision has to be your own, Midge. You know we'll always be here for you, whatever choice you make.'

By the time Monday morning had come around, Midge had made up her mind. Sitting down to breakfast with her family before leaving for the Swain's house, she announced her decision to them all.

'I've made my decision,' she said taking a deep breath. They all stopped eating and turned towards her. 'I've decided not to go. I can't bear to be away from you all, without knowing when I will be coming back.'

The family visibly relaxed and only Annie noticed a dark cloud scudding across the sun, momentarily plunging the kitchen into colourless shade.

*Why do I keep getting these strange sensations?*

She shook the thought away as the family swept her along in their chattering.

'You'll have to look for another job, Midge. I expect Papa will be pleased if you would do his books for him again, but you know he won't pay you much,' Annie pointed out to Midge across the youngster's heads.

'I don't mind helping him on the farm as well. Maybe he'll let me do the milk round again. But, can you ask around your friends and the church please, Mama? I'd really like to be caring for children again, but I suppose something to do with accounts would be good.' A glance at the clock made her rise quickly from her chair.

'Look at the time. I've got to go. Cheerio, Mama. Bye, you urchins. I'll see you next week.'

With a peck on Annie's cheek, she was gone.

## CHAPTER SIX

**1932...**
'We're going to have to get someone to do our book-keeping for us soon,' Halford told Ruby excitedly one morning. 'The business is growing so much. We can't cope with all the paperwork as well.'

Halford and his partner Jack had set up their back room as a workshop where they would repair bicycles, as well as providing safe space for the battery recharging. The space fronting on to the pavement would be an office with a bench for doing small repairs on clocks and watches. Having two rooms, the dividing wall had a window with a door to the side for easy access between them. They fitted a loud buzzer on the front door, so that they could be sure they wouldn't miss any customers coming in while they were working in the back. While Jack did the bicycle repairs, Halford travelled the surrounding area collecting and delivering the batteries. Local wireless owners were delighted with the service. The clock and watch repairs were building up as well. That was Halford's domain. They had agreed that the property would suit their purposes admirably.

Ruby suggested that she could keep her ears open for anyone who might be suitable to help them out. She was so pleased for her husband. He and Jack had worked very hard to build up their business. The extra money coming in now was such a help with their growing family.

Later that morning, Ruby sat at the scrubbed wooden table in her cosy kitchen reflecting on her life with Halford while enjoying a cup of tea after breakfast. Ignoring the crumbs and plates for a while, knowing she could see to that later, she surveyed the scene before her. Her children played happily together on the multi-coloured rag rug, bathed in the rays of the springtime sun as it beamed through the window. The kitchen gleamed brightly from her energetic cleaning. The cast-iron range shone like the coal that waited to burn and, on the mantel-shelf above it, the brass candle sticks were polished. There were two, one standing at each end with a tall white candle in each.

Memories of the birth of her three babies came flooding back to her. Each pregnancy had been difficult. Her first, in nineteen twenty-five had been devastating, ending in the still birth of her baby boy. They had called him Derek. Doctors advised her that it would be dangerous to have another child, but nature took its course, and three years later she discovered she was expecting again. She was packed off to Halford's father's house in Brighton for the duration of her pregnancy as it was thought the sea air would strengthen her. Her daughter, Beryl was born amidst much rejoicing and Halford welcomed her back home with joy in his heart.

Back in 1931 her doctor and family were more than a little alarmed when a third pregnancy was confirmed. Off to Brighton she went again, much to her dismay. She spent the months brooding and pining for her beloved Halford, until she gave birth to a son, Raymond.

*Ah, Halford!* she thought sadly as a flicker of unease shunted its way into her mind.

Ruby loved him despite his obvious disappointment that the child was a boy. She liked to please her husband, so she kept those thoughts to herself.

She poured another cup of tea and brought herself back to present. A small tickle of pleasure ran down her spine as she caught sight of her small daughter, putting an arm round Raymond's shoulder. Young Beryl was pointing to a picture in the book they were engrossed in, their blonde heads bent together. The child was already like a mummy to him, despite her own tender years.

With another glance round her kitchen, leaving her cup on the table and the breakfast dishes in the sink, she wandered slowly through her home, running her fingers lovingly along the oak hall stand that Halford had made. She liked the smell of the furniture polish. It gave her the satisfaction of a job well done.

Ruby's parents had moved into Oakley House when she was a skinny twelve-year-old, after they had retired from running the local public house. The place and everything in it was so precious to her.

When Halford had appeared in her life, she felt complete. After their wedding he moved into the house and established it as his own. He enjoyed carpentry and soon set about making pieces of furniture. Ruby often had an urge to pinch herself to believe that this young man had chosen her for he was that tall, dark, handsome man of a girl's dreams. He played the cello in the local orchestra and sang in the church choir. She knew beautiful ladies admired him and he could have picked any one of them. She stopped in front of the hall mirror studying her reflection and wondered how lucky she was to be his wife. She knew he thought her pretty with her halo of golden curls. He often told that he thought her beautiful especially when they were making love, but she wasn't beautiful. Not like those others. Or slim any more. On her wedding day, she had the tiniest waist, but three pregnancies had added some pounds.

A sudden shout from Beryl in the kitchen jolted her thoughts back to her duties as a mother. Little Raymond was struggling to breathe. He had a weak chest and been diagnosed as asthmatic. Beryl was patting him gently on his back while soothing him with her whispered words. Ruby knew that if she couldn't calm the child, or ease his breathing, then weeks in the hospital would follow. His pattern of life had already begun.

'Hello, anybody home?' called a voice from the front door.

Ruby groaned inwardly.

'Yes, we're in the kitchen. Raymond's had an asthma attack. He's not too bad now, thank goodness.'

She was sitting on a kitchen chair with Raymond on her lap, when her father-in-law walked in with the new lady in his life, Nora. His wife, Cecelia had walked out when she'd discovered the affair.

'Well, well, well. Feeling better are we now, old chap? Hope so. Now, Ruby,' he said, turning his face close to hers and reaching out a hand to Raymond's back.

'Looking pretty as a picture as usual I see.'

He leaned forward to kiss her. As his puckered mouth advanced towards hers, in revulsion at the thought of his lips on hers, Ruby swiftly averted his intention by turning her head slightly. The kiss landed on her cheek.

'Hello, Bill. Nora, how are you? We haven't seen you for a while.'

Nora nodded her head in greeting while glancing round the kitchen at the unwashed breakfast dishes and the bread still out on the board. Noticing her disdainful expression, Ruby apologised for the mess. Ruby's home was usually spick and span. She was embarrassed to have been caught out in this way, especially by stuck-up Nora.

'I've not had a chance to clear away with Raymond not being well.'

An offer of help wasn't forthcoming, so Ruby settled Raymond down on the carpet with Beryl while she scurried around in an effort to clear the remains of their breakfast off the table.

'Would you like a cup of tea?'

'Love one, my dear. What about you, Nora?'

'No thank you,' she replied with a curled lip as though the very thought of drinking out of a cup of Ruby's was too distasteful.

'Haven't you got a cuddle for your old Grandpa, Beryl?'

Beryl obediently skipped happily, stretching out her arms. He flung her up in the air and spun her round rather alarmingly. Ruby glanced nervously behind her to see what he was doing. Putting Beryl down, his attention turned to Raymond.

'What's wrong with you, young man, cat got your tongue, has it?'

Raymond continued wheezing and concentrating hard on the wooden toy car he was zooming around his feet.

'Too quiet that boy, Ruby m'dear. Too quiet by far.'

Ruby was uncomfortable under the inspecting eyes of Nora, who sat with her hands folded on top of the smart handbag resting on her knees, surveying the scene with unspoken accusations. Finally, the tea was made and her father-in-law sipped noisily from the best china tea set. The children played quietly together and Ruby waited for the next announcement.

'How's that business of Halford's getting along then, Ruby?'

'Very well, thank you.'

'Good, good. Must be making a tidy profit by now, eh?'

'Things are improving. He and Jack are working very hard.'

'Mm. Yes.' After a pause, he stood abruptly and went over to the kitchen window. 'The garden needs some attention.'

'Yes, it does. Halford has been so busy with the business, there's never time to get out there, but he will. He loves the garden.'

*Why am I being so defensive? This is nothing to do with him.*

'We thought you would like to come to dinner on Sunday. What do you say? Can you come along?'

Nora shuffled uncomfortably, wiggling her perfect bottom on the chair as though it was uncomfortable.

'Thank you both very much. I'll have to ask Halford, of course and then we'll let you know.'

'Right, that's that then,' said Bill slapping his knees and nodding his head. Suddenly, he gave a shout, pointing across the room.

'Watch out, there's a mouse!'

The children sprang to their feet and Ruby's heart raced as she scanned the kitchen floor. Bill roared with laughter at his own joke. Of course, there was no mouse. It was just one of his little games that Ruby hated. She was always caught out by them and now Raymond started crying and wheezing again. Bill rose quickly from his chair.

'Righto. We'll leave you to get on. Are you ready Nora? No need to get up, Ruby, we'll see ourselves out. Hope to see you Sunday. Get that man of yours to let me know, eh? Cheer up, Raymond, old chap. Can't be all that bad, can it?'

And with that, they were gone. Ruby breathed an irritable sigh when she heard the front door slam and was left to comfort Raymond until his breathing was calm once more.

'Grandpapa is very funny, isn't he, Mummy?' said Beryl innocently.

Ruby forced a smile. *I don't think so. No, not at all.*

\*\*\*

Halford grinned triumphantly to himself as he wound his way down the country lanes of Essex. He'd sold his car and exchanged it for a trusty

Murphy van. It roared along. He was pleased with his mornings work. Four batteries delivered and collected from satisfied customers. That left three more to collect.

*This is the life!* he thought as the road rolled along beneath him.

The banks on either side were full of primroses and celandines poking their heads up in a race against the tide of nettles and cow parsley that would eventually swamp them out of sight. The hedgerows were brimming with life as the birds were beginning their courtships. It was a glorious spring day. One of those days that's full of promise, of the expectation of good things to come.

He mused again the idea of employing someone to work for them. He and Jack agreed that they needed someone to sort out the paperwork before it became impossible, but who could it be? Halford ran down a mental list of their acquaintances. No one seemed to be the book-keeping type. He was grateful for Ruby's wide circle of friends and their conversation that morning showed him that she backed him all the way.

*Good old Ruby.*

A picture of Ruby flashed into his consciousness, she would be at home caring for their children. Yes, he was sure she would come up with a good suggestion for the vacancy before long.

As he drew nearer the next village, he slowed down at the start of the long main street to search out his first call there. It was dotted with houses and about a third of the way along he found what he was looking for. It was a small farmhouse, standing amidst a rambling collection of outbuildings and barns, with a short garden in front. Halford stopped by the roadside. The warm spring sunshine seeped through his thick coat. He soon removed it, feeling relief from the weight, and ran his fingers through his dark hair. Stretching himself up to his full height, he opened the low gate and walked up the garden path. He knocked confidently on the blue door and stepped back. While he waited he looked round at the flowers that edged the path. He nodded to himself approvingly. A smile crossed his face as he noted the name of the farm was Blue House Farm. 'Perhaps it should be Blue Door Farm,' he chuckled to himself.

A few wallflowers were already flowering prettily, poking their velvety petals up towards the sun, wafting their scent into his nostrils. He breathed deeply, enjoying the moment. A lone bee, visiting each flower, savouring its nectar reminded him of his own garden and the work that needed to be done in it. That would have to be postponed for a while. He had enough on his hands at the moment. The sound of footsteps behind the door, prepared him for meeting his next customer. The door was opened by a tall man with a rather grumpy expression. A peaked cap covered most of his grey hair and he was wearing a brown overall, giving the impression that he'd been disturbed while working.

'Good morning to you, Mr Davies. A beautiful day!' said Halford, politely touching his forehead.

Mr Davies grunted.

'I've come to pick up your battery, sir.'

The old farmer lifted his cap slightly and scratched his head, then turned around when he heard a noise on the stairs behind him. As Mr Davies moved aside, Halford peered into the gloom to see what or who had distracted him. Coming slowly down the stairs, wearing a dark blue dress was a young woman. Her black hair was cut in a short bob with one side tucked behind an ear. She was the most beautiful woman Halford had ever seen. He stared up at her. Time seemed to stand still. He was startled out of his trance by the voice of Mr Davies.

'You can talk to Midge. I've got the cows to see to,' he said as he nudged his way past Halford before disappearing round the side of the house, leaving Midge and Halford blinking at each other. Midge reached the bottom of the stairs. Halford tipped his hat politely.

'Hello. Come with me. I'll show you where the wireless set is and you can get the battery. That's my dad,' she indicated with a nod of the head. 'Sorry about his manners. He's not very happy at the moment. It's nothing to do with you. I used to help him with the farm work much more before I went away to Europe. Now he has to pay some local lads to come in. What with one thing and another, he has a lot to contend with.'

Halford nodded and realised that he had not spoken a word.

'Er, what were you doing in Europe?' he asked her.

'Oh, I was a nanny to two American children while their parents were on a working holiday. Even though I was working. I had a wonderful time. We saw so many incredible places,' she laughed, adding, 'I spent my twenty-first birthday while we were staying at the Grand Hotel in Stockholm. Very grand it was too!'

Midge had led Halford along a dim hallway to the large country kitchen where the wireless was standing sentinel on a dark oak sideboard. Halford set to work disconnecting the battery.

'If you get another battery, next time I come I could simply switch them over. You won't be without your set with two batteries,' explained Halford as they returned to the front door.

'I'll see what I can do. My father doesn't like to spend money, and I don't live here,' she explained mischievously.

After agreeing on a date for returning the battery, they said good bye and she shut the door with a thud. He gathered himself together and loaded the battery into the van. Halford finished his afternoon calls and made his way back to the workroom. Jack was busy with the repairs.

'Any luck yet Halford?' he called out cheerfully.

Halford was unloading the batteries. He looked up with a puzzled expression. 'Luck?'

'Yes, you know... with the book-keeper search,' replied Jack a little impatiently.

'Oh that. Er, no, not yet, but Ruby says she'll keep her ears open for us.'

Halford felt slightly embarrassed as since meeting Midge, he'd not given the book-keeping a thought, and was now being brought back down to earth with a bump. What was he thinking of? Ruby was waiting at home for him with their two lovely children. He could be certain in the comforting knowledge that she would have a nourishing meal on the table, and that she would lend an attentive ear to all the details of his day. And a cuddle in bed at the end of the day! His slippers would be by the fire and Beryl and Raymond would be excited to see him. Beryl especially, tugged at his heart strings. She was the apple of his eye. Raymond's weak chest was rather a trial, though he tried to be sympathetic towards him. Thankfully, he knew he could rely on Ruby to deal with anything that happened to the boy.

His life was comfortable now and he berated himself for getting carried away with his thoughts of the Davies girl. Halford joined his partner in the workroom and the two men worked companionably towards closing time.

After talking over the next day's schedule with Jack, he left the building and crossed the road to head for home. The sun was disappearing and as is usual at that time of year, there was an evening chill in the air. He tugged the collar of his coat up to his chin and pressed his trilby firmly on his head. Relighting his pipe, he continued the short walk home where Ruby was waiting for him.

His heart missed a beat when he spotted their doctor's car outside the house. Quickening his pace, he reached the door just as it opened. Ruby looked pale but was thanking the doctor with a smile as she showed him out.

'Ruby, what's happened? Is it Beryl?' Halford asked with panic growing in his chest as the doctor bid him 'good night'.

Ruby smiled and tucked her arm through her husbands, leading him into the kitchen. 'Raymond had one of his attacks. Nothing too bad really, but I saw Dr Foster calling at Mrs Fletchers to check on baby Tommy and I asked him to come and see Raymond.'

'Oh, of course, his chest. I thought something had happened to Beryl,' sighed Halford testily. Smiling at Beryl, he bent down and tickled her neck. 'How's my little girl?'

She shrieked with delight and then clambered onto his lap as he sat down in his armchair by the fire.

'Now then, young man. What have you been up to?'

His son started to cry, raising his little arms towards Ruby. She picked him up and cuddled him to her breast.

'Now, now, Daddy's not shouting at you.'

Turning to their father, Ruby gently chided him. 'Please try not to upset him, dear. It really has been a trying day.'

Halford sighed.

'And then to cap it all, she continued, 'We've had a visit from your father, today. That was enough to upset us all,' she said with a sigh of her own.

'Did you? Was that woman with him?'

'If you mean Nora, yes she was here too. You know I'm not one to dislike people, but she is so, so...' Ruby shook her head and puffed out her cheeks.

Halford let out a disgruntled groan. 'I don't know what he sees in that woman. She's out to get all she can in my opinion. I can't bear to imagine what Mother must think of it all.' He paused thoughtfully for a few moments. 'I suppose she's better off out of his life. What did he want?'

'They've invited us over for dinner on Sunday.'

'Oh no. I'm not sure I can stand that torture. We'll have to think of an excuse not to go, won't we?'

'All right, dear.'

Raymond began to whimper again, and Ruby stroked his head.

'What's for supper? Is it ready yet?' Halford asked.

Ruby was flustered. 'I've been trying to get it on the go for the last hour. It is almost done but can you hold Raymond while I finish things off?'

She passed Raymond to his father but the child began to cry. With an impatient grunt, Halford put him down next to Beryl. He tried hard to love his son in the same way that he loved his daughter, but he had been brought up to believe that males of the species do not show feelings towards each other. He should have had sympathy for his child's asthma problem as Halford suffered with the condition himself. He simply didn't know how to relate to his son.

'Play with your brother, Beryl, while I serve up,' said Ruby as she bustled back and forth across the kitchen with dishes of home cooked food. They were soon tucking into their evening meal and chatting about the happenings of the day.

'Daddy, Daddy,' Beryl interrupted suddenly, tapping Halford on the arm. 'The doctor put a terrorscope on Raymond's chest.'

Ruby smiled at her. 'Stethoscope Dear.'

'Eat your meal now, Beryl. Don't lean across the table,' interjected her father, feeling slightly irritated by his young daughter's interruption. 'Don't you know, little children should be seen and not heard?' Then he turned to his wife. 'Ruby, did you manage to think of anyone for the book-keeping?'

'Sorry. Not today with the problems with Raymond, but I'll be asking around tomorrow when I do my shopping. There must be someone looking for work. I'm sure we'll soon find the right person. How did your day go?'

For some reason, he skipped over his meeting with Midge Davies in the next village, sticking to the more mundane events of the day.
*Well, I don't have to tell her everything.*

## CHAPTER SEVEN

**1933…**

Tuesday nights were for orchestra practice. A pastime that Halford looked forward to with relish, so after kissing his family he gathered up his cello and pipe and walked out into the cold night air to his van. He arrived at the village hall for the practice in plenty of time and was greeted by the other early birds. When they had their various instruments settled into position, they gathered together to wait for their fellow musicians.

He enjoyed the company of these people. They jelled well together with a camaraderie between the men and women who made up this rather well-known local orchestra. Now as the room began to fill, there was much jocularity and not a little flirting.

Halford had an eye for a pretty girl and wasn't slow with a ready chat-up line or an arm round a slender waist. He scanned the gathering group for a rather attractive lady violinist who had joined them a few weeks earlier. He remembered her name was Ida as he spotted her being cornered by Joe.

Joe was their percussionist, a big, rugged man and always popular with the fairer sex. Halford was about tackle the crush of bodies obstructing his path towards them when someone shouted a warning.

'Eh up! The governor's here.'

This caused a bustle of movement as the players made their way to their designated seats in readiness to tune up. Some had already made a start on tuning and others sat chatting to their neighbours. The cacophony of noise grew with a touch of excitement in the air. Sheets of music were being retrieved from cases, bags and the floor. Halford completed his tuning and turned to acknowledge anyone he'd missed earlier. Then, he felt ready. With the cello between his knees, and the bow in his hand, he knew that shortly he would be transported to another world.

Wesley Francis, the conductor took his place in front of this buzz of activity. Wesley was the archetypal music conductor with his wild white hair and seemingly flailing arms inside a slightly dishevelled jacket. But he had earned the respect of these people. He knew his business and it was his flair that had pushed them into the top league.

Now, as he stood before them, he raised his baton and made a few sharp raps on the table. The response was immediate as all minds turned to focus on the work in hand. Wesley confidently gave out his instructions and waited patiently until everyone had found the passage they were working on. Halford held his breath, poised for action like an athlete primed for the high jump, waiting for the magic to begin. His body tingled with anticipation. Those first notes rising out of the silence always did it. It really was magic. Wesley raised his baton and gave the nod to start. The room was instantly filled with music.

They played well, striving to attain the performance required by the conductor until the signal came to break for refreshments and another chance to relax and mingle. Ted and Janette, the viola players began a discussion with Wesley about a tricky part they were struggling with, while others were confirming various notes and sections of the piece.

The wives of two of the players had volunteered to come along each week to provide tea and biscuits. Halford always had a cheeky word for them, and so it was tonight. They laughed sociably together. As he turned to move away from the counter, he almost collided with Ida, who stepped back quickly with her hands held up in front of her.

'Oops! Almost had you,' Halford chortled. 'Let me get you a drink as a token of my sincere apologies. What would you like?'

'Tea would be nice!' Ida replied with a quirky smile, knowing full well that tea was the only option.

'Right, one minute please, madam!'

When Halford turned again, carefully this time, she took the cup and saucer from him and they moved out of the melee surrounding the kitchen hatch and found a space further away.

'How are you enjoying playing in our orchestra?'

While Ida expounded on her experience with this and previous orchestras, Halford had time to wallow in the sound of the rich lustrous tone of her voice coming from rosy red lips. Her blue eyes sparkled with laughter, contrasting with the darkness of her hair. He was becoming mesmerised when he was jolted with a start by the conductor's baton calling them back to their positions. Slipping his arm around Ida's shoulder, he guided her back to her chair before settling himself on the opposite side of the room. As he took up his bow, he glanced across at Ida. She was poised ready for action with her blue eyes fixed on the conductor.

'Right everybody. We're going to go straight through the next piece. Let's see if we can get it right up to scratch. There are only two more practices here, then the final rehearsal at the theatre before the big night, so let's get it spot on. All right? Quieten down everyone please.' He raised his baton and began to count them in. Wesley was a real pro with a perfectionist streak. They had an evening of orchestral entertainment scheduled in three weeks' time, so he didn't want anyone slacking. Not that they would as they were all committed to the orchestra and performed to the best of their abilities. Later in the year they would be performing at the Annual Village Fete.

By the end of the evening, they were all tired but exhilarated. Wesley thanked them for their effort and bid them good night. The room was quickly vacated and with final farewells the players dispersed. Halford caught up with Ida as she was about to cross the road.

'Can I give you a lift home, Ida?' he asked hopefully.

'No thank you, Halford. My fiancé will along any minute.'

Sure enough, at that moment a nifty Austin Healey sports car pulled up.

'Good night, Halford. See you next week.'

'Good night, Ida.' Halford tipped his hat and continued on his way.

Ruby was waiting up for him as usual when he arrived home.

'Your cocoa's ready for you. How did the rehearsal go?' she said, helping him out of his overcoat.

'Good, good. We're all ready for the recital now.'

'Mrs Willis says her daughter Ida has joined. She says she plays the violin. Have you met her?'

'Yes, I had a bit of a chat with her. Says she's enjoying it.'

'Apparently she's getting married next year.'

'Oh!'

'She's been engaged for about eight months. Someone she met in the last orchestra she played with. I think that one disbanded because of lack of support.'

Briskly Halford changed the subject. 'How are you getting on with the silk backings for the speakers?'

'I finished the batch for you yesterday. They're all ready.'

As a side-line and to make use of Halford's love of carpentry, he built speakers to sell for gramophones. To enhance the appearance of what was simply a box shape, using a fret saw, he carved patterns into the front panel. It was to the back of the panel that Ruby glued the silk fabric. Sometimes he really went to town and stood the box on elaborate barley twist legs. The speakers, being electronically attached to the gramophone were far more effective than the old-fashioned horned speaker and were proving very popular.

Ruby was excited to be involved in the business. She felt proud that Halford should want her to be part of this other world of his. This was another string to his bow and added to their income along with what came from the shop and workshop.

'Thank you, Ruby. I should be ready with another two by the end of the week. Putting the silk behind the panel was a good bit of thinking. Yes, you made a real contribution there. They are selling well.'

She puffed out her chest with pride on hearing her husband's compliment. By now though, it was getting late and she sighed deeply and yawned.

'I'm off to bed now. I'm weary to my bones. Good night. Are you going to be long?' she asked, laying her hands on Halford's shoulders and kissed him on both cheeks. It had been an emotional day, dealing with another of Raymond's asthma attacks.

'I'll be up soon my darling,' he said as he patted her on the back lovingly.

Ruby climbed the stairs and popped in to look at her sleeping children. She loved this time of day, when the children were tucked safely in bed with Raymond breathing easy and Halford home from his various evenings out. Bending over each child's head she planted a gentle kiss. After straightening out their covers she crossed the landing to the room she shared with her husband. Stifling another yawn, she snuggled under the bed covers. As her feet reached the cold sheets, she searched around for the hot water bottle that she'd tucked in earlier in the evening. She hoped Halford wouldn't be too long coming to bed to keep her warm. But, by the time he got in beside her, she was in a deep sleep. Before long, he too was sleeping peacefully, curled round his darling Ruby.

***

The search for help in the office continued and during the following week there were two enquiries from applicants who had seen the post card for help with the book-keeping in the shop window. The first was a skinny young girl who took one look at the invoices and filing that needed to be sorted out and flew out through the door like an escaping bird. The other was a man who Jack and Halford, when consulting later, both felt could not be trusted with their confidential business accounts. Ruby had still not been able to come up with any suggestions and neither Jack nor Halford had made any progress.

'How about this for an idea, Halford? We could ask every customer if they know of anyone who can do book-keeping. Perhaps we could get someone to fill in just for a month or so. It would at least tide us over and get this mess cleared up.'

'Sounds like a good idea to me, I'll start asking today. I've got some batteries to take out and you can talk to anyone here.'

He began to search through the papers and envelopes that covered the desk that they had positioned near the door of the workroom. Bicycle tires hung from hooks in the ceiling and parts of bikes were scattered round waiting to be repaired.

'This is really beginning to annoy me,' he grumbled. 'The sooner we get someone in the better as far as I'm concerned.'

After five minutes searching he found what he was looking for and ran down the list of addresses for the recharged batteries to be delivered, then checked the places for collection.

Halford loaded the last of the batteries in his van.

'I'm off now Jack. Wish me luck,' he shouted through the doorway.

'Yes, I will. I think we're going to need all the luck we can get to sort that lot out.'

Halford noted with pleasure that one of the batteries to be delivered was to Blue House Farm, where he'd met Midge Davies. He hadn't really given much thought to her since their meeting, what with work and orchestra rehearsal. Having a family to consider took up a lot of concentration too, but he was looking forward to seeing Midge again. He'd like to get to know her a little more.

At each of his calls, he made his quest for a book-keeper known with scant success, but everyone was more than happy to oblige by agreeing to ask their friends and neighbours. When he knocked on the door of Mr Davies's farm, he was greeted with stony silence. He stood back, perusing the garden, then stepped further back to look at the house for signs of life. Nothing stirred. He knocked again, louder this time. A noise coming from the corner of the house startled him.

It was Midge flying round the end of the house, clattering her hob-nail boots on the stone path. The blue dress she was wearing when he first saw her had been exchanged for a rather unflattering khaki jacket with baggy trousers tied with string tied round her waist. With the short hair and boyish appearance, Halford almost didn't recognise her. She greeted him with a smile.

'Thank goodness you're here. Father wants to listen to the news broadcast, so you're just in time. I've told him what you said about buying a second battery so that you can exchange the old one when you bring the recharged one. I'm not sure I've convinced him yet though. He can be very stubborn.'

'Well, most of our customers have found that having two works best. It depends how often you want to listen to your wireless set though.'

While Halford fitted the battery into the set, he chatted with Midge easily, explaining what he was doing. She seemed interested in the way he and Jack ran their business and came out to inspect his van.

'I've been driving for a while now. I've got a van I use to deliver fruit and vegetables around the villages. I used to deliver milk for Father with a horse and cart,' she laughed.

'The car is definitely the transport of the future,' Halford told her. 'I'm certain of it.'

'Oh, I'd agree with that,' Midge said as she walked back towards the house. 'I'll call at your workshop when we need the battery changing again, perhaps I'll have persuaded Father to buy another from you!'

Halford got into the driving seat of his van and started up the engine.

'Oh, I almost forgot. We're asking all our customers if they know of anyone who can do book keeping, filing and general office work. That sort of thing. So, do you?' he called after her.

She stopped and turned around to face him again.

'I have done a fair bit myself for the farm and I'm helping Mama with her accounts. I don't think I can take anything else on though. The family I went to Europe with have returned to America, so now that I'm helping Father here on the farm again and with the book keeping I'm already doing, and my fruit and veg round, there's not much time left. But, I'll think about it, I promise.'

'Well, even if you could only do a few hours a week it would help. The filing and paperwork is building up and driving us both potty. We can never find what we need and we're desperate,' he said with a pleading grimace. 'We would be for ever in your debt if you could just say yes.'

'Righto. I promise to think about it.' With a laugh and a wave, she turned abruptly to answer a shout in the background from her father.

\*\*\*

Back at the shop, Halford related his conversation with Midge to Jack.

'Let's hope she doesn't turn out to be as bad as the other two. With the lack of interest from anything decent so far, we have to persuade her to come in and help us. From what you say, she could be just the ticket. What's she like anyway?'

'Erm, she's probably in her early twenties I should think, with short dark hair - a real bobby dazzler!'

Jack knew Halford had an eye for a pretty face so he wasn't surprised when he heard his friend's description. His mouth broke into an easy grin.

'So, just the right credentials to get all this lot sorted out!' mocked Jack.

It was typical of Halford to notice her appearance first.

'No, it's not that. We got on really well. She's not just a pretty face. She sounds like a really hard worker. At the moment she's helping her father on his farm and more importantly is doing his books for him, so she's got experience in book keeping. Her mother left her father awhile back and runs a boarding house in Walton-on-the-Naze so Midge helps with her accounts too. The big question is, will she have time to come in and help us as well as these other commitments? She's obviously very close to her family and wants to help them first. Apparently, her father is still pretty upset about them all moving out. Understandable really, poor old bugger.' Halford paused to suck on his cigarette. 'So, she feels obliged to do what she can for him on the farm. She's got brothers, but I think the old man would rather have local lads helping him. I suppose he feels his sons have deserted him by going off with their mother. Ah, life is so complicated for some people. I'm glad I've got Ruby and my nippers at home.'

Halford gave a deep sigh. He knew what it was like to experience the heartache of a marriage breaking down. His own parents had gone through it and his father now had the new woman, Nora in the family home. She was quite a domineering character and Halford did not like her and needed no encouragement to stay away.

Over the next few days, Jack and Halford became impatient waiting for Midge Davies's decision. Finally, one afternoon as the frustration of both men was reaching boiling point, Jack was alerted by a buzzer that meant the office door was being opened. He peered through the workroom window before nipping through the doorway into the office to welcome a young woman. Instinctively, Jack knew this must be Midge. She fitted Halford's description perfectly. She wore a dark suit with a white blouse and smart shoes.

*Mm. This looks promising.*

He wiped his hand on a rag as he extended it to shake hers and then leapt back with an embarrassed laugh realising how oily and grubby it was.

'Hello! Jack Austin. You must be Miss Davies.'

She smiled. 'Yes. That's right. How did you know?'

'We don't get many young ladies in here and Halford had told me you were thinking about our situation here.'

He was standing at the door, with his hand on the knob.

'Would you like to come into the office?' he asked. 'Well, we can't truly describe it as an office, but there is a desk somewhere under all the papers and things.'

'Actually, I've come to pick up a spare battery.'

'Oh Lord,' said Jack, covering his eyes with his hand. 'My apologies, my apologies. I thought you'd come about the book-keeping.'

'Well, I can have a look while I'm here.'

Midge pursed her lips as she sucked in her breath when she saw the chaos. Jack looked at her expectantly, wincing plaintively, like a little child waiting for approval from an adult.

'I see what you mean about needing some help. This really is a mess. Oh sorry, I didn't mean to be rude.' A flush of pink coloured her cheeks. 'I'm not sure if I can cope with all this in the time I have. Oh dear, I'm so sorry, but this needs at least a whole week of constant sorting simply to make any sense of it and I just haven't got that sort of time.'

Turning from the pile of correspondence on the desk, she caught Jack's downcast expression. He put his elbow on top of the filing cabinet, dejectedly ruffling his hair. As he leaned heavily on a sheaf of unopened letters they slid and toppled over his feet. Seeing Jack staring down at the papers that were now scattered across the floor, Midge was suddenly fearful that he would burst into tears. She hastily gathered up the fallen letters and placed them on the table with the other papers.

'Look, I'll see what I can do to help,' she said kindly with more conviction than she felt. 'I've got to go now. I need to drop the battery off to the farm and my mother is expecting me to go through some papers with her. Once we've sorted her accounts, things should be a bit easier over there so fingers crossed, I'll have more time on my hands. 'I'll see what I can do. Cheerio,' she added with warm encouragement.

After Jack had collected the battery he opened the office door for her with such a despondent air that she dare not catch his eye. He gave a deep sigh as he placed the new battery in her van.

Halford returned from his deliveries later that day, to be met by a glaring, angry Jack.

'What's the matter with you?' asked Halford, feeling nervous.

It was so unlike his friend to be unhappy. Usually, he was very positive and easy going.

'Your friend came in this morning. She doesn't think she's got time to sort all this mess out. She took one look at it and said she'd need a solid week to get it sorted. What the hell are we going to do, Halford?' He slumped down on a chair.

'Blast. That's a blow. I was sure she would help us out. Jack, did she say she definitely wouldn't do the work?'

'As good as.'

'Yes, but she didn't actually say no. Is that right?'

'Well, no, I suppose she didn't actually say it. As she left, she did say she would see what she could do.'

'There you are then. Have faith old boy. Our mess will be sorted. Now then, how about a cup of tea?'

Halford felt confident. When he arrived home that night, he couldn't wait to tell Ruby all about their good luck.

'Of course, we still don't know for sure if she'll do it but I feel confident that Midge will be the one to join us.'

'Oh, my dear, that's such good news. Things will be so much better when you don't have to worry about the letters and filing. You can get on with more important things. I'm so pleased. Let's hope your troubles will soon be over,' she added after a moment's thought, innocent of all doubt in her husband's faithfulness.

\*\*\*

Midge stood in the small space that was the centre of the so-called 'office'. With hands on hips, lips pursed and a deep frown furrowing her brow, she surveyed the scene of chaos that, if it was possible, appeared even worse than when she had first encountered it two weeks ago.

'The first thing I'm going to do is make a cup of tea,' she announced, taking charge of the situation. 'That always helps to get the job done. Where d'you keep the kettle and cups, Halford?'

Embarrassed, he shifted tools and dirty rags to reveal a rather grubby saucepan perched on top of a gas ring with two equally grubby cups and a teapot with a cracked spout.

Midge peered over his shoulder.

'Mm. Do you think we could afford to replace those things? I'll chip in to the cost.'

'There's no need to do that. I'll pop back home and dig out some cups and I'm sure Ruby has another teapot. I'll bring some milk over too,' Halford replied quickly.

Three hours later, having smoked several cigarettes and supped almost as many cups of tea, Midge leaned back in her chair. A smile of satisfaction spread across her face. She could now see the desk top and there were several stacks of papers that were the invoices, letters and bills neatly sorted ready for filing. She had pestered Jack with requests about this or that item that didn't fit into an obvious category during her mornings work. A further pile waited for Halford's return containing unknown items such as scraps of paper with scribbled addresses and notes that she could only assume might have some importance. Midge didn't want to risk throwing anything away that might be needed but there was a waste paper basket almost overflowing with empty envelopes and old newspapers. The filing cabinet was her next task and as she rested now, she began to make notes of further questions she had for her new bosses.

'Hello again, Midge, how are you getting on?' called Halford as he returned from his morning delivering and collecting the wireless batteries. As he put down the calibrator he was carrying, he turned to discover a tidy desk.

'Blimey! I hardly recognise the place. Well, you have been busy.'

'Ah, just the man I've been waiting for. When you've got a few minutes, can you go through this pile of papers with me? Jack says he doesn't know what they are, so I'm hoping you can help me. I must go through a few other queries I have with you both before I finish today.'

When the three were sitting down over yet another cup of tea in the now cleared room, Midge put all her questions to the men. She suggested they use a diary, a message book, an order book and an address book and promised to sift through all the bits of paper, transferring the information into the correct book.

'Once you get the hang of using the system, you'll find you are organised and business-like. I promise you, it will make all the difference.'

Halford and Jack had to agree that it all made sense, so Midge made a list of purchases that she would buy before she arrived for her next day's work. As she gathered up her handbag at the end of the day, Jack offered his hand to Midge.

'Thank you so much for coming to work for us, Midge. You've made such a difference already. Hasn't she, Halford?'

'I'll say!' replied Halford with enthusiasm, then an idea struck him,

'We're having a picnic on Frinton beach on Saturday. Would you like to come along? Gloria and Jack will be there. Bring some of your family too.'

Jack agreed enthusiastically. 'Rather! The more the merrier. That's what I say.'

'Well thank you. I'd love to come and I'll see if any of my brothers or sisters would like to join us. They all enjoy picnics, especially when it means swimming in the sea.'

Having agreed on the time and place, Midge mounted her bike and set off for home, thoroughly satisfied with a job well done, and looking forward to returning. The filing cabinet was still untouched and she had a feeling that would be a big challenge. As she rode her bicycle along the road she thought about the picnic and was puzzled by her excitement.

*It's only a picnic, but still, it'll be nice to meet Halford and Jack's families.*

\*\*\*

Halford woke early on the day of the picnic, feeling full of energy. He flung open the bedroom curtains.

'Come and look here, Ruby. It's the most wonderful day.'

His wife rolled onto her back on the large bed before rubbing her eyes and sitting up. Struggling to focus on his shape, she was somewhat relieved that it blocked out most of the glaring sunlight. Ruby slid her feet to the floor and with great effort, sleepily shuffled to his side.

As her head cleared and Halford slipped his arm around her, she had to agree that it was the perfect day for a picnic. The morning sky already heralded good weather, and the ruffling leaves on the towering oaks across the road, told Ruby there was enough wind to keep her cool.

'I'm looking forward to meeting Midge. Do you think she'll bring any of her family?'

'She told Jack and me that they like picnics on the beach, so we'll probably see one or two of her brothers and sisters.'

'One or two?' laughed Ruby, 'How many has she got?'

'Oh several. She did tell us but I can't remember how many.'

They giggled cosily together, both anticipating a pleasant day out.

'Come on, let's dress and get the picnic ready before the children wake up,' suggested Ruby enthusiastically.

He opened the window, inhaling deeply in the clear morning air, his mind full of expectancy for the day, before turning to find Ruby laying out his clothes in readiness. For some inexplicable reason, her action caused him some slight irritation that he forced from his thoughts. He shook the feeling off, determined not to let anything spoil their day out.

Later, at the beach, Ruby watched her husband as he and their friends raced into the sea, shrieking with laughter and feigning terror as their toes touched the cold water. Everyone had changed into swimming costumes except for herself and step-sister Nell. She was self-conscious of her size since having the children and preferred to sit fully clothed in a deck chair watching over the youngsters, while Nell liked to keep her company.

Midge had brought along her youngest sister, Teresa who was sitting in the sand with Beryl and Raymond, helping them to make castles. Nell shielded her eyes with her hand and nodded towards the group in the sea.

'She's getting on well with everyone, isn't she?'

Ruby shifted her gaze from the children toward the scene. She could see Midge splashing water over Halford while the others were dashing in and out of the surf or swimming in the deep.

'Yes,' laughed Ruby. 'She's a good sport and Halford says she's already made a huge impact on their book work, so he's very pleased to have found her.'

She returned to chatting with Teresa and the children, while Nell continued watching her brother-in-law at play. Since the death of their father and more recently Ruby's mother, Nell had felt the need to protect Ruby. Observing Halford and Midge's frolics, she experienced a disturbing knot of concern growing in her stomach. Desperate to dismiss the implications of such notions she turned her attention back to Ruby and the children.

'D'you think it's time we set the picnic out, Ruby dear?'

'Yes righto. Teresa, would you be a good girl and go down to the others to tell them we're going to eat please?'

Teresa stood up and ran off in the direction of the sea, as the two women started to gather up the baskets and hampers onto the blanket. By the time the swimmers had returned in a flurry of water and sand, the food and drinks were all laid out.

'Now do be careful, don't get sand in the food,' Ruby shouted good-naturedly as Halford flung himself down beside her.

'Mm, this looks delicious. I'm ravenous. Anyone else for a sandwich?' he asked around the group.

Cigarettes and sandwiches, wine and apple juice were exchanged with a plentiful supply of good humoured banter thrown in until the merry band lay back to enjoy the afternoon sun. Even the youngsters were content to play quietly.

That night Ruby prepared wearily for bed. 'I like Midge very much. She seems a sincere person and so good with the children. Did you see how patient she was when Raymond was crying?'

'What! Who!' said Halford with a yawn.

'Midge, of course! Mind you, so was her sister Theresa.

'A good day was had by all,' he added a few moments later, turning towards her back and shuffling into a comfortable position with his arm across her hip.

'Yes, a very good day,' he repeated.

Before lapsing into sleep, a slow-motion image of Midge leaping in the sea, floated across his vision. Halford drifted away with a contented smile playing on his lips.

\*\*\*

'Good morning, Midge. How are you on this damp, grey day?' called Halford cheerfully as he manoeuvred his way into the office holding the battery he had collected.

'Don't put it down there,' snapped Midge as he headed towards the desk top.

'Oops. Sorry,' he said with a mock horror expression thrown at Jack who glanced up at the disturbance. Halford turned full circle and thought it a good idea to put it in the corner of the workshop that they had sectioned off as an allocated area where the calibrators were supposed to be stored safely.

When he returned to the office he noticed Midge was leaning on her elbow, with her hand supporting her head. Her other hand held a pencil that she was running up and down a column of figures. With a frustrated groan, she threw down the pencil, sat back in her chair and reached for a cigarette. Halford fished in his pocket for his lighter, stretched round her shoulder and lit it for her. She puffed out a long cloud of smoke.

'Is something amiss, Midge?'

She tutted and gave an exasperated sigh.

'These numbers just will not tally. I'll have to go right back to the beginning to find out what's wrong.' She stood sharply.

'I'm going to make a cup of tea first. Anyone want one?'

'No, you're not. You sit down and relax for five minutes. I'll make the tea,' said Halford, guiding her back to her chair.

Jack came in to the office and sat on the stool, the only remaining seat.

'You've been with us six months now,' then added with a shake of his head, 'what an earth did we do before you came in to save our bacon?'

The two men knew only too well that the changes Midge had made in the office had indeed saved their bacon. She had worked wonders and kept them on their toes when it came to filing and messages. The various notebooks she had introduced were proving to be lifesavers too. There were no more scribbled notes on tea stained envelopes or embarrassing customers who had arrived expecting work that hadn't been completed. Halford placed teacups in front of Jack and Midge before darting outside.

'I've just got to get something out of the van. Shan't be a tick.' A few seconds later, he returned with a bunch of flowers that he handed to Midge.

'Oh, my goodness. What…why…Oh, thank you.'

'We wanted to celebrate your first six months with us.'

'They're so beautiful,' she declared, burying her nose into the blooms. 'They'll really brighten the place up.' Holding the flowers, she searched the room. 'Oh Lord. What am I going to put them in?' she laughed.

Neither men had thought of that problem, but Jack spotted the answer in the tea-making corner.

'Over there look. You can use a milk bottle. '

Oh yes, Jack. Thank you. So elegant,' she exclaimed, her brown eyes sparkling.

While Midge was arranging the flowers, Halford scanned the figures on the page.

'It's nothing serious is it, Midge?'

'No, I don't think so. There's usually a simple explanation. I'll get to the bottom of it before long.'

Midge set the flower laden milk bottle on the window ledge so that she could see them while she sat at her desk. Sitting down to resume drinking her cup of tea, she casually studied Halford and Jack over the rim of her cup. She knew they had been friends for a long time and wondered how they had met. The two men were similar in build and height and, though Jack was fair-haired and Halford had a head of thick, dark hair, they could be brothers.

From time to time she had been witness to the good-natured rivalry they displayed whenever a question of religion came up. Halford sang in the choir of St. Michael's, the local Parish Church while Jack was the organist for the Baptist Church. The two buildings stood directly opposite each other on the High Street in the village, vying for souls to save. One a towering ancient stone monument, the other a small nondescript hall. As if to echo her thoughts, the church bell tolled.

'What church do you go to, Midge?'

'I go with my family to the Catholic Church in Clacton. My mother is very involved there. She's had a lot of support since she left my Dad.'

'Oops. We'd better watch our p's and q's when she's around, Halford.'

Jack laughed, winking at Halford.

The friends had an easy way of working together that complemented each one's talents. As Midge watched them now, she smiled and shook her head before returning to her books.

She was deep in concentration, her pencil travelling up and down the columns again. Receipts had been speared viciously onto a metal rod that was attached to a block of wood. Open ledgers were balanced all around the desk. Halford sauntered over to Jack. He nudged him with his elbow and gave a nod of his head in Midge's direction.

It was mesmerizing to watch, but all of a sudden, she let out an alarming groan, and once again threw down her pencil. The two men immediately busied themselves, turning away from Midge's wrath. Something was up. They knew by now that that action meant trouble, but who was in it? They would find out soon enough. A cigarette could be heard being lit and seconds later, a long-drawn-out hiss. Jack and Halford worked on.

'Right. Who did it?'

The onslaught had started.

'Someone has taken money and not written it down in the petty cash book.' She paused, waiting for an answer.

'Come on. Own up.'

There was silence as the men studied their feet.

'Do you know what? This is the giddy limit. I'm trying to do your books for you and all I get is this sort of behaviour. You're like a couple of children. Honestly!' she finished with a disgusted snort.

'Well?' she demanded angrily, when she still didn't get any reply.

The two friends eyed each other sheepishly. They both coughed and began to mutter at the same time. Halford ran his fingers through his hair.

Jack scratched his chin and adjusted his tie. They tried again. This time Jack spoke first.

'Er, I needed money for some cigarettes on Wednesday. Hadn't any change with me so …' His voice trailed away.

'So, you took it out of petty cash,' Midge finished for him, tutting loudly. 'Jack, the petty cash is for the business.' She clarified this fact as if she were speaking to a child.

'I know. I know,' he said, nodding his head vigorously. 'Sorry,' he added with a guilty smile, folding his hands to his chest and making a slight bow.

'Righto,' said Midge thoughtfully, her eyes narrowed, her lips pursed. 'A packet of cigarettes doesn't cost that much, so where's the rest of it?'

'The flowers,' mumbled Halford.

Midge had a slight deafness in one ear and hadn't understood. 'What do you mean, the power,' she asked with a puzzled expression.

'No. The flowers. We took the money to pay for the flowers.'

Midge's mouth dropped open. Her reaction ranged somewhere between embarrassment and anger. A touch of relief was hiding somewhere in there as the mystery of the missing money was solved. She spun abruptly back to her books with a sound that echoed a terrier being deprived of its bone.

The three colleagues worked on quietly. The wireless played in the background and occasionally, Jack or Halford would whistle a tune or even break into song. Midge's high emotions gradually thawed and she successfully completed her task with the accounts. Harmony was resumed as the three colleagues chatted during their lunch break.

'How is your garden plan coming along then, Halford,' asked Jack.

'Very slowly actually. It's taking longer than I thought. I was hoping to get it all ready for planting in the spring, but I can't see it happening,' came his rather disheartened reply.

'I can help you,' suggested Midge.

Halford shot a glance in her direction. 'Yes, but…'

'I love gardening,' she interrupted.

'Yes, but you're a…,' he began.

Exasperated, Midge interrupted again.

'You think because I'm a woman I can't do it. Hah. Let me tell you, Halford Rivers, I have worked on my father's farm since I was a nipper, lifting hay bales and working twice as hard as some of his farm hands.'

She sat back and folded her arms indignantly.

Halford held his hands up to his shoulders in surrender.

'Whoa there. All right. I believe you. Bloody hell, keep your hair on.'

It was Jack's turn to interject. 'Come on you two. What's got into you both? Halford, it sounds to me as if an extra pair of hands could be just what you need.'

Halford got to his feet and crossed over to Midge. 'I'm sorry, Midge.'

'You're forgiven. Now, when would you like me to come and help you?' she said smoothly.

Midge looked up at him and patted his hand. She had sorted her parents accounts now and only needed to see to them once a month. The van had been sold as she'd given up her fruit and vegetable round. It wasn't profitable enough and during the winter it was not pleasant.

'Saturday would be good if it's not raining.'

'Righto. I'll be there.'

Peering round the flowers out of the small window in the office, Midge wondered if it would ever stop raining. Cycling to Thorpe le Soken from Walton on the Naze and back was not her idea of fun and there had been too many wet days lately. She sometimes wished she had kept the van. Jack and Halford had insisted that during the winter months she should finish during daylight.

She liked to leave at about two o'clock and pop in to see her father on her way home. On these darker evenings of course, her time was limited and her father's continuing gloomy outlook on life made her visits far from a cheery experience. But she persisted out of love and respect for him.

## CHAPTER EIGHT

**1934…**
Saturday morning dawned bright and crisp, and seeing the weather conditions, Midge happily donned her favourite chocolate brown corduroy trousers, a thick shirt and an old fair-isle sweater.

Annie glanced up as her daughter came into the kitchen. 'Good morning, Midge! You're just in time. Bacon and eggs?' she asked while hoisting the frying pan towards Midge's nose.

'Mm, yes please, that sounds like a good idea. It smells delicious. I'll get a plate.'

'Where are you off to today? I didn't think you were helping your Papa.' Annie asked, noticing Midge's clothes.

'No, I'm not. I'm going to help Halford with his garden. Apparently, he's been struggling to get a rockery built ready for planting when the weather warms up. Ruby's busy with her housework and the children so she can't help him, so I offered,' she explained enthusiastically.

Wanting to voice her opinion on the subject of Halford Rivers, Annie took a breath to speak, but had second thoughts on seeing Midge happily tucking into her breakfast.

Ruby opened the door in answer to Midge's knock with the children clinging to her skirt. Raymond had his face buried in its folds whereas Beryl gazed up at Midge's brown eyes with her blue ones.

'Hello Midge! It's good to see you again. Come in, come in and make yourself at home,' Ruby said with a good-natured smile.

'Hello Ruby! Thank you,' said Midge, grinning down at the children.

'Come through to the kitchen. I'll just try and dismantle myself from these two limpets,' laughed Ruby as she shuffled her way down the hall.

Once in the kitchen, Midge crouched down level with Beryl.

'You remember me, don't you? I came to your picnic with my sister Teresa.'

Beryl gave her a pretty smile, slowly nodding her head.

'Is this a little tiger hiding away?' Midge teased, stretching round Ruby's legs to give Raymond a gentle tap on the shoulder.

'He's shy. He's only three,' Beryl, finding her tongue.

'Would you like a cup of tea before you start, Midge?'

'Yes please, Ruby. Milk and one sugar,' Midge answered, raising her head with a nod.

Ruby rummaged round in the cupboard. 'I've got some camp coffee. Shall we try that for a change?'

'Oh, marvellous.'

As Midge sat down, she took a bag off her shoulder, and scrabbled round inside it.

'I've brought something for you two. Now where have they gone? Ah, here we are.'

Curiosity got the better of Raymond's shyness as he glanced up at Midge with half a smile. She pulled out two small spades.

'Oh, my goodness. I can see Midge is expecting some work out of you two. What do you say to Midge?'

'Thank you, Midge.'

Ruby put her hand on Raymond's arm saying, 'Come on now, Raymond, you can play with your sister while Mummy and Midge have a nice cup of coffee.'

Beryl took Raymond's hand and led him over to a box of toys. They wasted no time in their investigations and were soon happily engrossed.

As Ruby put the cups of steaming coffee on the table, Halford walked in. 'Ah here you are, Midge. Good morning.'

'Hello there, Halford.'

'So, what are your plans for today, dear?' Ruby asked her husband.

'I want to get the hole dug for the pond. It's not deep enough yet. It's hard going because of all the rocks in the way, but they'll make a marvellous rockery, and we can use the earth we dig out to raise the ground.'

'Mm, this coffee is good, Ruby,' said Midge. 'Have you drawn a plan at all, Halford?'

Halford laughed loudly, making the children look up with startled expressions.

'It's just like Midge to think of that, Ruby. She likes everything to be noted down.'

They laughed together companionably. As soon as they had emptied their cups, Midge and Halford disappeared outside to the garden. Beryl and Raymond toddled out after them in their Wellington boots, declaring they wanted to help so that they could use their new spades.

'Right,' said Midge. 'I believe we could do with some extra diggers, couldn't we, Halford? Where are you going to build the rockery? You'd better explain what your plan is before we go any further, or else we'll have to move everything again.'

Halford pointed out how he imagined the garden would appear when it was finished. He drew patterns and shapes over the ground using his hands and measured distances with his feet. Midge put in some suggestions of her own.

'Yes, yes. You've got some good ideas,' enthused Halford as he listened, nodding his head. 'I can see we're going to work very well together. Your mind ticks like mine.'

As they laughed, the two children who were shovelling minute spades of soil into a wheel barrow next to Midge, giggled as well. It wasn't long before Halford realised how hard-working Midge was. She was equal to him in her efforts to remove the earth.

'Anyone like a cup of tea and a scone?' called Ruby from the back door, later in the morning. 'You've been working so hard, all of you. I thought you might like a break.'

'Oh yes, rather. I never say no to tea,' answered Midge.

All the gardeners shook off their boots by the doorstep and headed for the scullery to wash their hands.

'Having Midge here to help has made all the difference. I feel as if we've made some real progress. Don't you think so, Ruby?'

'Mm. I can see it beginning to take shape now.'

In one hand Midge held her cup and in the other the beautifully risen scone that Ruby had spread with fresh butter and homemade strawberry jam.

'These scones are delicious. Will you give me the recipe?' she said, finishing off her first mouthful,

'Yes. I'll write it down for you before you go home.'

Draining her cup, Midge handed it back to Ruby and stepped outside again where she stuck her feet in her boots. She lit a cigarette and inhaled deeply. Putting her hands to the small of her back, with the cigarette dangling from her mouth, she leaned slowly left then right, easing the tension in her muscles. Halford, standing in the kitchen doorway behind her, watched with interest. She made him jump when she turned sharply towards him and caught him.

'Come along then, we'd better get cracking,' she ordered playfully.

Ruby glanced out of her kitchen window now and again as she happily pottered about in the kitchen, preparing the lunchtime meal. Halford and Midge were getting on like a house on fire, having contrived a routine to make the task run smoothly. She was surprised at Midge's strength, considering her to be almost masculine. In her opinion, women should be home-makers. Still, Midge was helping to make their garden take shape, so she wasn't about to make any adverse comments, and besides that, she liked the girl.

'Lunch is ready. Midge, you'll stay, won't you?' she called.

Midge suddenly realised she was very hungry so, stabbing the spade into the soil, she ran towards the house. 'Are you sure you don't mind an extra mouth to feed, Ruby?'

Ruby quickly responded. 'Oh no. It's the least we can do. It's all done and Beryl's laid the table and put a place out for you.'

Beryl appeared at her mother's side and looked up at their visitor.

'You can sit next to me,' she said as she led Midge to the table. Then, looking down at her hand, she exclaimed, 'Urgh. Your hands are all dirty and now mine is too.'

They all laughed at the child's frank remark. Midge and Halford held their hands out for Beryl's inspection. Despite the fact that they had worn gloves, they had to admit to having rather grubby hands. Midge darted towards Beryl and Raymond, wiggling her fingers like spider's legs. They both screamed in delight and ran away to hide behind their mother.

As Halford scrubbed his nails, Raymond in his excitement bumped into his legs. He was irritated and swung round roughly.

'Pipe down, Raymond. Sit down at the table now.'

The adults chatted through the meal while the children ate, obediently quiet. Ruby and Midge were getting to know one another and Halford savoured the atmosphere. Midge introduced brightness into the room. There was laughter here, where normally these days there were awkward silences. He noted thoughtfully that he and Ruby had lost the art of conversation somewhat. To Halford, Midge was a breath of fresh air. Now as the two women talked, his mind drifted off until he was snapped back to present company by Midge's voice interrupting his thoughts. Both Midge and Ruby were staring at him expectantly. He shook his head and shifted his position uncomfortably.

'Sorry. What was that?'

With a grin Midge repeated her question.

'Are you going to put some fish in the pond?'

He coughed. 'Er, yes. I was just thinking about that. We'll have some goldfish, won't we Beryl?'

Beryl's head shot up from inspecting the remaining food on her plate. She gazed at her father, not knowing quite what to do. His speaking to her at the dinner table was such an unusual occurrence, she was dumb struck.

'Won't we, Beryl?' he asked again.

'Yes, Daddy,' came the amenable reply accompanied by a wide grin.

Ruby began to collect the dishes and Midge rose to help her.

'Leave that, Midge. Ruby will do it. We need to get out to the garden again,' Halford called as he stepped through the doorway.

They smiled and Midge shrugged. 'Sorry, Ruby. He's the boss.'

'You go along out there. I can manage in here,' she answered, her blue eyes twinkling.

Midge put her boots on as she reached the door.

'Are you coming to help again, Beryl?' she asked.

The child looked quizzically at her mother.

'You can help if you want to. Put your coat and hat on. Raymond's going up for his nap soon, so you go and help Daddy and Midge.'

When Beryl hesitated, Ruby insisted.

'Go on then, shoo,' clapping her hands towards her daughter.

By three o'clock, they had made very satisfying headway, amply fortified by a steady supply of tea and biscuits, only stopping occasionally for a quick cigarette.

Ruby stood in the bedroom, holding Raymond who had just woken up from his afternoon sleep. From the window, she had a splendid bird's eye view of the developing pond and rockery. Halford had already flattened an area by the house, where he had laid crazy paving. A pathway curved from that through the garden. To one side of the path she could see where they were now working. Further down the garden, the fruit trees stood sentinel in strict rows.

Holding Raymond carefully she opened the window. Midge and Halford were sharing a joke while Beryl was running around Midge's legs. Ruby called down to them.

'You get a jolly good view of your efforts from up here. It's really taking shape. Come on up. Raymond's awake now.'

The little group all looked upwards.

'Righto, we'll come in now. I think we've done enough for today and Midge will need to get home before it gets dark,' Halford called to his wife.

\*\*\*

After cycling home and storing her bicycle away, Midge went into the house. She took off her gloves and coat, hanging them on the hall-stand, removed her boots and headed for the living room fire. Annie was sitting in the fireside chair, knitting needles clicking away at her latest creation. Without stopping, she glanced up.

'Hello Midge! You're back safely then. Come and sit down by the fire and get warm. You must be cold.'

'Yes, I am a bit. It's been such a lovely day, but now that the sun's gone down it was quite chilly on the bike.'

'How did your gardening go then? Did you manage to get quite a bit done?'

Midge smiled.

'Oh yes. We finished digging the hole for the pond. The children were digging for England too. Well, Beryl at least. Raymond does have a very bad chest. He started wheezing after a while. Ruby was kind enough to ask me to stay for lunch. She provided a never-ending supply of tea and biscuits, and the most wonderful scones. She's given me the recipe.'

'How are you getting on with Halford Rivers? What with doing his office work and now helping him with his garden, you're seeing a lot more of him.'

'Fine. Why do you ask?' returned Midge suspiciously.

Annie put down her needles and wound the loose yarn round the ball. Studying her daughter's face, Annie's voice was low.

Be careful, Midge,' she warned. 'I've heard stories about Halford Rivers.'

Midge folded her arms defensively across her chest.

'What do you mean? What sort of stories?'

'Well, darling. Some of my friends in the Thursday lunch club told me they'd heard that he likes to chase the ladies. He has an eye for a pretty girl.'

She stretched her arm towards Midge and patted her knee.

'Sorry dear, but that's what's been heard.'

'For goodness sake, Mama, that's just tittle-tattle and gossip. Surely you don't believe all that nonsense. He's a perfect gentleman. Very polite and on top of all that, he has Ruby and the children. No! I don't believe a word of it and you shouldn't either, Mama,' Midge retorted breathlessly.

Annie picked up her knitting again. She and Midge so rarely had a cross word between them that Annie sniffed back a tear.

'I'm only trying to warn you, dear,' she added quietly.

Midge jumped up, suddenly feeling hot and bothered.

'I'm going to make a pot of tea.'

She was so pleased to see Teresa in the kitchen that she totally forgot to make a cup for her mother. She'd arrived home in a pleasantly elated mood that Annie had dampened so she hoped Teresa would be able to restore her to a lighter frame of mind.

\*\*\*

Midge continued travelling over to Thorpe le Soken every Saturday. On one of those days Halford brought in a package that had arrived with the postman.

'Here's something we can get our teeth into, Midge,' he said, setting it down on the table.

'Oh, what's that then?'

Tearing open the brown paper, Halford handed her a seed catalogue.

'It's time to start planting, don't you think?' he said, lighting his pipe.

As he concentrated on getting it burning, Midge flicked through the pages.

'There are plenty of ideas in there. Oh look, here are Hollyhocks. And Delphiniums. We must grow some Wallflowers too. This is wonderful, Halford. Look, Ruby. Have you seen this?' she shouted enthusiastically.

Ruby came in from the scullery, wiping her hands on a towel, glancing briefly at the pictures.

'That's nice, Midge,' she replied rather blandly.

At that moment, Raymond, who had been sitting on a chair at the table, started alternately banging and clapping his hands.

'Raymond. Stop that noise. We are talking,' Halford said with an edge to his voice.

Ruby stood behind the child and grabbing him under his arms whisked him away.

'You can help me, Raymond. I've got some sheets that need folding. Come along.'

'Now what do you think, Midge, apart from what you've just suggested?' said Halford, bringing his concentration back to the catalogue.

'Let's make a list.'

Halford smiled as he recognised Midge's organised mind. She caught his expression.

'What are you smiling about?' she exclaimed with a curl of her lips.

'You.'

'What do you mean,' she asked, raising her eyebrows in curiosity.

'You're always so...' he paused and grinned again teasingly.

'What?'

'You're always so organised.'

'Oh, for goodness sake,' she huffed. 'Let's have a look at the catalogue.'

With paper and pencil, they sat down shoulder to shoulder, head to head, inspecting each page with its pictures and directions on times and conditions for planting. Before long they had a sizeable list and Midge began to tot up the cost.

'Mm,' said Halford, scratching his head. 'I think we'd better curb our enthusiasm a little, don't you?'

Midge laughed and, head to head again, they went through the list for a second then a third time until they had a more realistic order.

'Shall I fill in the order form, Halford?'

\*\*\*

As the spring had changed into summer and September approached, the pond was finished, with goldfish and water plants introduced. The plants that Halford and Midge had grown from seed filled the rockery and an herbaceous border. They had constructed a low wall as a border to the path that wound through the garden. In an area beyond the pond and rockery were the lawns that Halford took great pride in keeping neatly trimmed. A high privet hedge separated that part of the garden from the fruit trees that now were promising a bumper crop of apples, plums and pears.

'Now, Midge dear, we're having the family and some friends over for a Christmas meal on the 20th December and Halford and I, and of course the children would like you to join us,' announced Ruby one day a few weeks before Christmas.

'Oh yes, I'd enjoy that very much. Would you like me to help with anything beforehand?'

Some weeks earlier, Midge had moved in with the family. She had been spending more and more time in Thorpe le Soken, working with Halford and Jack as well as helping in the garden behind Oakley House, despite her mother's foreboding. The weather had become nasty as winter settled in and she was finding the journey by bicycle quite hazardous at times. So, it naturally evolved that Midge should come and live with them, returning home to Walton on the Naze every other weekend.

Beryl and Raymond, who had overheard the conversation ran to Midge and flung themselves onto her lap.

'Hooray,' they cheered, both grinning from ear to ear.

'There is something you can help me with and I'm sure you'll like to have the recipe. My old mother passed it on to me. It was always a family tradition to make it at Christmas,' said Ruby thoughtfully.

'What's that then, Ruby? I'm intrigued. Do tell me.'

'Every Christmas we would have homemade ginger wine,' said Ruby confidentially, whispering with her voice bright with anticipation. The children thought this was a big secret and leaned in to listen.

'Shall we go together this afternoon to buy the ingredients? Will you be able to come with us, Midge?'

Ruby loved this time of year with family and friends gathered. She would be organising the children to make paper chains soon in readiness to hang in the dining room. As the day dawned, she was up early in order to get everything done in readiness for their guests. She laid the table with sprigs of holly, their blood red berries glossy. And Christmas crackers that would cause such hilarity, especially the dreadful so-called jokes. The best cutlery and china would appear, beautifully polished.

*Yes, this will be a good one especially with Midge joining us.*

It was a wonderful dinner party. Everyone was impressed that yet again Ruby had produced a splendid meal, not forgetting to compliment Midge on her help. They were especially complimentary about the ginger wine as they raised their glasses in a toast to 1934 and to the coming new year.

Later that night, after everyone had left to wend their weary way home, and Halford and Ruby were preparing for bed, he praised his wife for her efforts. She was pleased and enthused.

'I couldn't have done it without Midge's help. She is such a blessing. A lovely girl. I'm so pleased she's come into our lives. She feels like one of the family now. What with the business, the garden and the way she helps me out, I don't know what we did before she arrived, do you?'

Halford agreed wholeheartedly.

## CHAPTER NINE

## 1935...

'Midge, Midge, come and see what Halford has made.'

When she heard her name being called, Midge came leaping down the stairs. Ruby laughed anxiously and put her hand to her throat.

'You make me so nervous when you charge down the stairs like that. I'm always frightened you'll fall.'

The two women smiled fondly at each other.

'You'll never make a lady out of me, Ruby, however hard you try.'

Feigning vexation, Ruby propelled Midge out into the cool April morning. Halford was putting into place a rustic seat he had been making over the last few weeks.

'Halford, how clever of you,' congratulated Midge. 'Now we can sit outside and relax.'

'I've got something else on the go that I think you'll like too,' taking her by the arm and leading her towards his work shed. Ruby admired the seat and didn't notice that they'd walked away.

'Isn't Daddy clever, Mummy? What's he going to show to Midge? Is he building something else?' asked Beryl.

'I expect so, dear. Shall we make a nice cold drink for everyone? Has Raymond woken up from his sleep yet? Let's go and see.'

In the dimness of the work shed, Halford stepped over pieces of timber that were lying on the dusty floor and reached for his latest creation.

'What do you think?' he asked as he held a post on which he had attached an ornate bird table.

'I think it's a marvellous idea, Halford. How are you going to make it stand up?'

'Always the practical one, aren't you, Midge?'

Their eyes met. Their expressions changed, but it wasn't simply that. Something extraordinarily powerful had surged between them. Something that Halford had tried to deny to himself for several months and at that moment he knew that Midge had been denying it too. The sensation he felt now, looking at Midge was nothing like anything he'd ever had before, not even with Ruby.

After what Midge felt was an interminably long time, she broke the spell by turning and fleeing from his gaze. Her heart was pounding like a machine gun. Halford hadn't meant it to happen. He recalled his first meeting with Midge, but the feelings he'd experienced then, had been suppressed and locked away. He couldn't deny that he often flirted with the ladies. Yes, had even gone further than flirtation with one certain lady when Ruby had been absent having her babies in Brighton. But those liaisons had been passing titillation. They were just a bit of fun.

Thankful that Ruby was nowhere to be seen, Midge sank down onto the new seat that Halford had made. She hoped he wouldn't come out of the work shed for a few minutes so that she could get her breath back and compose herself. She dug into her pocket for her cigarettes, lighting one with shaking hands. Drawing in deeply, she struggled to calm her nerves, not wanting Ruby to see her in this state. With her eyes closed, she gulped for air. Suddenly she felt something touch her knee. She gasped as she opened her eyes, thinking it was Halford, but it was young Raymond who had toddled outside. Stamping her cigarette under her shoe, she caught hold of his hand. She loved the two children and now felt the urge to hug him closely to her.

'Let's go and see what Mummy and Beryl are up to,' she said as she took him inside.

Ruby was standing at the table with her hands deep inside a mixing bowl, with Beryl standing on a chair trying to help. She had her own little apron with bees and honey pots that was now covered with flour.

'What's Daddy making now, Midge? Did he show you?' asked Beryl.

Midge laughed a little nervously.

'Maybe it's a surprise. You'd better ask him yourself when he comes in.'

Beryl was easily satisfied with the information. She tapped Midge's arm.

'Will you play tiddly winks with me now, please?' she asked in a sweet voice.

'Yes of course, but first you must ask your Mummy if she needs us to help with anything else. Go along.' Noticing flour on her sleeve, Midge called out, 'You'd better wash your hands first.'

When Halford entered the kitchen, he was met with a picture of homely comfort. As he washed his hands at the sink, he felt that it was as if that earlier collision of souls had not occurred.

*Yes, it was a collision. Like being run down by a steam roller, but in the nicest possible way.*

Halford noted that Midge resolutely avoided eye contact with him.

*Does that mean that she is experiencing the same feeling?*

'Dinner will be ready in about ten minutes, Halford.'

He was staring into space, sipping the cold drink she had given him.

Ruby repeated herself.

'Oh sorry my dear, I was miles away. I'm ready when you are. I'll just go and read the paper while you finish off.'

He made his way past the kitchen table.

'Look, Daddy, Midge and me are playing tiddly winks and I'm winning.'

Halford put his finger under Beryl's hair and tickled her neck. She screeched with delight, screwing her head down to her shoulder. Raymond banged on the table, while Midge continued to avoid Halford's eyes. She stood sharply and crossed the room to collect the cutlery ready for the meal, effectively turning her back on Halford.

***

As Midge lay in bed that night, she dared to recall the event in Halford's work shed. Her mother's words kept repeating themselves in her brain, but she reassured herself that up until today, Halford had indeed been the perfect gentleman. He'd never even flirted with her. They had become good friends. Very good friends with such a lot in common. She couldn't think of any other person that she enjoyed being with more. They worked so well together in the business and in the garden. He was such good fun too.

Whenever she'd joined the family on picnics, Ruby never wanted to swim or join in the games, so Midge often found herself playing in the sea with him or partnering him in tennis. So, yes. She did like him very much but this new emotion was a mite daunting.

*Be honest. It's scaring me half to death.*

She tried to find a comfortable position, to think of something else, but after tossing and turning for several minutes, her mind began to drift back to Halford again.

*But he's married. To Ruby. Dear sweet Ruby. This is silly. I must have imagined it. In the morning, it will be all right again.*

A few moments later, she prayed.

*Oh God. Please don't let this be happening. Bless this family and bless all my family too. Lead me not into temptation. Thank you, Lord. Amen.*

She said a Hail Mary for good measure and finally fell into a fitful sleep.

***

In the spring of 1935, all the inhabitants of Thorpe le Soken were discussing plans for celebrating the Silver Jubilee of King George V and Queen Mary. Ripples of excitement ran through the whole village. Business owners vied for the coveted first prize in decorating their shop fronts as well as devising designs for adapting their lorries as floats.

Austin and Rivers was no exception. As Halford sat by the fire with Ruby and Midge one evening, he explained what he and Jack had planned for their float.

'We're going to dress Midge's father's lorry up as the coronation coach.'

Halford's description became more vivid. His animation grew. He waved his hands in the air as he pictured the bunting and flags and balloons that would fly. There would be a king and queen seated on a majestic throne. Ruby and Midge caught his enthusiasm and before long they were adding their ideas to the picture. Suggestions were thrown in and out, yet it always seemed to be that Halford took on Midge's ideas. Their minds worked in tandem.

'We could make a golden crown to fix on the front of the lorry.'

'Yes, and paint the wheels gold too.'

Midge worked with Halford and Jack in an effort to make the design for the shop front the best. All along the road, normal business had become secondary as the buildings adopted different fascia's. Residents were amazed at the transformation taking place each time they passed by. Bunting in red, white and blue of every size and description was festooned across driveways and streets, over houses and railings and gates. Jack had found a life-size cut-out of a harlequin clown that they placed outside the shop. The clown was playing a penny whistle. It made everyone laugh as they walked by.

One of the services that Halford and Jack had added to their portfolio was to provide sound systems for garden fetes or parties that took place in the village, so on this special occasion they were again conscripted to do the same. They spent many hours fixing the speakers to telegraph poles along the route the procession was to take. No one minded that their battery recharging was delayed or their watches and clocks failed to be repaired on time. The whole country was in high spirits.

On the great day, not one person stayed at home. Even the infirm were provided with some form of transportation. The children became fairies, clowns, postmen, soldiers and nursery rhyme characters for the fancy dress competition. Lorries were transformed into glossy coaches, ships, army vehicles and even the air, sea, rail and safety services were represented. Magnificent dray horses were there with their manes and tails plaited and the brasses shining in the sunlight, pulling the beer wagons, proclaiming their ale the best.

As the festivities reached a climax, all gathered to hear the results of the various competitions. Halford stopped the music that was being funnelled through the loud speakers. A hush descended on the crowd as the judge made his way to the podium. His voice carried through the microphone that Jack had set up, to the far reaches of the field, where the hundreds of revellers were gathered. Midge, who had been helping out behind the scenes, was sitting near Halford when they heard the judge announce that their coronation coach had won third prize. She was so excited that she leapt up and flung her arms around Halford's neck.

Suddenly feeling a tingling sensation rushing up her spine, she realized what she had done and quickly released him. Halford was laughing easily, but as she drew back, the expression she saw in his eyes said much more than spoken words.

\*\*\*

Midge enjoyed a second Christmas with the Rivers family and once again she helped out with the ginger wine and entertaining guests at their dinner party.

'It's becoming a tradition,' someone was heard to remark.

Halford remained a respectable distance from Midge.

\*\*\*

As spring slipped into summer, Midge and Halford enjoyed an increasing amount of time in each other's company now that she was living in the same house as well as working at the shop. The seeds they had carefully sown in the spring needed attention, just as the seeds sown in their hearts were crying out.

During the summer there were picnics and outings where Midge invariably found herself near Halford. In the hot nights, she would lie in her bed trying to fight the images that flitted through her brain, images of herself and Halford. There was no escaping her desire to be near him. In spite of her mother's warnings, he was a magnet to her as his aura drew her ever closer. Her life was too wrapped up in his for her to step away now. Though her conscience pricked like needles in her brain, whenever she tried to imagine life without him, she would feel an overwhelming sense of despair.

So, life continued. They tended the garden they had so lovingly created, hoeing out the unwanted weeds, transplanting and pruning. As the flowers blossomed, so did their relationship. They developed a deep understanding. They agreed on ideas for the garden or plans for a day out. Ruby wasn't deliberately left out, but she was content to care for Beryl and Raymond, taking a back seat while happily tending her home.

Halford's involvement with the orchestra and choir had waned slightly. One night during orchestra practice, a fellow musician noticed that he wasn't chatting up the ladies as usual.

'What's up, Halford? Losing your touch, are you?'

He grinned, brushing off his friend's observation. 'You're probably right. Must be getting old I suppose.'

They laughed companionably. Nowadays, Halford preferred the company at home.

*** 

With Midge's careful bookkeeping, the business was doing well. Then, in January 1936, something happened to change the situation dramatically. The residents of the village were roused from their beds by an alarm of fire in the early hours of the morning.

A neighbour saw flames coming from the workroom belonging to Halford and Jack. Luckily, he knew the danger of fire where there were batteries stored.

It was about 2.30 in the morning when Jack was woken by hammering on the front door of his home. Racing down the road to the workroom, Jack grabbed the sand buckets kept especially for emergencies and smothered the flames. Cameron, the neighbour offered to help.

'Cameron, can you fill that up with water now. We'll have to stop the flames reaching the accumulators. We might just do it if we keep filling up the buckets.'

As soon as the bucket was empty, Cameron filled another until at last they managed to dampen the fire down but not before several small explosions took place.

Once Jack felt the place was safe from further outbreaks of flame, he turned to Cameron. 'Thank you so much for your help. You go on home now. I'll just clear up a little.'

He went to the door with him and shook his neighbour's hand. 'Thanks again.'

Jack wiped the sweat from his face with his handkerchief before returning to the smoke-filled room.

'Why didn't you send for me, Jack?' groaned Halford when he arrived for work the next morning and discovered the mayhem.

They were standing in the midst of the debris. Jack shook his head.

'There wasn't time, old thing. Cameron helped me with the water and then afterwards, without any electricity it was difficult to see anything. Thought we could sort it out now.'

'Right. I see. Well we'd better get cracking and clear up the mess. Find out what's the damage.' He removed his hat and swept his hair back with his hand, swearing under his breath as a clump of hair came away.

At that moment, Midge popped her head through the open doorway. 'Oh, my lord, what a mess.'

The three colleagues worked steadily all day to clean the blackened walls and smoky windows. The sand and water used to douse the flames proved very difficult to shift. When they had finally brought everything back to some sort of order, they assessed the damage. Several pieces of equipment and some of the accumulators would have to be replaced.

Jack looked at Midge with a worried frown. 'Is our insurance policy up to date?'

'Oh yes, of course.'

'It's just as well you've been taking care of our accounts, Midge. If it had been up to us, it wouldn't have been done, and then we would have been playing on a sticky wicket.'

They were all shaken by the event and sat for a while in the gathering gloom at the end of the long day, smoking in companionable silence.

The fire marked a shift in the relationship between Halford and Midge. Inexplicably, their passion was inflamed to such an extent that it was almost unbearable to be in the same room together. Nevertheless, they hid their emotions so well that no one who was with them noticed anything untoward.

\*\*\*

Halford drove his car slowly along the road. He had picked Midge up in Walton on the Naze where she had been staying for a few days with her family.

*If he goes any slower we'll come to grinding halt,* thought Midge.

She cast a sideways glance in his direction. His face looked drawn and pale. Ghostly, was the description that came into her mind. As they reached the open countryside, he slowed the van down even further until, with a deep sigh, he pulled over and switched off the engine.

For a few moments he leaned forward, staring at the road ahead. He held the steering wheel in a vice-like grip and as Midge turned to face him, she could see the muscles in his cheeks twitching. She suddenly felt scared, very scared indeed.

'Wh-what's wrong, Halford?'

He flung himself back onto the seat and ran his fingers through his hair, puffing his cheeks out as he let out a long breath. He turned to look into Midge's eyes.

'I'm in love with you, Midge. I've tried to ignore what's inside me. Tried to tell myself that it mustn't happen, but I can't deny it to myself or to you any longer. I love you, and I want to spend the rest of my life with you.'

He shook his head slowly. His eyes closed momentarily. Suddenly he caught hold of her hands and held on tight, stroking her fingers with his thumb.

'Say something, Midge. What are we going to do?'

'I've been battling against it too. I really don't know what to do. I hate to hurt Ruby and the children but, yes, I love you too.'

'Let's get out of the car for a minute and have a walk. My head's spinning. I can't drive yet. We have to talk about this.'

He got out and went around to open her door. They strolled quietly down a track that was branching away from the road-side verge.

Midge marvelled at the fact that nature was carrying on as usual. Despite the overwhelming situation that had developed between them, the birds were still singing, insects were going about their business. There were cows chewing their cud in the field on the other side of the hedge, oblivious of the monumental decisions that these two people must make.

For the first time, Halford put his arm around Midge and drew her to him. The physical contact was painfully sweet. They had spent so many hours in close proximity, in the office, and Halford's home and garden, that now the bond was too strong to break. They gazed into each other's eyes, until neither could bear it any longer. Their lips met. They clung together, both fearing to let the other go, neither wanting to break the spell. Eventually, they strolled on until they found a stile and sat together, thoughtfully smoking their cigarettes, silent, yet now thankful that the truth had been told. Neither had any ideas about what they would do next, but it was good to know how they felt about each other. A flock of starlings swooped and wheeled, hedgehopping like some black giant phantom in silhouette before them.

'Look at them, Midge. Could we fly away together?' He blew out smoke before turning to see her reaction.

'You mean leave everything behind and just disappear? What about Ruby and the children? They're your family, Halford. How can you simply leave them?'

Tears came to Midges eyes.

'They're like family to me too, you know. Oh Gosh! Mama would be devastated and I dread to think what my father would say.'

With each sentence, her grief grew stronger. With a sudden jerk of her head, she turned to look into his eyes, and gripped his shoulders tightly.

'I'll go away. I'll write to Mrs Swain and ask them for my job back. If they agree, then I'll go out to America to look after the children again and you can get on with your life with Ruby and Beryl and Raymond.' Taking his face in her hands, she sighed deeply. 'I can't ruin the lives of so many people,' she said breathlessly, struggling against the emotions inside her head.

'No, Midge,' Halford shouted angrily. 'Don't say that. I can't bear to live without you. I might as well be dead if I have to carry on here.'

Midge stared at the scene displayed before them. She puffed out a long stream of smoke and shook her head sadly.

'Please Midge, don't even think of leaving on your own. I mean it. I don't want to live without you.'

As he spoke, Halford pulled Midge into his arms and gently rocked her. She realised then, that he was sobbing as though his heart would break.

'Promise me, you'll stay with me for the rest of your life, Midge. Promise me that?' he stuttered through his grief, gripping her arms and staring into her eyes.

Midge's emotions got the better of her at that point and she broke down. They clung together for several minutes, kissing desperately, savouring the salty taste of their mingled tears, until finally they drew apart.

'The only way as I see it, is for us to go away together,' Halford emphasised. As Midge shook her head, he insisted urgently, 'No, we can't stay. We have to leave them.'

Midge was quiet.

'I suppose there's no other way. Maybe we could come back in a few years, once the scandal has died down.'

Halford took another puff on his cigarette.

'Maybe,' he agreed doubtfully.

She grasped his hands and stared into his eyes. 'I can't live without you either, I just wish there was another way. My darling Halford, I love you so much.' Her brown eyes filled with tears again.

Holding her tightly, Halford whispered, 'I love you too. I've never felt like this about anyone before, even Ruby.'

Suddenly, Halford broke away and walked on up the track.

'Midge, you're so pure and innocent, I don't want to spoil you in any way,' he said, spinning back to face her. Wrapping his arm around her waist and pulling her close, he stroked his fingers through her dark hair and stared deep into her eyes. 'We must work out what we are to do. It's been making me feel ill, having to keep my emotions under control. I know my feelings aren't going to change.'

'No, nor are mine.'

Coming back to the stile, Halford eyes travelled to a nearby tree. Taking out his penknife he leaned forward and began to etch their initials within a crude heart. It seemed such a juvenile action, yet one of profound importance to the couple at that moment in time. Midge leaned against the stile, quietly smoking while watching him with a warm glow in her heart. He blew away the debris and stood back to inspect his handiwork.

Midge peered over his shoulder at the initials.

"HR x AD, Halford Rivers loves Annie Davies." She spoke the words aloud, as if to confirm their reality. Halford grabbed her hand and pulled her close once more to enfold her in his arms.

"Come on, we'd better get back on the road again."

They released each other with difficulty and made their way back to the car, to continue their journey back to Ruby waiting at home for them.

\*\*\*

Over the following weeks, Halford and Midge continued to work in unison in the garden and in the business, sharing silent glances, sometimes managing to stroke hands and occasionally taking a stolen kiss. They were pretty successful in maintaining the charade of being good working companions. But, the only thing on Midge and Halford's minds was how they were going to get away whilst causing the least amount of pain to their families.

It loomed up in every situation and threatened their concentration. The very idea of leaving their families without causing them distress became an obsession. They came to realise it would be an impossible task. None of them would escape being deeply hurt. The ripples of their decision would be felt for decades by more than just their immediate relatives.

Later that day, sitting at the table for the mid-day meal, Halford had very little appetite for the delicious food that Ruby had cooked. He noticed that Midge was picking at her food as well. As Halford looked round at his family, a lump came to his throat at the thought of hurting them.

*Ruby, so good-natured, a wonderful mother,* thought Halford.

His attention turned to Beryl. The lump in his throat became more uncomfortable. *My Beryl.* He wanted to cry, to reach out and touch her. *She's so precious.* As he looked at Raymond, he felt a tugging at his heartstrings. *Raymond. He can't help being weak. I wish I could love him more.*

***

One day in May, Halford and Midge were working in the sunken garden they had created. In the centre well, stood a sundial. Roses circled the upper level. The scent of the roses was captured in the well of the garden as they paused for a smoke on the rustic bench that Halford had made.

It was a garden of tranquillity, but Midge sensed that Halford was uneasy. He crossed his ankles and stared at his feet.

'We've got to leave, Midge. Soon! I feel so ill. If we don't go soon, I'm sure I'll do something desperate.'

Midge noticed that his hand shook as he held the cigarette to his mouth.

'Couldn't we just stay here and live together somewhere. That way, you'll still be able to be near Beryl and Raymond?' Midge suggested tentatively. In her heart she knew they could never do that.

'We can't stay around here. Can you imagine it?' Halford spread his hands as though displaying the newspaper headlines. All the local gossips would relish the story. "Local Catholic girl lives in sin with married man." Do you think you could live here with that going on? I wouldn't want that to happen to you. I couldn't live with it.

The couple were silent for several moments, then Halford announced, 'We'll have to withdraw some money from the business account.'

'No, Halford. We can't do that.' She was horrified by Halford's suggestion. She folded her arms tightly around her legs as if to ward off this unwelcome idea.

'Ruby will have her share of the profits because she is part owner. She'll be all right financially. She'll be better off without me. Look Midge, we're going to need all the money we can get hold of to start our life together. We'll drive to London and then sell the van. That will give us some cash. Maybe I can get something from Father as well.'

'I've got some savings that will help for a while, but we'll have to get jobs pretty quickly. Oh Lord, this is terrible. I never wanted it to be like this. I can't bear the thought of leaving Ruby and the children,' said Midge. She was too scared to think of her own family's heartbreak and shame.

They didn't know what else to say and continued sitting in silence for a little longer, until Midge rose and returned to the planting she had been doing.

***

'Halford, I think you ought to go and see the doctor, don't you?' Ruby said. 'You've not been yourself for a while now.'

He listened to her as he stood in front of the hall mirror. His cheeks had a gaunt shrunken look and his hair was thinning at an alarming rate. He couldn't remember when he last enjoyed a meal.

'Yes, I suppose you're right. I don't feel myself at all. Maybe he can tell me what's wrong and give me something for it. I'll pop into the surgery this afternoon after I've done my deliveries.'

When he returned home later that day, Ruby asked him what the doctor had said was wrong with him.

'He says it's caused by stress. Says I have to stop worrying about things.'

Ruby looked at him curiously, and chuckled. 'What have you got to worry about, Halford? Now that you've got the insurance claim from the fire sorted out, the business is doing very well.'

He made no reply, simply shook his head.

***

In the office, Midge was filing invoices when Halford came in after delivering batteries. Jack was in the workshop dealing with a customer buying spare bicycle parts. Halford stood behind her and put his hands on her shoulders.

Keeping his eye on the window through to the workshop, he whispered quietly in her ear.

'Next Friday, Midge. I'll tell Ruby that I'm going to London to see a specialist about my hair loss.'

She stopped what she was doing and shut her eyes. Midge could almost taste the familiar smell of his pipe tobacco that he was so fond of. His hands felt strong and firm. A gasp escaped from her mouth as she leaned back against him with her hands resting on the open filing cabinet drawer.

'I'll take the van and leave early Friday morning. You could go home on Wednesday afternoon. Thursday is your day off so it won't seem odd. I thought you could tell your family that you are going to Ipswich on the train on Friday to pick up some parts for the business. When you get to the station, I'll be there waiting for you.'

Halford risked a fleeting tender glance in her eyes, before glancing towards the window to see what Jack was up to.

Midge continued to stand silently.

'Say something.'

'Darling Halford. You've worked it all out, haven't you? I thought I was supposed to be the practical one,' she said with a feeble laugh.

Jack seemed to be finishing his sales talk to the customer, so there was no time to continue with their plans.

\*\*\*

'Ruby, Doctor Foster wants me to go and see a specialist. I've got an appointment next Friday,' Halford announced during their evening meal.

'Righto. That's good. Maybe at last we'll find out what's wrong. Beryl, can you pass the salt please?'

Inside his stomach, snakes writhed a merry dance. 'I'll have to drive the van up to London.'

'Oh, will you have to stay overnight?'

'Possibly. I'll take a few things with me in case I have to.'

\*\*\*

On the Sunday morning, five days before his supposed appointment, Halford suddenly took his family by surprise.

'Put your warm clothes on, we're going to the beach.'

'What are you talking about, Halford? It's not a very nice day. Why do you want to go to the beach?' asked Ruby, puzzled by his sudden announcement.

The children were excited at this fresh circumstance, and ignoring Ruby's pleas to wait, they had donned coats and hats and found the buckets and spades that Midge had given them when she first arrived at Oakley House.

'Mummy, hurry up. Where's your coat and hat? Daddy's waiting.'

'I'm here now,' said Ruby as she struggled breathlessly into the van wearing her winter coat with its thick fur collar. Beryl was already sitting, waiting impatiently, while Ruby hoisted Raymond up onto her lap.

'We're off,' laughed Halford.

Arriving at the beach, the children tumbled out of the van and headed off to play. Halford stood and leaned against the railing, watching the children shouting and jumping in the sand. He drank in the sight, wanting to capture their laughter and take it with him. Calling them to him, he positioned them seated on the steps that led from the promenade to the beach, ready for a photograph.

'Smile please, say "cheese",' he called as he pointed his camera towards the little group. Beryl and Raymond had removed their shoes and socks so that they could play on the sand. When his family were ready, Halford placed his trilby hat on the steps next to Raymond and stepped back to take a photograph. He knew that there was no appointment with any specialist. What the three people in the frame did not know was that this would be their last outing together. They might never see him again. He thought his heart would break.

***

Midge was sitting in the garden, chatting with Annie and Teresa. It was a bright Thursday afternoon that had popped in after weeks of damp grey weather. The sunshine seemed to mock her sadness on what she knew would be her last days with her family. She felt a lump growing in her throat. She turned her face away, so that they wouldn't see the hint of tears in her eyes, closing them as if she was letting the sun warm her face. Desperate to let them in on her secret, she struggled to think of ways to explain her feelings for Halford. She was suddenly aware that Teresa was speaking to her.

'Midge, look over there. Can you see the little Jenny Wren? Isn't it beautiful?'

The opportunity was gone before it was even there. Midge couldn't answer, the lump in her throat was so huge. She shaded her eyes with her hand, but the wren had flown away.

'Oh, you've missed it. What a shame.'

Later, while Teresa was helping her mother prepare the evening meal, Midge sat in the bedroom that was now her younger sister's but where she slept when she stayed with her family. She took out a pen and paper from her handbag and stared at the page. Blank and white like virgin snow. What should she say to her mother? How could she begin?

*Dear Mother,* she wrote.

No, that was too formal. She tore the sheet from the pad and folding it carefully, placed it inside her bag.

*My dearest Mama,* she tried again. Her hand hovered over the paper as she stared out of the window. She could hear her mother and sister talking and laughing in the kitchen. Homely sounds of crockery clanging and spoons stirring in saucepans. Such noises of contentment and security. The smell of mint sauce wafted up to tickle her taste buds causing her to wish she felt hungry.

*Oh, dear God. Help me to do this. Please help me to find the right words,'* she prayed.

She read what she had written.

Just three words.

What else to say?

How to say it?

*Dear Mama, I'm running away with a married man. I didn't listen to a word you said, so here we are. He's wonderful and I want to spend the rest of my life with him.*

She didn't write those dead, hard, cold words. She tore the page up and placed it with the first one in her handbag. She would burn them later. Even though she and Halford had talked of coming back eventually, she knew in her heart she would never see her father again, nor Grit who was living in London, nor Frank who was in the Navy. She was thankful that at least she could spend time with Mama, James, young William and Teresa before disappearing for good.

The day before, Midge had gone with Teresa to spend some time by her beloved sea. The yachts were tacking in the wind, their colourful sails billowing in the breeze, almost like butterflies.

*Will I ever be able to sail again?*

She linked arms with her young sister as they strode along the promenade before tugging Teresa round some of her favourite spots.

'Are we going home now, Midge? I'm getting cold. Why are you taking me round to all these places?' complained Teresa with a shiver.

'I want you to know all the best places in town. I don't get over here much now, so come on, don't be a spoilsport. We'll see the rest as we make our way back home.'

At each place, they paused and Midge breathed in deep. Like Halford with his family, she wanted to plant the image of it all in her mind. There would be many times in her life when she would crave the smell of the sea or strive to conjure up the picture of one of her favourite places in her home-town. Even more strident would be the agony in her conscience when she tried to recall her mother's face or voice.

Now back home, having failed to write her letter and still with her mind in turmoil, she went downstairs to join her family for what was to be their last meal together.

\*\*\*

Halford became increasingly stressed and restless as Friday drew nearer. He snapped at Raymond for the slightest, even imagined misdemeanours and was bad-tempered with Ruby. Only towards Beryl was he considerate and loving. Ruby innocently put it down to his being nervous about the appointment with the specialist.

'I'll need to leave early in the morning, Ruby, with it being such a long drive to London.'

After tossing and turning all night, he rose from their bed, washed and dressed quietly without disturbing Ruby. He went into Raymond's bedroom and kissed him good-bye. Next, he went to Beryl's bedroom and hugged her tightly to him, kissing her over and over.

Ruby came downstairs in her dressing gown, her long hair flowing over her shoulders and down her back as Halford stood at the front door. He put his arms round her and held her for a long moment.

'Try not to worry too much, Halford. Everything will be all right. I'm sure the specialist will know what to do for you. Now drive safely. Have you got everything?' she ventured, reassuringly patting on the back. She adjusted his collar and brushed a speck off his jacket.

'Yes, yes, everything's on the passenger seat of the van. I wish I still had our old car. It would have been more comfortable. Ah well, beggars can't be choosers.' He gave a nervous laugh and fidgeted with his driving gloves.

'Oh. I'll have to dash upstairs again, I have forgotten something,' he stammered, as he was about to jump into the van. He took the stairs two at a time and rushed in to see Beryl again. Catching her up in his arms, he hugged and kissed her again and then, dragging himself away, he turned at the doorway and blew her a kiss. She would remember that moment for the rest of her life.

**CHAPTER TEN**

## May 1936...

'Mummy, is Daddy home yet?' asked Beryl, sleepily rubbing her eyes on Monday morning as she came into her mother's bedroom.

'No, Beryl, not yet. I expect the doctors are trying to find out how to make him better.'

Beryl climbed onto the bed and cuddled up to her mother. As the weekend had dragged on, Halford's non-appearance gave Ruby an uneasy feeling in the pit of her stomach. She worried that the doctors had found something unexpectedly wrong with him and that he had been kept in. But, why hadn't he found some way of contacting her? Whenever a motor passed by the house, she stopped what she was doing, to listen for the slam of the car door and Halford's voice calling out to her. But it didn't happen. The children were abnormally subdued. They had that childish intuitive ability to sense their mother's growing anxiety.

\*\*\*

At around 9am that morning, Jack made his usual way to work and he felt good. The business was flourishing and his day was mapped out with plenty of repairs to keep him busy. A hymn that he'd played in church the day before came into his mind. It was one of his favourites because he and the congregation could belt out the chorus. He began to sing it now with gusto as he unlocked the door and let himself in.

'Then sings my soul, my Saviour God to Thee, how great Thou art, how great Thou art.' He happily hummed the remainder of the hymn. He knew Midge would soon appear and hoped she had been able to get the clock parts they needed.

As he sat at his workbench, he thought about Halford, wondering how he'd fared with the London specialist. He had been rather distracted lately.

*Definitely not himself. Preoccupied, I'd say. This thing with his health must be a hell of a worry for him.*

Jack looked at his watch and realised it was well past the time when Halford should be joining him and there was still no sign of Midge.

'Probably gone straight out on the road. But where's Midge?' Realising he was muttering to himself, he tutted, made a cup of tea and settled down to his morning's work.

\*\*\*

At Wrigley and Partners, solicitor, Clive Wrigley took the mail from his secretary as he strode through the reception area towards his office. Always a punctual man, he was pleased to see that the time was exactly 9.30 am. Flicking through the pile of correspondence, he sat down and tasted his first tea of the day.

Eventually after perusing the normal formal communications, he stopped at a hand-written letter and noted the signature as W. H. Rivers. He tried to put a face to the name but couldn't. Never one to let anything get the better of him, he decided to tackle that letter later in the morning. In the meantime, there was other more pressing business to attend to.

\*\*\*

Nell walked briskly down the path from her front door. It was a beautiful May day with a clear blue sky, but just enough of a hint of crispness in the air to let her know that summer hadn't yet arrived. She was about to get into her car when the postman pulled his bicycle up by the door.

'Morning to you, Samuel. Beautiful day isn't it?' she called, winding the window down.

The postman dug deep inside his bag that was laden with letters and packages and answered merrily.

'Yes, isn't it, Miss Deal? Truly magnificent. Ah, here we are. A letter for you today. Cheerio then. Best be on my way.'

He cycled away, whistling cheerfully to himself.

Studying the envelope, Nell tried to decide who it could be from. It had a London post mark and the script looked vaguely familiar. She inspected it with a puzzled frown. Suddenly remembering why she was in her car, she looked at the time. 'Goodness me, it's almost ten o'clock. I'd better be on my way too, else I'm going to be late. That wouldn't do at all.' She tucked the letter inside her handbag as she started up the car. The letter would have to wait.

***

The telephone trilled out over the sound of the wireless in Austin and Rivers where Jack was bent over one of the bikes he was repairing. For a few moments, he left it ringing having forgotten that Midge wasn't there. Its continuing call forced him to turn around and swear silently to himself.

As he stalked across the office and stretched out his hand to lift the receiver, he spotted an envelope lying on the blotting pad on the desk. The words on the front diverted his attention from the conversation. It was addressed to Ruby. Dragging his thoughts back to the caller, he hurriedly closed the discussion and replaced the receiver.

He recognised Halford's tiny scrawl but was baffled as to why he should have left the letter here in the office.

'It must have been here all day Friday because Halford left early that morning. I never even noticed it. This is very odd.'

Jack noted the time. It was 11.05. A customer was due to collect a repaired bike at 11.30 so he'd have to wait for him before he could take the letter across to Ruby.

'Yes. I'll go and take the letter to her as soon as Mr Watts has gone.'

He set to work again but was still bemused by the envelope. He attempted to concentrate on the job in hand, but his mind kept straying back. A tiny ripple of something close to fear started to creep into his chest, up the back of his neck and into his head, causing his body to stiffen and tense.

\*\*\*

The meeting was tedious. Time dragged on as Nell struggled to keep her interest alive. The clock face, perched high on the wall of the lecture hall showed 11.35. A whole hour had passed drudgingly by while the speaker, an old man with an indescribably monotone pitch, rambled on, causing people to fidget. Chairs creaked, feet shuffled and not a few coughs developed. Nell could definitely detect the sound of gentle snoring coming from somewhere behind her.

At long last at 11.50, the chairman stood and, holding the older man by the elbow, whispered in his ear. The speaker coughed and thankfully, Nell thought, quickly wound up his talk. Everyone clapped courteously, before noisily leaving the room. Nell made her excuses and rushed back to her car as fast as it was polite to do so. She avoided all attempts by colleagues to speak to her and delay her further. Driving away as quickly as she dared, she couldn't wait to get back home so she could remove her shoes, get a bite to eat, sit down with a cup of tea to read the letter that was burning a hole in her handbag.

\*\*\*

Jack's customer was late. Minutes ticked by. He became increasingly fretful and anxious. Thirty minutes overdue, Mr Watts came into the shop. As hard as Jack tried to get rid of the man, the more he talked. Another time, Jack would have been only too pleased to enjoy a person's interest in his work, but not today. Not now. He made his way to the door, and opened it wide, hinting that he should be on his way, but the man couldn't seem to take the hint.

Eventually his patience gave way.

'I'm terribly sorry, Mr Watts. I've got to go out now. You'll find the bike in perfect order now. Thank you. Goodbye,' he said.

Puffing his cheeks out, he breathed a long sigh, snatched up the envelope, locked the door and made his way down the street towards Oakley House.

*\*\*\**

Nell put on her spectacles and tore open the envelope as she waited for the kettle to boil and then unfolded the single sheet of notepaper. A quick glance at the signature told her who had written it. She began to read. All thoughts of cups of tea and food vanished. The water steamed away unnoticed. Her legs wobbled, forcing her to sink into her fireside chair. Her hand went to her mouth as she scanned the page. The writing was an untidy scrawl, hastily written. It was difficult to make out the words, but she understood enough to realise the significance of the message.

'The cad! What an utter cad!' Nell spat.

Halford was instructing her to go at once to see Ruby. He had underlined the words, 'at once' to stress the urgency of his request. Sitting alone in her kitchen she re-read the letter aloud carefully to herself. She wanted to make sure she understood exactly what Halford was saying:

*Dear Nell,*

*I want you to go down to Thorpe le Soken le Soken <u>at once</u> to see Ruby as I shall not be going back again. I'm afraid my brain must be turning but I know she will be alright as she has the children to care for and love.*

*We have formed a Ltd. Co. Ruby will receive £3 a week as a Director, so she will be all right financially.*

*I won't offer any excuse for my action and know none can be given, but I ask you to forgive me. I shall not forget her as she has always been the best of wives to me. Please do your best for them all. I know little Ray and Beryl will be looked after.*

*I shall not be able to repay the Wilson Trust but will repay you through Mr Wrigley at my earliest.*

*Thank you for all you have done for me.*

*Halford.*

Nell squinted her eyes in an effort to read the footnote that was so small as to be practically unreadable.

She thought it said: *Tell the children I am ill in London, don't let them know...* She couldn't make out the last word.

Putting the letter on the small table beside her chair, she removed her glasses and sighed heavily.

'What has the silly bugger done this time?'

She was well aware of Halford's little escapades in the past. The pattern followed that when he became bored with his flirtations, he sought comfort once again with Ruby. But now this. This letter was worrying.

'I wonder if Ruby knows yet. Right, I'd better get cracking.'

She folded Halford's letter carefully and placed it in the envelope before putting it in her handbag. Next, she telephoned the school where she was head mistress. The secretary answered, expressing surprise at hearing her boss's voice.

'Ah, Miss Grant, good afternoon to you. Miss Deal here. I've been called away on urgent business. As I'm likely to be absent for a few days, would you ask Mr Reeves to take up his position as deputy?' Nell waited for the secretary's confirming answer. 'Good. Are there any messages for me, Miss Grant?'

After dealing with the few queries, Nell replaced the receiver. She suddenly remembered the kettle and dashed back to the kitchen. The water was boiling angrily. She grabbed the pot holder and removed the kettle from the stove.

'I've no time for tea now. I must get to Ruby as quickly as I can.'

Plucking her coat and handbag from the hall stand, she noticed the time was coming up to twelve thirty. Locking her front door firmly and trying to hold down her anger, she made her way out to the car.

\*\*\*

Ruby had been very busy that morning in the washhouse and now a row of sheets and clothes was hanging rather limply along the line that stretched down the garden. The day had started brightly enough as she took Beryl on the bus to school, but now the sky had turned grey.

She stood at the sink, staring out of the kitchen window. Anyone watching her would have assumed she was deciding whether it was worth leaving the washing out there. The reality was that her mind was far away from the laundry and the weather.

Keeping herself occupied was the best way to stop worrying about Halford. Now that her jobs were finished, her thoughts drifted back to him. With a sigh, she turned towards Raymond who was sitting at the table with paper and coloured crayons. The hall clock chimed once, reminding her that he would probably be hungry.

'I suppose I'd better find you something to eat, hadn't I?'

She smiled and ruffled his hair affectionately, planting a kiss on his soft downy cheek.

'Dinner time.' He rubbed his little hand over his tummy then held up a piece of paper. 'Look at my picture, Mummy. It's for Daddy.'

She stood behind her son and looked at the childish drawing he had made. Tears sprang to her eyes as she saw the swirls of colour. He had clearly drawn flowers that he knew his Daddy loved. 'That is so beautiful, Raymond. Let's put it on the cupboard door so that Daddy will see it as soon as he walks in. He'll be so pleased. What a clever boy you are.'

She found some pins and fixed it up. Raymond stared up at his artwork with pride. As Ruby set to work making some lunch, Raymond carefully laid his crayons in the wooden pencil box that Halford had made for him. Just as she was putting the plates on the table, Ruby was startled by a knock at the door. Telling Raymond to begin eating she went into the hall to see who was calling on them.

She was surprised to see Jack Austin standing on the doorstep. He removed his hat as he greeted her.

'Hello Ruby.'

'Hello Jack. Come in, won't you? We're just having a bite to eat. Would you like to join us?'

Jack seemed nervous. 'No thank you, Ruby. I've come over with a letter for you. It must have been on the desk since Friday but I only noticed it this morning. I'm so sorry, I should have come earlier.' He reached inside his coat and pulled out the envelope. 'It's from Halford.'

Ruby stared incredulously at the envelope. 'What…why…why has he…why did he leave it in the work shop. I don't understand. Jack, what's going on?'

'I'm sorry, Ruby. I have no idea. All I know is that he went to London to see the specialist on Friday.' He nodded his head towards the letter. 'Perhaps you'd better open it. See what he says, Mm?'

'You're right. Of course, that's what I must do.'

The clock merrily sang its half-hour tune.

\*\*\*

On her journey from Walton on Thames to Thorpe le Soken, Nell was making good progress, until she turned a corner and almost collided with a flock of sheep in the narrow road. They were being led along the road to fresh pasture by the farmer and his dog. There was nothing she could do but follow on slowly behind them.

Finally, the sheep were herded through a gateway into a field and she was able to speed up and be on her way again. She glanced at her watch. It was just after two o'clock. If she could keep moving now, she should make it by two thirty.

\*\*\*

Ruby's whole body shook as she fumbled with the envelope containing Halford's letter. It was folded up into a small square. She opened it out carefully and began to read. She had to hold the paper with both hands so that she could focus on the words.

*Dear Ruby,*
*I hardly know what to say to you. I know I am doing a cowardly thing, but if I did not do this, I might have done something far worse. I ask you to forgive and forget me. I am not worth worrying about. You have been the best of wives, but I'm afraid I have an inherited streak in me. God knows how I have tried to overcome it.*
*I have left instructions with Mr. Wrigley to let you do as you like with the property. I have left half of the cycle shop to you. Put the tools away for*

*Ray to have when he is old enough to use them. See that Jack doesn't buy too big. Keep your eye on things up there. If any difficulty see Mr Pawsey. I have left you £40. You will be receiving £3 per week, you will be alright financially. I am sorry about the Wilson Fund but I will repay both Mr Wrigley and Nell at earliest.*
*Now don't worry. I am sure you will be happier without me. I feel at times as if I shall go mad but I fight the feeling as much as I can. God bless you and the children. Kiss them for me each night. H.*

Ruby read through the letter three times. Jack talked quietly to Raymond while he waited for her reaction, not knowing what news the letter contained. He was about to learn how his life was going to change.

'Halford's gone away, Jack. He says he's not coming back.' Ruby's voice was a whisper.

She stood stiffly and pushed the letter towards him. 'Read it for yourself, it's going to affect you too.'

Her voice was so low that Jack could barely hear. All the emotion she had held within her throughout the last few days had caused her muscles to tighten. She was conscious of a pulsating pain passing behind her eyes. The emotion was still there yet her body felt numb. She moved across the room as though in a dream. She grasped the sink with both hands and leaned heavily against it.

Ruby couldn't think of any more to say. Her mind wasn't functioning at all. She jumped when Jack suddenly spoke.

'I think I would like that cup of tea after all, Ruby, if you don't mind.'

Thankful for something to do with her hands, Ruby filled the teapot with boiling water and set it on the table. Automatically, she put another cup and saucer out for Jack and began to pour. They sat in silence, staring into space, sipping their tea while young Raymond munched on his sandwich.

'Mummy, I've finished. Look.' Raymond was holding up his empty plate as proof. He flashed a beaming smile at his mother then turned to show Jack. The child's eyes were magnified behind the lenses of his spectacles.

'Oh Raymond, what a good boy you are.'

He held out his arms towards her as she leaned forward to pick him up. She hugged him almost fiercely.

Jack felt a lump rising in his throat as he watched.
*How could Halford do this to his family?*
The consequences to his own life hadn't even entered his head yet. For the moment he was concerned for Ruby and her children.

The hall clock struck two. Neither Ruby nor Jack wanted to talk about the letter and what it meant to them. They sat in silence. Ruby slowly rocked Raymond back and forth while Jack sipped his tea. The only sounds in the room were the ticking of the clock and the creaking of Ruby's chair.

Suddenly the back door was flung open. Raymond began struggling to his feet in excitement.

Ruby leapt out of her chair.

'Halford?'

When she saw it was Nell, Ruby almost collapsed into her arms. Nell was a strong, masculine-framed woman who was well able to support both mother and child, but Jack leapt up to help. Together they manoeuvred the pair into the sitting room and settled them down on the sofa.

'Have you got any idea where Halford has gone, Jack?' asked Nell.

Jack shook his head. He stood with his back to the dark empty fireplace.

'No. I'm sorry, Nell. I found an envelope addressed to Ruby and brought it over as soon as I could get away from the work shop.'

'Where's Halford's letter?' Nell asked Ruby gently.

Ruby shifted her position, but Jack interrupted her attempts to get up.

'I'll get it. It's on the kitchen table.' He returned a few moments later with the letter and handed it to Nell. As she read it, she pursed her lips and nodded her head. She noticed Raymond shifting restlessly on Ruby's motionless lap.

'Come along, little man, let's get you upstairs for your nap.'

He loved his Aunty Nell and gladly allowed her to sweep him up. She raised him high above her head where he giggled cheerfully, totally unaware of the drama unfolding. Nell left the room, but popped her head round the door again, holding her own letter from Halford out towards Jack.

'You might as well read this one that he sent to me. It runs along the same lines,' she said abruptly.

Jack scanned the letter quickly, feeling embarrassed to have been drawn into this intimate situation, before handing it to Ruby. After reading it, she laid it down on her knee and leaned back in the chair with her eyes closed.

'I don't understand any of it. It must be something I have done. He wouldn't go off and leave us like this without a good reason.' She lapsed into a weary silence again as Nell sang a lullaby to Raymond.

Ruby suddenly opened her eyes and looked at Jack.

'Wasn't Midge in the office today? She'll be able to tell us where he's gone,' she said hopefully.

Before he could reply, Nell came back into the sitting room to join them.

Hearing Ruby's comment, she said briskly, 'Well, of course. We'll soon find out where he is and bring him back home to you, I'm sure. What do you think, Jack?'

'I certainly hope so. I don't know how any of us will manage without him. Our business has been picking up, so I'm wondering why he should want to leave now. It certainly is a mystery.'

The clock struck three and Jack looked at his wristwatch in alarm.

'I'd better get back to the shop. There are still some repairs to be done. Will you be all right, Ruby?'

She answered with a weak smile. 'Yes, thank you, Jack. It was so good of you to come over and stay with me.'

'Don't worry about her, Jack. I'll make sure she's all right.'

Nell saw Jack to the door and then returned to her half-sister who now appeared to be brighter with a little colour returned to her cheeks. 'I'll go and collect Beryl from school for you.'

'Oh yes. She'll love that. A ride in your car, eh? That will make up for her Daddy not being here. Let's not say anything yet about him not coming home. Not until we've talked to Midge.'

'Yes, I agree with that. Good thinking.'

As she drove away from the house, Nell couldn't help but think to herself that Midge might know more than they realised, but perhaps she was being unfair.

'We'll see. We'll see,' she muttered under her breath.

\*\*\*

At precisely 3pm, Clive Wrigley placed his gold-rimmed spectacles on the end of his nose and inspected the hand-written letter from W H Rivers. He pressed a button on the intercom on his desk.

'Yes Mr Wrigley.'

'Miss Winterbottom, will you bring in the file on W H Rivers, please?'

'Certainly, sir.'

Clive Wrigley was very satisfied with the endeavours of Miss Winterbottom. She had worked at the solicitor's office for ten years now and knew all the nuances of each partner. With her punctuality and formality, she was ideally suited to the business.

Within a couple of minutes, she was standing at his desk with the file in one hand and a cup of tea in the other. Clive Wrigley could be certain that the tea would be exactly to his liking, a good dark colour, one spoonful of sugar and piping hot in a china cup on a china saucer. His favourite bourbon biscuit was resting on the saucer – a morsel he indulged himself in just once a day.

'Ah, thank you, Miss Winterbottom. Efficient as ever.'

She placed the tea cup and saucer on the mat that was positioned specifically for that purpose. As the woman turned away, he fixed his attention on the letter. It read:

*Dear Mr Wrigley,*

*Please find enclosed copies of letters I have today forwarded to my wife, Mrs Ruby Rivers and her sister, Miss Nell Deal. It is with great sorrow that I have come to make my decision to go away but it has to be done.*

*I came to see you a short time ago in order to form a Ltd. Co. with my partner Jack Austin, to be called Austin and Rivers. My wife was made a director and I would now like her to acquire 50% ownership. Thus, I would be grateful if you would set up payment of £3 a week from the profits so that she will be financially secure. I also leave instructions for her to do as she wishes with the property.*

*I will be contacting you again at my earliest in order to settle my account.*

*Yours sincerely, W H Rivers*

Clive Wrigley removed his spectacles, laying them gently on his blotting pad.

'Well, this is a rum do.'

Leafing through the file he found the paper work that indeed proved that Mr Rivers had set up a Ltd. Co. with Jack Austin. He pressed the intercom button again and called the secretary back in.

'Miss Winterbottom, it appears that Mr Rivers has gone away, according to his letter here.'

He picked up the letter and waved it in the air as if in confirmation.

'I'm sure I don't know what it's all about, but we are here to follow his instructions. Will you please set up a weekly payment of £3 for Mrs Rivers from their business account?'

He handed the file and the letters with attachments. 'The details are all there. Thank you, Miss Winterbottom.'

*** 

When Ruby awoke on Tuesday morning, she turned over and automatically reached out for Halford. She felt a warm body beside her, but as her sleep-filled eyes opened, the blurry sight of blonde curls snapped her back to the reality that Halford wasn't there. Beryl's little body lay sprawled across his space.

She gazed at her child's innocent face. An intense feeling of deep sorrow touched her heart as she struggled to come to terms with the enormity of what had happened to them. But then, she remembered that Midge would be back today. She decided to call at the workshop on the way home after taking Beryl to school.

*Funny, I can't remember her saying she wouldn't be back yesterday, but of course, I was worried about Halford's appointment so maybe I missed it.*

Nell crept in with a cup of tea for Ruby.

'Good morning, dear. Drink this while it's hot. Did you get much sleep?'

Ruby yawned. 'Oh, I dropped off eventually. Mm, thanks. This is good.'

Driving to school in Aunty Nell's car was a very exciting prospect for Beryl, and Raymond joined in the furore of getting ready. Warm coats, hats and gloves were donned before they piled onto the back seat. Raymond began to wheeze. Beryl held his hand and pointed at interesting things to see through the window, so he settled down obediently beside her. They rattled and rolled along the road to Beryl's school where she skipped through the gates to greet her friends.

Nell patted Ruby's arm. 'Let's go and see Midge,' she said, as she caught a glimpse of her sister's downcast expression.

Ruby smiled gratefully. 'Yes, righto. Let's go.'

'Hold tight, Raymond. Would you like to see Aunty Midge?'

Raymond clapped his hands. 'See Aunty Midge. Yes. Hurrah,' he shouted. He tapped his knees and kicked his feet up and down, then called brightly to his mother and aunty. 'I love Aunty Midge.'

Reaching Austin and Rivers work shop, Nell pulled up and turned off the engine. They walked in to find that Jack had arrived a few minutes earlier and was filling the kettle.

'Good morning, ladies. Will you have a cup of tea with me? Midge isn't here yet, but she should be along soon.'

Ruby gathered up the cups. 'Here, Jack, I'll make the tea. I'm sure you've enough to do without waiting on us. I feel a bit better with something to do.'

'Righto, Ruby. Thank you very much. If you don't mind, I'll make a start.' He began to go into the workshop but with a change of mind, turned towards Raymond. 'Do you want to sit up here and watch me do some repairs, young man?' Jack said, winking mischievously at the boy. There were small parts of bicycles he could work on, while keeping the child amused.

Raymond glanced at his mother, then back to Jack, nodding madly when he saw his mother smiling encouragingly. Jack found another stool and the child clambered up beside him. Ruby called a cautious warning across the room.

'Now don't touch anything, Raymond.'

'Oh, I'm going to give him a job to do. We can't have him sitting doing nothing, can we Raymond?'

The tea was made and drunk with still no sign of Midge. Ruby's stomach was churning. She didn't want to even consider that Midge might be with Halford.

*No, surely that couldn't be what's happened. It's just a coincidence that they're both away.* The thought cartwheeled round and round in her head.

Jack set the bicycle chain he had repaired to one side. He went to the desk to retrieve the repairs book to enter the finished job.

Suddenly, Raymond's piping voice broke the silence. 'Mummy, when is Aunty Midge coming?'

'We're not sure, Raymond. We'll wait a little longer, shall we?' she answered, trying to sound hopeful.

'It's half past nine. She should be here now,' murmured Jack.

He sat for a few seconds with his head bowed, then straightened up, having made his decision.

'I'm going to telephone Midge's mother, maybe she can help.'

Not wanting to voice his opinion that it was possible that Halford and Midge had disappeared together, he reached for the telephone. Sitting on the edge of the desk, he held the receiver to his ear, listening to the shrill ringing tone, waiting for an answer. He was about to replace the receiver when he heard a breathless voice.

'Hello, Annie Davies speaking.'

'Hello, Mrs Davies. It's Jack Austin here.'

'Oh hello, Jack. I'm sorry. I was upstairs making the beds and couldn't get to the telephone any quicker. How are you?'

'Quite well, thank you.'

'Do you know, I was only saying to Midge the other day that I haven't seen you for quite some time?'

'Er, yes that's right. Have you seen Midge then? Is she there now?'

'Oh, now let me see. When did we see her? She wasn't here for the weekend, but that wasn't unusual. Friday, she went to Ipswich. Oh, you know that already. She'd gone to get...'

Jack interrupted her, trying to be patient. 'Mrs Davies, can I speak to Midge? Is she there with you?'

'Well, no. She's not here. Isn't she there, at work with you?'

'No, Mrs Davies, that's why I'm telephoning you. She hasn't arrived for work and I've received no word from her.'

'Oh dear, that's not like her at all. Oh... Well, wasn't she with the Rivers' over the weekend?'

'No, apparently not. Will you please ask her to telephone me the minute you see her? It's very important that I speak to her as soon as possible.'

'Yes, yes, of course I'll ask her to telephone you.'

'Thank you very much, Mrs Davies. That's very kind of you.'

Ruby, Nell and even Raymond watched as Jack carefully replaced the receiver in its cradle. Listening to his side of the conversation they had soon gathered that Midge's family had no idea where she was and hadn't seen her for several days.

Nell gave Jack's shoulder a gentle pat. 'You were right not to tell her about Halford's letters. No good worrying her yet. You never know, they might still turn up with a simple explanation.'

Ruby sighed. 'I hope so, Nell. I hope so,' she said mournfully.

Collecting her gloves and handbag, and pulling her coat snugly round her shoulders, Ruby held out her hand for Raymond as he slithered off the stool.

'Come along now. Say thank you to Uncle Jack.'

Raymond looked up at Jack. 'Thank you, Uncle Jack,' but then turned accusingly towards his mother, tugging at her arm.

'Mummy, I want to see Aunty Midge.' His face crumpled into a cry that turned into a wail. That set off his wheezing and as Ruby gathered him up she prepared herself for the asthma attack that would surely follow.

\*\*\*

Annie Davies replaced the receiver on her telephone with a thoughtful frown on her face.

'Mm, I wonder where Midge can be. I hope she's all right.'

Returning to the bed making, the thought lingered for a few minutes, but before long it sank into the mass of distractions that were part of running a boarding house. As she was crossing the landing to go into another bedroom, Annie heard a noise downstairs.

'Is that you, Midge?' She was surprised when Grit's upturned face appeared at the bottom of the stairs.

'No, Mama it's me.'

Expressing wonder and joy, Annie hurried down to join her daughter who had by now gone into the kitchen. Mother and daughter hugged each other tightly before Annie pushed Grit to arm's length.

'What are you doing here, Grit? I didn't think you were due to have time off yet. You're not ill, are you? You look terrible. What's happening?'

Grit laughed gingerly. 'No, Mama, I'm very well, but I needed to come home and see you.'

She turned away quickly and busied herself with the cups and tea-pot. When she put the cups and saucers down on the table, her pretty round face was troubled. She pushed her dark hair behind her ear nervously.

'You'd better sit down, Mama. I have some news for you.'

Annie sank onto the nearest chair, her hand flying to her forehead.

'You're not pregnant, are you, Grit? You and Boy are getting far too close. You are cousins after all. It's not right…'

'No, of course not, Mama.' Grit interrupted before her mother could get started on her tirade against their romance. 'This has got nothing to do with me or Boy.'

'Well, that's a relief,' retorted Annie, fiddling nervously with her pearl necklace.

'I've had a letter this morning.' She took a deep breath. 'From Midge.'

'Oh, thank goodness. Jack Austin has been on the telephone asking for her,' said Annie with relief.

Relief was only momentary though as Grit went on.

'Mama, listen to me. Please. Mama, Midge has written to me to say she's never coming home again.'

Grit gulped back her tears as the words hit Annie who felt as though she had been struck in the stomach with a sledgehammer. Leaping up from her seat, Grit rushed to Annie's side. Their tears mingled as they held each other close.

'Can I see the letter please, Grit?'

Grit went into the hall to find her handbag and brought the letter back to her mother. Annie blew her nose loudly with a handkerchief she retrieved from inside her apron pocket. Taking in gulps of air to waylay the nausea that was building, she held the letter with trembling fingers. The words became blurred through her brimming eyes.

'Oh Grit, it's Halford Rivers. He's bewitched her.' She thumped the table angrily. 'I warned her about him. I told her he had an eye for the ladies, but she hasn't listened to a word I said.'

Sitting in silence for a few minutes, Annie read Midge's words again.

Grit watched her mother's face with concern. 'She says she loves him, Mama.'

'Yes, she does, but Grit, what about Ruby and the children. They love him too and his responsibility is towards them. What on earth can he be thinking of, running off with a young girl? And a Catholic one at that.'

'I don't know. Midge never said a word to me about any of this, and I thought we shared everything.'

Annie's mind raced through the many consequences of Midge and Halford's actions.

'I'd better telephone Jack Austin. This is going to affect their business. Oh dear, we'll have to tell your father as well.'

She was thinking aloud and as another horrific thought struck her, she faced Grit with a shocked expression.

'He's not even a Catholic. He'll probably get her pregnant and any kiddies they have will be illegitimate. How will she be able to live with herself? It's a sin, Grit. That's what it is. Oh, may God forgive her,' she added passionately, with her handkerchief pressed against her mouth.

\*\*\*

The telephone rang in Jack Austin's workshop as he struggled to concentrate on the repairs that needed attention. Wearily he crossed the workshop and in to the office to answer it.

'I see, Mrs Davies. Well, thank you for letting me know.' Jack replaced the receiver and swore under his breath at the mess Halford had left behind.

Annie Davies had said she would come up to see Halford's wife. Jack thought it appropriate to deliver the news himself sooner as it would be a few hours before Mrs Davies could get there.

It wasn't a task to be envied, but it had to be done.

*Thank goodness Nell is there with Ruby.*

It was mid-day when Jack locked up and went to Oakley House. As he walked, the full impact of Halford's desertion began to hit home.

*God knows how I can keep the business going on my own. No partner and no assistant.*

He kicked out furiously at a stone and sent it leaping along the pavement. His mood matched the overcast sky. By the time he reached Ruby's house, the first few drops of rain had begun to spatter the ground.

Even the spring flowers seemed to be forlornly poking their heads out of the ground near the garden gate. They went unnoticed by Jack as he lifted the knocker and rapped firmly. It sounded much louder than he intended. He stood waiting with his chin on his chest, shoulders hunched.

Nell opened the door to find a very dejected man standing with his hands thrust deeply into his raincoat pockets. The expression she saw on Jack's face did not bode well for good news.

\*\*\*

It was with a sense of relief that Annie Davies replaced her shoes with her comfy slippers before she sat down beside the fire in her sitting room that night. The day had proved to be one of the most horrendous she had experienced, ranking alongside the time of Veronica's death.

After her telephone call to Jack Austin, she had determined to make the journey to Thorpe le Soken to visit Ruby and the children. On the way, she had called in to see Will at Blue House Farm. Thinking back to their conversation, she shuddered and wiped her eyes for the umpteenth time that day at the words he'd used about Midge, his own daughter.

When she had arrived at Ruby's, she found that Jack had already broken the news and her half-sister had everything under control. Understandably, Nell's reception was cool, but she found Ruby's welcome deeply touching. Again, she asked herself, how could Halford desert his wife and children? Midge had spoken often, so lovingly about Beryl and Raymond, and Annie knew that Ruby regarded her as part of the family. Annie shivered and put a shovel of coal on the fire.

She was pleased Grit had offered to stay another night at home. Grit and Teresa, her two remaining daughters, had clung together when the younger girl had been told the news. No one had known what had been developing between Midge and Halford. Her normally sensible girl had so clearly made a terrible mistake. The man was a philanderer and would probably get her pregnant then move on. Where they had gone was a mystery that would accompany Annie Davies to her grave.

***

A week after Halford and Midge had disappeared, Jack Austin sat at his work bench with his head in hands. He was angry, frustrated and scared and was having difficulty breathing. He wanted to hit something very hard or scream out, very loudly, but he didn't have the energy. A telephone call from his bank manager had informed him that the cheque he had written a few days earlier had not been honoured. The man instructed Jack, in a most officious tone to "attend a meeting tomorrow at 2 o'clock sharp, in order to discuss your financial situation". Until that conversation, Jack had believed his finances to be in order, but now it seems something had gone wrong.

*First Halford and Midge up and disappear and now the bank manager's calling me in to his office. The bank must have made a mistake somewhere in the calculations.*

He fought to slow his breathing and calm himself down. His mind was racing and in turmoil. Working on the repairs brought him out in a clammy sweat, so after several failed attempts, he decided to call it a day.

The next day when Jack arrived home after his appointment with the bank manager, his wife, Gloria was shocked at his appearance. He seemed to have aged by twenty years. Normally of a robust, cheerful disposition, now he looked a broken man with stooped shoulders, laboured breathing and haunted eyes.

'Get me a glass of whisky, will you please, Gloria love.'

She watched as he drained the glass. Suddenly he was stricken with a terrible bout of coughing.

'I'm calling Dr Foster, Jack. Just sit yourself down here and try and make yourself comfortable. I'll just be a few minutes, love.' She was trying to hide the panic in her voice.

She still had no idea why the bank manager had wanted to see him, but she had noticed that Jack's cough had been developing over the past week. As she came back into the room, she found him leaning back with his eyes closed and his breath laboured. His hands gripped the arms of the chair so tightly that his knuckles were white.

He opened his eyes as she came towards him.

'It appears that we are ruined love. Halford's gone off with all the money. He's cleared the bank account out.' His words came in a whisper as his energy drained away.

Gloria didn't know what to say. She was bewildered and baffled by their friend's actions.

'How could he do this to us?' she moaned.

'The bank manager says we should get the police involved,' Jack said meekly as he tried to stir himself

Gloria went across to her husband and knelt in front of him. She held his hands in hers and kissed his forehead lovingly.

'We'll get through this somehow, love.'

Searching her eyes, Jack sighed deeply which made him start coughing all over again.

'Bill Rivers, Halford's old man came in the bank as I was leaving. It seems that Halford has run off with some of his money as well. I still can't believe it. It's a nightmare,' Jack added.

Later that day, Gloria followed the doctor into the kitchen where Jack had remained since arriving home.

'I'll be all right, doctor. I've just had a terrible shock and it's knocked me for six.' He tried to resist the doctor's attempts to check his pulse but the doctor insisted.

'You need plenty of rest Mr Austin. I'll come back and see you tomorrow. Keep an eye on him Mrs Austin and if his condition deteriorates, please call me at once,' the doctor instructed, after listening to Jack's chest,

'Righto, Doctor Foster. I'll certainly do that,' she answered, relieved that it was nothing serious.

As the doctor made his way out to his car, the thought crossed his mind that he wouldn't be surprised if his patient didn't succumb to TB. His symptoms were certainly taking that course. With that in mind, he made a mental note to keep a very close watch on Jack Austin.

A few days later following a frantic telephone call from Gloria Austin, Jack was admitted into intensive care, suffering from TB.

PART TWO

A NEW LIFE

## CHAPTER ELEVEN

**1945…**
It was July 1945, a hot summer day at the end of WW2. In the sitting room of the semi-detached house just inside the Welsh border the curtains were drawn, shading the room from the blinding sunlight. A soft breeze fluttered through the open windows, wafting the curtains like sheets blowing on the washing-line. They reminded him of another hot summer's day. Bill Hard's hands were shaking as he wiped the sweat off his head with a clean white handkerchief, tutting at memories he didn't like and certainly didn't welcome.

The house was too quiet. He couldn't sit down, couldn't keep still. His thoughts raced. *What could be wrong? It hadn't been this quiet with the others.* His mind traversed the journey he and Mary had made together over the last nine years. *Is that all it's been? Nine years.* It seemed a lifetime since they'd made that fateful decision.

He wished he hadn't recalled that time. Such was its magnitude that he and Mary preferred to keep it deep in the recesses of their minds. But for the moment he allowed his thoughts to back track. They'd had a journey of nightmarish proportions from London to Chester, their chosen destination. Mary had secured the position of managers of a wool shop in Chester's ancient city centre. It came with living accommodation consisting of one room that acted as sitting room, bedroom and kitchen, with a lavatory behind the shop, so at least they had a roof over their heads. They believed that it would be, if not a brilliant starting point, then an adequate one to their new life together.

Before long Mary was producing crocheted and knitted garments to sell and Bill discovered that he too could work with yarn. He created a beautiful tapestry picture of scarlet poppies and used his skill to make fire screens. They hit on a winning idea when Mary, using her French language skills, translated knitting patterns purchased from France, into English so that Bill could create the chic dresses and jackets. He also found time to make articles in wood, using marquetry as his main medium. The business was beginning to take off in this picturesque part of the old city almost beneath the clock bridge.

All went well for about eighteen months, until Mary found herself pregnant. It was delightful and worrying in equal measure as they knew this meant the end of their days in the wool shop. Sitting in the poky room above the shop they mulled over their options. It didn't take long to conclude that they weren't many. Bill would have to find a job and they would need somewhere else to live.

A few months later, Mary was in the shop taking stock of the yarn, when Mike Fielding, the representative from whom they bought yarn, walked in with a cheeky grin.

'Hello, Mrs Hard. I've got some wonderful new silks here for you. Only the very best!'

'Hello there, Mike. I'm afraid we won't be needing anything this time. We are leaving in a couple of weeks.'

'Oh, deary me, deary me.' A concerned expression appeared in his eyes. 'Have you got anything lined up yet?'

'Well, with my condition, we're looking for something for Mr Hard. We're not having much luck yet though.'

He leaned one elbow on the counter and with the other he scratched his bald patch.

'Now then, I can't promise for sure, but I think I might be able to help you and your husband out.'

He pursed his lips and was so serious that Mary was touched at his concern. Mike told her that he had a mate who was in the vacuum sales business, looking for someone to cover an area in Cheshire.

'West Kirby, it is. I'll get in touch with him and give him your telephone number, shall I?'

Mary suddenly felt emotional and thanked him very much and then became emotional all over again later as she recounted the tale to Bill.

Mike's mate came up trumps with a job and the use of a room in his house in West Kirby.

It was in that cramped room that Mary gave birth to her first child, a girl they named Veronica Mary who soon became known as Ronnie. The couple barely had enough money to buy bread and milk even though Bill was working hard at selling the vacuum cleaners, thankfully picking up a small commission with each sale.

As time went by, with Mary's thrifty nature, she miraculously managed to save enough for them to afford to move on to more suitable accommodation in Birkenhead. It was at that house that they had a shattering experience. Returning home from work one day with his next-door neighbour, Bill turned the corner into their street, to discover that their neighbour's house had been demolished by a bomb. The man, frantic with fear that his wife and family were killed, went into total shutdown. He couldn't move a muscle.

Bill, feeling his own panic rising ran forward to a group of people gathered quietly on the pavement ahead of them. With racing pulse, he pushed through the small crowd. Immediately, strong arms held him and it was then that he saw Mary holding Ronnie tightly in her arms, his neighbour's wife and family huddled beside her. They were shuffling wearily down the street.

Bill wanted to rush up the road to bring Mary to safety but was held back by a burly policeman. Without another thought, he turned and ran back to where his paralysed neighbour remained transfixed to the spot where Bill had left him.

'Nick,' he yelled into the man's face. 'They're all right. They're all right. Do you hear me? Come on, man. Come with me. They're over here, Nick.'

With a supreme effort Bill dragged the man forward as his wife came careering down the street, her children floundering behind her as fast as their feet would carry them.

Beyond the excited crowd now gathered round the happy family, Mary walked slowly towards him, tears streaming down her cheeks. They hugged as if they would never let go with little Ronnie squashed but safe between them.

Thinking about it now in his kitchen while waiting for news of Mary's third labour sent a shudder through his body. Following the bomb damage to their street the house was no longer safe to live in so they had to move on and this time they found a semi-detached house in Meols. He and Mary were proud of their achievement in affording this house, having worked their way up from living in those single rooms.

But sadly, Bill remembered how unhappy he was. He wanted to be working with his hands and began to loathe each morning he had to go out on the road again. Three years earlier he had lost all of his hair and with the nature of the job, he was forced to speak to potential customers. A phobia began to emerge. Even thinking of it now made the back of his neck prickle. It became harder and harder for him to get out on his rounds. He dragged himself round the streets, forcing himself up each garden path to face a front door with his palms clammy, his pulse pounding and beads of sweat seeping into his hatband. At home with Mary and Ronnie, tempers were frayed. Mary scoured the papers for a job and finally found one in a jeweller's shop in Chester that she hoped would suit his personality.

The soft thud of footsteps crossing the room above broke into his thoughts. He strained his ears for a sound to comfort his aching brain. Then it came. At first a low groaning then a moaning rising to a wail. More footsteps. Then more silence. He couldn't contain his panic any longer. Flinging open the door, he took the stairs two at a time almost running into the buxom figure of the midwife who was barring his way. Nurse Jones stood with her feet planted firmly in their sensible black shoes, arms folded across her ample bosom.

'Now then Mr Hard, what's all this?' she demanded before he could take another breath. 'Your wife is fine. No need to worry. I'll call you up when the job's done.'

She had a brusque manner, as if she was of the opinion that all men should be shunted off the face of the earth.

Bill retraced his steps, dejectedly muttering to himself.

'If it wasn't for us men, you'd be out of a job, madam.'

Nurse Jones had said not to worry. How could he not worry? Mary was at this very moment giving birth to their child. He felt an insignificant item in the whole procedure of labour, so helpless in the face of Mary's pain. He sat on the bottom stair and lit his pipe, listening again for any further sounds, yet not wanting to hear. The shouts followed by silence had been going on for hours it seemed to his weary body.

*Shouting, silence, shouting, silence...* his mind kept repeating. He put his head in his hands. Then he detected the midwife's voice. Not the words, but the change in tone, now intense and urgent, that attracted his attention. It sent alarm bells ringing in Bill's brain. Suddenly Mary roared triumphantly, then there was silence again, then a sharp slapping sound, then a baby's cry. What a cry! Bill held his breath, almost choking on his pipe smoke.

He stood up and put his pipe down in the ash tray on the small hall table. Turning to look up the stairs, he waited for the midwife to give him permission to enter his own bedroom to see Mary and their new baby. That's the way things were and he accepted it. He thought it was probably a bit of a messy business and was better off waiting in the wings. But the waiting was agony too.

*What is going on now?*

The minutes ticked by.

He could hear movement and low voices as the two women talked. Finally, the bedroom door opened and Nurse Jones appeared.

'You've got another daughter, Mr Hard. Now go and put the kettle on and brew up some tea.' Bill's jaw dropped as he was about to speak. 'And fill the kettle right up. I need plenty of hot water.'

He desperately wanted to go to Mary's side but he wordlessly obeyed this domineering woman. She was most definitely in charge and he wasn't going to annoy her if he could help it.

As Bill waited for the kettle to boil on the hob, his thoughts drifted back again to 1940 when he had taken up the position of watch and clock repairer in Chester. He remembered how selflessly Mary simply got on with the job of packing everything up and going along with him to the very house in which they now lived. Bill had been so thrilled with the work. Brenda and

Margaret, the two unmarried ladies who worked there soon took him under their wing, making him welcome and showing him the ropes.

The first few weeks he muddled through, quickly remembering all he had picked up as a younger man working in a repair shop, until he began to find his confidence. Always embarrassed by his lack of hair, he was thankful to be working in the back room, where he didn't have to come into contact with the general public. *Oh yes, they were happy days.* Then a cloud gathered over his face as he remembered how he foolishly allowed himself to be talked into resigning from that uncomplicated life to take up a position in the local aircraft factory. "Working for the war effort," it was called.

He had already worked himself almost into the grave during the First World War. Much to his family's horror he had faked his age and joined up to fight for his country in France in the Royal Army Medical Corps. So, it was with a sour taste in his mouth that he was suddenly brought up to the harsh reality of his life now. It was during this time, a time when they could scarce afford any extra expense that their second child had been born. William John Raymond's birth was during an air raid. Bill, now compelling his concentration onto that night, tried to bring some warmth into his mind. But it was a traumatic time for all of them, what with the war going on and having to work in that awful place. He failed to find anything comforting to recall.

'How's that water coming on, Mr Hard?' yelled a voice in the present.

With guilty thoughts still in his head, Bill spun round abruptly.

'Just coming.'

By the time Bill appeared sheepishly at the bedroom door with the tray Mary had brushed her hair and changed into a clean nightdress. Nurse Jones was bustling round gathering up dirty linen and generally tidying up. The baby was now sleeping in Mary's arms, wrapped cosily inside the tight swaddling sheet.

Mary looked up as Bill edged his way in, trying to find a clear spot to put down the tray. She pointed to a space that Nurse Jones had cleared on the dressing table. The midwife seemed a little more human now as she helped him with the tea tray.

'Go and see your daughter then.' She nodded towards the baby.

While the midwife poured the tea, Bill glanced gingerly at Mary, propped up on a pillow. Taking a few steps forward, he leaned over to plant a kiss on Mary's lips.

'Well done, darling.'

Then for the very first time, he tenderly touched his new baby. A second daughter.

'She looks just like you,' he whispered, glancing towards Mary.

*A sentiment expressed by countless fathers before him,* thought the midwife, grinning to herself.

\*\*\*

'Oh Mary, she's such a bonny baby,' cooed Alma. 'You're making me broody now.' She bustled in with Ronnie and John in tow.

Mary was in high spirits now that her labour was over.

'Hello my darlings,' she said turning to smile at her children who came in to the room a little shyly, not sure what they would find.

'It'll be you next then,' Mary chuckled.

She stretched out her free arm towards her two other children.

'Come up on the bed and see your baby sister,' she encouraged gently. Ronnie felt rather grown-up being a big sister as she stroked the baby's downy hair.

'How was it, love?' Alma asked in a confidential whisper.

'Oh, you know Nurse Jones. She was her usual business-like self, so she kept everything under control, including Bill.'

The two women chuckled. Alma knew Nurse Jones from personal experience. She thought how good it was to see her friend looking so bright and cheerful. They had first met a few years earlier when Mary and Bill had moved in to the house across the crescent from their own home. She'd helped Mary settle in and was there for her when John was born and Mary reciprocated when Alma had her baby daughter, Anne.

She and Jay had an older daughter, Elizabeth. They were a warm-hearted couple and even Bill found himself melting in their relaxed company. The two couples discovered a lot in common, more than Bill and Mary cared to admit, even to their new friends. The two women would share patterns and tips for dressmaking, knitting and crochet while Bill and Jay lost themselves in discussions about radios and motor engines. They enjoyed inventing mechanical devices and often disappeared into Jay's workshop to puzzle over some problem of engineering.

Now Mary looked up from her baby to meet Alma's eyes.

'Alma, thank you so much for taking care of Ronnie and John. They love coming over to play with Anne. Don't you?' she added, turning toward her two older children.

John nodded his head then cuddled back into his Mummy's side as close as he could while Ronnie agreed confidently.

Alma walked to the bedroom door and turned back to face her friend. 'If there's anything else I can do, you know you only have to ask. Right, I'll be off now then. It sounds like Bill's getting some food ready. Cheerio then.'

Later that night, after Ronnie and John had inspected their new sister, smothering her with kisses and now both sleeping soundly, Bill lay on the bed with Mary. He gazed down at this precious new life that had just joined their family.

'What shall we call her, Mary? We've got Veronica Mary for Ronnie and William John Raymond for John. They're all names to keep memories alive. We should do the same for this little one, so what about Dorothy after...'

Mary put her fingers on Bill's lips. 'Ssh, let's not talk about that. Anyway, I'm not keen on the name.'

With a final glance into the cradle, she snuggled down and they had soon drifted into sleep. Mary dreamed of a large family. Though she couldn't make out any features, they seemed somehow familiar, as if she knew them well. She was running, running to get away. Their outstretched arms grabbed at her clothes. They were calling her to come back, but she ran on. Her feet were lead weights treading water. But in a strange way, as frantic as she was to run away, at the same time she was trying to get back.

At the point where she had to choose whether to go back or force her way from their grappling hands, she woke up. It was the same every time and Mary had lost count of how many times that dream had recurred in various guises.

She knew what it meant and desperately wanted to erase the memories it evoked. The fears and guilt were sometimes too much to bear. As she sleepily turned to look at her stirring daughter, she wondered how she could be so blessed with her three wonderful children and this man sleeping beside her. She wished the dreams would stop torturing her.

Now fully awake, Mary picked up the baby and suckled her to her breast. Once settled, she began to think about the name they would choose for her. She knew Bill was right to keep a family name, but not Dorothy. She played around with the name, working others out. She had a friend called Dorothy, but no, the baby didn't look like a Dorothy. Or what about Doris? She whispered it as she stroked her baby's cheek, trying it out. It still didn't feel right. Then she remembered a name she had read in a book.

*Doreen. Yes, I like that.* She smiled to herself. *I'll tell Bill in the morning.*

By the time baby Doreen had satisfied her hunger and was clean and dry, Mary was yawning and put her back gently in her cradle. They were both quickly sleeping deeply, preparing for Doreen's second day in the world.

Bill was awake early the next morning feeling the tension pulling at his muscles as he knew he must face the day. At forty-eight, he was thirteen years older than Mary and felt protective over her, though he was vulnerable himself. His job at the aircraft factory provided a steady income, but the end of the war brought a decline in the need for engineers working on the Spitfires. Bill longed for the day when they didn't need his services any longer. He dreaded the thought of going to work with the other men who, he thought, were joking about his baldness behind his back. Bill was a loner, relying heavily on Mary for his comfort and security. He was grateful for the time he had worked in the jewellers where he could work alone most of the time and had thoroughly enjoyed his time there. He had improved his knowledge about watch and clock repairs that would soon stand him in good stead in the future.

With this in mind, he was keeping his ears and eyes open for a new venture they could look into. Both he and Mary were entrepreneurial spirits, working well together and enjoyed being their own boss, despite the hazards it entailed. But first things first. They had a baby to name and baptise.

***

'No. I'm sorry Mr and Mrs Hard. Doreen is not a saint's name. I can't baptise her into the Catholic faith with that name.'

The priest was adamant when they visited him to make the arrangements for the baptism. Bill and Mary looked at each other in dismay.

'What shall we do now?' asked Mary.

Bill remembered the conversation they'd had on the night of Doreen's birth.

'Back to Dorothy?'

She was about to object, then caught Bill's arm.

'You know I'm not keen on that but if we changed it to the Latin, it would be Dorothea. You registered her as Doreen Mary Eugene, so we'd have to change all of her names.'

Turning back to the priest she said, 'Dorothea Maria Eugenia. Can you baptise her with those names, Father?'

The priest nodded his approval. 'Oh yes that would be most satisfactory.'

On the way home Bill grumbled.

'Why on earth did he have to be so pedantic? What does it matter if it's not a saint's name?'

As he rambled on, Mary sighed deeply. Whenever Bill had anything to do with church, especially of the Catholic faith, he would become exasperated. He'd been brought up by staunch protestant parents. His father allowed only bible reading on Sundays between services. Mary's family were strict Roman Catholics. In later years they were to tell their children that their two families were so opposed to their union that they had been driven to run away together. That was the reason for them having no grandparents.

Mary listened now to Bill's tirade against her faith. She was saddened to think this was one area they could never agree on. Bill no longer went to church and brooded if she went without him. She complied with his wishes rather than suffer with his black moods, so her attendance at mass was now limited to Christmas, Easter and the baptisms of her three children. Mary didn't feel like defending her faith this time and she let her mind drift away.

*How did I manage to get myself into this situation? This man beside me is not the man I knew him to be when we met thirteen years ago. He's changed beyond all recognition. He used to be outgoing and confident. Now he's introverted and insecure, yet I do still love him so much.*

The baptism was a low-key affair that went without a hitch. There were no relatives to invite and they had few friends. As soon as it was over Bill and Mary set to work on their mission to find their next undertaking.

Every week Mary scanned the adverts in the newspapers, searching for a suitable business that they could work at together. Just as they were beginning to despair, she spotted it. Only a few lines, yet enough to give her reason to make further enquiries. The advert described a large house to rent, suitable to be run as a guest house and set in the pretty countryside of North Wales. Even from the short description, it sounded perfect. Mary had some experience in helping to run a guest house and knew about keeping records. She believed Bill would be in his element working in the garden. He was good with his hands too so she could rely on him if any maintenance work was necessary. She was so excited that she couldn't wait to tell him her good news when he came home from the factory.

'How would you like to live in a big house in the country?' she asked Ronnie on the way home after collecting her from school.

'Yes please!' Ronnie shouted eagerly. 'Will I go to a new school as well?'

'Can I come too?' piped her little brother eagerly.

'Of course you'll be coming, silly,' retorted Ronnie, tutting at his childishness. 'You're only three. If you don't come with us, where will you live?'

John gripped his mother's hand tightly, suddenly feeling anxious. Ronnie felt very grown up, for in her seven years she had already experienced moving house.

'We've got to speak to Daddy about it yet, so don't get too excited,' Mary quickly interrupted, realising she should have talked it over with Bill first. Yet she felt very confident that like her, he would want to make further enquiries.

## CHAPTER TWELVE

**1946...**

Before Doreen was a year old the family moved into their 'new' three hundred years old, three-storey house in North Wales. It was called Coed y Brain (as in Brian) that means Wood of Crows. The original building had been divided in two, the greater part being the one that Bill and Mary were allowed to rent. The front door opened onto a large hallway, to the left of which stood the oak room. This was by far the most elegant room in the house, it's walls being lined with oak panels, and an immense open fire surrounded by blue and white tiles. The parquet floor was dotted with rugs and towards the rear of the room was the dining table. Not only were the guests able to eat in here but with comfortable lounge chairs arranged near the fire, they could also sit back and relax. Overlooking the front garden was a bay window with leaded lights, through which the guests could contemplate the peaceful scene of open fields and woodlands with not another house in sight.

On the first floor were two bedrooms. One of these echoed the bay window of the oak room. It was a large room with a double brass bed and as with most houses of that ilk a small fireplace was installed to keep out the winter chills. The other room was also quite large with a fireplace that many a guest was thankful to have lit on a cold winter morning. The bathroom was conveniently placed on this floor, being easily reached by all rooms. It had the luxury of a bathtub, a sink and an Elsan toilet. A spacious airing cupboard was another luxury Mary enjoyed where all the bed linen could be aired and stored. From the large landing that was big enough to hold a bed if needed, a second flight of stairs led up to the top floor landing which was as large as the first one, but intriguingly this one had four doors even though there were only three bedrooms. Two of these rooms were for the family's use, unless there were extra guests when Bill and Mary would sleep downstairs on a bed settee.

The family entrance was through the back door that led into a passage. Off it, were their sitting room and the enormous kitchen that was the hive of activity. There was a pantry with many shelves for the bottled fruit and preserves, a scullery with a large sink and cupboards for dishes and crockery. They were all excited when they discovered a cellar. That housed the vegetables and fruit that needed to be kept cool. In the front hall there was a door marked 'private', which was the family's route into the main part of the house.

On that first day, the door was held open by a heavy weight, and Ronnie and John ran through it. Up and down the wide staircase and in and out of the rooms they went. It was a cold February day, but nothing could dampen their enthusiasm. There were five large bedrooms to explore and they wasted no time at all in their quest to discover every nook and cranny. What an adventure.

'Mummy, Daddy. There's an extra door upstairs – and it's locked. What is it? Where does it go? Is it a secret door? Is there a secret passage behind it?' they shouted as they jostled their way down the stairs.

Mary stopped unpacking for a moment and sat back on her heels.

'Well, that's strange. I wonder what it can be. What do you think, Daddy?'

'You'd better show us. Come along.'

Grabbing Ronnie's hand, he led the way. Up the stairs they trooped. John followed behind his Daddy, with Mary at the rear with Doreen. When they reached the top landing, Bill put his fingers to his lips. 'Ssh,' he hissed. Creeping forward, he slowly opened each door until he came to the one that was locked. He put his ear against the wood, bending low as if listening. They all jumped when he stood up and turned to face them.

Suddenly pulling a scary face he stretched out his arms, wiggling his fingers.

'Maybe it's where the bogey man lives,' he roared.

The children screamed in feigned fear and turned and ran down the stairs. Mary and Bill laughed contentedly.

'Don't go through the gate to the farm, you two rascals,' Mary called as she heard them race outside.

They ran panting and laughing, to explore the secrets of the walled garden while Mary returned to her chores, putting Doreen back in her pram. Before long the child began to get restless and grizzly.

'It must be time to stop for lunch,' noted Mary.

'I'll take Doreen out to find Ronnie and John.'

As Bill stepped through the back door with the baby in his arms. He was almost knocked off his feet by the children as they tore around a corner. He caught hold of John's arm as he raced by.

'Now, stop chasing round like wild animals. Mummy is getting lunch ready so go inside now and wash your hands.' John wriggled around trying to free his arm from his father's grip. Bill let him go with another warning as the boy scampered off in search of his sister.

'Daddy, what is that door upstairs really for?' Ronnie asked when they sat down to eat.

'I told you, it's where the bogey man lives.'

'No, really. Why is it locked?'

'What you think are two houses here, is actually one house. So, that door on the landing leads through to the other part of the house. That's all it is. It keeps us separate from our neighbours,' Mary explained patiently. 'Are you happy now?'

'Mm, yes. I see now. Daddy was just teasing us.'

***

Bill endured the work at the aircraft factory for a while longer, but it was proving to be difficult for him. Each journey required a bike ride to and from the station which on top of the train ride made a very long day, yet his wages were still necessary until the guest house business took hold. Things were brought to a head when one evening on his way home, he waved to a neighbour and in doing so, lost control of the bike. He fell in a heap at her feet, with a bloody nose, a bruised neck and a rather battered bicycle, not to mention his shattered ego.

Without the bike, the trek into work and back home became unbearable. A few mornings later he was still wincing with pain from the accident.

'I can't do that journey every day any more, Mary. It's bad enough putting up with those fellows in the factory, but now...' His voice tailed off and Mary could see he was struggling to explain himself.

'We'll manage somehow. We've been through much worse so I'm sure we'll be fine.'

So, Bill stayed home with Mary and could soon be seen cultivating the garden, wearing an old tweed suit, a flat cap on his head and his pipe comfortably between his teeth. He was happy with the solitude of tilling the soil and often stopped to gaze at the picturesque view of the Welsh mountains.

Sometimes he would become absorbed in watching a friendly robin perched cheekily on a fork handle or in a nearby low branch waiting for a juicy worm to be uncovered by his turning the earth. He was rightly proud of the vegetables he was producing for Mary's table. After inspecting the gardens one day, he came into the kitchen in a greatly animated state.

'I've just uncovered gooseberry bushes and raspberries and redcurrants. With a bit of pruning, I think we'll get plenty of fruit in the autumn.' His mouth watered at the thought of the pies Mary would bake.

'That's marvellous. It'll certainly help boost the meals.' She caught his enthusiasm.

'Have you noticed the stone shed in the corner by the wall?'

'Yes. What are you cooking up now, Bill?' Mary enquired with raised eyebrows.

'I've had a good look inside and I believe it will make an excellent work room. I thought I could use it to start mending watches and clocks and maybe do some woodwork in there.'

Mary was pleased Bill had begun to explore ideas for himself. When he finished at the aircraft factory, he seemed at a loss as to what to do with himself. She was happy to encourage him with this new venture.

'It sounds like an excellent idea to me.'

On further investigation Bill discovered the shed to be waterproof and once he'd fixed up a workbench, he moved his tools into their new home. The word got around and people were soon asking him to look at their broken timepieces. Bill repaired his bike and began expanding his business by visiting customers in their homes, regulating their grandfather clocks and doing any necessary repairs.

One day, in payment for some work he did for a customer, he was given a chest of drawers. Not wanting to look a gift horse in the mouth, he calmly thanked the man and balancing the piece of furniture on the pedal of the cycle, he wheeled it several miles home. He made plans to convert it into a bureau, with two drawers and a drop-down lid on which to write. It was to become a family heirloom.

Mary was well prepared for business. She had been advertising the guest house for several weeks so the diary was filling up nicely and the rooms were ready for her first visitors.

'Come in, come in. Welcome to Coed y Brain,' Mary encouraged warmly, as the Murphy family struggled through the front door. 'Darling, will you take the children outside to play while I show their Mummy and Daddy to their room? There's a good girl,' she said, turning to Ronnie.

Stretching out her hand she introduced herself and the young couple each shook her hand in return.

The man had an open friendly face. 'This is my wife, Kathleen and I'm Patrick,' he said with a smile.

She recognised his Irish accent and immediately warmed to this pleasant couple. The children, he said were twin girls called Brigitte and Bernadette.

'They're four years old now and we've managed to survive so far,' he said with a laugh.

Mary showed them to their room and while they unpacked, she returned to the kitchen where she continued to prepare the evening meal for them and her family.

Ronnie skipped off obediently, eager to show her new visitors around, with Bridget and Bernadette scurrying behind. John tagged on to the little convoy, not wanting to be left out. Being of a similar age they were eager to outdo each other in a game of follow my leader. She led them a merry dance down the narrow paths, beside the stone wall towards their Daddy's work room. She stopped abruptly, remembering her duties as the eldest and drew herself up to her highest height.

'That's Daddy's workroom. You are not allowed to go inside there. He will be very angry if you go in and touch anything, won't he John?' she said in the most mature voice she could muster.

John nodded his head vigorously, recognising the truth behind his big sister's words.

The twins stood in silence. Their blue eyes, identical as gems in a necklace widened in awe of this solemn statement. Ronnie stared down at them and was suddenly taken aback by their mirror images. She had been so busy racing on ahead, leading them on, that she hadn't properly looked before.

'Thank goodness your mother has given you different coloured ribbons for your hair. Which one's which?' she asked, switching her gaze from one to the other.

They pointed to each other and both started talking at once. In a fit of giggles, they tried again without success until all four were rolling along the path making a riotous noise.

'Stop, stop,' called Ronnie breathlessly. 'Tell us which one is which?'

Bridget pointed to Bernadette. 'Bernadette is called Bernadette Poppy, so she always has a red bow.'

'And Bridget is called Bridget Primrose, so she always wears a yellow bow,' added Bernadette.

John was fascinated by these girls. He'd never known twins before and the masses of curls that bounced and swayed with every movement of their heads intrigued him. The twin's hair was like their Daddy's whose glossy black curls shone like coal, unlike their own Daddy who had no hair at all. Both John and Ronnie had quite straight, brown hair and their baby sister had hardly any at all.

The children were dressed warmly against the cold winter weather but today the sun shone and there was an azure blue sky. They had fun blowing 'smoke' out of their mouths as they followed Ronnie up onto some stones that Bill had left ready to build into a rockery. They were shrieking with laughter and John, perched on the highest one was shouting at the top of his voice.

'I'm the king of the castle and you're the dirty ...' when their father's voice cut through the air like a knife.

'Get down from those stones. Don't you know how dangerous that is?'

The twins looked pleadingly at their leader, while she helped them all clamber down and led them to stand in front of her father. John stood a little way back, the laughter and camaraderie of moments before, now dashed away.

'Sorry Daddy,' Ronnie said meekly.

Their father glared down at them.

'Just make sure you don't climb on them again.' He was about to return to his task in the workroom, when he waved his hand towards the twins. 'Who are these?'

'They're Bridget and Bernadette, come to stay with us from Ireland. Their Daddy's Irish,' she added for good measure, relieved that the focus had been detracted from her and her brother.

'Right, well you'd better take them in now. It must be almost dinner time.'

Later, in the evening when the twins and John and Doreen were in bed, Ronnie revelled in her precious time cuddled up on Bill's knee in his favourite chair in the kitchen. His harshness of earlier in the day was forgotten. It was a cheery kitchen, big enough for the family to share their meal round the table, with a range where they could warm their toes. She loved the feel of his tweed jacket on her cheek and the smell of his tobacco mingling with the aroma of delicious food that Mary had cooked for their dinner earlier that day.

'Will Mummy be able to get a proper cooker soon, Daddy?'

She worried that Mary was trying to cook the meals for the family and their guests on two small primus stoves and had heard her saying how difficult it was. She knew she could talk to her father about these important subjects and at times like these she felt very special. They stayed wrapped in each other's company for a while. Ronnie stared into the flames of the fire, listening to her father's gentle voice.

'I'm sure we will soon. Mummy and Daddy have to work just a little longer until we can afford one.'

Suddenly, Ronnie sat up straight. 'Look there, Daddy. Can you see that horse?'

'What's that, chicken?' Bill answered lazily.

'There, on the wallpaper over the cupboard. There's a horse.' Jumping off his lap, she grabbed his hand and pulled him to his feet. With her finger she drew the outline of what she could see as shaped like a horse.

'Well I never did. She's right you know, Mummy,' he declared with a wink in Mary's direction. 'Where's a pencil? We'll draw it in.'

'Can we really?' Her brown eyes were wide in disbelief.

'Yes, go and get a pencil quickly, while I search for some more shapes.'

She dashed off to find her pencils before he could change his mind. After discovering several other shapes, father and daughter sat back down to contemplate their efforts. This activity was to become a regular feature of their evenings together, cementing the bond between them.

After a while Mary put down her knitting.

'Come along, you sleepy head. It's been a busy day. You need to go to bed.'

Ronnie gave Bill a big hug and a kiss, then catching hold of Mary's hand she left him to his thoughts.

'I love this house, Mummy. Are there going to be any more children coming? We've had such fun today. It would be good if there was someone my age come to stay, wouldn't it?'

Her mother agreed.

Once Ronnie was settled into her bed, Mary sat in a chair in the room as her daughter drifted off to sleep. Her mind wandered back to another bedroom and another child the same age as Ronnie now.

Banishing the thought from her mind, she rose to give Ronnie another kiss before returning to Bill and the warmth of the kitchen. He too had caught his mind meandering back in time to another family as he stared into the fire.

She entered the room and went straight to Bill. She stood behind him with her arms circling his neck and placed her lips on top of his head. He clasped her hands in his and turned to kiss her. They both sensed the others emotions. No words were necessary.

*\*\*\**

The Hard family adjusted well to the routine of their new life with the comings and goings of guests, and once the summer was over they began to make preparations for Ronnie and John to start their new school. It was to be John's first day.

Bill walked with them on that morning, pushing his bike. He kept their minds off the long walk by pointing out various flowers and playing eye-spy. On reaching the school gate he gave instructions.

'Stand up straight, shoulders back. Do as you're told and don't get into any fights.'

John looked up at his Daddy, then at all the other children chasing round the playground. With a gentle nudge to his shoulder, John was shunted forward.

'Off you go,' said Bill. 'Look after your brother,' he instructed Ronnie. Then with a nod of his head, he mounted his bike and pedalled off down the road, to make his first call of the day.

John's eyes scanned his new school. It was an imposing building constructed of red brick with high dark windows, and as he stared in dismay he wondered what terrors lurked inside. The sound of a shrill whistle startled him and before he could gather his wits, pandemonium broke out around him. His sister grabbed his arm.

'John, hurry up, it's lining up time,' she yelled in his ear.

Feet were pounding, bodies jostling, elbows shoving until as if by magic the children were standing in three neat rows, class by class. A girl with black pigtails stood in front of him, her long grey socks already round her ankles and her shoes scuffed and muddy. As John tried to make himself invisible, the boy behind him started to jab him in the back. One finger jabbing, jabbing. He twitched one way then the other.

'Stand still boy,' yelled a loud, stern voice from the front of the line.

John felt all eyes on him.

'Eyes to the front, hands on heads!' Thirty-nine pairs of eyes pierced the back of their neighbour's heads. Thirty-nine pairs of hands shot to their heads.

'Line one, march in!' The order was repeated, until all the children had disappeared inside to their classrooms.

The girl with the pigtails who told him her name was Iris showed John where to hang his coat and took him to his desk. As his classmates were settling into their desks around him, John inspected the room. The ceiling was so far above him that he felt like a little ant. Through the high, narrow windows, only the sky and the tops of the trees were visible. The walls were painted shiny cream, but he could see darker patches spreading downward from the great height.

Above the teacher's desk he saw a vast map of the world which had been fixed to the wall and in one corner stood a large blackboard leaning back on its easel. In the opposite corner was a small chair that faced the wall. John wondered what that could be for. On this cold September day, the big stove was lit. It was about half way down the room and took up a large area. The children who were lucky enough to sit nearby were as warm as toast. John's desk was a long way off, near the door. He sat and shivered, wondering what would happen next, his bare knees knocking. Reaching down to his socks, he yanked them up as far as they would stretch in an effort to warm at least some part of his body. A sudden gust of cold air when the teacher entered the room made him jump. He watched as she walked between the desks to her own high desk at the front of the room. Every child stood to attention, making their chairs scrape the floor, so John followed suit.

'Good morning, Miss Roberts,' they intoned as one voice.

'Good morning, children. Please sit down and take out your slates and chalk.'

With a clatter of desk lids, they prepared for the lesson. John was relieved to find his very own slate and chalk. He decided he liked the look of Miss Roberts. She was very pretty, dressed in a dark suit with a brooch shaped like a butterfly on her lapel.

So began John's first day of education. At the end of the afternoon he was glad of Ronnie's hand to hold as they walked home in the gathering gloom back to the guest house and the security of his mother's arms. Mary listened attentively to John's account of his first day at the village school. The events of the day came tumbling out as she prepared the tea.

Ronnie was eager to tell of the gory events of the day. 'A boy was poking John in the back at lining up time so at playtime I told him to leave my brother alone or else. The big bully.'

Their mother dreaded to think what the 'or else' might mean and hoped they weren't heading for trouble.

*** 

The days grew shorter and as Christmas approached, the children's excitement grew. In the oak panelled dining room there was a raised platform in front of the bay window.
'This would be just right for a stage, John,' Ronnie said as she studied it. 'Perhaps Mummy could fix up a curtain and we could do a play. Hilary and Doris might help.'

Hilary and Doris were two local girls that Mary employed to help with the housework and cooking. They loved to play with the children if they had any spare moments, so when they were propositioned later by two big smiles they laughed and both agreed. Hilary even suggested that her younger sister could join in and Doris added that she would ask her brother if he wanted come and be in the play. Mary soon concocted a stage curtain out of a couple of spare sheets.

'We've got some visitors coming just a few weeks before Christmas so why don't you do a Christmas play? There will be three children too so they could join in.'

'Can we have costumes to wear like real actors?'

'Oh dear, what have I started now?' asked Mary with a twinkle in her eyes.

And so it was, that as Christmas drew nearer, Mary, Hilary and Doris found themselves surrounded by various articles of clothing that somehow, with a bit of ingenuity they were creating into costumes. They sat round the dining room table, the roaring fire taking the chill out of the big room.

Doreen, testing her walking abilities, daringly lunged from one chair to the next. It was good that she was protected from the fire by a large guard.

'I'll just go and check on the mince pies, shall I, Mrs Hard?' asked Hilary.

'Yes, please love, they should be done now.'

'How many sausage rolls are you going to make, Mrs Hard?' asked Doris.

She stopped to think. 'Well, let's work out who is going to be here. Gracie Edwards and Liz Barry are going in the top floor twin bedroom, Mr Gordon in the single room and Mr and Mrs Hamilton and their three kiddies in the first-floor rooms. How many is that so far?'

'I make it eight,' answered Doris with a smile.

At that moment Doreen shouted 'eight' in perfect mimicry of Doris. They all turned with delight as Doreen chuckled, knowing she was the centre of attention.

Mary scooped her up. 'What a clever girl you are.'

Then turning to Doris and Hilary who had returned from the kitchen she continued her counting.

'Add that to the five of us, plus you Doris with your brother George and Hilary and young Linda.'

She looked thoughtful as she did the calculations.

'I'd say we'd better make about three dozen. Better to have extra in case of unexpected callers. We'll have to get cracking soon. Oh, I mustn't forget to ask Mr Hard to pick up the ingredients for my ginger wine. I'll have to check we've got enough coupons for everything.'

'Thank goodness for old Mrs Evans and her chicken farm. At least we can get some meat occasionally, and her eggs are always so fresh and tasty,' Hilary said. 'That new cooker is an improvement on the primus stoves, Mrs Hard. I'll say that for nothing! It's making life much easier with all these mouths to feed.'

They all agreed with that comment. So much to do and think about, but Mary was enjoying her life and looking forward to the festivities. Their last Christmas had been so miserable, not knowing how they were going to manage. She was determined that everyone would have a fantastic time, even Bill, who was facing it with some trepidation. There would be too many people for his liking but Mary had a surprise up her sleeve for him, one that would mean he could enter into the spirit of things without feeling exposed.

The guest house was a hive of activity with everyone involved in the various projects. Mary had helped Ronnie to write the words of their play that Hilary's sister, Linda would be reading. All the other children would act out their parts.

'Mummy, this is going to be my best Christmas ever,' Ronnie said to her mother one day as she helped to make the beds.

'I'm sure you're right, chicken.'

Ronnie loved to help with the jobs that needed doing when they could have their cosy chats. 'Do you think Daddy will like our play?'

'Of course he will. He'll be so proud of you.'

The young girl thought back to her previous Christmases when money was scarce and there was no one to celebrate with.

'Mummy,' said Ronnie with a thoughtful frown on her young brow. 'Nancy, my friend at school says that her Grandma and Granddad are coming to stay with them for Christmas and then on Boxing day they're all going to see her aunty and uncle. Why can't we do that?'

Mary sat down on the bed and pulled Ronnie into her arms. In her mind, a battle was raging.

*Is this the time to tell her about…?*

But caution, or maybe fear won.

'All your grandparents are dead now, and we didn't have any brothers and sisters so you don't have any aunts or uncles.'

Ronnie's eyes widened. She had asked her father a similar question but he had said with an uptight hint in his voice that he was too busy to answer and changed the subject. At eight years of age Ronnie had already learnt not to push too many questions in her father's direction. Discovering this new revelation from her mother, she now ventured a further question.

'Where did you live when you were a little girl?'

'With my parents on a farm in the countryside.'

'They're dead now though, aren't they?' She couldn't imagine life without her brother and sister or her parents. 'You'll always have me, Mummy,' she said softly, putting her arms round her mother's neck.

They hugged tightly and Mary's eyes filled up with tears.

'My goodness, look at the time. We'd better finish off these beds or the Hamiltons will be here and we won't be ready for them.'

Over the next few days the house began to fill as the new guests arrived. Mr and Mrs Hamilton had travelled up from London with their brood on the train. Ronnie and John met them as they tumbled out of the taxi that had picked them up at the station. They were immediately struck by the size of them.

'Like roly-poly dolls!' Ronnie had commented to John later.

The three children all had chubby, rosy-red cheeks just like their parents and they kept up a noisy chatter, everyone talking at once. The words they used were strange to Ronnie's ears.

'What country do the Hamilton's come from, Mummy?'

'Mm, what do you mean? They're from England.'

'Well, they don't sound as if they do,' said Ronnie in disbelief.

'They live in a big city called London. That's what people who live there sound like. Just as Welsh people sound different from us.'

'Oh,' she answered, wide-eyed.

When suitcases, teddies and toys had been unloaded from the taxi onto the garden path, Mary came out to greet them. Mr Hamilton removed his hat as he introduced his family.

'Good morning to you, Madam. Cedric Hamilton. Pleased to make your acquaintance. This is my good lady, Molly and them's me nippers. Alfred my eldest, Winnie the middle one and Harry the baby.' He patted each child on the head playfully.

'Hello,' they each said in turn very politely, with gap-toothed smiles.

Mary returned the introductions. 'Let's get you all inside out of the cold. Ronnie, will you show them to their rooms?'

Everyone struggled through the door and eventually with much huffing and puffing they reached the top of the stairs. Their jostling and laughter could be heard all round the house. Mary, downstairs in the kitchen laughed herself but hoped that their exuberance wouldn't be too much for the other guests, specifically Mr Gordon, the single gentleman.

'Thank goodness I put him on the top floor. At least he's a bit further away from them,' she declared to Doris. They grinned and tutted at the uproar the Hamilton's were causing.

There were three more days left before the two young ladies and Mr Gordon were due to arrive. During that time Mary put the finishing touches to the Christmas cake she had baked and made her ginger wine as well as the thousand and one other jobs that were required to make the celebrations run smoothly.

Gracie Edwards and Ruth Barry turned up in the local taxi, dragging their heavy suitcases into the hall. Bill appeared at the door to help them up the wide sweeping staircase. They gazed around in awe, glancing through the open door to the oak room on the left. Mary came out through the interlocking door, wiping her hands on a towel. After introductions were exchanged she left Bill in charge. He led the girls upstairs to their room then touching the peak of his cap that was firmly tacked on his head, he left them with quizzical expressions on their faces.

As he closed the door he heard them giggling. Convinced their amusement was at his expense, he could feel the back of his neck prickling in embarrassment. Once again, he cursed his baldness that now blighted his life, robbing him of his confidence, and scurried away to his work room where he remained for the rest of the day. Only inside his hideaway did he begin to relax as he inspected the wooden toys he'd been creating over the last few months. All that was needed now was a final touch of paint and they would be ready to put under the tree on Christmas Eve.

Mr Gordon's arrival caused a flutter of amusement amongst the guests as he turned up on a bicycle with a rather large rucksack on his back and a suitcase tied with string onto the rack over the rear wheel. Later, they discovered that he had come by train from Liverpool, intending to investigate the Welsh countryside, photographing the winter scenery and wildlife. He proved to be a shy lonely figure, disappearing each morning and only returning for the evening meal. However, much to everyone's surprise he accepted the children's invitation to watch their play.

When all the guests had been settled in, Ronnie got to work with the children who would be in the play. Alfred Hamilton was a year older than she was but didn't seem to mind being told what to do. He and Doris's brother, George hit it off immediately. Together with Alfred's young sister, Winnie who was seven and a half, as she liked to remind everyone, their younger brother Harry who was six, and John, they soon learnt what they were supposed to do and turned out to be willing actors. Linda, Hilary's teenage sister excelled herself in her role as narrator.

The night before the big day – the day planned for performing the play, Mary and Bill sat in the kitchen enjoying a quiet nightcap and a smoke. She turned to face him.

'Darling, I know it's hard for you with all these people here, but I've had an idea.'

Bill stiffened and let out a low groan but before he could object she continued quickly.

'The children would love to have a visit from Father Christmas, you know.'

At this point she took out a paper carrier bag from a cupboard and speaking firmly, not wanting him to notice how nervous she was she held the red jacket up against his chest.

'Look. I've made the costume already!'

She let it drop onto his knee as she delved into the bag for the trousers, and a wide black belt. The piece de resistance was the white curly beard and wig under a large red hood. She gazed into his eyes pleadingly.

'What do you think? I've searched for weeks to find the head gear.' She paused briefly for breath. 'Just try the things on, please. Please. For the children,' she urged quietly.

He sighed, resigning himself to the inevitable. 'I suppose we'll have to see if they fit me.'

***

The play was a roaring success. Even Mr Gordon clapped enthusiastically, and Gracie and Ruth who had brought along two handsome lads they'd discovered living in the village, cheered and whistled much to the pleasure of Ronnie and her entourage.

Bill watched at a discreet distance sitting on a chair behind everyone, disappearing as soon as the last word was spoken. He found the costume where Mary had left it ready for him and soon was transformed into his new identity. By the time the 'actors' had taken their bows and the audience could clap no more, Mary announced the surprise arrival of Father Christmas.

Just as she anticipated, the children were ecstatic. They couldn't believe what they were seeing. Mary watched with tears in her eyes as they lined up to tell Father Christmas their wishes and receive the small gift from his sack. After he'd made his exit, Mary served up the sausage rolls and mince pies with ginger wine.

With shouts of 'Congratulations!', 'Well done!' and 'Grand Costumes!' ringing in the air, the little gathering gradually dispersed. Everybody agreed that they'd had a marvellous time and thoroughly enjoyed their visit to Coed y Brain.

In a few days it was time for the visitors to leave and the family's own celebrations to begin. They had been such a lively lot that Mary and the children felt quite sad to see them go as they waved goodbye. Bill made himself scarce, explaining he had last minute clock repairs to do.

***

On Christmas Eve, after the children had eventually tired themselves out and been put to bed, Bill and Mary shut themselves in the dining room and set to work transforming the room into a winter wonderland. Earlier, Bill had brought in a large pine tree which now occupied the position where the children's play had taken place. Soon the room and the tree took on a magical atmosphere.

They stood back to admire their handiwork.

'Shan't be a minute,' Bill said as he disappeared through the door.

Mary was puzzled but continued to put some finishing touches to a garland of holly and ivy that she'd set up over the mantelpiece. She was arranging some gifts from the guests beneath the tree as Bill pushed his way awkwardly into the room holding a large cardboard box.

'Oh darling,' declared Mary in surprised pleasure. 'You have been busy,' she said as she peered at the toys in the box. 'These are incredible! So beautiful. The children will be thrilled.'

When Ronnie and John crept downstairs the next morning to discover the decorations and the tree with all the gifts, their eyes almost popped out of their heads. Bill and Mary came in with Doreen, laughing at the kiddies faces.

'Happy Christmas everybody,' they chorused.

All the gifts had been labelled with their names that Ronnie started to read as she handed them round. They ripped the brown paper off in a frenzy. Even Doreen had her own present to unwrap, shouting enthusiastically when she uncovered the tipper truck that Bill had lovingly crafted. There was a paddle steamboat for Ronnie and a wooden pull along train for John that went 'choo choo' as the wheels turned.

Ronnie flung her arms round her Daddy's neck. 'Thank you, Daddy, I love it.' He kissed her then turned to pick Doreen up for a cuddle.

'Haven't you got a thank you for Daddy?' he said, looking down at John.

John whispered his thanks, looking from his Daddy to Mary for support. Doreen squirmed out of Bill's embrace to be on the floor with her brother and sister, anxious to follow their example now that she was gaining courage with her walking.

Out of a cupboard Bill produced another package. He handed it to Mary as he leaned down to kiss her. 'Happy Christmas, darling.'

'Oh gracious! No wonder we've hardly seen you these last few weeks.' She opened her gift to reveal a wooden jewellery box that he had decorated in marquetry. He had designed an intricate pattern with the different shades of the veneer. She appreciated the work that had gone into the design and creation. Her fingers traced the patterns. Lost for words, her eyes brimmed with tears.

Mary had been busy too. She'd made pretty dresses for Ronnie and Doreen, a bright red scarf and matching hat for John and a fair-isle cardigan for Bill.

There still wasn't a lot of money to go around so they were thankful for each other's talents at creating something almost out of nothing. With so many items still being rationed, they had to find ways of being creative.

Once the presents had been opened and they had enjoyed their special meal, they spent the rest of the day relaxing together with the children playing contentedly with their new toys.

## CHAPTER THIRTEEN

**1947...**
With the challenges of their first Christmas in the guest house over, the family stepped into the new year.

In the winter months they found time to relax and have fun together, building snowmen or tobogganing in the fields on a sledge that Bill had made. In the evenings with a warm fire glowing and the heavy curtains drawn to keep out the winter chill and cold winds they would play cards or chess, and sometimes draughts or charades would keep them occupied.

Long glorious summer days were spent helping with the hay making on the farm, eating picnics in the countryside or taking long walks up Moel Fammau. This was the highest mountain in the Welsh range that could be seen from the house and was regarded as a local beauty spot. It was easily picked out by the silhouette of an old ruin perched on its highest point looking like a top hat.

The Hard family were often joined on these escapades by any guests who happened to be staying with them. They took pleasure in the charms of the Welsh landscape and each other's company.

As the seasons wafted and waned they saw some of their visitors returning for further holidays becoming regular guests, declaring they'd had the very best time.

Ruth, who had originally come with a friend and then brought her parents along, actually fell in love with a local lad. She married Delwyn and settled in the village with him, bearing three strapping children.

One bright morning a young couple arrived with their daughter, Susan. That evening after everyone had retired to bed, Mary was relaxing, the clicking of her knitting needles and the ticking of the carriage clock on the mantel piece being the only sounds. She recalled an incident that had happened during the day.

'That couple with the little girl that arrived today are acting a bit strange. There's a lot of tension between them.'

Bill glanced up absent-mindedly over his newspaper. 'Mm,' he said absent-mindedly, before shaking the paper and continuing his reading.

Two days later, Ronnie came running into the kitchen calling for her mother.

'Mummy, Mr Knapper is sitting on the stairs and he's crying. Come quickly.'

She tugged urgently at Mary's sleeve. As they reached the stairs, sure enough there was the man.

'Mr Knapper, whatever is the matter?' She stretched out her hand and gently rubbed his shoulder.

'It's Jean, she's gone.'

His sobbing became louder. He stood up suddenly and almost knocking Mary over, staggered across the hall. Before she could get her breath, he was out through door and running down the lane. She chased after him, calling his name, but he simply ran on without looking back.

As she came breathlessly back into the house, she spotted Susan crouching on the top step of the stairs, sucking her thumb. Mary raced up the steps as fast as she could and held the child close to her, stroking her blonde hair.

'Ronnie, can you make Susan a nice warm drink. She's had such a shock, poor little thing. Fancy having to see all that going on.'

Fortunately, a few days later, Susan's mother turned up again, and thanking Mary and Bill profusely, she swept the child up and disappeared, never to return again.

***

'Have you noticed Doreen rubbing her ear at all? I had to get up to her in the night because she was crying and said her ear was hurting,' Mary asked Bill one day

'Yes, come to think of it, now that you mention it, she was in the shed with me yesterday and kept putting her hand over her ear.'

Just at that moment Doreen started bellowing, her little face flushed and damp. Mary placed her hand on Doreen's forehead.

'She's got a temperature. Come here, chicken. Sit on my lap.'

She turned to Ronnie, trying to stay calm in front of the children.

'Get your bike and quickly go to Mr Evans the taxi. Ask him to phone Doctor Moss. Tell him about Doreen's ear and tell him it's urgent. Go on now. Be quick but be careful,' she shouted as Ronnie pulled her coat on and ran out.

The youngster was pleased to help and having done the job set off on the return journey home. She was anxious to get back and rounding a corner at a furious rate she suddenly found herself sliding along the gritty road with the bike in a crumpled heap behind her. Somehow, she managed to pick herself and the bike up and with a bloody lip and bruised face, knees and elbows, she limped home.

There wasn't much sympathy for her though, as by the time she got back, the doctor had arrived and was examining Doreen's ear. He announced that she had a burst eardrum and should be taken to hospital as soon as possible where the ear could be operated on.

Two distraught days were passed until during Mary's visit on the evening of second day, she was told that their daughter could be discharged.

Bill stood impatiently at the garden gate. While he waited in the night, he leaned way back, scanning the heavens, awe-struck by the myriad of stars glittering like jewels with the clear moonlit sky making a canopy above his head.

As he thought about his child in the hospital, he was transported back several years to another child and another hospital. He dragged deeply on his cigarette, until at last he saw the flickering lights of the taxi trundling between the hedges along the lane. As Mary opened the car door he was relieved to see the bundle in her arms. Soon tucked up in her own bed, sleeping soundly, the toddler was none the worse for wear after her ordeal.

'Is everything all right now?' asked Bill tenderly when Mary came back downstairs.

'Yes. She's fast asleep. The doctor said there should be no after effects, so there's nothing to worry about.' She suddenly felt exhausted. 'I'm dying for a cup of tea. What an experience that was. Poor little mite! She really struggled when they put the rubber oxygen mask over her face before the op. She didn't like that at all. I hope she doesn't get nightmares from it. She looked so defenceless.'

Mary shuddered at the thought of her baby being held down by the nurses in the pre-op room. She flopped down in an armchair and took out her cigarettes.

'Well it's all over now. I'll get you a cup of tea.'

She suddenly remembered her other daughters tumble from the bike.

'How's Ronnie's mouth now?' she asked Bill wearily as she removed her shoes.

'She's got a nasty gash on her top lip and her face is a bit grazed but she'll live.'

Suddenly Mary gasped in horror. 'Oh no. I've just remembered Ronnie took her 11 plus exam today. I'm sure it was today. What date is it?' she asked Bill desperately. 'I must go and see how she is. Oh, I feel terrible. How could I have forgotten? Poor child, she must be thinking we don't care.' She dashed to the stairs.

'What about your tea?' called Bill, his voice fading as she fled from the room. *Ah well, that's just like her to put the children before herself.*

The 11 plus was a vital exam in determining whether Ronnie would attend a grammar school or go to the local secondary modern. There had been such trauma happening at home that she had been unable to concentrate sufficiently to pass, but Mary was reluctant to send her eldest daughter to a secondary modern school. She hankered for her children to have a Catholic education.

With this in mind she made enquiries about a Catholic school run by nuns in a nearby village and managed to secure a bursary for Ronnie's attendance there. In September of 1949, Ronnie started travelling the journey on two buses to St Saviour's.

At the same time, it was the turn of Doreen, the baby of the family to start school and she happily skipped along with her brother. John took her on a short cut he had discovered, across the fields, through a wood and over a stile. Doreen kept crouching down to investigate stones and holes in the undergrowth.

They crossed the main road and stopped by a wild area of Old Man's Beard, blowing its whiskers in the wind and waving their arms wildly about in an attempt to catch them. Then they trudged breathlessly up the steep hill on the other side of the valley.

'Come on slow coach. We mustn't be late or we'll get the cane. Hurry up,' John shouted impatiently.

With a great deal of huffing and puffing, Doreen finally caught up with her brother and they reached the top of the hill. There was the church to pass, a few houses and then they would be there. She was walking past the church, lagging behind her brother again when a boy leapt out from behind a wall.

'Watch out for the bats!' shrieked the skinny boy leaping in front of her face. The thick lenses in his glasses made his eyes larger than life, and his spittle sprayed her cheek as he guffawed at his own joke. She flinched as he fluttered his hands over her head.

He was shouting crazily. 'They fly in yer 'air and get tangled up and you 'ave to 'ave all yer 'air cut off.'

Doreen put her hands on her head and ran as fast as her short legs would take her to catch up with her big brother. With a friendly arm around her shoulder, he hurried her into the correct line in the playground, making it just in time before the bell rang for the start of the day.

She settled in quickly, making friends readily, deciding that despite the fact that not all people meant well, she would enjoy going to school. She liked the story at the end of the day that the teacher, Miss Roberts read to the class.

On the way home that afternoon, even though John was beside her, she walked as quickly as she could past the church, her heart pounding in her chest. She kept her eyes on the trees and the church tower, searching for any possible signs of bats, terrified at the thought of one of them getting caught in her hair and having to cut it all off. She really believed the boy, as she trusted everyone to be telling the truth. She especially loved to listen to her Daddy's tales, unquestionably taking in every word. At that tender age little did she know that even her adored parents were experts in the art of deception, but in those days she and her siblings were blissfully innocent of their parents' secret.

By the time Doreen had joined her brother at Nannerch Primary School, Mary had made a success of running the guest house and Bill had built up a reputation for having an excellent knowledge of watches and clocks.

One day, as he and Mary were enjoying a smoke and a cup of tea, he shared with her an idea he'd been mulling over.

'I've been thinking about opening a shop in Holywell. There'd be more business as people could bring their watches and clocks in to me. That way I'd be able to fit more into the day. It would save such a lot of time.'

Mary dipped her chin in thought.

'Have you seen anywhere that might be suitable?'

'There's a room on the High Street to rent. It's over the chemists. Do you know the one I mean?'

Bill exhaled his cigarette smoke.

'Yes. Yes, I know it. That would be a good position. People could pop in while they're in town doing their shopping. But what about large things like the grandfather clocks that can't be moved so easily?' Her interest was growing.

'Well now that we've got the car, I could shut the shop once a week and go out to the houses to do those sorts of jobs.' He was already one step ahead of her.

'Right, let's find out what the rent is and get cracking. Hopefully it'll be within our limits,' Mary said enthusiastically.

Before long Bill's shop was up and running in the nearby town and the family relaxed. Things were looking up. They were on solid ground again.

'It almost feels too good to be true,' he exclaimed, feeling in a good mood. Spotting one of the farm cats hovering near the door he was reminded of the one he'd had as a child and felt the urge to share a story with his children.

'When I was a boy we had a parrot. My Dad loved to play tricks and make jokes, so he taught it to shout "cat's meat, cat's meat", and as the cat came running in through the door, the parrot would swoop down and nip its tail!'

Ronnie had already left to catch her bus to school. But his two remaining listeners laughed hysterically at the notion of the naughty parrot.

Doreen ran around the table flapping her arms like a flying bird.

'Cat's meat, cat's meat,' she screeched, imitating a squawking parrot until everyone was breathless.

It was in the midst of this merriment that Mary went to answer a knock at the door. Still chuckling to herself and straightening her skirt, she opened it to find the landlord standing there looking alarmingly embarrassed. His expression brought Mary down to earth with a bump.

Iain Davies whisked off his cap and twisted it round in his hands.

'Good morning, Mrs Hard. I wonder if I might have a word with you and your husband. Sorry to trouble you like.'

'No, no, it's no trouble. We've finished breakfast and the kiddies are just going off to school. Come on in,' she said as she showed him into their sitting room. 'Sit down. I'll go and get Mr Hard. I shan't be a minute.'

She wondered if he could hear her heart beat, it drummed so hard against her ribs. She left him there and hurried through to the kitchen where Bill was chivvying the children off to school. Mary poked her head round the door and whispered over the children's heads.

'Darling, Iain Davies is here to see us.'

As the children passed by her she kissed them. 'Off you go and don't dawdle. You don't want to get the cane for being late again.'

'Cheerio Mummy, see you later.'

'What does he want?' Bill muttered when they had gone.

'I don't know. We'd better go and find out but I don't like the look on his face.' She nervously tucked a stray hair back over her ear.

As they went in to meet their landlord, he stood up and began to fiddle with his cap again.

'Morning, Mr Hard'

'Would you like a cup of tea? There's one in the pot,' Mary asked him, desperate to delay whatever bad news he was bringing.

Bill jumped in even quicker with his offer to make it. Iain and Mary sat down at opposite sides of the fire place. He accepted the cigarette she offered and as she drew deeply on hers, she tried to calm her racing thoughts.

'How's Mrs Davies?' she said, trying to compose herself.

'Fine, fine thank you.'

'How are your son's wedding plans going?'

'Er, very well. Yes, very well. Er, thank you.'

His Welsh accent was alien to her. He was stressing every vowel, giving her the impression that he was as uncomfortable as she was. She was relieved when Bill reappeared and nervously put the tray down before handing the tea cups round. A hush descended on the room as the landlord picked up his spoon and began deliberately and slowly to stir his tea. Mary hands shook as she drew on her cigarette for comfort. It didn't help. They were all staring at the spoon going around and round, mesmerized.

Time seemed to stand still.

Iain tapped the spoon on the side of the cup, snatching the moment away. He took a long slurp of tea and sighed as he put the cup carefully back on the saucer. His ruddy face was grim. His mouth set in a severe straight line.

He leaned back in the chair and looked at the ceiling, then breathed in deeply. As his words came out, Bill and Mary both felt as though he had hit them with a hammer.

'I need to have the house back. As you know, my son Owain is getting married. He's going to need somewhere to live see, and this house is the obvious choice. He's got to be near the farm 'cause he's helping me run it, you see. So, I'm sorry to bring bad news, but there you are.'

Bill started to speak but had to clear his throat. 'How long have we got?'

'I can give you a month,' he answered with an embarrassed cough, avoiding eye contact.

Mary gasped. 'I've got guests booked in for the summer. What am I going to do?'

His reply was harsh. 'The wedding's in three weeks, see, then they've got a week on their honeymoon. Sorry.'

The weak apology in his sing song accent did nothing to assuage her frustration and anger.

The man carefully replaced the cup and saucer on the nearby table and stood up. He made his way to the door, awkwardly shuffling round the furniture.

'I wish you could have told us sooner. Really, I ...' then shook her head as Bill put his hand on her arm. She looked away as her words trailed off. She felt lost. The landlord took the opportunity to make a quick exit.

'I need another cigarette. I can't believe he could do this to us. Everything was going so well. It's so unfair,' wailed Mary as she slumped down in the chair. 'I told you it all seemed too good to be true.'

Bill tried to find comforting words without success. He was as devastated as she was. The whole of that day was spent in a state of numb shock, neither of them wanting to face up to the situation.

That night as they tossed and turned in bed, their thoughts raced and spun. Suddenly, Mary clung onto Bill, sobbing bitter tears. She was trying to speak but Bill struggled to understand her muffled words. He heard 'God' and 'punish'.

'What are you saying, Mary?' he asked her fearfully, holding her away from him, trying to see her face in the darkness of the night. It was no good, he couldn't see her face so he pulled her racking body close again.

'Darling, what are you saying?'

She breathed deeply, struggling to control herself. 'I can't get the thought out of my head that we are being punished for what we did, Bill?'

He paused, trying to find comforting words. 'You can't go on through life thinking that.'

'But it always happens. Just when we're making headway and when we start to relax, thinking everything's going well, something else goes wrong. I can't stand it.'

As she started to weep again, Bill folded his arms round her. 'You've said many times that we'll get through whatever happens as long as we're together, remember? We will do again. I love you. Just remember that.'

Gradually as Bill tenderly stroked her hair, the tension in Mary's body softened and though he remained awake, she slept. Her words had touched him deeply and with his heart aching for his own guilt he wept silently until at length he too, drifted into a fitful sleep.

Next morning with a heavy head, Bill rose to face the day, uncertain what it would hold. He went downstairs to the kitchen and lit up a cigarette while he stoked up the stove and waited for the kettle to boil.

Mary woke with a start realising that the nightmare she thought she'd had was actually real.

'Tea's up! How are you feeling?'

'About the same as you by the look of your face,' she said managing a weak smile, 'I thought I'd had a bad dream.'

He put his cup down on the bedside table and climbed under the blankets beside her.

'We need a plan,' Mary said. 'There's the money we've managed to save. It might be enough for a deposit and with your earnings perhaps we could get a mortgage. I'll get the paper today and see if there's anything worth looking at.'

'The clock repairs should keep the wolf from the door for a while, but you're right, we'll have to set to work to find another house.'

Later that day, after Mary had spent an hour scouring the paper, she pushed it away.

'I was hoping we could find another guest house, but for a start we haven't got enough time to search around and then of course we probably wouldn't have enough money to pay for it if we did find one. Oh,' she added with a shudder and a shake of her head. 'I'm so angry with that man for putting us in this position.'

Bill sighed. He had to leave the search to her. They couldn't afford to lose his business so he had to keep up with his work, but he made sure he kept alert for any opportunity that might materialise.

A few days later as he was driving home from the shop, out of the corner of his eye he spotted a sign he hadn't noticed before, stuck in the hedgerow next to a gate. He stopped the car and walked back to have a closer look, uncertain as to why it should have attracted his attention. Standing in front of the sign with hands in his pockets, he read the words that had been painted on a crude wooden board. It said simply FOR SALE - TEL 112.

The gate by the sign was barring the entrance to a long lane. He peered down its length but could see nothing that could be the subject of the sign. He was torn between leaping over the gate in order to investigate further and dashing home to tell Mary. Knowing that she would have a meal ready for him, his stomach told him he should head back. They could come out later and look together.

Later that evening, leaving the children in the capable hands of Doris and having no idea what they might find, Bill drove Mary back to the gate.

'Look here,' she called as he turned off the engine and followed her. 'I've found another sign.'

She was peering at a dilapidated sign almost hidden in the weeds. The wood was badly split making it difficult to read but with closer inspection she could just make out the words "Llwyn y Cyll" etched into the surface.

'It's in Welsh. Good heavens! I wonder how you say that.'

Bill struggled with the gate until finally with a lift and a push it moved far enough for them to squeeze by. Mary felt a tiny flutter of anticipation developing in her heart as they made their way down the rutted, stony lane. It was badly overgrown with grass reaching several inches high along the centre. The hedges hung loftily over their heads. After a few minutes they reached a right-hand bend beside a small copse of trees.

As they turned the corner, they both stopped. There, nestling at the end of the lane sat a stone cottage. To the right of it was a green field sloping downhill, on the other side a wooded area that rose upwards and away into the distance.

They set off again descending the slight hill at a brisk pace, glancing at each other for reassurance. Another couple of minutes and they had reached the property. As they surveyed the scene before them, they didn't know whether to laugh or cry.

In front of them, spread between the cottage and an outbuilding was a very large heap of cow dung over which swarms of midges danced in the early evening warmth. Keeping their distance from it as far as possible they ventured closer to the cottage.

'It's empty all right. It doesn't look as if it's been lived in for years,' Mary pointed out to Bill as they peered through a dirty windowpane.

Bill cast a critical eye over the structure. 'It certainly looks solid enough. Look at the walls. They've been made to last.'

The cottage was built in the typical Welsh style of a long cottage, constructed of thick stone walls and having a room at either side of the central front door. Attached to one end was a lean-to type of structure again made of stone and at the far end were two barns. All attached in a long row. At the front of each of the buildings was a low stone wall surrounding a small area.

'I expect that's where the family would have kept a pig or a few hens years ago,' observed Mary as she peered over the wall.

They scrambled round the back of the cottage but couldn't see anything except the beautiful view across the green rolling fields with Moel Fammau in the distance.

Suddenly Mary pointed towards the distance fields.

'Our guest house must be just across there.'

They laughed when they realised how close it was, yet because this cottage was so secluded they hadn't known it was there.

'What do you think?' they both said at the same time, laughing as they disentangled themselves from the brambles and bindweed to reach the front of the cottage again.

'It's worth finding out what they want for it, isn't it?'

'Definitely.'

Mary suddenly felt hopeful again, though she knew that now she would have to tackle the difficult task of telling Hilary and Doris they were to lose their jobs. The guests who had booked holidays would have to be informed, not to mention having to tell the children.

As she and Bill retraced their steps, Mary paused to have a last glimpse of the property. She wondered if they could raise enough capital to convert the barns into holiday accommodation but kept her thoughts to herself for the moment.

Over the next few days, they negotiated the owner down to a more realistic figure. They badgered the bank manager into giving them a mortgage, paid the deposit and picked up the key. Mary had dropped the bombshell to Doris and Hilary and written her letters to the guests but still hadn't told the children.

Exactly ten days after Iain Davies had delivered his devastating news, Mary opened the gate at the end of the lane leading to their future new home. As she got back into the car the children were bouncing around on the back seat, demanding to know where they were going.

'Shall we tell them?' she asked Bill with a chuckle.

'Well, I suppose they'll have to know sooner or later,' he teased.

'Tell us what?' yelled Ronnie, about to burst with curiosity while attempting to stop her brother and sister falling on top of her as the car jerked over the bumpy surface.

By the time the car had reached the bend and the buildings came into view, the children had become frantic with excitement. Bill stopped the car causing them to fall silent.

'That,' he announced in a dramatic voice. 'That is our new home.'

There was a wail from the back seat. 'But we don't want a new home.'

'I don't want to move. I like it in Coed y Brain,' John ventured bravely.

Doreen started to cry in sympathy even though she didn't quite understand what was happening. The two children slumped back in the seat with grim faces and arms folded, so Doreen followed suit.

Bill glanced over his shoulder and winked at Mary as he caught her eye. Curiosity got the better of them as soon as they reached the end of the lane and Bill had turned off the engine.

'Don't go anywhere near that muck heap,' their mother yelled at their backs as the two younger ones chased after their big sister.

After heaving open the front door that needed a good dose of oil on its hinges, they picked their way over the rubble. On closer inspection, the inside of the house was in a worse state than they had realised from their speedily arranged initial visit when they had been somewhat hastily rushed round. There actually wasn't much to see. The two rooms downstairs were almost identical, one with an open fire hearth, the other with a blackened cooking range. From this latter room, the stairs led up to the two bedrooms, the first of which had to be crossed to get to the second. Each room had a window facing the yard. There were no windows at the back of the cottage.

'What's it been used for do you think? It's absolutely filthy.'

Bits of paint that had flaked off the windowpanes were mingling with dead flies amidst thick sticky cobwebs on the deep window sills. As Mary was about to look into the other room she heard Bill calling.

'Come and look at this, darling.' He had gone back outside and was inspecting the small lean-to building. As she went out to join him he took her through a door into what appeared to be a washhouse.

'I see it, but what's all the excitement for?'

'Well it's a good size,' Bill suggested as he led her inside. 'Big enough for a kitchen.'

Mary laughed. 'Yes but you can't have a kitchen separate from the house,' she pointed out patiently.

'I know. So, I could knock a hole in the wall here and open it up into the room between the stairs and the range.' He patted the wall with the flat of his hand.

'Sorry, but I can't see how it would work. There isn't even a window.' She didn't want to curb his eagerness, but...

Undaunted, Bill countered. 'We could put a window in the front there.'

Slowly Mary began to catch his enthusiasm.

'It'll be hard work but knowing us I'm sure that won't stop us. First thing though is to make sure those rooms are habitable and we've only got a couple of weeks to do it in before we're made homeless! Come on, we'd better round up the kiddies and get them home and off to bed.'

With that they made their way carefully back to the car where Bill called the children from their explorations. They chattered eagerly all the way home about what they had found and then on until they fell exhausted into bed. Mary took her usual position looking out of the window while they slid into their dreams. She let her thoughts drift to the property they were investing in. It would be another phase in their life together. They had pooled their resources again and she hoped with all her heart that they could succeed in this new venture.

A wild fear suddenly struck her and she gave a start, her hand over her mouth. *What venture? Bill has his watches and clocks to repair but what am I going to do? There'll be no guests bringing extra money. I can't see us ever being able to afford to convert those barns.* She allowed her memory to slip back to a time when her family had a farm where there were always two or three dogs with puppies that needed homes. *Now there's a thought.*

The next day was Saturday, when her final guests would be leaving, so she had a lot to do and would not be able to make a start on cleaning the cottage.

Bill had some homes to visit with clock repairs.

'I'll go to the cottage later today and make a start on clearing some of the mess out. I'll be home in time for supper,' he said as he left home that morning, stopping briefly to kiss her.

After seeing to the guest's breakfasts, Mary helped them downstairs with their luggage.

'We're very sorry to hear you won't be here any longer. We really wanted to come back to stay again next year.'

'Thank you so much,' Mary replied graciously, with tears in her eyes.

Mrs Robinson gave her a quick hug. 'Goodbye, dear. Look after yourself and that family of yours. Best of luck to you.'

As they drove away Mary dabbed a handkerchief to her nose and dashed back inside ready to help Joan and Albert Shaw. They had stayed for two weeks with baby Tommy. He was a sickly baby and they wanted him to have some good clean air as an antidote to the smog of Manchester where they lived in a crowded terrace. Albert's Dad had won some money on the horses and had promptly donated his winnings to his son and daughter-in-law for their holiday.

Mary held baby Tommy in her arms and smiled as he sucked his fingers. Indeed, he did look better and seemed more content than when they first arrived. As the young parents piled their suitcases into the taxi, Mary rocked Tommy.

'He's going to be a bonny bouncing baby before long. His cheeks are already plumping up.'

Joan gazed at him adoringly. 'Yes, thanks to all this fresh air. I've felt so relaxed here, I'm almost dreading going back. You've been so kind,' she said sniffing and wiping a tear away with her sleeve. 'Ronnie especially has been so helpful. She'll make a good mother one day,' she added.

Mary's three children lined up to kiss Tommy's head as he lay sleeping in her arms. Once Joan and Albert were ensconced in their seats, Mary gently transferred the baby into his mother's arms.

'Cheerio and thanks again.' Joan waved until the taxi was out of sight.

Mary was close to breaking down. Farewells were torment to her, resurrecting painful memories she could not control or erase. But she wouldn't let her family witness her inner agony, so she ushered them back inside with breezy words.

'Righto. Who's going to help me strip the beds?'

They all made a dash for the stairs.

'Last one up's a silly goose,' called John looking down on them as he reached the top.

'Oh, that's not fair. I'm always last,' grumbled Doreen.

'That's 'cause you've got little legs,' teased John as he raced on ahead of everyone.

By the time they joined him on the top floor, he was bouncing on the bed.

'Everybody calm down. Let's get this job done.'

They soon finished and piled all the bed linen in the wash house ready for Doris and Hilary to work on when they came in on Monday.

'Ronnie, will you look after your brother and sister, while I start the supper? Take them outside to play until Daddy gets home,' she suggested, hoping to get them out of the way for an hour.

When they'd gone outside she sat down and lit a cigarette. Thinking about all the washing that needed doing she was so glad that Doris and Hilary had agreed to stay on to help until everything was ready for the move. *Thank goodness they took it so well.*

The meal was almost ready when Mary heard an almighty rumpus going on outside. Rushing out to see what was wrong, she was met with an hilarious sight. Bill was frantically scratching himself, his hands flailing all around his neck, arms, legs and body, unable to reach every part at once.

The children were racing round in hysterics thinking he was playing a joke or making up a new game but he was shouting wildly.

'Mary! Quick! Do something. I'm being eaten alive by fleas. That darned cottage is infested with them. What can I do?'

'Go in the wash house and start stripping off. Ronnie run in and fetch a big towel from the airing cupboard,' she ordered, taking control of the situation with as much seriousness as she could muster.

As soon as Ronnie reappeared with the towel, Mary handed it to Bill and he shut himself in the washhouse where he began to remove his clothes.

'Ronnie, take Doreen and John into the house now.'

Once the children had disappeared, she poked her head into the washhouse.

'I'll go and get you some clean clothes and hot water. Put everything in the boiler.'

Bill was still hopping around, slapping his hands all over himself when Mary returned with a large bucket of hot water that she threw over his head. This did the trick and after a couple more buckets and a soaping down, he was able to rub himself dry with the towel. Then she disappeared again for a last bucket, returning to pour it into the boiler. Tucking himself into a corner while Mary dowsed the floor, he managed to get the clean clothes on.

When they eventually went into the house, they found that Ronnie had taken care that the meal wasn't ruined.

'Thank you, chicken. You've saved the day. That would have been the last straw to have the food spoiled. Such a clever girl,' said Mary, wrapping the child in her arms.

Ronnie's heart swelled with pride at the praise from her mother.

'John laid the table.' she pointed out, not wanting her brother to miss any glory.

'And what did you do, pet?' Bill asked as he swung Doreen up into his arms, ignoring Ronnie's words.

'She got in the way,' retorted Ronnie.

'Now then let's not have any of that talk,' demanded Bill with a dark glance.

Over the next two weeks, the couple toiled long and hard to make the cottage fit enough to make their home. They trekked back and forth across the fields from one home to the other, carrying buckets and mops, dusters and brooms, tools and toys. The rooms were fumigated, scrubbed and distempered. Bill repaired the windows, filling in the gaps, cleaning the glass and painting the woodwork. The floors were cleared of debris and the cobwebs were swept from the walls and ceilings.

There was no running water in the cottage, so they had to draw water from the well they discovered hidden away in the corner of the garden, though as yet Bill thought it couldn't be described as a garden.

'More like a rubbish heap,' he remarked to Mary one day. 'We'll need to clear that muck away from the yard as soon as we can, else we're going to be plagued by flies, not to mention the smell. The good thing is, though, it'll be marvellous for the plants.' Bill already had plans in his mind about the land that he had been mulling over while working in the cottage.

They began to bring a few small pieces of furniture and bags of clothes but eventually the date arrived when they had to vacate the guest house. The landlord helped them by driving them round in his open lorry. Mary had to swallow her pride, still feeling angry as she did.

'I hate to have to ask him for help, but I don't know what we'd do without it.'

The back of the lorry was piled high with their belongings and after three journeys the job was done. They had been forced to sell quite a lot of their furniture not only to boost their finances but also because most of it wouldn't fit into the cottage and Iain's son had been only too ready to agree to purchase anything they offered him. By 4 o'clock that afternoon, Iain had driven Bill round for the last time and Mary was helping them to unload at the cottage.

As usual, coming home from school, Doreen had lagged behind John. She picked flowers and gazed at butterflies, getting further and further behind him as he marched on up the hill towards their new home. He remembered his mother's warning that they would be at the cottage from now on.

By the time Doreen reached the turning to the lane leading to the guest house, he was nowhere to be seen. That didn't worry her, she was used to finishing off the journey on her own. She continued dawdling along, stopping at a gate when she spotted some cows. They considered her with their big brown eyes edged with long lashes while they swished their tales and chewed on the cud.

'Bye, bye cows,' she called as she tripped away happily. She let herself in through the big gate and with a few carefree skips reached the back door. Her hand went up to the latch but when she pressed it down, nothing happened. She tried again. Still the door didn't do what it was supposed to do. This was very odd, as she had never known the door to be locked.

A tiny flutter arose in her tummy as she ran to the front of the house and tried that door. The same thing happened. As her panic grew, she retraced her steps to the back door. By now she was becoming frantic. She hammered on the door, screaming and shouting for her mother. She was crying so much that she didn't hear the lorry coming along the lane towards the farmhouse.

Suddenly, a voice called out from behind the gate.

'What's going on? What's the matter?'

'Mummy and Daddy aren't here. I can't get in.'

The voice belonged to Iain and he had returned from the last drop at the cottage.

'They're at the cottage. Did you forget you were moving today?'

'Oh yes. I forgot. Sorry. I'll go across the field,' she said with little catch in her voice.

'Will you be all right?'

'Yes, thank you.'

He watched her climb the stile and head off along the edge of the field, standing still until the girl had disappeared from view. With a shake of his head and a smile, he made his way to his house.

When Doreen was almost at the cottage, she could hear raised voices. Well, one raised voice. Her father was shouting at John.

'Where is she then? Why couldn't you have waited for her? We've told you over and over again to stay together. You should know better at your age. We can't trust you to get anything right.'

At that moment Doreen made her entrance and stood in the doorway, waiting for her father to notice her. He had his back to her and she could see his neck looking red. It always did that when he was angry.

Mary spotted her and shouted over Bill's voice.

'Here she is.'

Immediately, Bill swung round, yelling in her face.

'Where the devil have you been? We've been worried sick.'

Doreen tried not to cry but with the trauma of thinking they had gone off and left her and then the relief of finding everybody in their new home, her emotions got the better of her and she let out a wail.

'I thought you'd gone and left me. There was no one at home,' she accused them, her face wet with tears.

Mary put her arms round her youngest child until her sobs had quietened. She cast a warning glance toward Bill.

'Let's all have a nice drink and calm down, then you can help get your bedrooms sorted out. You can put your toys in them, can't you? It's been a very tiring day for your Daddy and me. We need lots of help. I tell you what. I think the first thing we should do to this place is change its name. I can't even say it, can you?'

Doreen soon forgot her fright and started dancing round the room singing, 'Cluewin a click, cluewin a click.'

'That's not the way the Welsh people say it. It's Llwyn y Cyll. You have to put the tip of your tongue behind your teeth and blow through the sides of it,' Mary called after her, laughing good-naturedly.

By the time they had all tried it they were in hysterics, tears rolling down their cheeks.

'We'll have to ask Doris if she knows what it means and perhaps we can change it to a name we can pronounce. She speaks Welsh so she should be able to think of something else.'

Several days later, Bill looked up from the letter he was reading as Mary came in.

'What's the matter?' she asked, seeing his black expression.

'It's a letter from the council. They're saying they won't connect us to the main water supply. It's bureaucracy gone mad.' He threw the letter across the table towards her.

Mary read it carefully. 'They say that if we get a trench dug to the main road and lay the pipes, then they'll connect us up.' she said after a few minutes thought.

'Well that's generous of them, I'm sure. Darling, how can we afford to pay someone to dig a trench?' Bill retorted sarcastically.

'We'll do it ourselves.'

'What? Are you mad? For Pete's sake. Have you actually noticed how far it is from the cottage to the road?' After another glance at the letter he pushed his chair back, and snapped angrily, 'I need to get to Holywell and open the shop,' and stormed out leaving Mary sitting at the table contemplating this latest hiccup.

Mary read the letter again, then putting the official-looking paper back in the envelope she went outside to make a closer study of the lane. Since moving in to the cottage they had been drawing water from the well, but Mary regarded this to be a daily chore they could do without.

*After all, this is the nineteen-fifties. People have running water these days.*

As she stared down the lane, she had a sinking feeling. She had to admit that Bill was right. It was a long, long way and from where she was standing she couldn't even see the end of it.

'Still,' she argued with herself, 'we never let hard work get in our way before,' and with that she donned some old trousers, the thickest pair of gloves she could find and started digging near the wall of the cottage.

Sparks flew as her spade hit rocks and stones, and by mid-day she had a mound of rubble to show for her efforts. Unfortunately, she hadn't made too much impression in the trench department and what's more her body ached in muscles she didn't know she had.

But, undaunted, after a quick lunch and a cigarette she returned to her task. The mound of stones and earth grew and so did the size of the hole, but Mary realised they would need some heavier tools. The stones were coming out easily enough but the rocks required something much stronger than her spade and fork. She would talk to Bill when he came home.

'What are you doing Mummy?' asked John when he came bounding through the gap in the hedge from the footpath they followed across the fields behind the cottage. It cut off a large corner of their journey to and from school.

'I'm digging a trench so that we can have water from a tap, instead of having to carry those buckets every day. You can help me if you like. See how many stones you can pick out as I loosen them. Doreen can help too. Ah, here she is. Good boy, for waiting for her. Now, go and find some buckets and see if there is another spade or a trowel. I'll loosen the ground, and then you can shovel the earth and stones on to the side.'

They were making progress, albeit very slow progress, when Mary heard the sound of Bill's car as he returned from the shop. Slamming the car door, he marched over to them and putting his hands on his waist he shouted, 'what the...?'

Doreen dropped her trowel and jumped across the gap.

'We're digging a trench. We're helping Mummy,' she interrupted enthusiastically.

'Humph,' grunted Bill as he turned on his heel and made for the kitchen. Ronnie got out of her side of the car and came over to have a look.

Mary suddenly remembered that she hadn't given a thought to the evening meal.

'Come along children, leave that now. Let's go and get washed. I'm starving,' she said, trying to keep the tension out of her voice. She struggled to move her aching limbs, making her way stiffly to the cottage. The children leaped like young goats.

Bill pounded out of the kitchen, almost knocking them over.

'Why didn't you wait and ask me first?' he demanded with a face like thunder.

Mary glared back at him and turned deliberately to the children.

'Go in and get washed will you, and Ronnie, peel some potatoes please.' Wheeling round to face Bill she retaliated.

'What else are we going to do? We can't go on carrying water from the well. We need running water. I have spent all day digging. My back is breaking in two and now I'm going in to make our supper.'

With that out of her system she marched into the cottage, aches and pains fleetingly forgotten in her anger.

By the time Bill came in, Mary and the children had cleaned up and there was a delicious smell of sausages. Potatoes and carrots were simmering on the range and Mary was preparing gravy. The children had laid the table and were now sitting, scrubbed up like little angels, silently watching his every move. Not a word was spoken. He sat down as Mary began to serve up the meal.

'Thank you, Mummy,' said each child, nervously keeping their eyes on their plates.

Bill said nothing.

They began to eat.

The silence was abruptly broken by Doreen remembering something that had happened at school. 'Guess what happened to ...'

'Don't speak with your mouth full, Doreen. Little girls should be seen and not heard,' prompted Bill. 'John. Don't slouch. Sit up straight.'

He had a strict regime regarding mealtimes. The children had to sit up straight, keep quiet, cut their food neatly, take a fork full, then while chewing the food with closed mouth, they should put knife and fork down on the plate and place their hands in their lap. Tonight, they did just that.

Over the next few days Mary continued her digging making steady progress. Bill continued his silent treatment.

*Two can play at this game, he'll come around.*

Sure enough after four days, he came out and quietly started helping her. They would offer each other a cigarette or a cup of tea until the atmosphere thawed and Bill arrived home from the shop one day with a crow bar, a pick axe and dynamite. This last caused a stir of excitement in the family, but he had realised the rocks were impassable without the extreme measure of blasting through them.

After two weeks of tough labour they reached the main road. An inspector from the water board stamped his approval on their endeavour and the pipes were laid. Bill had installed a sink complete with tap in the lean-to wash house that was to become Mary's kitchen and they were ready for connection.

The whole family stood transfixed before the tap. First, they heard the water gurgling along the pipe, and then they saw it splutter from the tap. To start with it was a sludgy, brown colour, but after a few minutes it ran sparkling like a spring shower of rain. The children danced around each other clapping and singing.

'Hooray, hooray, the water has come today.'

What a triumph!

However, having water was one thing but the opening in the wall from the cottage that Bill had spoken of had yet to materialise. Mary was still waiting for the kitchen he had promised her.

'We've got the tools. We've got the water. So I suppose there's no excuse now. I'd better get cracking and make you a kitchen,' he said sheepishly.

The "hole in the wall" turned out to be a six-foot-long tunnel which Bill and Mary painstakingly hammered and chiselled through the solid stone. The family christened it the Mersey Tunnel when it was completed. Bill knocked a hole in the wash house wall and put in a window. He fitted a new door and built cupboards and shelves. With a good coating of white distemper on the walls and lino on the floor, Mary had her kitchen with the luxury of running water.

Their enthusiasm was slightly dampened when Ronnie came home from her school with a note during the last week of the summer term.

'This letter says that St Saviours is closing down and the teaching nuns and the pupils will be transferred to another Catholic school. What a shame. Ronnie's been doing so well there,' Mary said to Bill.

'Good lord. Another change of school.'

'Yes,' admitted Mary thoughtfully. 'It can't be doing her education any good. But, if they're having the same nuns then she should be all right.' She paused hoping for a sign of confirmation from Bill. When none came she continued. 'D'you think we might as well send all the kiddies there? They could go together on the bus.'

'Well I suppose if they're together we'll know where they all are. We'd better get it sorted out ready for them to start in September.'

A few weeks into the autumn term in the new school, Doreen was helping Bill to dismantle a clock, chattering in her usual way.

'Daddy, how old are you?'

'What on earth do you want to know that for?'

'Our teacher wanted to know our Mummy's and Daddy's ages. We have to write about our families.'

Bill felt a sensation of unease creeping up his spine, prickling the back of his neck. Not wanting his young daughter to notice, he joked. 'Er, tell her I'm one hundred years old.'

He had forgotten how Doreen took everything anyone told her quite literally. Next day when she came home from school she was indignant.

'When I told Sister Wilomena that Daddy is a hundred, she laughed and all the class laughed as well. She didn't believe me even when I said that Daddy had told me. He is a hundred isn't he, Mummy?'

'Doreen, you shouldn't believe everything your Daddy tells you.'

Her mother's answer was rather puzzling to the young girl.

'We've got to take in a photograph of you getting married. Have we got any pictures of you getting married, Mummy?'

'No, darling. We didn't have any photos taken.'

The little girl didn't notice the tremor in her mother's voice as she answered.

To Mary's relief that was enough to satisfy her inquisitive mind and she happily went off to play. During the family evening meal, Mary noticed that Ronnie was not herself. She had a vacant expression and seemed to have the world resting on her shoulders.

'D'you want to tell me what's the matter?' Mary asked kindly when John and Doreen had gone to bed.

Ronnie glanced at her mother sheepishly and rested her chin on her hands.

'You know my friend Bronwyn at school? She's one of the orphans.'

Her mother nodded. The orphanage was attached to the convent and run by the same nuns.

'Well, she told me that she's always hungry. They only get bread and water for their tea and sometimes the nuns hit them. Just as she was telling me, Sister Paul came up behind us and heard her.'

At this memory, Ronnie's eyes pricked with tears but she strived to control her voice. 'She grabbed hold of Bronwyn's ear and dragged her away. It was awful. Bronwyn was crying and struggling to keep up with Sister.'

Mary held Ronnie to her, kissing the top of her head and rubbed her back until her sobbing eased. 'I keep having bad dreams about it.' Another sob snatched at her breath.

'I hate it there, Mummy. I don't want to go to that school any more, but what about Bronwyn and her little brother? What'll they do? They haven't got anyone to take care of them.'

Mary spoke softly. 'We'll see what we can do. There must be a better place for you all. I'm sorry about the orphans, but there isn't anything we can do to help them, except you could remember them when you say your prayers.'

Just then, there was a shout from the bedroom upstairs.

'When's Ronnie coming up to bed, Mummy?' Doreen was trying out her usual stunt of not going to sleep until her big sister went up to share their big double bed.

'She'll be up in a minute. You get to sleep now.' Mary answered.

She smiled down at her eldest daughter but was saddened that she had to witness such cruelty. Without a doubt, she knew that Bill would agree with her that the children would have to be moved yet again. She just could not condone that type of discipline to innocent vulnerable children.

When Mary told Bill what had happened to cause Ronnie to have nightmares, he heartily agreed with her.

'Let's go to Holywell convent and see whether they can take the children there. I know you're keen to send them to another Catholic School. I just hope this one works out.'

Mary was adamant that was what she wanted, so when they received a letter of acceptance from the Mother Superior, she was delighted. Though the journey was further, it was easier in that it required travelling on only one bus. The three children took this latest change in their stride. It was all part of a big adventure, though the first day usually brought with it a flutter of apprehension.

## CHAPTER FOURTEEN

**1953...**
'Look at that, Mary. Can you believe it? We've actually done it?' said Bill with disbelief.
 'I know. It doesn't seem possible does it? Worth all that hard work though. Look at the colours. You wouldn't have thought we had an earthly chance of making such an improvement. The place really lives up to its name now. I'm so pleased Doris came up with that new name. Llwyn Teg, Beautiful Grove!'
 Bill and Mary were sitting on the wall outside their cottage surveying the changing contours of the garden they had created out of a midden. It was early 1953 and they had now lived in their Welsh cottage for three years, improving the place until it was almost unrecognisable.
 There was a rockery built high to screen an old building where Bill kept their three-wheeler Robin Reliant and Mary did her washing in the dolly tub. Up the centre of the rocks they had built steps so that they could sit in an elevated position and have a wide panoramic view of the garden. Against one end of the barn, Bill had constructed a water garden complete with waterfall. In place of the muck heap was a green lawn. There was a vegetable garden and even the children had each been given their own plot to work in.
 The two buildings that were attached to the cottage now housed the product of Mary's new ventures – one with her breeding dogs and their litters and the other containing one hundred chickens. Both were proving

profitable. Certainly, the notice she had placed at the end of the lane was a useful point of advertising as the eggs were selling well. She loved the dogs best of all and was making a name for herself in the breeding and show world with her dachshunds and cocker spaniels. The children were enrolled to help with all the activities that were going on, whether it was collecting eggs, helping to feed the puppies, or going on visits with their father to repair customer's clocks in their homes. They even helped in the watch and clock repair shop he was successfully building up or doing jobs in the house and garden.

Mary sighed contentedly. They had weathered the various trials with regard to the children's education. Ronnie was due to leave school at Easter after her fifteenth birthday and was keen to commence nursing training. Doreen had started ballet and tap classes in Holywell during 1952 because dancing was what she lived for. John was…Mary struggled with her thoughts of him. She loved him so much, but she was continually the ombudsman between father and son. Lurking deep within her was a suspicion that their good life would crumble around them before long. He was growing up fast, pushing out the limits of his independence, and testing his father's patience.

Later that year, on the day of the Coronation of Queen Elizabeth in June, John and Doreen were on an errand for their mother at the village shop when Nain stopped them for a chat. Nain and Taid were like grandparents to the children who often visited them for a drink and a piece of Nain's delicious home-made cake.

'Hello, cariad,' she said warmly to John. Oh, you're fetching something for your Mam. Such a helpful boy, you are. Indeed you are.'

John swelled with pride at this unexpected compliment.

'Do you want to come and watch the coronation on our new television set?'

They stared in disbelief. They'd never seen a television set, though they had heard some of their friends at school talking about such a thing.

'Yes please,' they chorused.

'We'll have to go home and ask Mummy first though, won't we, John?' Doreen reminded her brother.

He shrugged his shoulders.

'Don't be long now. We'll see you later.'

The children ran home and breathlessly asked for permission to go back to Nain and Taid's to watch the television.

'All right, but you must be home in time for tea at six o'clock.'

They were so thrilled. Chattering and laughing they turned around to head right back.

'Don't forget – six o'clock,' Mary called as they vanished down the lane.

The children sat mesmerized in front of the television set. All thoughts of time banished. When it was all over and they were stuffed with Nain's delicious cakes and pop, they happily skipped off home in a blur of pageantry and crowds, horses and carriages, wanting to share their experience with everyone. They bounded into the kitchen to be met with stony silence and a very angry father. Their laughter abruptly stopped when they spotted his scowling face.

'Where do you think you've been?' he bellowed.

John's eyes fearfully shot round the room then down to the floor.

'Look at me when I'm speaking to you. Well, where have you been? Your Mother told you to be back home at six o'clock and it's now gone seven.'

John stuttered unintelligibly. Doreen held John's arm and began to speak.

'Be quiet, Doreen. I'm asking John.'

John tried again, but he was so nervous, nothing came out clearly.

'Right, you can both write out one hundred times "I must be home by six o'clock".'

Spotting the paper and pencils on the table, Doreen sat down and quickly began to write. John took a step forward to follow suit but Bill's hand came down roughly on his shoulder as he spun him round.

'You young man, are coming with me first. That can wait.'

He marched John through the Mersey Tunnel and through the sitting room into the far room that was their parent's bedroom. As Doreen started to write her lines, she could hear the thwack of the leather belt as John received his punishment. Her hand trembled and she could barely see the words that she wrote through her tears. Would she be next?

Mary stood at the sink before a bowl of dirty dishes, hiding the tears that streamed down her own cheeks. She wanted to rush in there and grab the belt from Bill. She had tried so hard to ease the tension between them, but it always made things worse. Whatever task John was given, Bill would not be satisfied. These constant admonishments did not bode well for a future of peace and harmony. This was not what she had imagined when they had first met and fallen hopelessly in love. It seemed like a lifetime ago. It was a lifetime ago. Another lifetime entirely. Sometimes she sadly thought he seemed like a completely different man.

Even Doreen was stretching her wings. One day, she was skipping in the playground with Megan, her best friend.

'Can you come to our house after school? We've got a surprise to show you,' Megan asked.

Doreen waited in anticipation for the end of the school day so she could discover what this exciting thing could be. When they arrived at the house, Megan's mum came out to meet them at the gate.

'Have you come to see our new lavatory, Doreen?' she asked proudly.

'Lavatory?' Doreen cast a puzzled glance in Megan's direction.

*What's so exciting about a lavatory?* she thought.

At home their lavatory was a big old oil drum with a wooden seat balanced on it and newspaper cut into squares. As Megan and her mother walked briskly round to the back of the house, Doreen's curiosity won and she followed them.

'Look at that,' exclaimed Megan, stretching out one arm while dragging Doreen forward for a closer look. As she peered into the gloom, she saw two holes in a wooden bench over a box.

*That's not much to look at.*

Then Megan dived inside and reached up to a chain that was hanging from another smaller box attached near the roof. Confidently she pulled hard on the chain. There was a loud splashing noise as the water flushed around under the wooden bench. Doreen's mouth opened wide in astonishment. Megan laughed victoriously at Doreen's expression.

She couldn't wait to tell her family about this new invention. Unfortunately, she'd forgotten that she should have gone home first to ask permission. After several goes at pulling the lavatory chain, the novelty wore off so the two friends ran off to play in the fields. When she arrived home two hours later, she found Mary pacing up and down and looking none too pleased.

After giving her a sharp ticking off, Mary softened.

'We won't tell Daddy this time, but you must come home before you go off somewhere after school. I was very worried about you.'

\*\*\*

Bill arrived home one hot summer's day, waving a piece of paper in front of Mary.

'What have you got there?' she asked curiously, knowing how he loved a new venture.

His watch and clock repair business was doing well but he knew Mary was anxious to improve her contribution to the family coffers.

'It's details of a lock-up greengrocers for sale in Flint. It's already a good little business and I thought it would be ideal for you.'

'Mm.' Mary replied carefully. It was true. She did need something a bit more lucrative. She read through the details and concluded that it was worth a look. The latest puppies had been sold leaving them with Yana, a short-haired black dachshund and Flinders, a golden cocker spaniel. Too many chickens had been lost to rats and the eggs failed to sell because of the continuing mysterious disappearance of the sign they had erected at the end of the lane. Bill suspected that John had something to do with it, but there was no proof. The chickens had been replaced with mushrooms. A smile spread slowly across her mouth.

'Right, when can we take a look?'

Within a couple of weeks, they unlocked the door of the tiny shop. They would sell fruit, vegetables, fresh fish, nuts and dried fruit. The whole family lost no time in arranging all the products decoratively in order to entice the customers in. Having studied the accounts, Mary knew that the business had been doing pretty well and there were many regular customers so it didn't take long for her to establish herself as the new owner. She enjoyed her days welcoming customers and getting to know the regulars.

A few months later, Bill had another idea that he put to Mary one weekend.

'We could get a van.'

'We can't afford to run two vehicles. We'll have to get rid of the three-wheeler,' Mary interrupted sadly.

'I would carry on with the clock and watch repairs, but I was thinking that we could use a van to deliver fruit and vegetables to people's homes. I could shut the Holywell shop up early once a week and then come over here and go out to deliver the orders. What do you think?'

'It's a good idea but are you sure it won't be too much for you, trying to run two businesses at once?' Her face held a concerned frown.

'John can help me. He's old enough now.'

She had to agree that he was old enough, but there was a deep sense of foreboding lurking within her heart. Bill and John working successfully together was questionable.

\*\*\*

'Mummy,' called Doreen as she came bounding in to the shop on one hot day during her summer holidays. 'Can I go and play with Jennifer?'

'Where are you going to go?' She was not yet comfortable with her youngest daughter wandering about the town. The child travelled alone on buses to and from school and even to Chester and back for her dancing lessons but was keen to stretch her independence further.

'We're going to go to the pictures or the fair.'

'I'd rather you didn't go to the fair, Doreen.'

'Oh Mummy,' wailed Doreen. 'Oh, all right but can I have some money to spend please?'

'You'll have to do a job for me first. You promised you'd bag those nuts up for me.'

Reluctantly she did as she was asked quickly, before holding her hand out for the coins that Mary handed her.

'Thank you, Mummy.' With a kiss, she ran out of the shop before her mother could say any more.

Fourteen days later after Bill had already left for his shop, and Mary was preparing breakfast for the children, Doreen came downstairs complaining of feeling ill. Her skin had a sickly pallor and was moist to the touch. On closer inspection, Mary discovered a rash developing behind the girl's ears and face.

'It looks like measles to me. John can you go on your bike and get Mr Evans to telephone for Doctor Moss. What a good job it's the holidays. At least we don't have school to worry about, but I won't be able to open the shop.'

She laid her hand on Doreen's forehead.

'Mm, you've got a temperature. You'd better get back to bed.'

Without complaint, Doreen clambered back upstairs.

John soon arrived back. 'Mr Evans said that Doctor Moss said he'll come later this morning when his surgery finishes,' he panted, breathless after his speedy bike ride.

After a while, Doreen crept down the stairs again, appearing more cheerful and certainly less pale and feverish. Mary had the radio on and Doreen began to sing then gaining energy, she tapped her feet on the lino.

Suddenly they heard the recognizable sound of the doctor's car approaching down the lane.

'Quick,' urged Mary. 'Go in there and lie down on our bed,' she whispered as she shoved her rapidly recovering daughter into the bedroom. 'And look ill for goodness sake.'

Rushing across to the door, she hastily tidied her hair and dress and almost bumped into Doctor Moss as he let himself in. She hoped that Doreen had done as she'd been told.

The doctor confirmed it was a case of measles and working backwards to discover the root of the contagion, Mary realised it was the time Doreen had gone with her friend to the cinema. It suddenly dawned on her that she had never asked her daughter what film she had seen or if indeed she had been to the pictures. As soon as the doctor had left the cottage, Mary confronted Doreen with her question. Doreen owned up that they had gone straight to the fair and not seen a film at all. Mary was confused and disappointed that she had been lied to and sent Doreen up to her bedroom for the rest of the day. Measles or not she had to be punished. The youngster soon bounced back to health and had to be restrained from doing too much but before long, life got back to normal.

'I'm afraid we're going to have to get them to Clatterbridge Isolation hospital, Mrs Hard. They're very sick children,' said Dr Moss as he put away his stethoscope. 'They both have a severe case of Measles. The rash isn't coming out, you see. I'm sorry but there's nothing we can do for them here. We must get them away as soon as possible. Is there anyone who can look after your youngest, while you take them to Clatterbridge?'

Mary was at a loss for words. Bill had already gone out when Doreen came down alone for breakfast. Running upstairs, Mary had found both of her older children looking feverish and miserable and she'd had to send Doreen to Mr Evans to call for Doctor Moss. She knew of no one who could look after her youngest child.

'No, I can't think of anyone. I'm sorry,' she said, struggling to contain her emotions.

The doctor smiled kindly.

'Tell you what. She can come back to the surgery with me and sit in the waiting room until you get back. Mrs Jones, my receptionist will see she's all right.'

'Well if you say that's all right. Thank you.'

'Right. Young lady, go and wash your hands now. We can't have you going to my surgery looking like a gypsy, can we?' the doctor ordered, briskly taking control of the situation.

With a heavy heart, Mary reluctantly let Doreen go with the doctor while she settled her other two children in their old car. 'What a good job it was Daddy's day to do his clock repairs and he took the van. We'll soon have you there.' She was trying to keep up a cheerful appearance. 'Tuck yourselves in and keep warm.'

For Ronnie and John, it was the beginning of a nightmare. They were ensconced separately in secure rooms and allowed no visitors for several days. The nurses and doctors entered through a separate, small anteroom where they would don special overalls, gloves and masks, looking like strange creatures to the two frightened youngsters.

John's twelfth birthday was coming up and Ronnie had recently left school at the age of fifteen. They couldn't understand why their family didn't come to see them and no one told them what was happening. There were no comforting words with nothing to do and on top of all that, they both felt very ill.

Once the quarantine time was past and they began to recover their strength, they were allowed to visit one another and at long last the day came when Mary arrived to pick them up. They hugged her as if they would never let go, yet though feeling weak, the sight of their mother and the warmth of her arms gave them the energy to make their way to the car and be taken home.

As soon as Ronnie and John felt strong, Bill made an announcement at dinner.

'Ronnie, you're going to have to help us out now that you're old enough. A customer of mine, Mrs Evans needs some help with her young family. She's just had a baby and has three other children. She'll want you to live in and come home every other weekend. The money you earn will help us keep the wolf from the door.'

The girl sat in stony silence. She gritted her teeth, struggling to breathe, feeling as though she was about to have an asthma attack. She knew it would be useless to argue or tell her father that actually she wanted to be a nurse in a hospital. It had already been decided.

Mary put her hand gently on Ronnie's arm. 'You know how you love babies and you're so good with children. Look how you've helped me with your brother and sister. I know you'll be all right, darling.'

That night, Ronnie went to bed with a heavy heart. She lay awake while her sister slept soundly beside her. Her father had told her that he would take her along to Mrs Evans' home next Monday morning to start.

***

Doreen counted the bags of peanuts she'd filled and called out to her mother. 'I've done twelve bags of peanuts with two ounces in them. Shall I do any more?'

When there was no reply, she turned in the direction she knew her mother was standing. Mary was deep in thought, counting out the day's takings. Doreen practised a few tap-dancing steps across the shop, and with a shuffle ball change landed at her mother's side. She tugged her mother's arm.

'Shall I do any more bags of peanuts, Mummy?'

'No thank you,' answered Mary distractedly. She was holding a small pile of pound notes in her hand.

'Can I help you count the money then?' pleaded Doreen, as that was her favourite job.

'I think that might be a very good idea. I can't make the money agree with what I've written down in the book. That's the second time this week it's happened. Here you are, let's see what you make of it.'

Mother and daughter stood together and counted. The young girl's total agreed with her mother's. Mary scoured the floor beneath the counter in case any money had been dropped, but there was nothing there.

'You haven't taken any money out of the till, have you, Doreen?'

The child's eyes widened, as she answered truthfully. 'No, Mummy.'

Over the next few weeks, Mary found more discrepancies. She became increasingly worried as they could scarcely afford to be losing money. Bill was working flat out with his clock repair business, as well as toiling round the streets in all weathers, selling fruit and vegetables from the van and delivering orders. Recently he had developed a hacking cough and was struggling with increasing weariness. She had a troublesome thought that when she told him about the disappearing money, it could push him over the edge.

Matters were brought to a head one day, when she was tidying John's room. She picked up a pair of trousers that were pushed down the side of his bed, to discover several pound notes stuffed into a pocket. Sitting down on the bed, she held the notes in her hand and stared in disbelief. Her mind was spinning, her whole body stiff with tension. What was this going to do to Bill's state of mind? And what is John doing?

Rising slowly to her feet, she went downstairs to face Bill with her discovery. It was Sunday afternoon and John had been sent out to collect logs for the fire from the nearby wood. He would be back soon to face the music. Mary dreaded it.

Bill's reaction to the news was as bad as Mary had expected. He cursed and stormed around the room, with promises of what he would do to John when he came back home. Mary's own feelings were running riot. She was intensely angry with her son, but also deeply hurt that he could have stolen from her. Her stomach churned as she listened to the ranting and raving coming from Bill.

As soon as John opened the door, his father glared savagely at him. He picked up the cash, shaking it in his fist.

'What the hell do you think you are playing at?' He threw the money back onto the table in disgust. 'You've been stealing money from your own mother. "Bugger you, Jack, I'm all right." That's your motto, isn't it?' 'Pointing towards Mary, he continued his tirade. 'How can you do this to your mother, after all she's done for you. Eh?'

John stood silently, his lips set in a thin line. His face was red and his hands, hanging down by his sides were squeezed into tight balls. Having been caught out, he didn't have a thing to say in his own defence.

Bill sat down heavily. 'You'd better apologise to your mother, and then go up to your room before I knock your block off.'

John kept his eyes down and with a mumbled word in his mother's direction he marched between his parents and ran up the stairs.

Mary's legs began to buckle beneath her, forcing her to find a seat quickly.

'You know what this is, don't you?' she asked gravely.

Bill looked up. As their eyes met, she answered her own question.

'It's the penalty we're paying for what we did,' she whispered tremulously, holding her handkerchief to her mouth.

Instead of comforting words, Bill shot back savagely. 'Oh, don't start that again. That's all over with. We can't change the past. It happened. It was what we both decided. We can't change anything.'

His words cut through her and she began to sob quietly, shaking her head and rocking backwards and forwards in her chair.

Bill stood, scraping his chair back with an angry rasp.

'I'm going across to the work room,' he snarled.

She listened to his racking cough as he stormed away from the cottage.

\*\*\*

John lay on his back on the bed, staring at the ceiling. His breathing was heavy and laboured. He forced himself not to cry even though his eyes prickled painfully.

*Think, think, think,* he repeated over and over in his head. He wanted to rush downstairs and scream at his father. 'I hate you, I hate you.' That's what he wanted to say but he knew he wouldn't do it. He had to think what he was going to do. 'I don't want to stay here, that's definite,' he swore angrily.

He'd stashed other money away and sitting bolt upright, he leapt across to where he'd hidden it. He'd have to be careful now. Don't make them suspicious. Tomorrow morning instead of going to school, he would have his bag packed with spare clothes and run away.

*If only we had grandparents or an uncle somewhere, I could go and live with them. It's not fair, everyone has relatives except us. I bet the old man's an axe murderer or something. He'll murder me if he gets the chance now he knows I've stolen the money.* And so, his thoughts rolled and tumbled through his troubled young mind.

Downstairs in the sitting room, Mary sat stone-like, staring into the flames of the fire. She felt old beyond her years and was weary from looking over her shoulder, exhausted by the continuing war between Bill and John and tormented by the perpetual shame over her past actions.

*What does God think of me now?*

Out of the corner of her eye she saw a movement, and slowly raising her head, she watched Bill shuffle towards the chair on the opposite side of the fireplace. He was gasping for air and Mary feared he was about to collapse. She rushed to their bedroom to grab his inhaler. After a few puffs of the medication he leaned back and closed his eyes waiting for his breathing to ease. Bill tried to talk, but he had to sit for several minutes before he could manage to speak.

'I haven't got the energy to cope with him anymore. I'm so tired. I can barely walk. What are we going to do?' he asked pitifully, staring into her eyes.

'Let's talk about it in the morning. We've got some of the money back. In the morning I'll ask John if he has any more tucked away, then we can take it from there. Things will look better in the morning,' Mary answered with more conviction than she felt.

Next morning, John was up extra early. He came into the kitchen where Mary was preparing breakfast, went straight to her and put his arms round her.

'I'm so sorry, Mummy. I promise I'll give all the money back to you and I'll never do anything like that again.'

Since there was no sign of his father, he gobbled his toast quickly and slurped down the milk Mary had put ready for him.

'I've got to go into school early today. Mr Ellis wants me to help him with something before lessons,' he informed his mother blithely.

He pulled his cap down hard on his head, wrapped his scarf round his neck before hoisting his bag onto his shoulder. Kissing his mother quickly on her cheek, John carefully avoided eye contact as he was sure she would know he was up to something.

As soon as he was on the lane leading away from the cottage, he began to run despite the weighty bag bumping against his back. He wanted to get as far away as he could before his father came trundling along in the old van on his way to the shop. He felt like tossing his school cap over the hedge in defiance. It would be great to watch it fly through the air, but he thought better of it. Someone might be on the bus that would make a fuss and ask too many questions. *No. Keep everything looking normal. Just let the early bus come on time.*

John needn't have feared his father catching up with him that morning, because Bill didn't go out in the van and it would be many months before he would drive again.

When Mary took in a cup of tea to the bedroom, the colour of Bill's skin scared her. His pyjamas, the sheets and pillowcase were soaked in sweat. She put the cup down next to the bed and rushed back to get a wet towel. While she dabbed the cold towel over his face and neck, she spoke quietly to him. When she realised she was getting no response from him, she knew it was time to call the doctor.

As she waited for a reply, she silently thanked God that they had finally decided to get a telephone installed. Today it was proving its worth. Doctor Moss gave Mary assurance that he would call and see Bill as soon as he could get away from the surgery. At that moment, Doreen came skipping down the stairs, ready for her day at school.

Seeing her mother's worried expression, she stopped in her tracks.

'What's wrong, Mummy?'

'Oh nothing, chicken. Daddy's not feeling too good today so Doctor Moss is coming to see him. It's nothing to worry about. You go and have your breakfast. You mustn't miss your bus for school.'

As Doreen ate her toast, she wondered where her brother was.

'Where's John?'

'He said he had to go to school early to help Mr Ellis.'

Doreen shrugged her shoulders. 'Huh, he didn't say anything to me. Oh well, I'll just have to go on my own. I don't care.'

She put on her coat and shoes and gathered up her satchel ready to leave for school. 'Can I go and say "good-bye" to Daddy?' she asked brightly.

'Yes of course you can. Just go in quietly and give him a kiss. That'll help cheer him up.'

Obediently she slipped silently into the room, tiptoed to the bed and planted a gentle kiss on her father's sleeping face. She felt the burning heat of his skin and jumped back in alarm.

Bill opened his eyes and smile weakly.

'Hello, chicken,' he whispered.

Doreen giggled. 'It's "good-bye", silly. I'm going to school now.' With a toss of her long ringlets, she left the room.

*** 

The early bus arrived on time and to the conductor's enquiry as to the boy's unusual travel arrangements, John gave the same reason he'd given his mother. The story satisfied the man's curiosity. His usual school journey involved catching two buses. Today though, second bus he needed would be travelling in the opposite direction. This meant waiting at a different bus stop. It proved to be a tricky manoeuvre.

As John stood there in the gathering brightness of the day, looking expectantly down the street, he spotted a familiar car. It belonged to the man who owned the little shop in the village where he lived, who knew everyone's business and loved a juicy bit of gossip.

'Not mine though,' smirked John. 'I'm going to the seaside. And no-ones gonna stop me.'

Dipping his chin down to his chest, he spun round to peer inside the nearest shop window. He hoped the driver hadn't seen him and would go past and even more avidly, he hoped the bus wouldn't arrive until the man was well on his way.

Heaving a sigh of relief, he heard the car engine fading as it progressed down the street. As his heartbeat slowed, the sound of a noisy motor heralded the arrival of the bus. John waved his arm wildly at the bus driver and leapt on as the thundering beast pulled up before him. He bounded up the stairs and flung himself on the back seat. Throwing his bag on the floor, he suddenly felt exhilarated, spying the world from the lofty heights of the top deck. He was king of the castle, full of confidence now and feeling very proud of himself.

He was running away. No more rules. No more teachers and no more parents to boss him around. He quickly pushed an image of his mother out of his mind. He didn't want to hurt her, but he hardened his heart. The bus lurched and swayed towards its destination while he stared out of the window. The Welsh landscape raised no passion in him. Catching sight of his reflection in the glass, he snatched his school cap from his head and shoved it inside his bag. He wouldn't need that now.

The bus conductor climbed the stairs, expertly leaping onto the floor of the top deck. The man collected the money from passengers seated in front of John and then stopped beside him with his hand outstretched. John handed him some money. 'Single to Rhyll, please.'

The conductor wound a handle on his machine, producing a ticket.

'Having a day out are we, sonny?' he asked jovially.

John nodded and gave an uptight laugh. He wished adults didn't have to try to make jokes that were so obviously not funny.

Beyond getting to the seaside, he had no further plan. In his naivety and rashness of youth, he hadn't thought further than that. He had his money hidden in his bag. *Plenty of it,* he enthused. At fifteen years of age, John was a tall, good-looking, intelligent youth. Unfortunately, he had never been able to prove his worthiness to his father. From an early age he'd been put down and criticized. Try as he might, he could never win his father's approval. *Well now I don't have to listen to him anymore.* Feeling comforted by that thought, he settled down to enjoy his freedom.

*** 

It was 11.30 when Dr Moss turned into the long lane that led to Llwyn Teg. The weather was cold but pleasant and he whistled happily as he drove. He thought about the patients he'd seen in surgery that morning, shaking his head in amusement at Mrs Lewis's stunned silence when told she was pregnant for the sixth time.

Little Betty Crowther's hacking cough was improving, and the rash on Elizabeth Jones's hand was clearing up nicely. There were more of course, and Dr Moss was always on hand to treat his patients kindly, many of whom he'd delivered as babies.

Pulling up in front of the cottage, he stopped briefly to admire the garden, silently reminding himself to congratulate Mr and Mrs Hard on their hard work. He smiled at the synonym as he knocked on the door. Dr Moss let himself in as he always did. This was a privilege his position warranted, and one that he used with all home visits.

It took the doctor only a few minutes to realise that his patient's condition was far more serious than a chest infection.

He spoke gravely.

'I'll need to telephone for an ambulance, Mrs Hard. We must get him to hospital as soon as possible. When I've done that, I suggest you telephone the Sisters of Mercy. They'll come out and help you with anything you need. Caring for the children, doing housework, that sort of thing.'

Mary nodded meekly. She sat in mute silence as the doctor used the telephone.

'Mrs Hard, the ambulance will be here in about twenty minutes. Would you telephone the convent now, please? I've written the number on the pad there for you.'

Automatically, Mary dialled the numbers and heard Sister Agnes's voice as if she was speaking of or to someone else.

'Of course, my dear. There's no need to worry. I'll come around in my old jalopy and see to everything. What time do the children get home from school?' she was saying.

Having told Sister Agnes all she needed to know, Mary sighed and followed the doctor to the door. The doctor took Mary's hands in his. 'The ambulance will be here shortly, Mrs Hard. He'll soon be in safe hands.'

She knew Bill would normally hate this. Having strangers looking at him would be anathema to him. When the ambulance men appeared in the bedroom and hoisted Bill onto the stretcher, he was too ill to protest. *Thank the Lord for small mercies.* She wasn't sure if that was the right expression to use in this instance, but she was thankful that her husband hadn't become stressed and had meekly allowed the men to do their duties around him.

*\*\*\**

As John journeyed to the seaside, his excitement grew. Now that he was alone, he shoved his hand deep inside his bag to pull out a sweater. He had to change out of his school blazer to avert suspicion. While rummaging around, he found a small packet, and clasping his fingers tightly round it he smiled as he brought it out. He'd almost forgotten he'd bought this the day before. Placing the packet carefully on the seat beside him, he quickly discarded his blazer and pulled the sweater over his head. The jacket was stuffed away before any other passengers came up the stairs to see him.

Now for his little treat. Squeezing the packet between his fingers, he extracted a small white cushion-shaped block of chewing gum. As his tongue savoured the taste of the mint flavour, John imagined himself to be an American cowboy he'd seen in a film once. He chewed the gum with his mouth open, knowing with satisfaction how that would have angered his father. He wouldn't allow them to have chewing-gum.

'When I've got enough money, I'm going to buy me one of those big American cars and I'm going to be a Teddy boy,' he whispered to himself. He slicked back his hair at the sides and pulled a lock of it down his forehead.

'Yeah,' he said, imitating an American accent, 'I'm gonna get me some drainpipe trousers and crepe-soled shoes, too. Oh yeah.' He was suddenly thankful he'd persuaded his mother to buy him long trousers for school. Most of his friends had started wearing them now and the teachers had given in to the boy's dissension at being treated like kids.

\*\*\*

'Ah, Mrs Hard. Yes, your husband has been taken to the waiting area. Staff nurse is just getting a bed organised for him.'

She had arrived several minutes after the ambulance and followed the nurse's directions to find Bill. He was in a corridor on a trolley, still very hot and now glaring angrily around him. When Mary took his hand, he looked pleadingly into her eyes, trying to pull himself up into a sitting position.

'Mary, what is this place? It's a nightmare. People are rushing round everywhere, but no one's coming to see me. Can you take me home now?'

'I'll see if I can find out what's going on. The doctor's bound to come and see you soon.'

Bill went into another fit of coughing, so Mary waited until it was over.

'I'm going to find matron. I won't be long. I'll try and get you a drink as well.'

Feeling increasingly concerned about his welfare, Mary hurried to the nurse's desk to find out what was happening. There was frantic activity everywhere. Nurses in fancy caps and tight belts were scurrying about, holding clip boards to their chests or pushing trolleys. Doctors with stethoscopes dangling round their necks, their white coats flying in their wake like wings, were dashing up and down the corridors. There was no one at the desk.

*Bill's right, this is a nightmare.*

'Can you please help me?' she said as she grabbed a passing nurse by the arm.

The nurse rushed on. 'I'll be with you in a moment,' she called out as she disappeared.

Mary tried the same tactics on several more people but received a similar reply each time. Then a glance down the corridor in Bill's direction told her that he was finally being seen to. Rushing as fast as she could, she reached him as a nurse began to wheel him away.

'Where are you taking him?' she called out as they marched on at an alarming rate. She was almost running in an effort to keep up with them.

'Ward 7,' replied the nurse briskly.

The trolley banged through double doors and Bill was wheeled into a small room. Mary almost collided with the back of the nurse as she came to a sudden halt. The woman turned and glared at Mary.

'You can't come in here. This is an isolation ward.'

The door slammed in Mary's face. She stood for a few seconds in stunned silence, not knowing what to do. On the brown door was a notice that said, "Authorised Entry Only. Isolation Ward 7".

Sitting herself down on a wooden bench that ran along the wall outside the brown door, she tried to collect her thoughts. Someone in authority would surely come along soon, so she decided to wait and see what would happen next. A glance at her watch informed her the time was two o'clock. Mary sent up a silent prayer that Sister Agnes would have arrived at Llwyn Teg by now.

*No more complications please Lord.*

***

John could barely contain his excitement. He'd been to Rhyll a few times before and could remember some of the landmarks. He fidgeted about on his seat, turning this way and that, and stretching forward in an effort to see the sea. He'd chewed on three pieces of the mint-flavoured gum and was now feeling slightly sick. His stomach churned, and he realised he was hungry. As soon as he reached the seaside, he would get himself a big bag of fish and chips.

The bus was filling up with more people as they neared the town. A large man sat next to him and lit up a cigarette. John liked the smell and decided that after the fish and chips, he would buy himself a packet of cigarettes. He'd tried smoking with some of the other boys on the way home from school and after a lot of coughing with the first attempt he'd soon got the hang of it.

\*\*\*

Minutes crept by as Mary sat and waited. The nurse had come out of the room with the brown door several times only to return without so much as a glance at Mary. She wondered why the woman had to be so harsh. Nurses are meant to be caring, she'd always thought. Feeling light-headed with lack of food she caught a flurry of movement. A white-coated doctor was hurrying towards the brown door, steadfastly avoiding eye contact with her.

Mary stood up ready to speak, but she'd barely taken a breath before the doctor swept importantly past her and the door once again slammed shut in her face. Slipping back down onto the bench, she decided she would feel much better if she had a cigarette. Shaking one out of the packet, she lit it quickly and took a refreshing drag.

After the third puff, Mary had recovered some of her senses. Just as she was slowly exhaling, filling the air around her with a blue haze, the brown door opened and the harsh nurse loomed over her.

'Mrs Hard,' yelled the nurse. 'We do not allow smoking in here. This is a hospital.'

Searching round the floor for somewhere to stub out the offending cigarette, Mary was embarrassed to find no such place. Leaning over as low as she could, she pushed the remainder of the cigarette under the bench and squashed it under her heel.

The nurse chose that moment to make her announcement.

'Come this way. Mr Hopkins will see you now.'

Mary noticed the disgust in her tone of voice.

\*\*\*

John bounded off the bus, relieved to have reached his destination without mishap. First stop would be fish and chips. His mouth watered and tingled at the thought of the salt and dripping vinegar. He was definitely going to eat them out of the newspaper too. That was something that he would never be allowed to do normally. Making his way to the sea front where he remembered seeing the chippies, he passed a newsagents' and dived in to buy a packet of five cigarettes and some matches. He hoisted his bag on his back and lit up the first cigarette. Filled with confidence, he marched briskly towards the promenade. The wind whipped the smoke around him, bringing tears to his eyes.

Fish and chips out of the newspaper, he decided was delicious with plenty of salt and vinegar. He found a sheltered spot while he picked out each mouthful before licking his fingers clean. When the last piece of batter was gone, he pushed the paper behind the bench where he sat and glanced round to see what he could do next. There weren't many people around and the few that braved the weather were bracing themselves against the wind, wrapped up warmly in thick coats, boots, hats and scarves. John pulled the sleeves of his sweater down over his hands and shivered. He hadn't thought to put in his duffle coat, not realising that the sun doesn't always shine at the seaside.

He wanted to run in the sand and even paddle in the frothy sea, but when he ran on to the beach, the sand was being tossed about by the wind. Pieces of paper were swept along, frolicking in the northerly gusts. This wasn't quite the fun John had anticipated. Climbing back up onto the promenade, he spotted the amusement arcade. That would be a great place to shelter out of the weather. Maybe he would get lucky and win even more money. After the arcade he would go in search of somewhere to stay. There was plenty of time and he had all that money in his bag. He wasn't worried. His mind made up, he ran towards the colourful building where the music welcomed him.

***

The nurse's shoes squeaked each time she put her feet down on the polished hospital floor, and once again, Mary was almost running to keep up with her.

'Ah, Mrs Hard,' said the consultant, shaking Mary's hand warmly.

Feeling a little more encouraged, Mary smiled weakly and sat on the edge of the chair that was near his desk. She noticed a photograph of a woman sitting with two children and assumed they must be his family. The picture of the family helped to relax her a little. The surface of the desk was cluttered with files, medical books and various mysterious instruments. Mr Hopkins sat back in his large leather chair, and then leaning forward onto the desk he made a steeple of his fingers, tapping them gently together.

Mary waited. Her heart seemed to stand still and her stomach was somewhere it shouldn't have been.

The consultant inhaled deeply through his nose and pursed his lips.

'Mrs Hard, your husband has contracted TB so he will have to be kept in isolation until the worst is over. After that he will need to convalesce in order to gain his strength. Nurse Mason at the reception desk will give you the details of visiting hours.'

He stood up, not waiting for a response from Mary, shook her hand again, indicating that the meeting was over.

'Thank you, doctor,' Mary said gratefully as she left the room.

Somehow, she managed to find her way back to the reception desk, where the nurse gave her a sheet of paper with details of visiting hours printed on it. There was also another sheet telling her that she would have to scrub up and wear protective clothing whenever she went into Bill's room. Visiting was strictly only one person at a time for ten minutes duration. No children allowed.

'Can I see him before I go home,' Mary asked the duty nurse hopefully.

'Sorry, love. Visiting time is over now. You'll have to come back tomorrow. All the times are on there,' she said pointing to the paper she had handed Mary.

*Oh well, I suppose it's all necessary for his treatment and recovery.*

Looking at her watch, she was surprised to see it was now 5.30 and the night was closing in as she made her way to the car.

\*\*\*

'Sorry son. We haven't got any vacancies here. Try Mrs Thomas at number 35,' said the woman on the doorstep of a house that advertised B & B in its window. This was the third house John had tried. His legs were aching and he was cold and hungry again.

At number 35, a tall, thin woman came to the door. Examining the boy standing on her step, she sucked hard on the cigarette that dangled from her painted lips.

'Come in then, love. Don't let all the cold air in.'

John remembered his manners.

'Thank you very much, Mrs,' he said and plunged through the doorway.

She slammed the front door and squeezed past him.

'You want a room, do you?'

'Yes please.'

'Righto, come this way.'

The hallway was dimly lit, with one bare electric light bulb. The lino on the floor and stairs was worn and shabby, and as John followed the woman up to the room, he noticed how the walls were dark with the dirt of numerous coats that had slid up and down against them. On the landing were four doors, each with a number. She showed John into number two.

'Here we are, son. This is your room.'

Although she had flicked a switch, John could barely see inside. Taking a step forward, he peered round in the gloom. The smell of damp and the odour of previous tenants attacked his nostrils. He shuddered uncomfortably, but knowing he had run out of choices, he put his bag down and mumbled his thanks to the landlady.

'The bathroom's the door at the end of the landing. Breakfast is between 7 and 9 in the morning.'

As soon as she had gone, John jumped on the bed to test it out. At home he had a feather bed with plump pillows and warm blankets. In this room, an inspection of the covers revealed rather grubby sheets, one thin pillow and a threadbare blanket. The only good part that encouraged him was when he spotted a gas fire with a slot meter beside it. He guessed if he put some money in, he might be able to get warm. He felt in his pockets for some change and put the coins in the slot. He wasn't quite sure how it worked but noticing a small lever, he twisted it round with his cold fingers. There was a sudden hissing and a strong smell of gas. Quickly turning the lever back again, he grabbed the packet of matches out of his pocket and tried the lever again. This time, he managed to get a meagre flame burning.

Next to the bed was a small chest of drawers and beside it stood a lopsided wardrobe with one door hanging off its hinges. John sat on the floor, huddling over his knees and took out his cigarettes. If he wasn't going to have any more to eat, he might as well have a smoke. At last he started to warm up and looked round the room for something to do. He was feeling bored and slightly disillusioned and began to think of home, his Mum and his sisters. He wondered whether they had missed him yet. Thinking about his Dad made his heart beat a little faster.

'I hope he's getting really mad. It serves him right,' he voiced through gritted teeth. He thumped his knees and then wrapped his arms tight around himself, rocking back and forth in a gentle rhythm.

*** 

The sky was pitch-black as Mary drove home from the hospital. She was relieved to see a car parked outside the cottage as she pulled up.

*That must be Sister Agnes's old jalopy. Thank goodness she got here.*

'Mummy, John hasn't come home yet,' Doreen said as she kissed her mother on the cheek.

'Thank you for coming, Sister,' Mary said, greeting the nun as she unbuttoned her coat. She turned to look at her daughter, concerned by her news.

'What do you mean, Doreen? He must be home by now.'

A glance at her watch told her it was almost six thirty.

'No, he's not here and he wasn't on the bus.'

As she took off her coat she was overcome with fatigue, almost collapsing onto the kitchen chair. This latest blow was the last straw. Her hands went to her head as she leaned heavily on the table.

Sister Agnes bustled round, making comforting comments. She placed a bowl of hot soup in front of Mary with a hunk of bread.

'You need some food inside you. I suppose you've not eaten all day, and with all the worry, you'll be feeling faint.'

The nun's gentle lilting Irish brogue soothed Mary's emotions and as she took her first mouthfuls of the steaming soup, she could feel her tension easing.

'The boy'll be safe tonight. You need to get some strength back in your body now. You won't be any use to anybody if you get ill, now will you?'

As soon as Mary scraped the last of the soup from the bowl, Sister Agnes put a plate of stew in its place.

Mary stared at the food.

'Have you eaten, Doreen?'

'Yes Mummy, and Sister Agnes has been playing snap with me. Shall I get your slippers for you?'

Mary nodded her head and slipped off her shoes. Her mind wouldn't function properly, she felt as though she was in a fog. When she'd eaten all she could, she began to think more clearly. Suddenly she heard Doreen's voice.

'Mummy, where's Daddy? I wanted to see him when I got home,' she was saying in a tearful voice.

'Oh, I'm sorry Doreen. I should have told you straight away. Daddy has had to stay in the hospital.'

'Really? Can I go and see him there?'

'No, I'm afraid you can't. They won't let children in, but maybe when he's feeling better, you'll be able to go. How about that?'

Doreen pulled a face but accepted Mary's reasoning.

After Sister Agnes had left Llwyn Teg that night, Mary brooded over the nun's advice to do nothing about John until the morning. She knew she'd never forgive herself if something happened to him and she'd done nothing, so she picked up the telephone and rang the police station.

The policeman confided that a child running away from home, especially a teenager was a relatively common occurrence and they usually turned up safely. Nothing could be done at that time of night, so she should telephone again in the morning and they would start making enquiries.

\*\*\*

Alone, hungry and thirsty, John tried to find a comfortable position in the hard, unyielding bed. He listened to a drunken couple yelling at each other in the street below and pulled the covers over his head to try and block out the sound. Someone was playing music in one of the other rooms and another person had a persistent racking cough. Maybe running away hadn't been such a good idea after all.

After a very restless night, John got out of bed and stretched his aching limbs. Still in the clothes he'd been wearing during the day, he picked up his bag and wondered what time it could be. He pulled the threadbare curtains apart to see the day. The sun was up but the people he watched hurrying by were well wrapped up.

The bedroom door creaked as he cautiously opened it. No one was about so he crept along to the bathroom. Then, smelling food, he decided to investigate downstairs. Following his nose, he found the dining room easily. As he put his head round the edge of the door, he was almost knocked over by a large woman struggling to reach round a big table that took up most of the room.

'Come and sit down, young man. Are you hungry?'

John's stomach grumbled as he nodded his head and squeezed his way to the other side of the table to find a seat. The large woman wore an apron that had seen better days and round her head was wrapped a scarf tied in a knot on her forehead. Underneath the scarf, John detected curling rollers. Dangling from her mouth was a smoking cigarette. Whenever the woman spoke, the flickering ash dropped onto the plate she was carrying.

Ignoring the black bits of ash, his mouth watered at the sight of the eggs, bacon, sausage and fried bread. He was starving hungry and could have eaten the breakfast twice over. He slurped down the tea from a large enamel mug as he sat with his elbows on the table. This action pleased him as he remembered his father's fastidious rules at the table.

There were two other guests sitting down with him. No one asked him any questions. In fact, they didn't speak to him at all or indeed to each other. The radio did the talking. Someone was giving the news bulletin. Suddenly, the scraping of chairs seemed to herald the end of breakfast and it was time to pay up and leave.

'Are you coming back again tonight, love?'

'I might,' John shrugged as he paid his money.

\*\*\*

For the first time since Mary had known Bill, she was facing a crisis alone. For twenty years they had lived and worked together. Not that she was weak and helpless without him, but she was accustomed to his companionship. Mary was a strong character, forever optimistic that things would turn out all right if you did your best.

But deep down, she held a fear that she was being punished. She couldn't accept a forgiving God and most of all she couldn't find forgiveness for herself. A decision taken twenty years earlier was still having repercussions in their lives now. Would she ever be free of the humiliating shame? All night long, the dark tormenting thoughts paraded across her mind.

It was with relief that she saw the morning light stealing away the night. Now she could get on with the day and the tasks that needed to be faced. Automatically, she went through her morning chores, her mind churning over how to go about finding John. She was startled out of her reverie by the arrival of Sister Agnes. Mary hadn't expected her to arrive in the morning, but the nun bustled in.

'Good morning, Mrs Hard. I'm sure you want to get started on finding your laddie, so I'll get the breakfast on the go for you and make sure the little lass gets off to school on time.'

Mary was about to object at the woman's apparent domineering stance, but then thought better of it. She was actually grateful for her company.

'Yes, you're right. Thank you so much for coming, Sister. I was just about to call Doreen down. It's time she was getting ready.'

As Mary sipped the cup of tea that Sister Agnes had handed her, she tried to collect her thoughts about the problem of John's disappearance. All night she had been trawling through every possibility of where he could be, but none of it made any sense.

There were no relatives that he could go to, and as far as she knew, he had no special friends that would take him in. Something he had been asking about for the last few weeks sprang into her mind. She recalled how he had been pestering her to take them to the seaside, to Rhyll. Her heart began to race as she imagined him travelling there alone. That was obviously why he had taken the money.

*If only there wasn't so much tension between him and Bill.*

Sadly, she knew only too well, that John was a thorn in Bill's side, but had never been able to get to the bottom of it. In her heart she conceded that history was being repeated. Shaking herself out of that train of thought, she stood up determinedly and reached for the telephone.

\*\*\*

By the time John walked out of the boarding house, a drizzling rain was filtering down through the grey mist. It covered his pullover in a fine cloak of dampness. His hair was soon causing small ripples to run down his nose and drip from his chin. The whole day stretched out before him. Miserably, he argued with himself over what he should do. He felt he had two choices, one to go to the amusement arcade then head back to the same bed and breakfast place, or the second option would be to go back home to his punishment.

As he traipsed along the street, trying to dodge the growing puddles and avoiding the splashes from passing traffic, he was very miserable indeed. But, his misery was soon dismissed when he turned a corner and heard music. Already the amusement arcade was in full swing. His mind made up, he quickened his pace and was soon happily putting pennies in the slot machines as his clothes steamed and dried.

So caught up in his world of winning and losing, he didn't notice that he was being watched. When his luck ran out on the machine he was using, he turned to move along to another. It was then that he noticed the policeman leaning on one of the columns that supported the roof. He almost looked like a statue, so much so, that John was startled when the man moved and strolled towards him. John searched round for a means of escape, but the policeman grabbed hold of him.

'Hold it right there, sonny. You're not going anywhere.'

Relaxing his grip slightly, he stared into John's eyes.

'Are you John Hard?'

His stare was so piercing that John was terrified of turning away and simply nodded his head.

\*\*\*

The telephone startled Mary as she sat at the desk in the bedroom, trying to make sense of the bills and bank statements that lay in a pile on the desk in front of her. Earlier in the day, she had given the policeman her idea of where John may have gone, so now she ran eagerly to answer it.

'Mary Hard speaking,' she announced breathlessly.

'Morning to you, Mrs Hard. PC Evans here from Holywell police station. Good news for you. My colleague in Rhyl picked up your son this morning. Your hunch was right, thank goodness. If you would like to come over here, he should arrive about one o'clock. You can take him home after we've asked him some questions.'

Mary's hand flew to her throat on hearing the news that John was safe.

'Thank you. Thank you so very much. I'll be there at one o'clock. Good bye.'

Her legs weakened and her head throbbed. At once Sister Agnes was at her side and with an arm under her elbow. The nun guided Mary to her armchair beside the fire.

'Let me get you a nice cup of tea, Mrs Hard. I take it they've found your boy? Ah, to be sure, that's a blessed relief, now isn't it?'

She nodded and closed her eyes. Her hands were shaking as she held the china cup and saucer, but as the hot liquid entered her body, she settled into a more comfortable position. Putting the cup and saucer down, she reached for her cigarettes, ignoring the nun's disapproving glance.

***

John was quite excited during his ride in the police car, but the long lecture by PC Evans in Holywell had him sufficiently chastised by the time Mary arrived to take him home. He stood in the policeman's office, with his head down and kept it down as he heard his mother come into the room. Mary's whole body was churning with emotion. Her soft side, the mother in her wanted to run to him and fling her arms around him, thankful that he was safe, yet another part of her was fuming with anger. She decided to keep calm, yet cool and in control.

'Thank you, PC Evans,' she said, addressing the man who now stood towering over her son.

Then she spoke to John in the coolest voice she could muster.

'Come along, John. It's time to go home.'

Turning briskly on her heel, she marched back along the hallway, past the counter and out of the door to the car. She opened the door for John before slamming it shut and then climbed in to the driver's side.

He slumped down in his seat, crossed his arms over his chest and glared out of the window.

'What have you got to say for yourself, John?' demanded Mary, suddenly allowing her anger to overflow.

'I'm sorry, Mum,' he muttered, almost inaudibly.

'Is that all you have to say?'

Gripping the steering wheel and straining forward, Mary suddenly turned to glare at her son.

'Is Dad very angry with me?'

Mary sighed heavily.

'Daddy doesn't even know. He's been taken to hospital. All the stress over the business and the money was too much for him. The doctor's say he's got TB.'

John was quite pleased with this piece of news as it meant that he wouldn't be punished. He couldn't wait to impress his little sister with stories of all the adventures he'd had in Rhyll.

## CHAPTER FIFTEEN

**1955...**
Over the next few weeks, Mary's life was a round of hospital visits, consultations with doctors, and trying to keep the greengrocery business going. There was also the difficult burden of unravelling the tangle of debts that had built up over recent months that hadn't been helped by John's stealing.

Sister Agnes continued to be a tower of strength in dealing with the practical everyday events. Ronnie helped out when she could get a weekend off from her job, giving her mother as much of her earnings as she could spare. She had now moved on from helping Mrs Evans and was working on a farm, out in all weathers doing the same jobs as the men.

Mary's business was suffering, with little money coming in.

It was with relief that she was able to tell her family that their Daddy would be coming back to their midst in the next few days.

'The doctors just have to do a few more tests and if he gets through them, he'll be home.'

'Does he have to do sums?' asked Doreen in a puzzled voice.

Their mother frowned, then quickly laughed as she realised what Doreen had misunderstood.

'Yes, he's got to do his twelve times tables first,' John laughed.

Mary tutted at John's tactless remark.

'No, darling, of course he doesn't. John's teasing you. It means that the doctors have to make sure he's well enough to come home.'

'Oh. Will he start mending his clocks again?' asked Doreen, wide-eyed. 'I like helping him with the clocks.'

'No. It's going to take a long time for him to get properly better. He's going to need lots of rest and no one upsetting him.'

This last comment was directed at John.

*That's not fair,* he thought selfishly.

***

As the days lengthened and Bill had re-joined his family, the months wore on and Mary, feeling disheartened and depressed, struggled to feed and clothe her growing son and daughter. With the help of Sister Agnes to care for the children and Bill, she was able to keep the greengrocery business going, but there had been many occasions when she couldn't open because of commitments at home, resulting in customers slowly slipping away. Now she feared every day that more creditors would be pushing her for payment of their invoices.

By September she was forced to sell up. They'd had to close the watch and clock repair shop in Holywell when Bill had gone into hospital and now there was precious little money.

It was a difficult time for the family not only financially but also emotionally. Relationships were strained and as Mary stood one night staring out of the window at the night sky while Doreen drifted off to sleep, she was hit by a terrible premonition of further disaster befalling their little family. It was almost as if she had been punched in the stomach. She felt the pain and instinctively pressed her fists into her abdomen. Resting her head against the cool windowpane, she squeezed her eyes shut wanting to rid herself of the vision she had seen.

Turning towards her sleeping child, she couldn't stop the sobs that erupted from her throat. Stepping quietly to the bed, she leaned over and kissed Doreen tenderly on the cheek and stroked her long hair away from her face.

Holding the candle carefully, she tiptoed across John's bedroom on her way downstairs. She yearned to put her arms around him.

'Don't stay reading too long now. Good night, John. God bless,' she said simply.

He shifted uncomfortably, with an impatient sigh, before shifting the torch he was holding over the Roy Rogers comic.

Downstairs, Bill was sitting at the table doing a jigsaw puzzle.

'Are you coming to sit down with me?'

'Yes, in a minute. I'm going to make a milky drink. Would you like one?'

A few minutes later, she settled down in her armchair by the fire and wrapped her hands round the hot cup. She was about to tell Bill about her premonition, but as she took a breath, she decided to keep it to herself.

\*\*\*

'Mummy, look. There's Daddy,' shouted Doreen, pointing to a figure beside the dark road as they drove home from Doreen's dancing lesson, one dark November night.

The rain was pouring down in sheets and Mary could barely see through the windscreen. The wipers were struggling to clear the window. She braked hard and peered out trying to make out who it was in the car headlights.

'Oh my God. You're right, Doreen. Quick, open the door and then climb in the back.'

As Doreen opened the door, she shouted as loud as she could, to be heard over the engine and the drumming rain.

'Daddy, come over here. Get in the car. Quickly!'

Bill raised his head and squinted in the bright light. He was holding his hat on, and Mary could see that his raincoat was soaking wet. As soon as he sat down and shut the door, she screamed in rage.

'What on earth do you think you're doing? Look at you. You're absolutely saturated. Have you lost your mind? You're supposed to be convalescing and you're out in this weather.'

Not waiting for an answer, she tore off down the road at break-neck speed, wanting to get him home as soon as possible to dry him off.

'You'll be lucky if you don't catch your death,' she cried as they tumbled in to the kitchen, bringing the rain and wind with them. 'What the hell were you thinking of, Bill?'

'I was coming to meet you,' he said, a suitably chastised expression crossing his face.

Mary groaned and turned her back on him.

'You'd better go and get yourself changed into some dry clothes and sit by the fire to warm up. I'll make you a hot drink.'

Doreen helped her lay the table, anxious not to upset her Mother any further. She was a bit frightened hearing her shouting at her Daddy like that. It was most unusual. Their younger daughter had little idea of the stress that her parents were experiencing. Mary screened her from problems of finances. It was her way of protecting her child from the horrors of the real world. She even went as far as allowing Doreen to continue with her dancing lessons. During the months of Bill's convalescence, though struggling to make ends meet, she put her dressmaking skills to good use making costumes for the shows that the dancing school put on in Chester.

Many an evening after school, Doreen would curl up next to her father and they would dream of the day when she would become a dancer on the stage. Bill and Mary found that concentrating on their daughter's aspirations was therapy to their weary brains and bodies.

The reality of their situation, however, would not let them escape. With threats arriving daily from creditors and banks, Bill and Mary realised that Llwyn Teg would have to be sold. This would free up some cash to satisfy a few of their creditors.

'We'll have to ask Ronnie to help us again, Bill. Now that she's started nursing she's getting a little more money,' Mary said to her husband on a particularly bad day. 'I've scratched my head and searched every avenue I can think of to raise enough to pay off these debts, but I've come to the end now. There is no other way.'

Bill groaned and sighed, shaking his head. He was still nowhere near full strength and even small problems created a crisis in his mind.

When Ronnie arrived home for her weekend off, she recognised immediately that her parents had come to a conclusion. After John and Doreen had gone up to bed, she sat before the fire with Mary and Bill. The room was cosy with the warmth of the open stove, yet Ronnie shivered.

'Can I do anything to help? Have things reached the point of no return? You know I'll do anything I can to help you get out of this mess, don't you?'

She glanced from one to the other and saw the look of despair that they threw each other. Eventually, Mary began to speak quietly, using her words carefully.

'Ronnie, we're going to have to sell Llwyn Teg, but even that is not going to be enough to keep the creditors and bank happy, so…' here she paused and looked at Bill for support.

He continued where Mary had stopped.

'So, we wondered… we thought…well what we mean is that, if you can lend us even a small amount we'd be very grateful.'

He coughed and took a sip of his tea, before placing the cup precisely on its saucer.

The couple gazed at their eldest daughter and she suddenly felt an enormous weight on her young shoulders. She had only recently started earning any money that she could think of as an actual wage. Now she was being asked to hand it over. Ever since she had left school she had given her parents her money. She had never questioned it, or felt in any way grieved by this expectation, and even now, she gladly nodded her head dutifully.

Despite that action, unselfishly taken by Ronnie at the young age of nineteen, Bill and Mary were declared bankrupt. The proceeds of the sales of Llwyn Teg, the greengrocery business, van and much of their furniture were used to satisfy the creditors.

***

Mary found a job as housekeeper for a well-to-do family in a town about ten miles away. The bonus was that a very smart house went with the job. Though John and Doreen were sad to leave Llwyn Teg, they were more than satisfied with the move to a modern house. They had their own completely separate bedrooms. There was a kitchen, dining room and a living room. The lights came on at the flick of a switch, so they wouldn't need candles or gaslights now, but the cause of greatest excitement was the bathroom. It had running water and a flushing toilet. The family wouldn't have to fill up the tin bath in front of the fire again and there would be no need to go outside to use the lavatory.

Before his illness, Bill had begun work to convert an outhouse that sat behind Llwyn Teg into a bathroom, but with the onset of TB and loss of money, the project had been scrapped. Now they had a home with all modern conveniences, set in the beautiful tree-filled grounds of the 'big' house.

A few months later, in September John began the new school year at the Secondary Modern school in nearby Ruthin. To his parent's great relief, he settled in well. He came home telling them how he was enjoying swimming in the school pool and that he had been chosen to be in the team. Bill and Mary relaxed with the comforting thought that he was finally growing up and taking more responsibility for his actions.

When the school year ended in 1957, Doreen, who had stayed with a dancing companion for the final term in order to sit the 11-plus exam, rejoined her family. She and John spent the summer investigating the fields and woods that surrounded their new home. The only black spot came with the result of her test. Mary opened the brown envelope and the family gathered round to read the letter.

'Oh, what a shame, you missed the pass mark by a few points. Never mind, chicken. You did your best.'

She put her arm round her daughter's shoulder in consolation as Doreen's smile dropped. After a few moments thought, the girl's face suddenly brightened.

'I'll be able to go to school with John.'

Mary silently hoped that wouldn't turn out to be a recipe for disaster. As she caught Bill's eye, she realised he was thinking the same thing. Still, John did seem to have settled in well and buckled down to study, so Mary prayed the trend would continue and he would prove a positive influence on his younger sister.

***

'If anyone asks you about a trombone, say you don't know anything. OK?' warned John to his sister Doreen.

She looked up at her big brother and nodded her head in agreement. In her usual way, she didn't even think to question what he meant. From a young age, Doreen had learnt that questions were answered with vague, non-committal replies from her parents. So now, she shrugged her shoulders and skipped towards the bus stop for her first day at her new school.

A few weeks later, Bill spotted some schoolbooks that he thought John had forgotten. He had little to do and decided to go along to the school with them.

'Perhaps I can talk to one of his teachers. See how they think he's getting on,' he said to Mary as he put his shoes on.

She was surprised to hear Bill's suggestion. He rarely had much interest in John's activities.

'Yes, darling. It sounds like a good idea. If we show willing, maybe it'll boost his confidence a bit.'

What she really wanted to say was that it would build up John's self-esteem to know that his father was doing something for him, but she knew better than to voice that opinion.

Bill made his way through the long hallways of the school. The place made him extremely uncomfortable. He wanted to disappear inside the walls when anyone came in sight. But, he forced himself to speak to a man wearing a black chalk-stained gown who was striding towards him.

'Can you tell me where John Hard's class might be, please?'

The man stopped in his tracks, his gown swirling round his knees. He scratched his head, muttering almost to himself.

'John Hard, John Hard. He's in Mr Howell's class I believe. Yes, yes, I'm sure that's right. Follow me. He's in the staff room.'

Before Bill could speak, he was chasing along in the wake of the black billowing cloud of the teachers' gown.

Mr Howell was a tall red-haired man who towered over Bill as he ambled from his chair across the room. He shook Bill's hand warmly.

'Very pleased to meet you, Mr. Hard. What can I do for you?'

Bill held out the books that he'd brought for John

'Er, good morning to you. John left these books at home this morning. He'll probably be needing them.' He coughed then smiled pleasantly. 'We're very relieved to hear that he is settling in so well. He's been telling us all about his swimming. His mother and I are glad he's been picked for the team.'

When he saw the puzzled expression on Mr Howell's face, Bill's smile disappeared.

'I'm sorry, Mr Hard. We don't have any teams in swimming.'

'Yes, but you do have a swimming pool, don't you? He goes swimming every Wednesday evening after school,' said Bill becoming increasingly alarmed.

The teacher spread his arms, palms upwards, shoulders high, shaking his head sadly. 'No. No. I wish we did. That would be the height of luxury for us,' he said with a laugh in his sing-song accent. 'Oh dear, I can't think why he would tell you those things, but I'm afraid there's no truth in what he's told you. I tell you what though, we do have a music club and John borrowed a trombone a few weeks ago. I should be obliged if he could return it soon, as others in the club would like to use it.'

Bill felt himself sinking. His knees shook and his heart was pounding. A tight girdle clamped itself round his chest. With all his strength, he forced his voice out, and heard his words as though they were coming from a distant place.

'His mother and I must have misunderstood what he said. I'm sorry to have bothered you, and I will ask him about the trombone. He never mentioned that, but I'll see that he returns it to school tomorrow. Good afternoon to you.' With a weak smile and a nod of his head, he left the room.

Mr Howell watched Bill scurry along the corridor. As he disappeared around a corner, the teacher scratched his head and with a puzzled frown stepped back into the staff room.

'What was that all about, Bryn?' asked a colleague.

Bryn Howell shook his head. 'I'm not sure. Not sure at all. The boy's obviously leading them a merry dance about what he's doing here. God knows why, though.'

Moving his sleeve back from his wrist he glanced at his watch. 'Is that the time? The little sods will be wrecking the place.'

Bill returned home with a heavy heart. Just when they thought things were improving, he'd discovered nothing could be further from the truth. He was boiling with rage that he had been made to look a fool, but equal to that was his disappointment that John had lied to them again.

So burdensome were his feelings that he walked the two miles home. Still not up to full strength, when he arrived back he could do no more than crawl into bed. He didn't want to face anyone. He didn't want to talk to anyone. He hoped the world would end and this nightmare would be over.

Pulling the covers over his head, he fell into a deep sleep, and dreamed of boxes piled inside one another, like Russian dolls. A woman with a familiar face was pulling the boxes out in a fury. One after another she threw them all around her. She was yelling, red-faced, just one word.

'Liar. Liar. Liar. Liar,' she screamed at him over and over again. Her hair was wild around her face and shoulders. Her clothes were rags. He occasionally glimpsed two small children cowering in the background. There seemed to be no end to the number of boxes, causing him to fear he would be smothered in them.

At the moment the boxes had reached his chin, the scene changed. The boxes disappeared and he thought the woman with the familiar face was calling his name, but it wasn't the right name. He recognised it, but it wasn't the right name. He shook his head, trying to speak, trying to tell her she'd got his name wrong, when he realised that Mary was shaking his arm and telling him to wake up.

Opening his eyes was painful. It was a great relief to realise it had all been a dream, but he was still shaking and weak. As Mary put her arms around him, he broke down and sobbed, clinging on tightly and burying his head in her shoulder. She rocked him like a baby, making shushing sounds until he began to relax and quieten.

'You've had a bad dream. It's all over now. It's all right. Shh,' Mary said gently, when he had stopped shaking,

As Bill's mind cleared, he recalled the horror of his meeting with John's teacher earlier that day. Now he told Mary. Her reaction was calm resignation.

'It's almost time for the children to come home. D'you feel like getting up now? I'll get us a nice cup of tea, and then we can work out how to deal with John,' she said, in her usual practical way,

She left him with a soothing cigarette. The doctor had banned him from smoking, but she hadn't the heart to remind him. By the time she returned bearing the tray of tea cups, he was sitting on the side of bed. He turned to face her with a stiff back and a defeated demeanour that filled her with concern. She knew he was not fully recovered yet and feared this latest knock could send him spiralling down once more.

Sitting down next to him, she turned to focus on his worried face.

'Let me talk to him. I'll see if I can find out where on earth he's put that trombone first. I certainly haven't seen him with one.'

Bill sighed deeply. He really was at the end of his tether and did not have the energy to deal with his errant son.

As Mary met the children at the bus stop, she told Doreen to run and see her Daddy. She waited until the girl had gone a distance away, before beginning to stroll slowly beside her son, back towards the house.

'Daddy went to your school today.'

No reaction came from John.

'You left some books he thought you'd need.' Taking a deep breath, she began to elaborate. 'He spoke to Mr Howell. Told him how pleased we were about you being chosen for the swimming team.'

She stopped walking and looked at him.

'Well, have you got anything to say about it?' she said quietly when he remained silent.

John shrugged his shoulders, and with hands in his pockets, he dropped his chin and watched his feet scuff the stones on the ground.

'Righto, so you have no answer for me? No apology? No reason for telling lies?' she asked him pointedly, wanting to shake him.

There was still not a word coming out of his mouth.

Expecting a reaction from her next question, she waded in abruptly.

'What about the trombone? Where is it, John?'

She was right in her expectation. His head jerked up angrily.

'Mr Howell said I could borrow that.'

'That was good of him, wasn't it? But where is it now,'

His head dropped and he began to kick stones again.

Calling on all her powers of patience, Mary continued.

'He said you've had it too long now and he'd like it back. Other children would like to borrow it. So, where is it, John?'

'It's in there,' John mumbled, waving his hand in no particular direction.

Puzzled, Mary looked towards the house.

'Do you mean in the house?'

'No, in there.'

This time Mary followed his waving hand that seemed to be pointing towards a tree.

'What? You mean it's in the tree?' Total disbelief left her almost dumbfounded.

He had returned to his job of shuffling stones.

Suddenly Mary snapped.

'Show me now.' Grabbing his sleeve, she pushed him forward.

He scrabbled up the bank, squirmed under the wire fence and to her utter amazement and horror, removed the instrument from a hollow in the tree trunk. Words now failed her. Quaking with anger, she frog-marched him home. When they reached the front door, she snatched the instrument and pointed up the stairs.

'Go straight to your room and keep out of my sight. Daddy and I will expect an apology from you later.'

'I don't suppose we'll ever get an explanation,' she muttered under her breath as she watched her son mount the stairs two at a time.

As John's door slammed, Doreen came bouncing into the kitchen, unaware of the drama that had unfolded.

'Look, Mummy. Look what Daddy's made for me.'

Tears came to Mary's eyes as she gazed at her daughter's happy face, then at the painting that Bill had done for Doreen. Knowing her love of dancing, he had created an oil painting of a young girl looking at herself in a full-length mirror. The girl was dressed in a dark school uniform, but when the mirror was opened, she was depicted as a beautiful ballerina.

During his time of convalescence, Bill had taken to oil painting, so this was a product of his new hobby. It was good to see that at least Doreen was relatively unaffected by their troubles. Bill and Mary had been successful in keeping their financial and emotional problems from their young daughter.

Later that evening, after waiting until Doreen had gone to sleep, Mary called John downstairs. With much puffing and blowing, he reluctantly made his apologies to his parents. Bill sat stony faced and silently brooding.

'You can take the trombone back to Mr Howell tomorrow and tell him you're very sorry you kept it so long.'

John nodded.

'Can you promise us you'll stop telling all these lies, John? All this worry is making Daddy ill again. There's no need for it at all and you're letting yourself down,' chided Mary.

When he didn't answer, Mary repeated, inflecting an urgent note into her voice and leaning forward towards him.

'Can you promise me, John?'

Squirming uncomfortably, John yielded.

'Yes, all right. I promise.'

He actually couldn't believe his luck. There had been no threat of the belt or even harsh words. In fact, John was slightly unnerved by his father's silence. He couldn't wait to escape any possibility of a sudden outburst.

'Can I go back upstairs now?'

'You'd better go and eat your supper first.'

Like a mouse breaking free from a trap, John bolted for the kitchen. Realising how hungry he was, he gobbled his food and then slipped softly back to his bedroom to lose himself in the excitement of an adventure book.

## CHAPTER SIXTEEN

**1956...**

Bill waited to meet Doreen outside the hall where she was having her dancing lesson. He smoked his pipe and tried to imagine what it would be like to live in this town. Earlier that day he had travelled from their home by the 'big' house about five miles away for an interview. There was a vacancy for a married couple to run a jeweller's shop with living accommodation in the flat above. His meeting with David Cohen the owner, had gone very well and Bill felt his confidence growing.

As his daughter emerged from the building in a flurry of girlish laughter with other dancers, Bill retreated self-consciously into the shadows. He waited until she was alone before approaching her. There was plenty of time until their bus left so they strolled down the High Street together. It was evening and most of the shops were shuttered and dark. One or two had lights illuminating the windows and they stopped occasionally to gaze at the displays.

Doreen chattered on about the show they were rehearsing until Bill paused outside the jewellers. Putting his hands round his eyes, he peered into the shop window where the diamonds glittered in the glow of the street lamps. There was a metal grille protecting the glass and a heavy iron gate fixed across the doorway. He stepped back and tilting his head, looked up to the higher windows above his head.

'How would you like to live here, Doreen?'

'Huh, no thanks. It's horrible,' she retorted as she scanned the street.
'I mean here, over this shop.'
Her mouth dropped open and sharp tears pricked her eyes.
'Do you mean we have to move again, Daddy?' Blinking hard, she tried to force her thoughts to take in this unexpected and alarming information.
Bill chose his words carefully.
'We can't stay at the big house any longer. There isn't any work for me there and I need to work with Mummy so that we're earning enough money.'
'Yes, but that house is so nice and this is so…' her words dried up and she couldn't contain her tears any longer. She walked quickly away from him towards the bus stop, not wanting to hear or say any more.
All the way home, Doreen sat facing the window, refusing to look at her father. Bill was stung by her reaction, not fully realising the extent of her fear. Starting again at another school meant being the odd one out again, trying to make friends, getting familiar with the new rules and regulations. Worst of all was having to stand in the middle of the class room, having to recite her name backwards – Hard Doreen. It always caused a ripple of sniggers.
As soon as she stepped through the door of the house, she rushed straight up to her room and flung herself down on the bed to sob her heart out.
Bill and Mary, shaking their heads, sat down to eat without her. John was out on one of his forays, preferring to disappear into the town alone than spend time with his family. He was determined to leave school and join the navy as soon as he was old enough.
'She'll come around,' Mary said in an effort to comfort Bill.
'If they offer us the position we'll have to take it. It's too good an opportunity to miss, isn't it?'
'Mm. I'll say.'
'And her dancing school is there after all. I would have thought she'd be thrilled to bits,' he added thoughtfully.
Just at that moment the telephone rang and Mary crossed the room to answer it. Bill watched her face, trying to work out who was calling. A thread of fear weaved its way into his heart as he saw her expression change. Her face paled.

'I'll get down there as soon as I can, Inspector.'

As soon as she put the receiver down, she leaned back against the window ledge. The muscles in her jaw tensed.

'That was the Inspector from Ruthin Police Station. They've arrested John for stealing a transistor radio.'

Mary suddenly felt incredibly tired.

*How much more of this can we take?*

Struggling into her coat, she was barely able to lift her arms. Seeing her floundering with the sleeve, Bill snapped out of his own thoughts and leapt to her aid.

'I'm going with you, darling.'

'No, I'll be all right. You stay here with Doreen.'

They had a quick kiss and a supporting hug, both needing to confirm the others' support.

\*\*\*

John was put on probation and ordered to report to the probation officer once a week. Bill and Mary despaired of finding a way to deal with the deceit and stealing that had been going on for so long now. They became tense and touchy with one another. Mary was continually filled with guilt, but had to bottle her feelings up, for she knew that Bill no longer had patience with that kind of thinking. She sometimes wondered what his real, true feelings were. Did he have the same guilt and the same fear that she had? He kept his thoughts to himself and wouldn't even discuss them. It was as if what they had done in the past and even what was happening to them now was not really occurring at all.

These days whenever the telephone rang, the atmosphere in the Hard household became strained. They dreaded what new event might have happened.

\*\*\*

After his interview with David Cohen, Bill had pushed any hopes of getting the position to the back of his mind, not daring to think he would be so lucky.

*We seem to court bad luck. Better to think the worst and then maybe I'll be surprised.*

When the telephone rang two weeks after his interview, he was more than surprised when Mary's face broke out into a huge grin.

'That was Mr Cohen. He wants us both to go and see him next week. He was very impressed with your knowledge of watch and clock repairs and says he wants to ask us a few more questions.'

'This could be just what we need to get us back on our feet. At least we'll know there's a regular income and of course having the accommodation to go with it is an extra bonus. You'd better pray that John behaves himself.'

After Mary had worked out her notice in the 'big' house, she and Bill, with John and Doreen in tow, moved into the small flat above the jeweller's shop in Mold. There was a small office cum workroom behind the shop where Bill repaired customers watches and clocks and Mary restrung pearls or bead necklaces and did the accounts. Behind that was a lean-to kitchen. The first floor was reached by a dark staircase lined with plates they'd hung up as soon as they moved in.

Bill and Mary slept on a bed-settee in the main room on the first floor. Each morning they would fold it up and the room would become their sitting room, with enough space for two armchairs and the desk that Bill had made out of a chest of drawers. It had moved with them when all around them was being sold. A small bathroom was on the same floor. Up another narrow flight of stairs was a large landing that became John's bedroom. He never felt comfortable in it as it wasn't even a proper room. It led to Doreen's bedroom that she shared with Ronnie on the weekend's when she was home from her nursing job.

The building was old and dark, with uneven floors and rotten window frames. The only space outside was a grey walled yard. Bill and Mary missed their garden and the countryside, but knew it was more important to have the security of money coming in, so they determined to be positive.

Doreen was ensconced in the local Secondary Modern School and finally they could afford the piano lessons that she'd been begging them to let her have. John had left school and begun working in a nearby aircraft factory. Once again, Bill and Mary sighed with relief that their children had entered into this new phase of their lives, they believed without too much stress.

On August 8$^{th}$ 1958, John made an excited announcement during breakfast.

'I'm seventeen now. I'm going to enlist with the Royal Navy.'

Mary looked up. 'Well, you've been waiting to do this, so you'd better get along to their offices and sign up.'

To her mind, this decision could be the making of him. Surely the discipline involved and the regimented life-style would leave no room for him to stray.

***

The dim lights above Mary's head, gave only a notion of the direction she should take. Her feet floundered in the sticky mud on the ground as she strained forward, using all her senses to keep alert. She had no idea where she was or where she was going. All she knew was that she had to keep on moving forward through the tunnel. As she struggled onward, her ears picked up a knocking sound. At first it was in the distance somewhere behind her but gathering momentum, reaching a crescendo of drumming.

Mary gasped and brought her mind into focus. She peered through sleep-filled eyes into the gloom and realised with relief that she was in her bedroom. The knocking had been in her dream. But no, Mary gasped again as the knocking started up again.

*What on earth is going on?*

Someone was hammering on the door of the shop. Whoever it was must be leaning over the heavy gate they fixed up every night. She turned to Bill and shook his shoulder.

'Wake up. Wake up.'

Bill turned his head round and mumbled sleepily.

'What's going on? It's not time to get up yet surely.'

'There's someone banging on the door. I'm going downstairs to see who it is.'

She pulled on her dressing gown and switched on the light. Squinting in the sudden glare, she pushed her feet inside her slippers and went downstairs.

Bill called out as she disappeared, 'I'll put some clothes on and come and help you with the gate.'

By the time Mary had reached the front of the shop, she could hear him breathing behind her.

'Who's there?'

'Police! Can you open the door, please Mr Hard? We need to speak to you.'

Mary's heart raced as she made her way back to the office where she flicked the switches for the lights and grabbed the keys. She knew Bill must be sharing the same emotions. How many times had she felt this sickening fear at the thought that their past had caught up with them?

The policemen were ushered into the office while Bill locked the shop door once more. One of them seemed nervous, which didn't help Mary's state of mind. She watched anxiously for Bill to come to her.

The two men glanced at each other. The older one coughed behind his fist. Looking from Bill to Mary, he spoke with grave formality.

'Are you the parents of William John Raymond Hard?'

They nodded together.

'I'm sorry to have to inform you that the body of a young man was found in the London Underground late last night. From belongings found, it is believed to be that of your son.'

Mary screamed and sank onto a chair, feeling as though every ounce of breath had been crushed from her body. She couldn't stop the scream from escaping through her mouth. Her whole being shook. She wanted to die right then. Bill's hands gripped her shoulders as his head bowed over hers, willing back the bile that was threatening to erupt.

Ronnie and Doreen came clattering downstairs to find out what the commotion was about. Stopping dead in their tracks, they took in the scene before them. The policemen stood awkwardly and their devastated parents were on the point of collapse.

Bill and Mary turned to face their daughters. Mary took a deep breath and spoke slowly. 'John's dead. He's had …'

'He's had an accident in the London underground,' their father finished. Ronnie threw her arms round Doreen.

Suddenly, Bill shot a glance towards the policemen. 'Are you sure it's him? There can be no mistake?'

The policeman coughed again nervously.

'Er…we're going to have to ask you to go down to London to identify the body, sir.'

Bill's stomach twisted into a tight knot as he fought nausea again.

'There were some effects found on the bo…on him that lead us to believe it is your son. We'll telephone you a little later this morning and let you know the arrangements.'

They began to shift their boots towards the shop door, concluding their business with further apologies for being the harbingers of such unfortunate news. Bill let them out and locked up again, mechanically going through the motions.

No one knew what to say. No one wanted to say anything. No one knew what to do. They were each in a no-man's land.

The family learned later that John had been thrown out of the navy. He hadn't revealed to the recruitment officer that he was on probation and was spotted by his probation officer who had then informed the officials. He was instantly dismissed. Dejected, he made his way to London where he had contacted an old girlfriend. Sadly, she no longer welcomed his company and turned him away.

The conclusion for the reason of his death was that he had been attempting to take a short cut through the underground tunnel from one station to another and been struck by a train. There was some suggestion that he had stepped in front of the train deliberately but the verdict of the inquest was accidental death.

The funeral was held in Mold, North Wales on an icy, snow-ridden January day in 1963. John was twenty-one years old.

\*\*\*

Picking up the pieces following the tragic death of her only son was, for Mary an almost insurmountable task. To have a child snatched from her in this way was surely the ultimate punitive blow. Her Catholic upbringing had forced punishment and penance deep inside her consciousness. She experienced a physical agony that reached into her very soul, and for a few brief moments allowed herself to remember another death in her lifetime. The memory brought on a tremendous need, a yearning to be able to hold her own mother, to tell her how she now understood their shared horror of losing a child.

'Will I ever be able to atone for the terrible sins I have committed or are you going to go on punishing me for the rest of my days?' she begged God in her prayers.

Worrying and fretting made its mark on Mary, dragging her down into ill health. Finally, her body cried out for refuge and she was rushed into hospital with shingles.

Bill refused to discuss Mary's worries about God's punishment, accusing her of being over-dramatic. He clamped his ears shut to her pleas for a comforting word and remained adamantly tight-lipped, ashamed to ever admit that deep down, very deep down, he was actually relieved that his son would no longer get into trouble, that at least those worries were over. He had long ago turned his back on God and didn't want to be reminded of his sins. No, he preferred to live his life without the hindrance of a higher authority.

By the time Mary had recovered from her stay in hospital, Ronnie was immersed in plans for her wedding to William Pearce. Now a district nurse and midwife, she was kept busy while her future husband was sailing the seas with the Merchant Navy.

Mary knew she had to pull herself together for her daughter's sake. As the wedding day drew nearer, excitement was mounting. But, so was the tension in the form of Bill's insecurity caused by his lack of hair.

It was to be a smallish gathering. The Hard family had no relatives, so with their few invited friends, the numbers were swelled only by the large Pearce family, coming from Wallasey, but Bill didn't care how many or how few people were invited. He would be happier staying at home. Voicing this opinion to the female factor of his family was met with a very chilly reception. For once, he was outnumbered and with their powers of persuasion working overtime, his obstinacy was weakened and he relented.

Euphoria prevailed in the flat over the jeweller's shop. Wedding presents arrived, along with cards and dresses. Bill had no hope of escape, except to keep his head down over his watch and clock repairs and stay out of the way.

For some years he had been building clocks, searching out the workings from broken down timepieces that he picked up. On one such clock he carved the Latin words "Tempus Fugit" meaning - "Time Flies". Looking at this clock while relaxing in the sitting room of the flat, he mused on the words and thought how apt the phrase was. It certainly had flown. He recalled the first time he had held Ronnie as a baby and now here she was getting married. But, even engrossing himself in his beloved clocks couldn't completely stop the gnawing in his stomach or the tightness in his chest whenever the image of himself walking down the aisle loomed in his mind.

The weather on the day proved exactly as the forecaster had predicted on the wireless the night before. It dawned bright and sunny with a cloudless blue sky. Perfect for an April wedding in the old Roman Catholic Church. During the wedding meal, Bill survived by keeping his hat on for as long as possible and when he had to take it off, he sat low in his seat, hoping not to be noticed. There was no "father of the bride" speech.

After the reception, Ronnie and her new husband drove off in a flurry of confetti to honeymoon in Devon.

***

With the wedding over and the honeymooner's returned from their sojourn to the sunny south coast, Mary sank into an unsettled mood. She still worked alongside Bill in the jewellers and on the surface, all appeared to be well. However, she was struggling with her conscience. Each morning she floundered in her attempts to come to terms with the loss of her son. Each night she tossed and turned until exhausted, she would be overcome by a haunted dream-filled sleep.

After several weeks following this pattern, Mary awoke from another restless night, but with a new determination. A determination to perform some action that would begin to alleviate this dark mood that had penetrated her emotions.

'Darling, I think we should have a holiday this year.'

Bill was surprised to hear her suggestion as they had never had much interest in going away, preferring to take day trips.

'Where were you thinking of going?' he asked cautiously.

She paused for several moments, taking a deep draw on her cigarette.

'I want to go back.'

The muscles in his face began to work overtime, so she rushed hastily on.

'I think it might help to lighten this awful weight I feel I'm carrying. I...I don't know if it'll make any difference or even what it is I'm hoping to achieve.'

She shrugged her shoulders sadly as tears filled her eyes. Her hands were gripped in a fist against her chest.

'I've just got this awful ache inside that I can't seem to get rid of. If I don't do something I think I'll go mad.'

Finally, she stopped speaking and stared down at the piece of uneaten toast on her breakfast plate. She hadn't felt like eating for weeks but had forced herself to nourish her family. Now she waited for Bill's reply.

He filled his pipe and took his time with the business of lighting it. When he was satisfied with it, he leaned back and folded his arms across his chest with the pipe gripped between his teeth. After a few moments, he took it out slowly and inspected it.

'Yes, I suppose we could go back for a short visit. It would be good to see the old place again.' He drew once again on his pipe. 'We ought to hire a car though. I don't want to go on a coach or the train and then have to walk round. It would be too risky.'

Mary visibly relaxed.

'That shouldn't be a problem, should it? I'll make some enquiries about it? We'll have to ask Mr Cohen if he'd mind if we shut the shop for a few days. I'm not sure he's going to like that.'

'Let's cross that bridge when we come to it, shall we?' Bill replied not wanting to have a dampener put on her sudden enthusiasm.

Over the next few days, Mary busied herself with plans for their holiday. She actually felt excited and expectant. Just the thought of going back was making her feel brighter and more positive. Even Bill warmed to the idea and by the time they talked to Doreen about it, the hire car, and bed and breakfast accommodation were already booked. Of course, the true reason for the choice of destination wasn't given to Doreen. She was simply told that they wanted to go back to visit Mary's place of birth and look around the area. Doreen innocently went along with what they told her.

\*\*\*

Bill stopped the car opposite one of the houses that Mary had lived in as a child so that she could take a photograph.

'Look over there. That was the house my father built,' Mary called over her shoulder to her daughter sitting on the back seat.

Doreen didn't even register the name of the house that was scribed on a sign above the front door. Mary was relieved that she didn't ask questions. Their daughter had learned well. Not asking questions was now an inbuilt trait of her character.

They drove on a short distance before pulling up in front of another house.

'This was the farm where I was brought up. Do you remember me telling you how I used to help with the hay making and milking the cows?'

Mary was rather dismayed that her daughter could only gaze blankly through the window, seemingly bored with the information.

*Still, better that I suppose than asking questions we won't want to answer.*

She blew her nose hard and dabbed the tears from her eyes. The trip was going well and they drove on to another village. They had swapped over, so now Mary was driving. Doreen had been puzzled and rather amused as she watched her parent's efforts to change places. For some reason she couldn't fathom, they were acting very strangely. They stopped the car on a stretch of the road where there were no houses and then scanned all round as if they were making sure no one was watching. After a few moments, they dived out of the car, ran around the front and leapt in as if their lives depended on it.

As the car approached the next village, Bill visibly shrank into his seat. He pulled his hat well down over his eyes. His mouth was dry and his heart drummed a manic rhythm. Mary slowed right down to a crawl and inched the car past a large, double-fronted white house, standing close to the side of the road.

Peering from under the brim of his hat, Bill wondered if…*No, don't even think of that.*

'Drive on. Drive on.' His hands gripped his knees as he drank in the sight of the house they were passing close the side of the road.

Oblivious to her father's agony, Doreen stared vacantly at the scene now passing beside her. There was an old house and an old pub beside an old church.

'What are we stopping now for?' she called impatiently from the back seat as Mary pulled up again.

'We're just looking round at our old haunts.'

Doreen couldn't see what could be interesting about a tiny, dilapidated shop, and let out a moan when Mary spoke again.

'Shall I turn around, Bill?'

He nodded in compliance but shifted uncomfortably.

'It'll be all right,' Mary said as she patted his knee.

Having turned the car round, Mary drove once again down the street. Reaching a junction directly opposite the double-fronted house where they had slowed down before, she manoeuvred round a tight left-hand corner. Bill let out a sigh of relief that there was no sign of anyone around to observe their visit. As he cast a last glance in its direction, he was somewhat consoled by the fact that his former home looked lived-in and cared-for. However, his relief was short-lived as they reached another reminder of his past. They were on a narrow road and Mary halted beside a tall hedge that fronted another property.

'It could have been all mine,' he cried as he stared at the house through blurred vision.

Suddenly Doreen's interest was alerted as she saw her father's shoulders shaking and realised that he was crying. She had never seen this phenomenon before and was shocked to hear his words. Even at John's funeral he hadn't cried.

Bill was equally shocked at his reaction to seeing the place again. He was on an emotional roller-coaster over which he was losing control. He shook his head and squeezed his eyes tight. Removing his glasses, he placed his hands on his face before returning to gaze at the house beyond the hedge. With a final wipe of his face he replaced his glasses, and fixing his sight on the road ahead, he directed Mary to drive on again.

'I need a cigarette. Do you want one?'

***

In 1965, two years after John's death and Bill and Mary's journey down memory lane, Doreen's wedding took place in the same little church that her older sister had used. For the second time, Bill was forced to wrestle with his self-consciousness in order to walk down the aisle, this time to give away his youngest daughter.

The day was a glorious Whit Monday in June. The sun shone on the happy wedding party as they gathered outside the weather-beaten Catholic Church for the traditional photographs. After the reception in a nearby hotel, the happy couple drove off to their honeymoon and a new life in the Midlands.

With the last of their brood flying the nest, Bill and Mary kicked off their shoes at the end of the long day. They had survived so far. Living together and working together.

Thirty years on, their love story continued.

Occasionally, in the years that followed, when they sat by the fire on a frosty winter afternoon, they would mull over the disappointment that their youngest daughter gave up her dancing days in favour of becoming a wife. At thirteen years of age, she had taken up piano and singing lessons, but now they had to face the fact that she would never go on the stage or become a concert pianist.

**PART THREE**

**A SECOND CHANCE**

## CHAPTER SEVENTEEN

**1980...**

'When are you gonna come and live over here with us, Gramma?' demanded Zoë excitedly during their monthly phone call to her grandparents in England.

This was a recurring question directed towards Mary and Bill by their four grandchildren since Ronnie had immigrated to Ohio in the States with her family some eighteen years earlier. Mary, smiling at her seven-year-old granddaughter's accent, repeated Zoe's question to her husband.

His usual reply echoed through the airwaves.

'When you've found us somewhere to live.'

It was a game they'd played as each of their four grandchildren had become old enough to ask the question. This time however, Mary sensed more excitement in the child's voice. Sure enough, as she relayed Bill's reply the child let out a shriek.

'We have.'

Zoe laughed raucously, causing Mary to laugh too, picturing her young granddaughter's vivacious personality.

At this point, Ronnie took over the phone call.

'We've found you an apartment. It's about five minutes away in Elmore Retirement Village.'

'Oh, my goodness.'

Ronnie went on to tell her mother more details until Mary interrupted her flow.

'Hold on a minute. Let me ring you back. We'll have to talk about it.' Putting the receiver down, she turned to Bill.

'Let's put the kettle on and I'll tell you what she said.'

There was a stirring of excitement within Mary that she hadn't felt for years. With cups of tea made and Bill's pipe lit, she related all the information that Ronnie had given her. Bill too felt a re-awakening of his taste for adventure.

They had been settled in Cohen's the jewellers for many years until Bill had retired in 1970. Leaving there, Mary found work as a book-keeper. They moved out of the small flat over the shop into a modern council house, where finally after years of sleeping on a bed settee in the living room, they now had a proper bedroom. Behind the house was a postage stamp garden where together they created an oasis of blooms with Hollyhocks, Delphiniums, Marigolds, Wallflowers and Roses of every hue. At every available opportunity they would take off in their little car to explore the back roads of Britain to satisfy their thirst for action.

'What do you think of the idea?' she asked Bill when she had finished. Her eyes shone with expectation.

She suddenly had the urge to hold a cigarette and savour the taste of nicotine in her mouth, but she'd given up smoking several years ago and had to make do with the passivity of inhaling Bill's pipe smoke.

Bill leaned back in his chair, crossed one leg over the other while Mary balanced on the edge of hers, waiting for him to speak.

'It could be the answer, but what about Doreen? What's she going to think about us disappearing 3,000 miles away?'

Sipping her tea, Mary relaxed back into her seat.

'She seems to be settled with her little family. We see so little of them, don't we? I've often thought we might as well be in America. We hardly know little Matthew and Suky.' She gave a small laugh. 'I think she'll be happy for us.'

Suddenly Bill slapped his knees startling Mary and making her cough so much the tea cup rattled dangerously on the saucer.

'Righto, let's ring them back. We need to find out what we have to do.'

'Yes, I bet there'll be all sorts of forms to fill in,' she tutted. 'After we've spoken to Ronnie, I'll give Doreen a ring.'

Mary prayed fervently that nothing would stand in the way of their emigration plans. She knew that only miracles would ensure a smooth passage. In her mind it would be a leap of faith to freedom.

'Mummy, I need a copy of your marriage certificate. The authorities have written to say I've got to prove that Daddy is my father. Can you send me a copy or even fax it to me? Every day counts now.'

It was one of Ronnie's many phone calls across the ocean.

'We haven't got one, darling.'

'What d'you mean? Every married couple has to have a certificate.'

'No, I'm sure we haven't got one. I'll have to try and get a copy.'

Putting the phone down in her dining room in Elmore, Ronnie was puzzled.

'She says they haven't got a certificate,' she said to her husband.

'That's a bit odd, isn't it?' he said dubiously. 'Although, having said that, they got married before the war, so it's just possible the document got destroyed in a bombing raid.'

Ronnie read the official request again.

'The letter says that if a copy is not available, they must obtain an affidavit from the Commissioner of Oaths. Maybe they can do that then. I'll give Mummy another ring and tell her.'

Mary prayed even more desperately when she heard this news. Perhaps an affidavit would be enough to keep the authorities satisfied. Both she and Bill knew there would be no marriage certificate forthcoming. They sat in silence. Mary prayed. Bill was deep in thought.

A booming clap of thunder startled them out of their pondering. Though still early afternoon, darkness descended rapidly. As they sat in the fading light, the flickering flames from the fire traced patterns on their faces. Another boom of thunder reverberated round the small dark room.

'It sounds like bombs exploding out there,' Bill remarked. He stood up and peered out at the darkened sky, before drawing the curtains. Rain dashed against the windowpane.

When Mary heard Bill's words, her eyes nearly popped out of her head. The mounting tumult of the storm fuelled Mary's imagination as she worked out her plan.

Bill sat back down and puffed on his pipe, wondering what life in America would be like.

'I've got an idea of how to get around this certificate problem. Do you remember...Oh, years ago...during the war, we read about Father Dempsey's church being bombed? It was St. Margaret's in Canning Town in London.'

His face was blank but Mary, undaunted and now warming to her plan, continued.

'I'll write to the priest there first and ask if they can find a marriage certificate.'

'What will be the point of...?'

She shook her head.

'Then I will write to the Commissioner in Chester explaining what happened. All the documents were destroyed - the church was totally destroyed during the war. Everything in it went up in flames. There shouldn't be any trouble at all.' Mary leaned forward, resting her elbows on her knees. 'Darling, it's going to be all right.'

Looking at her eager face, her eyes bright with anticipation, Bill tried to catch her enthusiastic optimism.

'I hope you're right,' he said gently.

Mary never ceased to amaze him. She was always positive and even-tempered, never one to complain. If a problem arose, ever the practical half of the partnership, she would gnaw away at it until she found a solution. She was his rock and he sensed a growing confidence that if there was a way to get them across the ocean, she would find it.

***

Feeling much younger than the grand old age of eighty-four on 6th March 1981, Bill put the key into the lock on the door to their apartment in Ohio, U.S.A. After six months of turmoil, taking ten steps forward then five steps back, overcoming each obstacle that stood in their way, they had said their goodbye to Doreen, now pregnant with her third child.

They boarded the plane at Heathrow departing their homeland, regretting nothing. The thrill of this new beginning rose inside them as the plane gathered speed on the runway. Feeling the sudden lift as they became airborne, Mary grabbed Bill's hand. Their emotions soared while they peered down through the wispy clouds to the disappearing island that had been their home for so many years.

As a young man, Bill had dreamt of emigrating to either Canada or the States and here was the dream coming to fruition. His eyes filled with tears that he fought to clear as he savoured England's green and pleasant land that for him would be the last time.

So here they were, very tired after their long, emotional journey, stepping through the door of the place they would call home. It was part of a complex of purpose-built properties. There was a living room, a kitchen, two bedrooms and a bathroom, all equipped with the elderly in mind. The complex had a hall where parties and meetings were held and help could be summoned at the click of a button.

Close friends of Ronnie's had been busy putting in essentials in readiness for her parent's arrival. In the bedroom was a queen-sized bed furnished with pretty covers. Bedside cabinets and a five-drawer chest were there for storage. A line of wardrobes fitted with limed-oak doors filled one wall.

Bill walked into the bedroom and through a door in the far corner into the bathroom.

'The bathroom is enormous,' he called and as he opened another door, he gasped. 'The cupboard in here is huge as well.'

They felt like little children who had been given surprise presents. Mary was investigating the kitchen.

'The kitchen has got ... let's see... sixteen cupboards and six drawers.'

She opened and closed them all and then it was her turn to gasp.

'Huh. They say things are always bigger in America. Did you notice the fridge and freezer? They're twice as big as our old ones,' she said with a laugh.

'It's marvellous.'

Standing together in the sitting room, they felt the cosiness and intimacy that the place radiated. In a few weeks, the crate containing their possessions from Wales would arrive. Then their contentment would be complete.

They spent the next day recovering, with upset stomachs and jet lag. Later in the day they had a stroll around the surrounding grounds of the complex. They were pleasantly surprised by the well-tended lawns and flower beds. They continued their walk into the main street a short distance away. As they turned the corner they were overcome with emotion when they spotted a large board placed high on the building.

"Welcome to Bill and Mary Hard from England".

Mary silently noted that it said England and not Wales, but they were both pleasantly pleased with the thought behind the message. Beneath it was a smaller message.

"Congratulations to the Pearce family on becoming citizens."

'They certainly know how to celebrate over here, don't they?' commented Bill, shaking his head in amazement.

Later, Ronnie bustled in with their family in tow.

'Gramma, why couldn't you come with us today?' Zoe, the youngest spoke for them all.

Ronnie frowned at her daughter.

'Oh Zoe, Gramma and Granddad are very tired after their long journey.'

'We're Americans now,' she announced proudly.

'Mom, when can we change out of these clothes?' pleaded Stephen pulling at the collar of his shirt with his finger.

'I must say, you are looking very smart, all of you. I'm sure, now that you are American citizens, we'll have to pay to visit you, won't we Granddad?'

There was to be a welcome party a few days later, so Mary made a chocolate cake. She enjoyed baking and preferred her own cakes to the American version that she declared, 'are nothing like our cakes.'

\*\*\*

As the days moved forward, Mary wanted to find some work to do. They were to receive their pension by cheque but so far there had been no word from the British pension department. Bill was frustrated that his tools were still en route somewhere across the Atlantic. Six weeks after arriving in the States, they received a letter from the Shipping Agent.

'Our goods will be arriving in New York on Wednesday. Thank goodness. I'll write to the Destination Agent today and ask when we can expect delivery,' Mary told him, showing him the letter.

'I hope it won't be too long. I want to get on and do some work.'

When the crates finally arrived, Bill examined the clocks that had been badly damaged in transit.

'This is tragic. All that work ruined. We asked for professional packaging so that this wouldn't happen, didn't we?'

Mary scrutinized the contents of their shipment.

'It's the giddy limit, the way they've sent them. I'm going to write and claim damages on the insurance. They can't get away with this.'

They had put the clocks on the kitchen table and Mary realised there was a great deal of work to do.

'Oh well I suppose repairing them will give you something to do. I'm sure you'll be able to put them right.'

'I fancy taking up painting again,' said Bill one morning. He had found the box containing his brushes and oil colours as he unpacked one of the cases that had been shipped over.

Mary looked up from the crochet square she was working on.

'That's a marvellous idea. We could make the small bedroom into a work room. You could do all sorts in there if we put a bench in.'

It was no sooner said than done. Their son-in-law set up a bench for him. In that little room he could be occupied for hours, sometimes painting, sometimes crafting pieces using marquetry with wood veneer. He was really pleased with it.

While living in Wales, Bill and Mary had developed a deep love of travelling. They had driven down practically every back road on the British Isles and Mary was determined not to be cowed by the Ohio drivers test. She couldn't wait to get out on the open road again, and Bill shared her impatience. They were tired of having to rely on others to take them out, so they used some of their savings to buy a second-hand car. It was a blue 1974 Matador two door automatic.

Before their first outing, Ronnie rushed in to the apartment with a warning.

'Now for goodness sake, be careful when you go out in it. It's not like Britain here you know. Make sure you keep an eye on your mileage or the time. Remember, however far you go, you'll have to drive back. These roads are so long and straight, you can travel miles and not even realize it.'

'Oh, we'll be all right,' Mary tutted at her daughter's fussing.

'Well, I'm just warning you,' Ronnie said. She had breathed a great sigh of relief when her father had announced that he'd resigned himself to no longer driving.

One day, they were out on a foray into the surrounding countryside, driving through a small town, about an hour away from home.

'Look at that, Mary! It's a baker's shop.'

Mary slowed the automatic down and sure enough Bill was right.

'That's a sight for sore eyes. Let's go and see what they've got.'

Walking into the shop, they were agog with pleasure. Their mouths watered, as the aroma of freshly baked bread and the spectacle of delicious pastries and cakes pervaded their senses.

The shopkeeper, wearing a spotless white apron came forward to greet them with an amused twinkle in his eye. The portly man bowed slightly.

'Velcome to Polski's,' he said.

'This is like being back home,' remarked Mary.

'Excuse me, vere is home? You are foreigners like me and my wife.'

'We've come over from North Wales. We've been here about three months now.'

Suddenly Mr Polski's face creased as he laughed jovially.

'We are from Poland. We live here forty years and we still foreigners. Our sons, they are American.'

His announcement was conveyed with pride.

'But,' he held up a finger, 'they still help their old Papa. We make all bread and pastries here. Every day, fresh.'

Mary moved over to a shelf full of loaves of varying shapes.

'We miss our fresh bread. We can't stand the fluffy sliced stuff they call bread over here.' She flapped her hands in front of her chest to show how disgusted she was.

Following their discovery of the bakery, they regularly made the two-hour round trip to Polski's bakery. In between times, Mary baked her own bread as well as cakes and scones.

They also discovered a traditional watch and clock repairer who was pleased to hear of Bill's penchant for the intricacies of clockwork. Bill enthusiastically resurrected his old tools and, for a while, worked on bringing the time pieces back to life once again. The extra money he earned went towards the motor expenses and tobacco for his pipe.

During the 1980's, travelling could be done in the States at very little cost. Petrol prices were low, or "gas prices", as their grandchildren kept reminding them.

'Granddad, you're in America now. You have to speak American,' they would reprimand in a gently way.

'Oh, get away with you,' Bill would tut, rolling his eyes skyward, 'we're British.'

Because of the inexpensive fuel, Mary drove many miles, hunting out non-American foods or clothes bargains. Bill particularly kept an eye out for old watch and clock workings. This was something he had done back home in Wales, using them to create new mechanisms that he placed within beautifully patterned cases. The cases, he made himself, fashioned out of wood and faced with intricate marquetry designs.

'I've made more friends since we've been here than in all the years we lived back in Wales,' Mary confided to Bill one evening when she returned home from a DBE meeting.

The Daughters of the British Empire had been founded for women of British birth or parentage, living in America. Once a month, they would gather to discuss topics of the old country. Mary soon became an active member along with Ronnie, enjoying the company of young and old alike.

Two of her friends invited them one year to go on holiday in Oregon. While there, Mary was browsing through the delicate pottery in the gift shop in a small town they were visiting. The shelves were crammed with every conceivable gift idea. Bill was at the other end of the store, gazing longingly at an array of old-fashioned clocks. Real ones, with real workings. To his eyes, the battery driven ones could never replace true clockwork and those new-fangled digital ones were unspeakable in his opinion.

In the far corner of the shop, Mary noticed a staircase and began to climb. As she reached the top of the narrow steps, she gasped at the sight that was spread out before her. The whole room, from floor to ceiling was awash with Christmas decorations. Gingerly turning around, she stole back to find Bill. She knew exactly where to find him and could barely contain her excitement.

'Bill.' Out of breath, she tapped him on the shoulder. 'Bill, come and see what's upstairs. You've got to see this. It could only happen in America.'

'What is it?' He frowned at the disturbance, but Mary persisted.

'It's June for goodness sake,' as she walked away.

His curiosity won and he followed her. Climbing the stairs again, she threw a warning over her shoulder.

'Be careful on the stairs, they're a bit steep.'

He made it safely up to the top. With mouth open and eyes wide, he held his breath as he surveyed the spectacle before him.

'Ha, you're right. It could only happen in America. Who but them would have thought of having Christmas decorations throughout the year? It's absolutely amazing.'

Meanwhile, in a hardware store, just two blocks away, a woman thirteen years younger than Mary, purchased nails and other materials that she needed to complete the building of her mountain home. A log cabin had been her late husband's dream, so now she and her four daughters with their partners were completing it. If Mary had ventured into the hardware store she would have come face to face with her mirror image. But it wasn't to be. Fate did not allow a meeting and Mary would never realise how near she came to the possibility of the healing of old wounds.

\*\*\*

When they returned home, Mary telephoned Doreen.

'You'll never guess what we've been doing,' she said with a chuckle in her voice.

'What have you been doing? Knowing the things you two get up to, I'm not even going to try and guess. Come on, tell me.'

'Daddy and I have been white water rafting.'

'Oh, good grief.'

'It was such an incredible experience. So exhilarating. But after we'd got off the boat, the chap running the place, casually asked for Daddy's age. When we told him he was eighty-six, he nearly collapsed back into the water. Apparently, there's an age limit and Dad was way beyond that, so he shouldn't have even gone. He wouldn't have missed it for the world.'

Laughing cheerfully again, she went on to tell Doreen about the all-year-round Christmas store, spectacular views they had seen and the wonderful food they'd eaten.

They received fewer letters than they would have liked from Doreen. But, they knew she was busy with her family and welcomed the ones they did get. One letter though, caused Mary such heartache that she wished it had never arrived.

Doreen wrote,

*Dear Mum and Dad,*
*I have some amazing news to tell you. Last week I became a Christian. I have given my life to Jesus. Since we moved to our new house in Nottingham, I feel like I have come home. The people in the Anglican Church I go to are so supportive and have welcomed me. We have bible studies every week and the services are very charismatic. I've realized that I can't agree with all the rules and regulations in the Roman Catholic church.*
*I hope you can understand and be pleased for me. Love Doreen.*

Mary read the letter twice before handing it over to Bill. She was stunned into silence. Her body felt weak and numb. She was angry and upset. Angry that her daughter seemed to think that she had not been a Christian all her life.

'What on earth does she mean?' Mary asked angrily. 'She's been baptised into the holy Roman Catholic Church. I just don't understand. Does she think I am not a Christian?'

'I'm blowed if I know,' Bill shrugged, shaking his head.

On hearing her Mother's discomfort, Ronnie guessed that things weren't as bad as they seemed, and a second letter was soon winging its way from Doreen to Mary.

This time her revelation was a little softer.

*I'm sorry if I upset you. I know I have been a Christian all my life, what I meant to say was that I have re-found my faith. I felt that I had turned my back on God and that He had given up on me, but now I know that He loves me and wants me to have Jesus in my life.*

Mary was slightly appeased by Doreen's words, but still couldn't understand what all the fuss was about. A few days later she spoke again to Ronnie about it, voicing her confusion. It seemed to her that Doreen was trying to say that Catholics had got it all wrong.

Ronnie tried to ease her mother's tension.

'You pray to God and believe in Him, so you don't have to change anything. You've always been a good person.'

'Oh, you don't know what I've done,' Mary retorted viciously.

Stunned at the force behind her mother's statement, Ronnie silently wondered what was behind the outburst.

By October of that year, Ronnie's petition for her parents to be established as permanent residents in the United States was accepted and after a medical examination they could begin to claim state benefits. These benefits together with the small pension received from taxes paid in Britain, raised their standard of living a little.

There were several scares as Mary's body yielded to the ravages of brittle bones, though she never complained. Her mind maintained its sharpness as she continued to create needlepoint pictures and even recovered her interest in the French and Welsh languages. Even though not physically fit, Mary was determined to keep her mind active and enrolled on various college courses.

'I'm going back to school,' she told her amused grandchildren one summer.

The courses on accountancy proved to be very hard work, but determination was her forte and she wouldn't let anything beat her. Even if it meant missing a few lectures because of illness, she always returned to her studies and completed the course.

One time when she was admitted to hospital with bronchitis, an English friend heard she was missing her English cup of tea. Mary couldn't believe her eyes when she saw Margery struggling through her ward door laden with bags.

'Hello Mary,' she puffed. 'Wait 'til you see what I've got for you.' She turned and smiled, her glasses slipping down her nose. Pushing them up with the back of hand, she proceeded to delve into the first bag. Out came a teapot with a pretty knitted cosy with a tea strainer and two cups. From another bag she pulled an electric hot pot, then followed milk and sugar.

'Margery, you're a marvel. This is wonderful.' Mary was grinning from ear to ear.

The water was soon boiling and before long a steaming hot cup of tea was waiting for Mary's delectation.

'Mm,' she said, breathing in the delicious aroma, 'This is making me feel better all ready.'

To complete the tableau, Margery reached into the bag again and withdrew a packet of real English wheat meal biscuits.

'Oh Margery, how can I thank you. This is so kind.'

'Oh, you're welcome. What are friends for, if they can't provide a little treat now and then?'

Mary was lulled into a sense of security as her friend shared a confidence with her.

'Jerry was such an angel. He really did rescue me like a knight in shining armour. My husband was an animal. Oh, my goodness me, yes. When I met Jerry, it was like I'd been transported to heaven. We just took off one day, and never looked back. Of course, I couldn't get a divorce or the brute would have been after me, so Jerry and I have lived together ever since. Oh, Mary, you wouldn't believe the shame I felt at first.' She stared into the distance. 'Huh. Do you know what, Mary? I've never told another living soul about that. I don't know what's got into me.'

Mary's heart beat faster. Could she trust this woman with her own shameful secret?

Suddenly, Margery checked the time, stood quickly and gathered up the things she had brought in.

'I must be going.'

'Thank you so much for coming, dear. It's been good to see you. You're a real friend.' The opportunity for confessions had flown.

***

Bill's good health continued to amaze all who knew him. He had even become bolder in his acceptance of other people and could often be found sitting beside their front door, basking in the warmth of the summer sun. There were roses round the apartment that he had planted soon after they had arrived from Wales. These were flourishing and much admired by the folks who passed by.

One particularly balmy evening, he and Mary sat companionably, enjoying the evening air.

'D'you know what I've been thinking?' he said, puffing on his pipe.

'No, darling, what's that?'

'If I live like this, I'll be happy if I reach my 90th birthday. Then I'll go contented.'

Mary smiled at him and took his hand. They had endured tragedy and toiled together in work. They loved one another without compromise and now, in the twilight of their lives they were content in each other's company. They were pleased that at least for the moment they could still remain independent. When the grandchildren came to visit, they felt blessed to have such a loving family.

Just occasionally, a sneaking doubt would creep into their dreams. A nagging sense of shame and guilt would assault their consciences, causing one or other to cry out in pain. At times like these, they would comfort each other with words of love and consolation.

'I'm going to start saving the money I get from the clock repairs instead of spending it on the car or tobacco,' announced Bill one summer morning, coming inside for a cool glass of iced tea.

He'd been sitting outside in his usual spot by the door watching the birds and enjoying the sound of the bees buzzing around the Petunias. He could hear the sound of music. Someone was playing the piano.

Immediately he was transported back many years earlier when Doreen had been learning to play the instrument. She was always making music and the sound of the piano now, pulled at his heartstrings. He longed to see his little girl again. His heart ached and he began to think of a way to make it possible for her to come to America to visit them. They hadn't even met their two newest grandsons yet. He realized then that he and Mary would have to help Doreen with the ticket money if they were ever to see her again.

'What are you thinking of doing with the money then, Bill?'

'I want to buy tickets for Doreen and the two young ones to come over here for a holiday.'

It was a bold decision and his confidence pleased her. They wasted no time in putting the idea to Doreen who excitedly agreed. It would be her first experience of air travel.

By early 1986, the tickets had been booked for Doreen's flight to Detroit with her two youngest sons, Mark and Martyn. Mary was inundated with suggestions from her friends of places to take their visitors on their first ever trip to the States. Maps were poured over in anticipation. They were determined this would be a holiday of a lifetime for Doreen and her boys.

Bill and Mary could barely contain their excitement at seeing their youngest daughter after five years separation. They, together with Ronnie and her husband arrived at Detroit Airport early so that they could be right beside the barrier as Doreen came into the Arrivals Hall.

At last, Ronnie spotted them. Mark was pushing his baby brother in a buggy and Doreen was struggling with a loaded trolley. Tired and stiff after their long and tedious journey, the three travellers were soon ensconced in a warm cocoon of hugs and kisses.

A friend had lent Ronnie a mini bus for the duration of Doreen's visit and another had given her a car seat for 15 months old Martyn. Four years old Mark clambered in energetically to sit at the back with his Uncle. It hadn't taken him many minutes to recover after the nine-hour flight. He wasted no time at all in telling his uncle what he'd seen as they arrived in the airport.

'We saw a real sheriff with a cowboy hat and he had a real gun.' His blue eyes were wide with the wonder of it.

As Ronnie drove along, Mary pointed out the various sights that were so new to Doreen. The enormous roadside hoardings advertising a store or restaurant that could be found by turning off the freeway, the skyscrapers on the skyline of Toledo as they crossed the bridge over the Maumee river then as they moved into the countryside there were the vast, flat fields of corn.

'In a couple of months those small shoots will be taller than a man. If you look very carefully, you might see a skunk or a ground hog in the fields,' Bill told them.

'Are you all right Doreen? You're very quiet.' Mary said.

'Mm, yes. It's hard to take it all in. It's so different. I'm just so tired after that horrendous flight.'

'You'll be all right in a couple of days. You can take it easy today and tomorrow, and then we want to take you out. There's so much to see,' Mary said cheerfully. Doreen smiled to hear her mother being as positive as usual.

True to her word, as soon as Doreen was over her jet lag and caught up on her sleep, Mary and Bill took them to Lake Erie. The children thought they were at the seaside and paddled and splashed in the waves that gently lapped the rocky shoreline. There was even a lighthouse. The sky was an iridescent blue against which the brilliant white walls of the lighthouse glistened. Doreen was entranced by the beauty of it all.

Another day they visited a nature reserve where Doreen and the boys climbed up to a high viewing platform. From the great height, Mark and Martyn were thrilled to see their Grandma and Granddad moving round like toy people down below them. They spotted Egrets and Cranes feeding in one of the pools and even two small deer, their beautiful docile eyes alert for danger.

'You did very well to climb up so high and then down again, didn't you? I wish I could climb like you,' Mary enthused.

From time to time, Ronnie would take her sister and nephews out for the day or they would simply stay home and enjoy each other's company, giving the children a chance to play with their cousins' dog, Oso. Martyn soon learnt to say her name and loved to lie down with his head resting on her chest.

It was also an opportunity for the older couple to catch up on their rest. Mary liked to think she was still a strong woman and would resist all attempts by her body to tell her anything different, but during a hot afternoon while they were watching Stephen and Zoe running in a track event, Mary almost collapsed. It was a warning of how vulnerable she had become. She hated to be reminded that she was getting old and frail and this was surely one of those occasions. Impatiently, she insisted she would be all right in a few minutes but was glad to get back into her cool home where Bill was waiting.

One day, Ronnie and Doreen came to visit them. The boys loved being with their Grandparents and Mark was soon telling them what they had been doing. Mary found some crayons and paper and settled them down.

'Why don't you draw pictures for us? Then when you've gone home back to England we'll be able to see them and think of you.'

Ronnie and Doreen bustled about in the kitchen making drinks for everyone. As the three women sat and sipped their tea, Bill carefully placed his cup and saucer on the small table beside his chair. He put the palms of his hands on his knees, smiled across the room.

'I remember the first time I met your mother. She was walking down the stairs in a blue dress. I thought she was the most beautiful girl I'd ever seen,' he announced in a clear voice, his blue-grey eyes twinkling.

Mary raised her eyes heavenward, tutting at his romanticism. Ronnie and Doreen glanced at each other. They leaned forward, eagerly awaiting his next words like baby birds waiting the next tasty morsel.

He sat quietly for a few moments while they held their breath, not wanting to interrupt his flow of thought, both daring to hope for more. Suddenly, Bill looked at them as if weighing up his decision to speak. He leaned back in his chair, crossed one leg over the other and ran a hand over his head.

'I discovered on my birth certificate that my name, my real name,' he emphasised, 'isn't Hard at all.'

'Wha...what do you mean?'

'It's not William Hard,' he replied nonchalantly, as though it was nothing to be bothered about.

'So, when did you find this out, Daddy?' asked Ronnie with a stunned expression.

He gave his answer simply.

'I needed my birth certificate when we came over here, so I had to send for it and that's what I discovered. It's William Halford Rivers.' Before anyone could react, Bill bent forward as though to get out of his chair, but a wave of dizziness almost caused him to fall. Ronnie leapt across the room to catch hold of his arms and gently guided him back onto the seat.

'It's probably the new glasses he's wearing. He's had a couple of these turns since he's been using them,' Mary explained.

Ronnie was not convinced.

'You should go and lie down, Daddy. You'll feel better after a rest.'

'I expect you've worn yourself out with all the trips we've done,' Doreen added. 'We've enjoyed them haven't we, boys?' Two blonde heads nodded in agreement. 'Come on you two. Have you finished your drawings yet? We need to leave Grandma and Granddad in peace now.'

With a few more strokes of their crayons, they held up the completed pictures. Everyone admired their art work.

'Those pictures are going straight onto the fridge. Thank you, Martyn and Mark.'

After kisses were given all round, Ronnie and Doreen made their way dejectedly home, still feeling shell-shocked by the revelations about their father's name and a cloud hanging heavily over their heads about his state of health. He was so rarely ill and since his bout of TB so many years ago when they were still living in Wales, neither of the sisters could remember a time when he complained of being unwell.

Left alone in the solace of her sitting room while Bill rested in their bedroom, Mary closed her eyes and re-ran the earlier scenario of his revelations. He hadn't discussed any of his thoughts with her and she was faintly annoyed by his impulsive speech. If she'd had time to prepare herself, she might have been able to reveal more, but it was such a shock and then with his sudden dizziness the moment passed.

And now here they were on the last day of Doreen's holiday. Mary thought her heart would break as she watched her daughter and grandchildren disappear into the tunnel that separated them. Bill and Mary had hugged them tight, not wanting to let them go, both silently wondering if they would ever see each other again.

## CHAPTER EIGHTEEN

## 1987...

'The doctor is admitting Daddy into hospital. His dizzy spells have got worse,' Ronnie said to her husband one day. 'Mum isn't well either. I don't know how I'm going to cope with all the running around as well as my work,' she added with a worried frown.

'We'll all have to help. Jonathan and Christopher will be able to visit Granddad in hospital and Zoe and Stephen can pop in and see their Grandma after school.'

A few days later, while Ronnie was visiting her father in hospital, the doctor called her into his office.

'I'm sorry, Mrs Pearce, we can't do any more for your father. He has a brain tumour that's inoperable. Can you make arrangements for him to be cared for at home?'

Ronnie was stunned into silence for a few moments, stumbling for an answer. Her mind struggled to find a solution as to how she could care for both parents, too ill to look after themselves. She suddenly became aware that the doctor was waiting for an answer.

'Yes, I suppose we'll manage somehow,' she blurted out.

The doctor stood and stretched out his hand. The meeting was over. She was being dismissed. Obviously, he had other patients to attend to.

'Er, thank you, doctor,' Ronnie mumbled as tears pricked her eyes. She turned abruptly and fumbled her way out into the corridor to return to her father's bed. Somehow, she managed to help him to dress and led him out to her car. They were both in a state of shock as she steered the car through the evening traffic. Bill was pleased to be going home but confusion filled his mind, while Ronnie was filled with apprehension about the situation she would have to deal with when she got there.

Ronnie spent the next few days scouring the local nursing homes. It had become obvious that the tumour was affecting his mind and he was too ill to be cared for at home. St. Nicholas's Nursing Home was the answer they had been searching for.

Bill was taken in and given a small room to himself and he was soon ensconced in their routine, chatting to the nurses and taking on a whole new persona.

On family visits they were surprised to see him eating salads and pasta, foods that he had steadfastly refused previously. The nurses said what a jolly soul he was – the life and soul of the party. Ronnie was mystified. This didn't sound like the father she knew. The tumour had changed his personality, but sadly it didn't last. Before long, he had to be transferred back to the St. Charles's Hospital where he spent his last days.

***

The battle was underway. But this was no ordinary war. There were no soldiers. There were no guns. Not a drop of blood was spilt. Yet it was a battle fought to the death.

Witnesses stood by in helpless confusion, fearful at the sight and saddened by the painful convulsions of the man. For this was no ordinary war. This was the final battle for the soul of William Hard.

The devil taunted the Lord God Almighty, spitting venom at his victim.

'This vile creature you call a human being is a liar and a cheat. He hasn't even had a single thought in his head about you in sixty years.'

'He's a good man, who loves his family. He has known the error of his ways. Despite what you say, I am giving this man - my child, a chance to make amends for all the pain he has caused in his life,' the Lord God Almighty replied.

Lying on his hospital bed, Bill had no conscious recognition of this tug of war. But his soul was alert. His soul, led by God fought with his conscience. His conscience was filled by the devil with guilt, unforgiveness and self-loathing.

'How can I ever be forgiven for the despicable actions I have taken?' his conscience cried out to his soul.

'I love you despite the wrong things you have done. I want to forgive you.'

Bill's body contorted, causing the witnesses to leap forward in alarm. His conscience wrestled fiercely with this consideration.

'There have been too many people hurt by my actions. They will never forgive me.'

'First you have to forgive yourself. Their forgiveness of you is not your concern. What they think or believe makes no difference to you now. Understand that, and forgive yourself,' said his soul with patience and gentleness.

As his breathing slowed and his body relaxed onto the pillow, the witnesses also relaxed and took up where they had left off their praying. But the battle wasn't over yet. The devil wasn't about to settle for defeat.

Bill's tormented conscience screamed.

'That's all rubbish. People's lives have been devastated by my decisions. I'll never be able to forgive myself.'

Another spasm hit Bill, stretching his weak limbs to their limit.

'Listen to me,' called his soul. 'Listen to the voice of the Lord God Almighty, your Saviour. Listen!'

The Lord God Himself then spoke.

'My Word says, "Repent of all your sins and your sins shall be forgiven." I gave my only begotten son so that your sins shall be forgiven. My Word is for you, my child.'

'Lies, it's all lies. You've told too many lies,' hissed the devil.

Suddenly, Bill's conscience was overwhelmed by the loving voice of God.

'Didn't I forgive the two thieves on the cross? Haven't I said that one sin is as bad as any other, and yet still I forgive if you repent? Remember how the prodigal son was welcomed back into his father's arms. That's how I want to welcome you.'

The devil was busy. He filled Bill's gut with foul, putrid bile and wheezed his rancid breath into his lungs.

'That's all your sin. You'll never be rid of it. You'll never be free. It's too late. You are coming with me into the infernal fires of damnation.'

Mary stopped praying and stared at Bill. Her hand covered her mouth as he gasped for breath. Her own breath was caught in communion with the man she had shared most of her life with.

Her son-in-law glanced in her direction. Sensing her agitation, he rose from his chair and reached out to put an arm round her shoulders in order to comfort her. Together, they watched helplessly as Bill retched.

As he tossed and pitched, Bill's conscience pleaded with God.

'Please forgive me. Take away this agony. I want to be free of this guilt and sin.'

With a final heave, Bill was free. His body sank into the bed. His face took on a new countenance of peace and well-being. Mary, who had sat beside his bed for most of the day, whispered a prayer of thanks. The battle was over. The Lord God had won.

## CHAPTER NINETEEN

**1995...**
Frail and vulnerable, Mary had arrived in the Riverview Nursing Home in Oak Harbor in December 1994, some three months earlier. The journey there was uneventful and unmemorable. She was trapped in her own nightmare world of pain and insecurity. Her electric wheelchair had been strapped securely into the Ottawa County Transportation Vehicle. This was a type of mini-bus for moving the elderly and infirm from one location to another.

As she sat, ensconced in her isolation, an uncharacteristic twist of bitterness sneaked its way into her thoughts. When she and Bill had emigrated from England to the States in 1981 to live near their eldest daughter, this was not how she envisaged her twilight years to be.

*Bill's probably turning in his grave.* She grimaced at the thought.

Nine years had passed by since Bill passed away. His funeral had been an unassuming event. Mary thought at the time that Bill would have been pleased with that (if the dead could be pleased with anything). He hated a fuss. She wondered how she had coped without him. There had been times when her whole being ached for his presence. Not in a sexual way. *No,* she smiled to herself. *I'm too old for that!*

She would be caught out during the loneliness of an evening spent in the silence of her small apartment. With only the television for company, she often found thoughts would steal in and sit heavily on her shoulders. The weight of them was sometimes too much to bear alone. She had wanted him there to share memories and to comfort her when those memories became too painful.

The ill health that she now experienced had crept up on her in the last few years, depriving her of her independence, and forcing her into the situation she found herself in now.

*Eighty-five years on this earth and nothing to show for it.* Mary pushed the unaccustomed bitterness away. It was she who had suggested to Ronnie that she should move to the nursing home. *The poor girls got so much on her plate at the moment, having me to cope with is all too much. I'll just have to put up with it.*

Ronnie's son, Stephen was seriously ill causing everyone a great deal of concern. It was a difficult time for her. She was being torn in several different directions between her mother, her sick son, her work and the rest of her family. Mary knew all this to be true and from personal experience, recognised the stress her daughter was under.

The mini-bus slowed down and the driver turned his head round briefly.

'Nearly there.'

The indicator clicked.

'Come in, come in, come in,' it ticked, causing Mary's nerves to jangle. Her stomach churned and her pulse quickened, but as she focused on the tableau coming into view, she couldn't help being captivated by its calm stillness.

The dismal, grey day unexpectedly brightened as the driver turned the vehicle into the grounds of the nursing home. As her sight adjusted to the sunlight, she took notice of her surroundings for the first time. The nursing home in Ottawa County, Ohio was a sprawling, single storey building. Built of red brick, it reposed in beautiful park land that spread down to the river bank. Mary's eyes glistened as she imagined herself becoming part of a scene on a Christmas card such was the appealing scene unfolding before her.

The pure white snow stretched away from the winding driveway, crossing the land and burying whatever lay beneath. Several hillocks offered suggestions of features that were hidden mysteries. As she followed the line of sight, her eyes stopped at three majestic conifers contrasting darkly against the brilliance of the deep blanket of snow that spread on the ground beneath their feet. Jack Frost had been busy sprinkling his icicles over the branches, becoming in her imagination, fairy lights. The wonder of it lifted Mary's mood.

Wanting to share this magical moment, she raised her hand towards the window.

'Look at those trees. Aren't they a marvellous sight?' she said to her fellow passengers. The three old ladies offered no response. No one moved a muscle.

Mary tutted at their senility. *I may be old, but I'm not dead yet.*

The driver steered the mini-bus along the sweeping drive. Not wanting to miss any of the spectacle, she gazed at the fast-flowing river beyond the trees. The ripples on the water shimmered, dancing for joy at the unexpected pleasure in the brief respite of sunlight.

Suddenly the view was hidden as the driver pulled into the covered forecourt. Mary sat and waited for him to release her from the confines of the vehicle.

*I wonder if I will ever get to see the gardens when the snow has gone.*

She fished inside her sleeve for a handkerchief when a rattle in her chest heralded an oncoming cough. Holding the hanky to her mouth she felt far from well. The journey had made her very tired.

Later, after all the admittance formalities had been dealt with, Mary lay on the bed in the room consigned to her. Someone had helped her to remove her warm winter coat and all the encumbrances necessary to protect her in the sub-zero temperatures of the Ohio winter. Now, she was too exhausted to even look around.

After a while, Mary became vaguely aware of someone moving round the room. She opened her eyes slightly and saw that it was Ronnie unpacking her bag. Feeling relieved that her daughter liked to take charge of a situation, she allowed herself the privilege of remaining quiet and still, composing her thoughts for a few for moments longer.

*Ronnie is such a good daughter. I know she means well and she's so caring and loving. Oh, she went through agony about me coming here, but we ran out of options.*

Mary determined she would make the best of the situation for the sake of her daughter. Now she opened her eyes.

'Hello Ronnie. Are you finding enough room for everything?' she asked cheerily.

They smiled and Ronnie came across the room and kissed her mother. The older woman's bony shoulder blades shuffled beneath Ronnie's hands, contrasting with the cushioning comfort of her daughters embrace.

'Yes, I've put most of it away for you.'

An anxious frown crossed Ronnie's face.

'I hope you're going to be all right here, Mummy.' Not wanting her mother to see her distress, she turned quickly away.

'Now then, I'd better tell you where I've put everything.'

It was an emotional time for all of them and they were filled with relief when they learned that Doreen had answered their plea to come over from England as soon as possible. She was due to arrive on Boxing Day, alone this time.

Christmas Day passed in a mist of loneliness as Mary counted down the hours to when Doreen would come.

'If only Bill was here,' she repeated to herself throughout that day. She had been expecting Ronnie and the family to spend some time with her but they had been called away urgently to Stephen's bedside. He'd taken a turn for the worse. As she prepared for bed that night, Mary prayed for her grandson. But as always, her plea was that she would have the courage and strength to reveal her secret to her daughters at long last.

***

On 27th December, Mary struggled into her electric wheelchair after checking she had all she needed to take a shower, and then made her way towards the shower room. The heat inside the building belied the snowy scene displayed through the large picture windows that stretched the entire length of one side of the corridor. A vision of thick, icy, unforgiving snow was captured in the frame.

'Hi, Mary,' called Tina, a nursing aide, waiting to help her. 'Gettin' all spruced up for your big day?'

'Yes, that's right. Doreen'll be here this morning. She flew in yesterday evening.'

Tina pushed open the heavy, wide door, leaning her back against it to let Mary through.

'What part of England does she come from, Mary?'

'She lives with her family in Nottingham.'

'Oh, I know, that's where Robin Hood lives,' said Tina with raised eyebrows.

'Yes, well "lived". It was a long time ago,' laughed Mary good-naturedly.

'Did you ever go back to visit your daughter, Mary?'

'Oh yes. I went over for Christmas, err, let me think. It was after Bill died. Oh gracious, it was four years ago. Would you believe, I travelled in my wheelchair? What an experience.'

Tina's mouth dropped open in disbelief. 'My, oh my!' she giggled, 'you sure are adventurous.'

'Oh yes.' Mary let her mind drift back. She'd enjoyed spending time with her youngest daughter, Doreen and her family.

When they'd arrived at Gatwick airport for her return flight, her plane had been delayed for twenty-four hours. All the passengers were put on a bus and taken to a hotel in Brighton for the overnight stay.

Thinking about that journey now, brought memories of Bill flooding back as she recalled passing the places where he had lived as a youngster. The whole episode had been a nerve-wracking occasion for her, vulnerable as she was, trapped in a wheelchair and unable to walk unaided. But she lived to tell the tale.

'How're you feeling today, honey?'

She jumped in alarm when she heard Tina's voice.

'Oh, same as usual, but I'm not complaining.'

Shakily, Mary stood in the shower room while the aide kept a steadying hand under her elbow until she sat her poor old, brittle bones on the special seat. Tina kept up with her friendly chatter, though now that Mary had removed her hearing aid, the words were an indistinct murmur. It suited her well. She wasn't really interested in the gossip. The water was quickly cooling down and Mary began to shiver.

'Sorry, honey, the water aint too warm today. Somethin' wrong somewhere, I guess. Gee, you'd think they'd fix it, wouldn't ya?' the aide shouted sympathetically as she splashed water over Mary's head.

Meanwhile Doreen was following the signs through the nursing home to the reception area. She walked with a straight back and head held high. Years of being instructed to 'stand tall, bottoms in' by her ballet mistress had put paid to any slouching. Now in her fifties, her upright posture was second nature. Her once dark brown hair, wore a powder puffing of grey. This was the subject of much teasing by her sister, for though seven years senior, Ronnie hadn't a grey hair in sight.

'Hello. I'm here to see Mary Hard,' she announced to a woman sitting behind the information desk.

The woman was dressed in a white uniform with her blonde hair drawn back from her face and tied in a pony tail. Suddenly, her expression changed into a beaming smile, revealing a row of large teeth.

'Oh, how are you? You must be Mary's daughter from England. I'm so pleased to meet you. She's so excited about you coming over. Janie, come out here, will you,' she called, turning her head round towards an open doorway behind her.

Janie appeared exposing an equally large set of teeth, looking quizzically at her colleague.

'This is Mary's daughter from England.'

The newcomer leaned against the door frame, folding her arms across her ample chest.

'Oh my God, you look just like your mother. Gee, you've got the same eyes and nose.'

'Yes, I suppose so.' Doreen muttered uncertainly, feeling slightly overwhelmed by the scrutiny. 'Can you tell me which room she's in, please?'

'Why sure, honey.' With her eyes still on the visitor, she spoke to her colleague out of the side of her mouth. 'Oh, will you listen to that. We just love your accent.'

'Thank you. Er, what room is it?'

'Just follow me. I'd be glad to show you, though I believe Mary is having a shower right now.'

Inside the room, Doreen sat down to wait.

'I'm certain your Mom won't be long now, she's been gone about half an hour,' Janie said as she turned to leave.

The woman pronounced half as 'haf', causing a nervous giggle to rise up in Doreen's throat. She glanced round the room that had now become her mother's home. It was large enough to occupy two residents and could be divided by pulling a curtain down the centre. On Mary's side were a single bed with the comfortable armchair on which she now waited, a small cupboard, topped with a TV set and a cabinet with a lamp conveniently placed next to the bed head.

Peering through the long narrow window, she took in the view. Not bad, considering the flatness of the Ohio countryside. There was no sign of the river from this part of the building, but in the small garden area, someone had attempted to insert some height with shrubs of varying heights and textures, that would be pleasing and relaxing to the eye.

Today though, it was all nestling under an eiderdown of snow. The overcast sky was bleak and grey, heavy with threats of further falls. However inside, the room was warm and snug, so Doreen removed her heavy coat and prepared to wait for her mother to come back from her shower.

Sitting there, in those closing days of 1994 she began to think back to her last visit to her parents and sister. An image of that time shot like a thunder bolt into her mind. The picture was so vivid, it was as if she were back in the room with her parents. Her father had become uncharacteristically emotional and open. He had been sitting in his favourite chair with Mary in hers beside him when he began to talk about his name…

At that moment, the sound of voices coming from the corridor outside interrupted Doreen's reverie. Mary turned the corner in her electric wheelchair, expertly manoeuvring it through the doorway into her room, cursing to herself.

'Damn shower was freezing cold. Bloody hell. What are they trying to do to me? Give me pneumonia I expect.'

Doreen stood up and stared in amazement. Her mother was well known as being such a gentle, patient woman, rarely given to complaining and even rarer to swearing. It was proof, if proof were needed of the stress her mother was feeling, what with being so unwell in addition to being away from her own home.

Mary suddenly noticed her daughter moving towards her.

'Darling, I'm so pleased you're here,' she cried, holding out her arms.

The two women hugged and kissed. Mary longed to hold Doreen close but was thwarted by the cumbersome wheelchair. She swallowed the lump in her throat.

'It's so good to see you.'

'It's been such a long time. How are you feeling?' Doreen struggled to keep the tremor out of her voice.

They both wiped away the tears as Mary reached into her bedside cabinet for her hairbrush. She rubbed her wet hair vigorously with the towel that had been wrapped round her neck. The effort of this action made her gasp and she had to stop to get her breath back. When she had recovered, she patted the last few drips away before brushing the silver curls into shape. Without answering Doreen's question, she continued to complain about the cold water in the shower.

Lowering her voice, she shook her head.

'I'm not staying here,' she vowed. 'I can't stand it anymore. You can tell Ronnie to bring my things for me so that I can get back home. The woman in the other bed doesn't stop grizzling and her snoring keeps me awake at night.'

Doreen had never heard her mother complain so much. It confirmed her strength of character. Her mother's usual patience was thrown off balance by the change in surroundings and the failure of her body to combat its weaknesses.

Brittle bones meant she had been unable to walk unaided for some time. She had given up smoking many years ago, but the constant inhalation of nicotine over the years had resulted in severe lung damage, the evidence of which lay in the oxygen contraption and various containers of medication beside the bed. Effects from the necessary medicinal drugs left her shaky and nauseous.

Mary was only half listening as Doreen told her news of her own family back in England, understandably being more concerned about getting back home.

'What are the nurses like here, Mum? Are they looking after you well?' asked Doreen as she gained no response.

Mary glanced darkly towards her daughter and felt the tension in her shoulders tighten. 'Well, apart from trying to freeze me to death, they're kind enough. I suppose the poor old girl over there', indicating towards the other bed, 'should be pitied. She doesn't have any visitors.' Stopping to catch her breath, she thought for a moment. 'Maybe they'll let me have a room of my own. That would be better.'

Doreen smiled. She recognised her mother's true personality shining through. Her mother hadn't lost any of her strength of character. Though her head was bowed and her shoulders sunk, she obviously still mentally pictured herself as a strong woman.

Both of her daughters admired Mary's tenacity and positive attitude. She had worked hard alongside Bill with unerring support through the many difficulties they had encountered in their years together. Ronnie and Doreen believed that their mother's capacity to endure emotional and physical pain without complaint was deserving of sainthood. Even in the aftermath of her disastrous hip replacement surgery when her leg was badly broken, she continued to work on her cross-stitch creations and crochet. As soon as she was given the go-ahead to drive again she was off on her jaunts.

'I noticed a chapel on the way through. Have you managed to go to a service at all?' Doreen asked her question carefully, trying to steer the conversation away from the subject of her mothers' discomfort.

Mary's eyes softened.

'Oh yes. I can go down there in my wheelchair. One week it's a Catholic mass then the next it's Lutheran that is like our Church of England, so yes, I can go. I've been waiting for a visit from Father Greg. Do you remember how he used to come to my home and give Holy Communion to us? I'm sure I told you at the time. Three or four of us would meet once a week for it. He promised he'd come and see me here, but he hasn't been yet.'

She tutted impatiently and was suddenly seized by a worrying fit of coughing. It took several minutes for her to gain her breath. Then she continued with a contemptuous flick of her hand.

'He keeps sending women from the Church, but I don't want to talk to them. I wish he'd come himself.'

Seeing her mother's eyes stare off into the distance and thinking to make her feel better, Doreen explained.

'That's what they do nowadays though. The priests or vicars don't do so much visiting personally. They often have a team of people who act on his behalf.'

'Well I prefer it the old way, when it was always the priest who you talked to.'

Mary had lived her life with a firm conviction of her faith and trust in God, respecting the authority of the priest in charge.

Mother and daughter lapsed into silence for a while. Their similar features reflected across the space between them. Mary was lost in thought in a world of her own. Her pale, old brown eyes stared unseeing through the window. She knew she didn't have long for this world and there was still one major commitment she had to fulfil. There was a pain in her heart so deep it was like a cork screw being twisted into the cork. If she didn't release it soon, she felt she would explode. She decided that now was not the time. Better to have her girls together.

It was a comfort to her that her daughters had developed a deep friendship in recent years. Of course, there had always been a loving relationship between them, but Doreen had been like an only child, with her sister having left home at a young age and the early death of their brother. Now in their maturity, Mary recognised their close bond.

She noticed Doreen glance out of the window and shiver. The sky had become ominously dark and she shivered again, adjusting her position.

'You'd better get back before it snows again. Have you driven here yourself?'

'Yes. Ronnie gave me a quick reminder before I set out, about driving on the wrong side of the road! I've managed OK.' Her laughter helped to lighten the atmosphere. 'Do you want me to get you anything before I go, Mummy?'

'No, I'm all right thank you, darling.'

Doreen suddenly delved into her handbag.

'I nearly forgot. I've a few little things here for you. I'll leave you to open them.'

'Thank you. Be careful driving back won't you.'

'Bye then, Mum. I'll come back tomorrow afternoon,' Doreen said as she leaned over to give a hug and a kiss.

Mary slumped back in her chair and appeared to shrink in size as Doreen turned to leave the room. The gifts lay under her limp hands.

Gulping back tears, Doreen retraced her steps past the reception desk where a different girl called out to her.

'Bye now. Have a nice day. Drive home safely.'

With heavy feet she went on down the corridor beside the chapel to the front entrance. The daylight was speedily drawing in and the air gave a cruel nip to her nose as the automatic doors slid open.

'Why do people have to grow old?' she asked herself crossly.

\*\*\*

As the days passed by, Mary's resolve to move back to her apartment weakened. She was given a room of her own that granted her some privacy, so she had gracefully conceded that she would be staying in Riverview Nursing Home. But, she wasn't ready to give up her fight for life just yet. There was still the matter of unburdening her heavy load to her daughters. Each time they had been together, Mary had baulked at speaking out.

On Doreen's last visit before returning to England, Mary had sat quietly listening to her two daughters chatting about their families, enjoying each other's company. Several times, she had been on the verge of telling them her secret, but her courage had failed her. Their time together came to an end when Mary was informed that dinner was being served. Ronnie and Doreen walked slowly beside her wheelchair as they made their way to the dining room.

Too late now for confessions of her secret, Mary's heart ached. She had a desperate yearning to cling on tight to her daughters and be hugged in return, but her legs could barely carry her any longer. Her bones were so brittle now that even a cough could break a rib.

They cross the dining room to Mary's usual table and were joined by two white-haired women who had befriended her. The women clucked around sweetly like mother hens at the news of Doreen's departure. Everyone knew deep in their hearts that this would be the last time that Mary and her youngest daughter would meet on this earth.

Ronnie and Doreen turned one last time at the door of the dining room, feeling the anguish of parting. With a final wave they linked arms and walked away. Neither dared speak lest their emotions spill out of control.

*** 

During the weeks that followed Doreen's departure back to England, Mary settled into the regimented routine that was necessary to run the nursing home efficiently. The staff admired her dogged determination in the face of pain and discomfort. Her sharp mind and willingness to be 'game for anything' and 'try anything once' kept them in awe and of course they couldn't get enough of her English accent.

They loved to hear her stories of how, despite being confined to a wheelchair, she and Ronnie would drive up to Canada to eat English sausages, steak and kidney pie or fish and chips. Other times she told them of trips with friends they'd made to Pennsylvania, West Virginia, Indiana, Oregon and the Maumee State Park. Her descriptions of the Fall colours, perfect weather, pretty countryside and wildlife were vividly painted in their minds.

Her fellow residents were enthralled by her well-spoken words. They even forgave her for having an enviable, fancy motorised wheelchair when others of their numbers had to be content with being pushed along. It had been provided by her medical insurance company because her income had fallen below the poverty-line.

Sometimes they were caught by surprise when her sense of humour bubbled to the surface. One such occasion was when she called to her friend who was also wheelchair-bound.

'Hold on, Clara.'

The old lady grabbed hold of the back of Mary's chair and they went cruising down the corridors in tandem.

That was one of her better days. For the most part, Mary was tormented with the fear that Father Greg wouldn't show up in time. She was certain she didn't have long left. Each day, as she became weaker, the pressure on her chest grew stronger and she knew that it wasn't simply that her lungs were caving in. The pressure came from something much deeper.

Mary repeatedly chastised herself at her lack of backbone in not disclosing the truth to her daughters. No matter which way she looked at it, she was a coward. Now her only chance for restitution was through the Catholic priest.

*I need to tell the truth. Over sixty years of lies. Oh God forgive me. Please forgive me. Send the priest soon. I don't know how much longer I can go on with this weight on my shoulders.*

Three months after arriving at the Riverview Nursing Home, Mary was dozing in her chair. She'd had a restless night, and now her mind was caught in a dream. She was riding bare back along a sandy beach. The horse's long chestnut mane whisked across her arms, just as her hair was windswept back from her face. The sound of its hooves splashing in the foaming water filled her head. Her breath came in short gasps of salty air, not from damaged lungs, but from the exhilarating ride. Free of weighty thoughts and regrets, pain and stiffness, she was transported back to her childhood days full of innocence and recklessness.

'Mary.'

Someone was calling. She heard a movement beside her, flushing away her reverie.

'Mary.'

A hand was touching her arm. She forced her eyes open and moved her stiff body slightly, turning her head to see who the voice belonged to. It was one of the nursing aids.

'Father Greg's on his way to see you, honey.'

As the young woman left the room, Mary pushed the dream away and prepared herself to greet the priest at long last. Making herself comfortable, she checked that her oxygen cylinder and mask were close at hand and prepared to greet him.

Father Greg walked steadily through Riverview Nursing Home, aware that Mary Hard had been requesting a personal visit for several weeks. He rarely made this type of call these days, preferring to leave it to his team of capable men and women, but his secretary had finally persuaded him to make an exception.

At the reception desk, he leaned his tall frame over the counter while he chatted pleasantly with the uniformed woman. She noted that he was a good-looking guy with his blonde hair curling around his ears and a charm that could melt the iciest of hearts.

*Pity he's a priest,* she thought wryly.

Striding down the corridor towards Mary's room, Father Greg recalled the many times he had given the sacrament of Holy Communion in Mary's home in the retirement village a few miles away. He recalled her gentle spirit and devotion to the Lord. She had such a positive outlook on life that was quite refreshing in a woman of her age. He calculated she must be in her eighties.

*Wasn't she learning a foreign language? Welsh or French was it?*

He pondered on what it could be that specifically required his presence. He guessed it had something to do with her approaching death. It was not uncommon for folks in their closing years to want to talk to a member of the church. It was as if they wanted to dot the i's, cross the t's and finish the last chapter of their lives with a full-stop – The End.

He knew from experience that he would give her all the time she needed, that he must be patient and give her his undivided attention. It was these characteristics of his personality that had made him such a successful priest. He was respected by young and old.

The priest tapped gently on the open doorway and stepped inside, shutting the door quietly behind him.

'Well, hello Mary. How are you?' He pulled a chair close beside Mary.

'Could be better, Father, but I mustn't complain you know.'

Her breathing was getting more difficult than ever, making it necessary to use her oxygen mask frequently and today was no exception.

'Thank you for coming, Father. I have been waiting for you.'

'What is it you want to say, Mary? You know I'm here to bless you for our Holy Father in heaven?' He tucked his bible onto his lap and leaned forward, crossing one knee over the other and linking his fingers together.

Only Mary knew how much her heart pined for freedom from the burden that lay so heavily on her shoulders. Now, she knew she was about to throw that weight off. The dread of unfolding her secret had loomed in nightmarish proportions in the past. She had come to realise that no one but the priest had the authority to bless her with forgiveness for her sins.

Mary's mouth was dry and she wondered if he could hear her heart pounding and if it would continue to beat long enough, a thought that added to her fears. She had rehearsed what she wanted to say, countless times, but now that the time had come, her mind was racing. It was ticking like a time bomb and she didn't know where or how to start. A strangled cry escaped her lips, as in the pain of childbirth while she struggled with her inner conflict.

Father Greg laid his large hand over hers. She felt the weight of it. It was a comforting, safe feeling.

'I'll pray for you, then would you like to make your confession?'

'Yes Father. I have sinned,' she said in a breathless whisper.

The formality of this exchange began to steady her heartbeat. When Father Greg ended his prayer, he removed his hand and sat back patiently until eventually his calmness transferred its presence to Mary.

The priest had a gentle smile and compassion in his gaze.

'Mary, why don't you begin at the beginning, that's often a very good place to start.'

'Mary, are you OK?'

For a moment Mary couldn't think where she was. She felt a hand on her arm and a warm voice.

'Mary.'

Turning towards the voice, she saw Father Greg and remembered.

'Oh. I'm sorry, Father. It felt as though I was right there again. James was always getting into scrapes…'

'Are you sure you want to continue, Mary?'

'Yes, I'll be all right. Just let me use my inhaler for a minute.' She gave him a weak smile, before placing the oxygen mask over her mouth and nose.

As Father Greg sat and waited, he prayed silently and wondered what her story was leading to.

Mary settled herself again. 'Right, Father, where was I...'

A persistent yet gentle tapping brought Mary back into the present.

'Shall we ignore that or would you like me to see who's there?'

Of course, the voice belonged to the priest. She nodded silently. He rose tentatively from his chair, keeping his eyes on her, trying to judge which part of his question she was affirming. When she nodded again, he crossed the room in three easy strides and opened the door. A young aide was standing behind a trolley. He was momentarily surprised to see the priest.

'Oh, I'm so sorry, Mary. I didn't realise you had a visitor,' then added brightly, 'would you like a cup of tea or some coffee?'

'Yes please. It's just what the doctor ordered. I'm spitting feathers,' said Mary with a small laugh.

The young guy gave them a puzzled glance as he left the room and shut the door behind him.

Father Greg laughed along with Mary, sharing her attempt at humour. Once again, he was amazed at her strength. He hoped the interlude wouldn't stop her continuing. But it seemed nothing could stop her now.

'If I hadn't taken the job, well...'

Father Greg watched as Mary sank lower in her chair. He wondered if it was all becoming too taxing for the old lady. Her cup sat precariously on its saucer, balanced on her lap with the tea only half drunk. Tentatively, he stretched out his hand, attempting to retrieve it before it crashed to the floor.

Mary was reliving the time when she had to make the most momentous decision of her life, knowing now, that the choice she did make, changed the lives of so many people. The heartbreak it caused all those years ago stabbed her again and tightened its grip round her chest. She felt the familiar sensation of a coughing spasm rising in her lungs that always accompanied her struggle for breath.

Stirring herself, Mary put her cup on the bedside table and reached once again for the oxygen mask. She fixed it shakily over her mouth and nose then inhaled deeply, trying to regain her composure. The priest prayed that Mary would not lose her will to fight on. After a few minutes, her breathing eased and she felt able to remove the mask.

'He was my life, you see, Father. We couldn't bear to be apart.'

Mary was doubled over in pain. Her whole body was shaking with the effort of her confession. She had been in this position for several minutes with the oxygen mask pressed tightly against her face.

Placing his hand gently on her back, Father Greg sensed she had reached a poignant milestone. He prayed aloud.

'Lord God. You are mighty, Holy God. With You, all things are possible. Please give Mary the will-power and strength to fulfil her desire to complete her confession. We praise Your Holy Name. Amen.'

The shaking ebbed away enabling Mary's tension to ease. She wanted to get everything out in the open. It had been hidden away for too long.

'Father, for the past sixty years, we have gone through heartbreak, tragedy, poverty and ill health. I believe we've suffered those things as punishment for the decision we made all those years ago. It was a decision made out of deep love. We deceived our families. Left them without a word and have never spoken to or seen any of them since the day we ran away.'

'Mary, have you ever felt the need to confess in all that time?'

'Oh yes. Countless times. That's why I'm so racked by guilt. I've never found the courage to tell anyone before.'

'You've never told another soul?'

'No, Father.'

'Well, you know, Mary, it sounds to me like you have a repentant heart. All you have to do is ask your Father God to forgive you, and this is most important, accept your forgiveness. Become like a child and receive God's gracious gift of a clean heart.'

As Mary's voice faded into silence, she gazed into Father Greg's eyes, as though searching for something.

*Was he speaking the truth? Could it be that simple?*

His eyes were filled with compassion and love. Yes, love. Was it the love of God, shining through this man? As she continued to gaze into the priest's eyes, she began to be filled with a glorious sense of peaceful calm. The feeling grew and grew. As it grew, she felt the weight of tension being lifted from her shoulders.

Slowly, she nodded her head and smiled.

'Thank you, Father.'

The priest took both her hands in his as a broad grin spread across his friendly face.

Two weeks later, as she sat with Ronnie, Mary paused many times in their conversation. She knew what was on her mind, but her courage failed her again. Still the risk of rejection was too great, exactly as it been on her mind for the past sixty years.

*What would my daughters think of us? Would Ronnie turn away with a look of disgust?*

'I'm sorry. I'm not very talkative today.'

She had to let it go. She had to admit to herself that she could never admit to her daughters what they had done. Her confession had been made to the priest and through him she had accepted her forgiveness and received her freedom.

Mary Hard was ready to leave the world. That night she entered the gates of Heaven with a pure heart.

Mary was buried alongside her beloved Bill in Elmore Cemetery beneath a shady tree with this simple epitaph -

Bill and Mary Hard

"Tempus Fugit"

**PART FOUR**

**A MIRACLE ON THE INTERNET**

## CHAPTER TWENTY

**2017...**
*A letter to my children, grandchildren and generations of children to come,
Since our mother passed away, your Grandma Ronnie and I have been on a quest to find answers to some of our many questions concerning the early lives of our parents, William and Mary Hard.
Why were there no photographs of their wedding day?
Why had we been so discouraged from asking questions?
Did we truly not have a single living relative?
Would they really have wanted us to find the answers to their secrets?
This last was a question that other people frequently ask of us, but I am convinced that Mum and Dad meant us to discover the truth. During their lives they had given us many small clues, though tantalizingly, the clues almost always lead to even further puzzles.
So now here we are, my sister and I three thousand miles apart and we have that miracle...*

**1999...**
I replaced the telephone receiver with a sinking feeling in my stomach. Perhaps "sinking" isn't quite the right word, because part of me felt quite elated, yet there was also a distinct disappointment coursing through my

mind. I had been speaking to Mrs Stanley, the old lady who had, almost a year ago kindly forwarded copies of the deeds to the properties owned by our mother's family.

It was at that time that Ronnie and her husband Bill had come from their home in the States and together we had visited the village where we knew our mother had lived as a child. Mrs Stanley is now living in the house that she told us had been built by William Davies - the man whom we assumed must have been our grandfather. She kindly invited us in for a cup of tea and as we left, I passed my address and telephone number to her.

My mind was reeling over the news she had just shared with me.

'Mrs Fisher, I just had to phone you to tell you that I've had a visit from an American family. She told me her maiden name is Davies just like you said your mothers was. And, she was interested in Blue House Farm as well. It's an amazing coincidence to have visits from you both within a year of each other when I've been living here for over twenty-five years.'

'Oh, I wonder if we are re...'

Mrs Stanley continued, 'She said her father had built this house. I think she said she comes from Idaho – er, somewhere in America anyway. She was here with her daughter and grandson, visiting another grandson who's stationed in the American Air force base.'

'That's fantastic. How amazing! Did she give you her name and address so that we can contact her?'

Mrs Stanley's voice dropped. 'I'm so sorry, but no she didn't. It was such a shock and with so many people here I just didn't think to ask for it.'

My heart sank. From being so elated, I felt as if someone had just hung a bag of stones round my neck.

'Well, thank you for letting me know, Mrs Stanley. It's very kind of you to think of us,' I said quietly.

Telephoning Ronnie with the news, knowing that she would be equally disappointed, my ear almost burned with the shock of Ronnie's anger. She was beside herself.

'How could she do this? Trying to find this family will be like looking for a needle in a haystack. They have to be closely related to us. Perhaps she's a cousin of Mum's. The woman could be able to answer some of our questions.'

'Mrs Stanley said that the woman told her that her father had built the house.'

'Weren't we told that Mum's father had done that?'

'I expect she got it wrong. Oh, I am so upset, I could scream. What on earth are we going to do to find this family?'

'We'll have to get praying.'

'We're going to need an almighty miracle to sort this one out.'

***

In desperation, I sent a letter to the Us Air Force Base in Lakenheath.

*Dear Sirs,*

*With this letter comes an appeal for Help, definitely with a capital H. I am attempting to trace the history of my mother's family and somewhere within your Base is a young man who may be either related to me or else knows information which will be very helpful to me. The information I have is so scant that it is going to be a bit like looking for a needle in a haystack. Please bear with me as I try to relate to you the bare bones of the facts as I know them and if you will, my appeal is that you might attempt to find him – here goes -*

*Last week, a young man of around 25 years of age, stationed at your Base, must have had some leave (around $25^{th}$ February) when he was visited by his family from Idaho. The visitors were a couple – possibly his parents, his grandmother and a boy of around 9 years. The whole group, including the young man, made a journey to see the house where his grandmother had lived about 50 or 60 years ago. The address of the house is VERONICA, Kirby Cross. His grandmother's name is DAVIES. The connection with me here is that my mother's maiden name was also Davies and she had lived in 'Veronica'.*

*My sister and I visited 'Veronica' ourselves last year and left our telephone number with the present owner who called me yesterday with the news about her latest visitors. Unfortunately, she omitted to get their names or address, and could only remember that the young man was stationed at Lakenheath and she thought the family came from Idaho.*

*So, it is a real shot in the dark and I'm sure you are very busy people, but I AM DESPERATE to trace this family who look 100% certain to be the only people who can give first-hand information about my mother.*
*I have enclosed a stamped addressed envelope with many prayers with the hope that someone in your office will have an idea or a spark of inspiration as to who this young man could be. (I know miracles can happen sometimes.)*
*Yours sincerely and hopefully,*

Yes, I was that desperate. I really was clutching at straws and of course I didn't receive a reply. I'm sure whoever opened the envelope and started to read that diatribe, quickly dismissed it as someone mentally unstable.

Ronnie too was desperate. She prayed to God, 'If you want me to find these people then you will help me.'

What we needed was a miracle. Read on for what happened next.

One week later, Ronnie telephoned me. I could see her in my mind's eye sitting at her dining room table looking out over the decking towards her garden.

'Doreen, are you sitting down?'

'Yes.' I was suspicious. 'Why, what's wrong?'

'You know that American family who visited Mum's old home last week?'

'Yes of course. How could I forget them?'

Ronnie's voice rose with excitement she could barely contain.

'I've found them and you'll never guess… the woman is Mum's youngest sister!'

'What? No! How can she be? Mum didn't have a sister.'

*What was she talking about?*

Ronnie told me how earlier that day she'd been trawling through genealogy web sites on the internet. She wasn't really sure what she was looking for but needed to do something practical to alleviate the stress she felt about the problem of how to locate the American family.

Reading through her emails she spotted one from her niece, telling her to visit a site with cute dancing hamsters. She clicked on the link and immediately found the site where indeed there were dozens of dancing hamsters. She smiled as they leapt and cavorted on her monitor. Just as she was about to close the site, she noticed a link at the bottom of the page, called Ancestry.com. Thinking it might be interesting she clicked and found herself in a site for family history research.

She thought it strange that she had never spotted that one before. Having spent hours trawling through genealogy sites, she was amazed to find a new one. The site asked for the name of the person you wanted to find. Her pulse raced as she typed in the names of our mothers' parents, "William Davies married to Annie Bedelia Fairweather" and hit the send button. To her utter astonishment, there staring starkly back at her, appeared the two names. Scrolling across the page, she was shocked to see that someone else was searching for anyone with information about these two long-dead people.

A cold shiver ran up her spine.

'Hm, this is odd. Have a look at this.' she called to Bill.

Her husband dragged himself away from the news programme he was watching to see what she had found on the internet.

'I've just put in the Davies's names and look what's come up. Someone called "dfields" is researching them as well. That's the email address if we want to contact them.'

Ronnie's stomach was churning as she typed an email to dfields.

'I hope this is genuine.'

The cursor hovered over the send button as she debated whether to contact this unknown person.

'Go on then. You might as well send it and see who it is,' her husband urged from behind her.

'OK, here goes.'

It was sent.

Minutes later...

'Oh, my Lord, we might have just received our miracle. Quick! Come here again. That email I sent. I've got a reply already.'

This time he was at her side like a shot and together they read the words that "dfields" had written.

The email was dated 6th March 1999 at 8.09am.

*Oh boy, this is great. Mom's line is busy, so I just keep redialling, but I know you are related to us. My Mom is Teresa, youngest in that family and*

*I have seen a picture of Midge. Mom has so wanted to know what happened to her. Mom's name is Teresa Mary Veronica Davies. Just got back from a visit to England the other day – only third since 1946. You have many cousins, in USA and others in NZ, France, South Africa etc. Still trying to get through to Mom...Denise.*

They read and re-read the email.

'It was the family visiting Kirby Cross. Can you believe it? It really is a miracle.' Tears welled in Ronnie's eyes. She quickly removed her glasses and wiped the tears away.

'She doesn't actually say how you're related, does she? But look at that - Teresa, has the same names as you,' he said thoughtfully.

Ronnie shivered. Her hands were shaking. She was desperate to call me but didn't dare risk losing the connection on the internet to use the phone.

At 9.31 a message flashed on Ronnie's monitor – another email had come through. It was from Denise again.

*Veronica, I just got through to Mom and she is VERY excited, not having heard anything in about 65 years. She will be writing you, and we are all excited to make contact and help fill in missing bits...The excitement in my Mom's voice was indescribable.*

It was strange to see her formal name of Veronica used, but now Ronnie avidly read this new email with her stomach turning somersaults. She sensed something big was happening here. There were still no details but obviously her mother meant a lot to this American called Teresa. She sat back on her chair. Bill rubbed her shoulders as he stood behind her.

'I'm going to make a cup of tea. My nerves can't stand the suspense.'

She groaned and headed for the kitchen. As she passed the window, she saw that the day looked exactly as it had done when she first sat down at the computer. It was only about an hour earlier, but it seemed like a lifetime.

'Just keep an eye on the screen for me while I'm out here,' she called as she found mugs and tea bags, 'I don't want to miss anything.'

The couple spent the next hour conjecturing what the connection between the families could be, until finally the computer bleeped and their waiting was over.

On 6th March 1999 at 10.51, Teresa Mary Veronica wrote:

*Dear Niece Veronica,*

*You have no idea how thrilled I am to find you and to learn news of my older sister, 'Midge' after 65 years! My daughter, Denise forwarded your email and also phoned me with your news. I sat down and cried with joy.*
*I was only 10 years old when your mother left home and none of the family ever heard from her or anything about her until now. It's so wonderful to learn that I have two nieces, her daughters. You undoubtedly were named for another of our sisters who was named Veronica but died as a young child. This was why Mother named the house that Dad had built "Veronica". Just over a week ago I was in that very house and visited with John Stanley and his wife. They mentioned that someone named Veronica had been there from the USA and enquiring about the place and Blue House Farm not long ago. Was that you? Would you be willing to give me your phone number? We have so much to talk about. I find it hard to believe that I will finally, after all these years, be able to learn what had happened to my sister. So many questions come to mind.*
*Welcome to the family. It's a big one! Aunt Teresa*

Once again Ronnie leaned back in her chair and breathed a long deep sigh. She felt as if her mind would explode with the knowledge she had learned in the last few minutes. Reaching for the mouse, she sent copies of the emails winging over the airwaves to me, printed off the three email messages and came off line.

That was when Ronnie phoned to tell me about our new family.

'Are you sitting down. We've got some incredible news for you.'

She went on to tell me all about the emails.

'Go and have a look at the emails I've sent you. I've no doubt she's telling the truth,' she told me.

I sat in stunned silence for a few seconds, not able to move.

'It's a miracle. I can't believe it,' I stuttered as we hung up our phones.

My phone rang again. I rushed to answer it. I'd been telling my husband the news of our discovery about our mother.

'Doreen, it's Ronnie. I've just got off the phone after talking to Teresa. You need to sit down again.'

As I sat at my kitchen table I stared at a photograph that stood on the Welsh dresser. It was of my parents sitting in their American garden, innocently holding hands.

'Are you ready?'

'Yes, what is it?'

'Well, Mum was the eldest of seven children.' I couldn't stop a strangled sob. My legs began to shake and my throat tightened.

'She ran away from home with our Dad.' She paused at this point, waiting for it to sink in. I was in speechless shock.

'Are you all right?' she said with concern.

'Yes, I'm OK. I just can't believe it. It's amazing.'

'There's more.'

'Right, go on,' I answered slowly, thinking to myself, *'What more could there possibly be?'*

Ronnie took a deep breath before unveiling the final revelation.

'Dad was already married with two children - a boy and a girl. Teresa thinks their names were Raymond and Beryl.'

She stopped, waiting for my reaction.

I couldn't speak. Tears streamed down my face. I held my head in one hand and clutched the phone in the other against my ear.

'Teresa doesn't know where they are or whether they still have the same surname. They must be in their seventies,' Ronnie continued, breaking the stunned silence.

'I can't believe it,' was all I could say.

We mulled over the shocking revelation that somewhere in the world it was just possible that we had a half brother and sister.

'Ronnie, I'm not sure I can cope with finding them yet. It's been unnerving enough finding Mum's family.'

'Mm, and of course we don't know what their reaction will be. No, I think you're right. Let's wait awhile.'

Unsurprisingly, Ronnie seemed reluctant to end the conversation, and we sat holding our phones for a few seconds in silence.

'Teresa didn't realize that Dad was the same person that Mum had gone off with because I'd said that our family name had been Hard. It wasn't until I mentioned that his birth name was Rivers that she recognized it. If he hadn't told us, we might never have known about his side of things.'

I gazed out of the kitchen window and recalled how upset I'd been when I'd discovered the change of name.

'I'd love to know why they chose the name "Hard". It's such a strange name. Ronnie, out of all the names available, you'd think they could have come up with something a bit more ordinary, like…Oh, I don't know…say Smith or Jones. Wouldn't they have been able to merge into the background a little more? How many Hard's are there about for goodness sake? It really bugs me.'

It reminded me of my school days when I had to stand and tell a new teacher my names backwards. What an odd name to choose, if they wanted to melt into the background.

Along with the emails, we had been given the names of our mother's siblings and now photographs were being revealed. Tears streamed down my face as I watched my monitor. I blew my nose and wiped my eyes. It was impossible to see the image that was slowly being revealed to me until I had cleared the tears away.

I saw the dark hair and high brow of a child. My hand flew to my throat.

'It's Ronnie, but no, it's Mum.'

Line by line the picture grew. To the left of Annie (known as Midge) my mother, *their big sister,* I mused, was a younger girl with blonde hair. There was nothing familiar about her features.

'That must be Veronica. She looks so healthy and full of life. How sad that she didn't live to grow up.'

Line by line the picture grew. Another dark head appeared on the other side of Midge, a smaller girl this time with dark curly hair. As more of the face came into view my tears flowed again. I needed a tissue to dry them away and began whispering to myself.

'This is incredible. That could be me yet it has to be Gertrude, the sister they call Grit. Oh God. It's amazing.'

The three sisters had all been carefully dressed in a similar style with a big ribbon tied in a bow in their hair. A baby sat on a chair in the centre of the group.

'So, that's their brother Frank.'

William and Annie Davies, in the year of 1919 could not have been aware that over seventy years later that photograph would be the cause of such emotional turbulence in the lives of their descendants.

Along with the photos Teresa wrote in an email –

*You've got Uncle James and his wife Miche in France, Uncle Bill and his wife in Sudbury, I'm here in Oregon with four daughters and their families and Gertrude (Grit) who moves between Reading where her son and his wife live and Majorca where her daughter runs a bar. Oh, and sometimes she goes to sea with her other son in his boat. You've got five cousins in South Africa who've all got big families. They're all offspring of Frank who died a few years ago.*

***

Once the whole family had been given the news, all those involved with the discovery were feeling more than a little shell-shocked by recent events and Ronnie summed up her feelings, writing one day…

*Here we are at the beginning of a new week, and how my life appears to have changed!!! It is with mixed feelings I view it all this morning. When my sister and I decided to trace our family and also to try to find out why Dad had changed his surname, we knew we had to find a paper trail. It began by trying to find out when he changed his name. We knew in 1938 it was Hard because that was on my birth certificate. We searched for a marriage license between Mary Davies and William Hard, or William Halford Rivers, but no luck. The next quest was to find his army records, to see what name he used then. But there was a hitch with that theory, and we had to wait to do something else. Also, we had been told about his business going up in flames and that the insurance company were suspicious of foul play, and that Dad may be the one, so we were trying to find some record of that, thinking that maybe this is why he had to change his name.*

*Doreen was able to find and obtain birth, marriage, and death certificates of grandparents and great grandparents but we were looking for answers for more recent dates, more about who was this man we called Dad, why the mystery, why didn't Mum have contact with her parents??? Always loads of questions but no answers. In all our searching and hoping we never expected to find living people who actually not only knew Mum but were her family. I guess we are both dealing with feelings of disbelief, sadness, and in some ways hurt that we grew up in such a sheltered life with no relatives and really, no close friends. We believed our parents.*

*Many times, I have told people my parents were 'only' children and our grandparents were dead before I was born. I blindly believed them, and then we knew the dates of our grandparent's births, that when I was born, they all could have been alive.*
*So now suddenly, we have almost all the answers and a family we knew nothing of, I am having a hard time coping with this. So many emotions are running at the moment, it will take time to digest.*
*I am happy for you, Teresa, and your brothers and sister that now you at least know some of Mum's story. You know the man she ran off with stayed with her until he was ninety. They had their problems, but they worked them out.*
*So, let me have time to come to terms with our newly-found family and the answers. Keep the emails coming. We won't lose track of you now.*
*Love Ronnie.*

Her words and thoughts were an echo of my own.

\*\*\*

An email from Uncle James came scudding into my computer with photographs of our mother as a child with members of her family. He gave the names of the people and I wanted to ring Ronnie straight away as one of the names sounded familiar to me.

'Can you remember the name of the priest that Mum told us had married them? Does Father Dempsey ring a bell? I'm sure that's the name.'

'It sounds vaguely familiar. Why d'you ask?'

I couldn't keep the excitement out of my voice.

'Well, I've just had an email from Uncle James with some photos. (It feels so peculiar saying Uncle James!) The pictures aren't very clear but what he said in his email has intrigued me. He's given the names of the people and one of them he says is Father Dempsey who was a family friend.'

Between us, we began to put two and two together.

'I bet you any money that Father Dempsey was working in St. Margaret's church in Canning Town in 1932. That was what was on the affidavit they had to get so that they could move over here to the States.

Mum must have known the priest was working there at that time,' Ronnie surmised.

'So, you think they were never married?'

'I'm certain of it now,' Ronnie answered.

'No wonder I couldn't find a marriage certificate. What a wild goose chase I've been on in my searches,' I wailed, feeling sorry for myself.

'Just think of the torment Mum must have gone through. Even as late as 1981 when they emigrated to live near us, she'd had to lie on oath to produce some form of identity. I know she wrote to the church because I've got the reply from them saying that many documents had been destroyed in the war. They couldn't produce Dad's birth certificate because his name wasn't the same as my maiden name. So, they had to find another way to prove he was my Dad. My God, talk about a tangled web,' Ronnie countered in awe.

We were both stunned into silence by this fresh revelation. It seemed that just as we picked up the pieces from one shock, another one hurtled its way in.

Three weeks after their first communication, our new Aunt Teresa telephoned Ronnie.

'Now, let me tell you some news, Ronnie. My brother, your Uncle James is coming to stay with me in May and we'd love to have you come and spend some time with us. What do you say?'

My sister hesitated before answering. Everything was still very raw and she wasn't sure of her feelings or emotions.

'Thank you for asking. Let me give it some thought, Teresa. I'll have to work things out first, OK?'

'I understand.' Teresa paused thoughtfully. 'Ronnie, I want you to know that your mother was loved and missed so much all these years. For 60 years she's been loved and sorely missed by me. Now I'm so anxious to meet you and Doreen. We have so very much to share. It truly is a miracle that we've found each other.'

***

Plans were put into place to fly out to Oregon as soon as Ronnie had accepted Teresa's invitation. It was all a bit surreal but there were further surprises in store for her. Her mind was in turmoil. She was apprehensive about meeting Teresa and James.

'Sometimes I wonder what the heck I'm doing, travelling all that way to see people I've never ever met before. It doesn't seem real. I think I must be dreaming and will wake up soon,' she said to Bill one evening as she packed her suitcase.

'It's amazing, isn't it? But I'm sure once you get there you'll be OK,' he replied in an effort to comfort her.

'I suppose so,' she said, staring out of the window to the garden beyond. 'I wish Doreen was going with me.'

As she watched the birds feeding on the seeds she'd hung on the deck outside the dining room door, her thoughts wandered back in time. She tried to recapture her mother's image. Suddenly, tears pricked at her eyes as she angrily cried silently.

*How could you do this to us? All the lies you told us. How could you leave your family all those years ago and never go back to see them?*

'I feel so angry with Mum and Dad. Why couldn't they have told us?' she cried to Bill.

He didn't have an answer and Ronnie hadn't expected one. It was enough for the moment to have been able to speak out her frustration and anger.

## CHAPTER TWENTY-ONE

## 1999...

Ronnie accepted the hugs and kisses that Teresa's family bestowed on her. Denise had offered to meet her at Boise Airport in order to drive her the 200 miles or so to Teresa's home in Oregon. She was the daughter with interest in genealogy who Ronnie had initially contacted.

Still in a dreamlike state, Ronnie arrived in Halfway, Oregon with her new-found family. It would be a couple of days before she could relax enough to appreciate the spectacular mountains that surrounded Teresa's log cabin home. The moment Teresa opened the door to her sister's daughter, she made her welcome, but Ronnie found herself surreptitiously inspecting her aunt and uncle for signs of family likeness. In James, she could definitely see the familiar features of her mother.

'It seems so odd, you being my mother's sister yet so American,' she confessed one evening, as she sat with Teresa. 'But the more I look at you and get used to your voice, the more I can see Mum in you, Teresa.'

Stories were shared and photographs examined. Little by little, questions were answered.

'One thing I really want to know is why they never got in touch with any of you?' said Ronnie one evening.

The whole family had gathered to sit in the garden. They relaxed in the beautiful, balmy evening air. Ronnie could clearly see the breath-taking grandeur of the mountains spread out before them across the valley, but she was struggling to come to terms with the fact that the parents she had loved and trusted all her life could be the same people who had run away from their families.

'That's something we'd all like to know, Ronnie. I guess they were scared of the reaction. Mother was devastated when she read the letter Grit had got from Midge saying she would never be back. So, I'm not sure how she would have reacted. But so far as her brothers and sisters were concerned why, we would have welcomed her with open arms.'

James agreed, adding his own observation.

'The thing was that Midge had run off with a married man. That was a situation that was absolutely frowned upon in those days. Mother was a staunch Catholic so it was a shameful thing to have done in her eyes.' He shook his head and shifted uncomfortably in his seat.

All too soon, their visit together came to an end. It was time to get back to the real world. Warm good-byes were mingled with sad tears and promises to keep in touch as Ronnie waited for her flight back home.

Bill was at the airport to meet her.

'I've got a surprise for you.'

'Oh no, what is it? I think I've had enough surprises lately to last me a lifetime.'

'It's in the car. Come on let me carry your bag, the car's way over in the parking lot.'

They hurried out into the night. As soon as he unlocked the car door, Bill reached inside the glove compartment and handed her a letter. With trembling fingers, she read the postmark.

'Oh Lord,' she said in a scared voice. 'I'll have to sit down. My legs are like jelly.'

The postmark told her that the letter was from Thorpe le Soken and there was only one person it could be. The historian, Pearl Lonsdale had replied.

In all the excitement of recent events, she had forgotten that a few weeks earlier, she had contacted someone about information regarding the battery recharging business that Dad had run in Thorpe le Soken. This was one of the snippets of information we had been given years earlier. According to this person, there had been such a shop in the village, operating under the name of Austin & Rivers.

'But,' he wrote, 'if you want to know more, then you should write to Pearl Lonsdale. She's the local historian and her book all about the area has just been published.'

With trembling hands, Ronnie read the letter aloud to Bill, her voice thick with emotion.

'She says she remembers Halford leaving. *He left his wife Ruby, daughter Beryl and son Raymond. Ruby is dead and...*Oh no, Raymond has died. He never enjoyed good health. Oh, this is incredible. *Beryl is married to Peter Clarke. They have a daughter and three sons and a grandchild.*' She gasped as she read the next sentence. *I have given her a copy of your letter. It was a shock to her, I'm sure she will write to you.*'

'It sounds as if Pearl might live quite near Beryl. She says she's given her a copy of your letter, not posted it, doesn't she? Wow, if Beryl is in her seventies now, it's hard to imagine what she must be feeling to hear about her father all these years later,' commented Bill.

'Look Bill, Pearl's put a phone number there. I'm going to call her. I can't wait for the mail. It's too slow. Let's get back home. Oh no, I'll have to wait until the morning to call because of the time difference.'

After a fitful night, Ronnie awoke early, peering at the clock beside her bed, willing it to be a suitable time to call Pearl Lonsdale. She had been glancing at the clock most of the night and now finally, it would be a reasonable hour in England.

'Hello, this is Veronica Pearce speaking. Is that Pearl Lonsdale?' she asked nervously.

'Oh, hello Mrs Pearce, yes you've got the right number,' came the high-pitched Essex accent.

'Thank you so much for your reply to my letter. I'm sorry to telephone you, but I just couldn't wait any longer.'

'That's quite all right,' interrupted Pearl happily. 'Beryl is so excited about all this. She lives a few doors away from me. She's lived in the village all her life. When I took the letter round to her, I told her she should sit down as I had some wonderful news for her. I got her husband to make a cup of tea and we all sat round the kitchen table. Well, when I showed her your letter, she started shaking all over. She couldn't believe it was true. After so long, to be able to find out about her father was nothing short of a miracle. And to know that she's got two sisters. My dear, she was dumbfounded.'

Ronnie choked back her tears.

'Yes, it is incredible. We are still finding it difficult to believe.'

'Beryl will be writing to you in the next few days and she definitely wants to meet you both. It's a shame you are in America,' Pearl continued boldly.

Hearing of such a positive reaction filled Ronnie with confidence.

'Oh, but my sister, Doreen lives in Nottingham so that's not too far away. I know she will want to get in touch with Beryl.'

Wild horses couldn't have stopped me visiting my new half-sister, Beryl. The name was strange on my tongue. We'd had a few telephone conversations and I liked the sound of her, though I didn't yet feel completely at ease when talking to her. But, I was looking forward to meeting her and Peter her husband.

## CHAPTER TWENTY-TWO

**1999...**
The weather was very kind to me for the four-hour drive from Nottingham to Essex. After driving through many pretty villages, I stopped off at a garage to buy a bunch of flowers for Beryl. The idea came to me while spotting the myriads of colourful spring flowers poking their heads up to the sunshine and blue sky.

Arriving in the village of Thorpe le Soken, I peered around expecting to remember some landmarks. Nothing looked familiar. I had driven through here with Ronnie and my brother-in-law Bill just a year ago and couldn't recall anything in the place, let alone from my holiday with Mum and Dad thirty years earlier. Of course, during both those visits I had no idea of its link with my father.

Beryl's husband Peter had given me directions for finding their home. I kept my eyes on the road as well as the buildings until I reached the roundabout that he'd had told me about.

'Don't turn left,' he'd instructed. 'Indicate to go right even though there's no road to go to. As you turn across the roundabout, you'll see the drive going through a narrow archway. You'll have to stop first as you'll need to pull in your side mirrors.'

I was puzzled when he told me on the phone, but now I could see that he was exactly right. On the low wall that shielded the front garden, I read the word, 'Archways' emblazoned in beautifully scrolled wrought ironwork. Butterflies fluttered a merry dance in my stomach as I carefully manoeuvred through the archway and down the long, narrow driveway. I wasn't sure whether it was because I was frightened of scraping the car or that I was about to meet a stranger who is my sister.

As I pulled on the hand brake, I let out a huge breath of air that had been gathering force in my lungs. Grabbing the flowers from the back seat, I turned to approach my new relation.

Beryl came out of her kitchen door with a sparkling smile, her blue eyes beaming. She instantly put me at ease.

'Hello, Doreen,' she called enthusiastically. Her arms were outstretched in an invitation for a hug, which I accepted. It was a warm embrace and I realized that I was already happy to know her. We stepped apart and I handed her the flowers. As she buried her face within the petals, I took a few deep breaths. My heart was still thumping.

'I expect you'd like a cup of tea after your journey, wouldn't you? Peter will be down in a minute. He's looking forward to meeting you.'

Beryl's silver, permed hair bobbed along as I followed her through the back door into the kitchen. As she prepared the tea, I glanced round the kitchen but I couldn't stop myself watching this lady. Her movements were twins of my fathers. It was mesmerizing.

'Do you like milk and sugar in your tea?' she asked, turning around to face me.

'Only milk thanks.'

Our eyes met and we smiled.

'You are so like Dad, Beryl. It's uncanny. Your eyes are his and your movements and mannerisms are just like his.'

'Are they?' she said with a slight shrug in her shoulders and a lift of the chin. There was the twinkle in her eyes, just as he used to have.

'Ah, here's Peter.'

Beryl's husband gave my hand a friendly shake and I felt accepted into the family. Little by little as the minutes tick by, we filled in some of the gaps. Sixty odd years was going to take some catching up though. It couldn't be done in a few hours.

'It's so sad that my brother, Raymond is no longer with us to meet you. He was killed in a motor accident, driving his Robin Reliant three-wheeler.' She paused, then... 'Didn't you say on the phone that you played the piano?'

I nodded in response then suddenly realised another amazing family coincidence.

Interrupting Beryl's flow, I blurted out, 'We had a Robin Reliant at one time too!'

'Well! Amazing isn't it?' said Beryl. Then continuing her thread of thought, 'Music must run in the family because Raymond loved to play the drums. He was always tapping away at anything he could get his hands on.' Beryl smiled as she remembered.

Her memories were coming thick and fast.

'Father was such an outgoing person. He belonged to the local church choir and played in the orchestra.'

My jaw dropped open.

'That doesn't sound like the man we knew. Dad, that is our father was very introverted and would never have played in an orchestra or sung in a choir. He was always so embarrassed about not having any hair.'

'Oh yes, he was losing his hair when he and Midge left. He told Mother that he was going to see a specialist and never came home.' She folded her arms giving a slight shrug of her shoulders and raised her eyebrows.

*There's his look again.*

We sat in silent contemplation for a while.

'What instrument did he play in the orchestra? He told us his mother was a concert pianist. Did he play the piano?' Because of my interest in music, I was keen to know.

'No, he was a wonderful cellist.'

I was amazed at what she was saying.

'Hah. We never knew that.' It made my heart heavy to know that he left behind his beloved music. 'No wonder he encouraged me with my music.'

'His personality certainly seems to have altered. I suppose it must have been the guilt at leaving us behind that made his hair fall out. So, didn't his hair ever grow back?'

'No, it never did and he just couldn't come to terms with it. He was ultra-sensitive about it. It blighted his life, and ours,' I added as I remembered how our family had been scared to refer to it.

'He was an excellent carpenter and gardener. Did you know that?' asked Peter.

'Oh yes, now that sounds more like my Dad,' I laughed.

While Peter set the table, I bustled round helping Beryl to dish up the dinner. It felt good to be with them. Nothing was awkward or uneasy. It seemed like I'd known them all my life.

After I'd been spoilt with Beryl's splendid roast dinner, we went out for a tour around the village. Beryl wanted to show me the house next door where she had lived with her mother Ruby and our father, Halford. (As we're talking about the time when he was Beryl's father it's easier to think of him as Halford. Otherwise it is terribly confusing!) Oakley House was a large double-fronted building, now occupied by a young family. They had sold it about eight or nine years earlier when repair work that was required to maintain the old house, had become a liability. The sale had included only part of the very large garden, and Peter had gained planning permission to build the smaller house in which they now live in the remaining portion of land. As we strolled by, I tried to imagine what it was like when Dad and his other family lived there. Beryl told me that it had been changed quite a lot inside, but the front remained much the same as it was.

'Except that when we lived there it had iron railings around the front garden. They went towards the war effort.'

I stopped to gaze at this house that my father had lived in.

'Shall we go and look at the shop where Father had his business?' Beryl didn't wait for an answer. She rushed off at lightning speed. I laughed out loud and called out to her.

'Beryl, you even walk exactly like him. He was always in a hurry.'
She turned around with a grin. 'Ha, do I really?' she said, looking pleased. Once again, I was struck by the similarity in her eyes to our father.

Crossing the road, we stopped in front of a small building that was now being used as a Chinese restaurant.

'This was Father's shop. That's where he and Jack Austin, his partner did all the repairs to the bikes and watches and clocks and the battery recharging.'

'Oh gosh, seeing it all in the flesh makes it all the more real somehow. It's still difficult to believe though. And to think that when we came here in 1963, it was all here and you were living in Oakley House. They must have been so nervous.'

I stared into the window, trying to imagine what it was like when Mum was there working with Dad when they first met. I was suddenly brought back to the here and now.

'Of course, it all fell apart after they left. With the shock of finding the money gone, Jack became very ill. He almost died,' Beryl was saying.

This was a startling piece of news. 'What money? What do you mean?'

'Oh, they took money out of the business account,' she says in her matter-of-fact way.

'Oh no, that's terrible.' I felt sick. This surely couldn't be my parents we were talking about. They were always so upright and straight-laced. I found it difficult to concentrate, but Beryl was moving away from the building and I strode out to catch up with her.

'Beryl, it almost sounds like we're talking about someone else, but I know that what you say must be true. It's just so hard to take on board.'

She linked her arm through mine.

'They must have been very much in love to do something so desperate. Obviously, they needed money, so they must have thought that was the only way.'

As we walked down the road together, Beryl enlightened me with more details.

'Father sent letters to Mother and Aunty Nell, her half-sister, telling them he'd arranged for money to be paid to Mother so that she would be financially secure, but within a few weeks any money we had was gone. We were almost destitute.'

We walked on a short way in silence. I didn't know what to say.

'Mother never stopped hoping he would come back. She never married again. Well she was still married to Father, wasn't she?'

'Yes, Ronnie and I have to accept the fact that our parents were never married.' I felt uncomfortable hearing this part of the story. I wanted to think of my parents as honourable people. What I was learning about them was upsetting.

'Let's cross back over the road and go to the church. It's where Mother and Father got married and where he sang in the choir.'

There were daffodils and snowdrops dancing like jewels in the grass amongst the gravestones. The brown and cream stones of the churches towering walls glowed warmly against the blue sky. Once again, I felt myself being taken back in time. We walked down the aisle and gazed at the stained-glass windows. I saw the organ and the altar and experienced a prickly sensation, knowing that he had walked on these same tiles and sat in the pews and choir stalls all those years before.

It was cold inside and I shivered. Beryl led me outside again into the bright sunshine and the relief of fresh air. I breathed deeply. We made our way back to Beryl's home where we had a cup of coffee with a piece of her home-made fruit cake. The rest of the afternoon passed quickly as we shared experiences of our own families.

I got out the old photos I'd brought with me of Mum and Dad. I was beginning to think of them as two sets of people now. Halford and Midge from Beryl's time and Bill and Mary as Ronnie and I knew them. I had one or two photos that dated back to a time before they ran away, and as we compared them, we could see that the snaps were taken at the same time and even on the same roll of film as a few of hers.

My heartstrings were pulled in all directions as I looked at images that were unmistakably of my mother, holding Beryl in her arms or sitting with Ruby and the children in the garden. In the snaps she was portrayed as a happy young woman. There were several where she was sitting close to Halford, our Dad, with Ruby his wife in the background.

'It's unbelievable,' I remarked as I shook my head.

Beryl handed me a photo of our grandmother, Cecelia Rivers sitting at a grand piano.

'She was a lovely, sweet lady. Grandpa Rivers didn't deserve her. He had many lady-friends and eventually, Cecelia had enough of him and left.'

I nodded my head sadly, remembering that our mother's parents had split up too.

'Who's this man?'

'That's Father's brother, Uncle Raymond. He was an amazing pianist. They named my brother after him. There's a picture of his sister Dorothy here somewhere as well.'

She rummaged through the pile.

'Ah, here it is.'

I laid the two photographs on my lap. I couldn't stop staring at them.

'We thought he didn't have any brothers or sisters.' I wanted to cry but swallowed the urge away.

'Our brother was called William John Raymond and my baptismal name is Dorothea, obviously after his brother and sister, but we were never told.'

The two images of my unknown aunt and uncle, sitting side by side on my knee stared back at me.

Beryl handed me more photographs, but I couldn't get the idea of those names out of my head.

'Don't you think it's strange that they used the name Raymond for his two sons? That would have been a constant reminder of who they had left behind.'

Peter had been sitting quietly watching and listening.

'Why do you think they used the name, Hard?' he now asked.

'Ah. I've thought about this a lot and come up with the idea that they took the first two and the last two letters of Dad's name – Halford making Hard. It seems to make sense to me.'

They both nodded their heads in agreement.

'Did Raymond and Dorothy have any children, Beryl?' I wanted to know.

'They both married but only Dorothy had any family. She has a son, Michael. I see him occasionally. He's getting on a bit now and his health isn't too good.'

Beryl handed me another picture, this time of Halford playing the cello.

'Did they use my name in any way?' she asked hopefully. Her blue eyes for once, looked sad.

'No, they didn't.'

'I expect it would have been too painful a memory. Father was always so fond of me. I can remember the day he left as if it were yesterday. He kept coming back into my room to kiss me. I think he wanted to take me with him.'

'I wish he had done,' I said, putting my arm round her shoulders.

Suddenly brightening, Beryl jumped up from her seat.

'Would you like a sherry?' she asked with the twinkle returning to her eyes. As Beryl stood she leaned over to hand me two envelopes. I immediately recognized my father's tiny scrawl.

While we sipped our Sherry's, I carefully unfolded the two letters my father had sent to Ruby and Nell.

*How could the man I had called 'Daddy' for so many years have written such lies?* I had to keep reminding myself that Halford Rivers, Beryl's father, was the same man as my father, Bill Hard.

That night I slept in the bedroom to the front of the house and after a peaceful night I woke early in the morning and went to the window. Flinging the curtains open, I contemplated the view. It suddenly struck me that what I could see, was the same view that my father would have seen when he opened his curtains each morning in the house next door. Just like me he would have seen the high white wall with its ornate gate set into the corner.

Ancient tall trees swung and swayed beyond the wall, and somewhere beyond them stood The Abbey. I wondered if he ever had cause to visit the mansion. Perhaps he recharged their batteries. Peter had told me the night before that the village had changed little over the years.

After breakfast, Beryl suggested we go and look at Blue House Farm and 'Veronica' and then into Frinton.

'There's another house I'd like you to see. We can drive by it on our way out.'

'Ok.' I was happy to go along with her idea and interested in what she was going to show me.

She asked me to stop outside a house that I noticed is called 'The Anchorage'.

'Who lived here, Beryl?' I asked while peering through the windscreen at another double fronted house, set behind a high hedge.

'That's where Grandpa and Grandma Rivers lived.'

'Huh. Something else we didn't know. We never did know where Dad had lived, apart from knowing that he was born in Sale. Well, I never. Huh.' I shook my head slowly in amazement.

We enjoyed a pleasant day out together and drank our coffee back in her sitting room.

'Did you know that your family, the Rivers' and mine, the Clarke's came over from France as long ago as the 17$^{th}$ century?' Peter asked as he put down the newspaper he was reading.

I shook my head.

'Oh yes. The Rivers' and the Clarke's. Of course, we were known as the Rivière's and de Clerkes in those days. The area all around here was occupied by the French. The place is steeped in history.' Peter was a fount of knowledge about the local towns and villages. He stood up, as his eyes widened and his hands waved excitedly. He continued apace. 'The Dumertons. Do you know of the Dumertons?'

'No, I've never heard of them.'

'Well, Tom Dumerton was your father's relative. He was an engineer and taught Halford and Jack Austin their trade. His family came over from France too. Ah, yes. The place is steeped in history.' He gazed out of the window for a few moments.

'Oh gosh, not more relatives,' I laughed.

Beryl laughed too.

'We don't really know how that family is related to ours. It must be way back in time. They weren't close relatives, but it was Uncle Tom who taught Father his engineering skills that he used in the shop.'

Soon it was time for me to return home and as we reached the car, Beryl and I shared a hug. We agreed that we're glad to get the chance to know each other.

'What a pity, things couldn't have been different and we'd met sooner,' Beryl said, as we stand back, still holding hands.

'It's amazing to think that the decision taken by Mum and Dad could have had such an effect on so many other lives. Ronnie and I, and our families wouldn't even exist if they hadn't loved each other enough to run away. So, I'm not sorry they did get together, just that I wish they could have stayed in this area, so that you would have had your Dad and we could have known each other.'

'Mm, we can't turn back the clock though, can we? I'm simply glad that we've met now. You'll come back again and see us, won't you, Doreen?'

'Oh yes, definitely. We'll keep in touch over the phone.'

In my car on the way back home, I mulled over the things I'd heard and seen during the few days staying with Beryl and Peter. I couldn't wait to get home and phone Ronnie...

## CHAPTER TWENTY-THREE

**1999...**
'Hi Ronnie, you need to come over here for a holiday. I've had a lovely letter from Aunt Gertrude or Grit is what we've been told they called her. She'd like to meet us. There's Uncle Bill too. Isn't it amazing that there are members of Mum's family still alive? Uncle James or Jim as he likes to be known has emailed inviting us to stay with him in his home in the south of France.'

'Wow, Doreen,' replies Ronnie. 'It's all happening so quickly. In a few weeks we have gone from being adult orphans to having this world-wide family. I'm losing track of it all! But you're right, I need to come over there. Oh, Doreen this is all so incredible. Do you think Mum and Dad are pleased we've done this?'

We are both still shell-shocked with so many new relations wanting to meet us, wanting to know the story. It's unbelievable that so many of our mother's siblings are still alive. I can understand my sister's concern.

'Yes,' I reply. 'I firmly believe they did set us a puzzle that they wanted us to solve, otherwise why would we have been given so many clues? Snippets were planted in our minds, like Dad's change of name and the names and places of Mum's childhood. So yes, I definitely believe they wanted us to discover the truth, but perhaps they were hopeful that it would only be after they had passed away.'

I'm excited to share all the news with Ronnie. The phone lines have been buzzing and emails are burning up my computer there are so many. I can't wait to copy Grit's letter onto the computer so that Ronnie can read it.

*29.3.99*
*Dear Doreen, Thank you so much for your letter. It was wonderful to hear after all these years. I only wish Midge and I could have met – however I am so glad she had a full and happy life. They really loved each other and guess they were great parents. I will write again when I can sort out some of the things we did and the kind of childhood she had. We all loved her and worried about her, talked of her many times. If only we had known she was Okay.*
*Mother kept Midge's last letter to me all her life and always prayed that Midge would come home.*
*Much love to you,*
*Aunt Grit*

It didn't take Ronnie long to arrange her flight back to the UK and we were soon on our way to meet our Aunt Grit in Reading for the first time. She made us so welcome and as we shared a glass of sherry, she regaled us with many stories of the childhood she had shared with Midge. As with Teresa and James we were mesmerised as we discovered our mother's features in Grits face, movements and expressions too. It was uncanny that we could even see aspects of our own characteristics in them.

We had also made plans to visit Uncle Bill. He was the only relative that we hadn't had communication with, but armed with his telephone number, we had called and arranged to meet him at his home in Sudbury.

It was a beautiful day as I drove towards the town with Ronnie giving directions. We both loved to drive off the beaten track, so we were especially delighted to be getting out into the English countryside that Ronnie missed so much.

'We're just like our parents' in this respect, aren't we? They always wanted to get into the small lanes, away from the main roads,' commented Ronnie. 'Look at it all. I love it,' she shouted happily. 'Here we are. That was a good journey.'

We were warmly invited inside to be met with several dogs. It was then that we realised what an amazing coincidence there was there. Bill told us that he was a breeder of Daschunds. Another family coincidence. So many, but perhaps not so surprising.

## CHAPTER TWENTY-FOUR

## THE FINAL PIECES OF THE PUZZLE

**2017...**
*We received our miracle. Our questions were answered. It's taken a long time to put the pieces of the jigsaw together, but we're almost there.*
*There was still a part of the puzzle that gnawed its way around my brain and that was - Why did Midge (who's birth name was Annie) and Halford choose the surname of 'Hard'? My original idea that they had used the first two and last two initials of Halford's name didn't sit easy with me. It didn't seem quite right.*
*The answer came to me in a flash of inspiration.*
*It happened just like a light bulb being switched on! I've often scoffed at that joke when someone gets a good idea, but that's how it's happened. One minute I was pondering yet again how my parents had concocted the surname of Hard, the next it hit me. It was an actual, physical impression in my body. The impact was of such a force that I jerked up out of my cosy nest in the bed.*
*Instantly I recognised that it had to be my mother's idea. We had similar minds when it came to solving problems and I can't believe I haven't thought of it sooner. The answer is so simple that a child could have solved the puzzle.*
*I know it has to be the answer.*

*The amazing thing is that the name they chose would be a continual daily reminder of their past lives. It wasn't just simply a name pulled out of the hat, chosen on a whim, or even the first and last letters of Halford as I had originally presumed. No, it had been carefully thought out. It was a code they believed only they would have the clues to open the secret.*
*I have finally cracked the code. I am so sure that this is the answer that even now, as I write this letter, I am tingling with excitement.*

    *Lovers love initials, don't they?*
    *That is it!*
    *Halford Rivers loves Annie Davies.*
    *Halford loves Annie loves Rivers loves Davies.*
    *Halford, Annie, Rivers, Davies.*
    *Their names entwined forever, for eternity – H A R D.*
    *Even that may not be the final piece but... It is enough.*
    *This is our history.*
    *It is your story for all time and for your children's children.*
    *From your loving Grandma,*
    *Doreen.*

## POSTSCRIPT BY THE AUTHOR

Dear Reader,

When telling people of the amazing discovery about our parents, without exception writing a book was suggested. This gave me the encouragement I needed to get started. As the writer, I have taken the bare bones of the myriad anecdotes and memories given to us by the surviving siblings of our mother Mary Hard and given them flesh.

Our father's siblings had already passed away, so the chapters depicting his marriage to Ruby were gleaned from Beryl's own memories, old photographs and my imagination! Any misrepresentations are fully accepted to be the fault of the author.

By the time of completion of this book, our mother's siblings are also deceased, but I hope that their story, our story will live on. I (Doreen) and my sister Veronica (Ronnie) want our grandchildren to know where they are from and whose blood is coursing through their veins.

But for the decision made by William Halford Rivers and Annie Mary Davies to desert their families, to disappear and become William and Mary Hard, Veronica and I would not be on this earth and neither would our descendants. Their monumental choice in leaving caused ripples in so many peoples lives, but all concerned are grateful to finally know the truth.

Thank you for reading this book. If you have enjoyed the story please take a moment to put a few words on Amazon. I'd love it if you would keep in touch. You can find me at unexpectedanswersblog.com facebook.com/familysaga.unexpectedanswers/
email: deeriversauthor@yahoo.com

*Dee Rivers 2018*